ASSASSIN'S CREED
THE MING STORM

A cold gleam suddenly flashed towards her, like a light. Like...

A blade!

Shao Jun drew her weapon in an instant. Anyone who was able to get this close without being noticed had to be dangerous. When he leapt, she guessed from his moves that while he was not a member of the Eight Tigers, he was at the very least one of Zhang Yong's henchmen.

His sword skimmed past her feet at incredible speed. *Crack!* The branch she was standing on suddenly snapped.

Shao Jun was fast, but her attacker was faster. After slicing the young woman's first perch, he quickly cut the second she had just landed on, and began sweeping the air with wide, slicing strokes. He leapt straight upwards towards Shao Jun to sink his weapon into her heart, only to strike at thin air.

Impossible! He swore. The young woman flew through the air like a supernatural spirit.

ALSO IN THE ASSASSIN'S CREED® SERIES

Renaissance
Brotherhood
The Secret Crusade
Revelations
Forsaken
Black Flag
Unity
Underworld
Heresy
Desert Oath
Odyssey

ASSASSIN'S CREED VALHALLA
Geirmund's Saga

THE MING STORM

YAN LEISHENG

Translation by
Nikki Kopelman

First published by Aconyte Books in 2021.

ISBN 978 1 83908 088 3

Ebook ISBN 978 1 83908 089 0

Cover art by Simon Goinard

Distributed in North America by Simon & Schuster Inc, New York, USA
Printed in the United States of America
9 8 7 6 5 4 3 2

ACONYTE BOOKS

An imprint of Asmodee Entertainment Ltd

Mercury House, Shipstones Business Centre

North Gate, Nottingham NG7 7FN, UK

aconytebooks.com // twitter.com/aconytebooks

Prologue

The waves blossomed across the sea, whipped up by the wind, like so many flowers of blue-green water on the surface of the swell.

Taki Choji admired the marvelous sparkle from his seat upon a rock at the water's edge, reminded of the canons read during his training as a monk in which the eyes of the Buddha were compared to the lotus flower. Excommunicated at the age of fifteen, he offered his blade in service to a lord before becoming a masterless ronin, then a pirate, and had banished his childhood at the monastery to the depths of his mind to best avoid any form of compassion. What was reviving such old memories now?

A white sail caught his attention. Keeping his eyes on it, he called out "Katana! Katana!"

A young man ran to him.

"Yes, Father!"

The young man, still wearing the clothes of a child, was an

orphan collected by Taki Choji at the start of his outlaw career. Back then, his band numbered only five and could attack only small, lonely trading vessels, until one day he decided to force destiny's hand by assaulting a large, stranded ship. He had scarcely boarded the ship when his nostrils were assailed by a terrible stench: the deck was strewn with the bodies of the crew, victims of a previous attack. As Taki Choji searched the vessel for any morsels of value, he discovered a small boy, unable to walk or talk and half dead from hunger and thirst, who weakly waved a katana as he approached. The child had survived five or six days among decomposing corpses, and still seemed determined to face a new pirate attack! This strength of character kindled something in the normally emotionless Taki Choji, and he chose to adopt the orphan, unimaginatively naming him Katana.

At barely sixteen years old, he could have been born to sail the sea. His swimming abilities and fierce temperament, forged through their piratical way of life, made him an essential member of his adoptive father's crew.

Taki Choji rose and pointed at the small sail on the horizon.

"Katana, that's likely Chief Sun. Tell the others to get ready."

The adolescent shaded his eyes as he scanned the sea in turn.

"Isn't that Wang's ship?"

"No, Wang's sails are ashen."

While his men were vagabonds with no attachments or resources of their own, Taki Choji was slightly more educated. He had learned it was in his interest to limit the disturbances he caused at the edges of the Ming empire. To this end, he had concluded agreements with some coastal villages. Each month they supplied him with some of their harvest in exchange for being left in peace. He ended up settling down on a small island with a source of fresh water, and expected Sun, one of the local chiefs, to come to pay him tribute any day now.

Best to remain on his guard, nevertheless. Taki Choji had made this island his base for a decade: it was not only home to his crew, but also to a small pier where small boats were safely moored, allowing him to run to sea at short notice. He always watched for imperial troops, who would have no moral scruples with disguising themselves as Chief Sun for a surprise attack. The Wang mentioned by Katana was another pirate haunting the seas between Japan and the Ming empire, counting both bandits and traders in his fleet. Taki Choji dreaded the imminent end of their peaceful coexistence. They had agreed, for mutual prosperity, to avoid interfering in each other's affairs. Recently he had some minor involvement in business where Wang also had an interest, meaning a future conflict was inevitable. He was reassured that the approaching vessels did not carry Wang's colors.

Taki Choji's men, around a score of ronin produced by the chaos of the times, spent their time between raids drinking and gaming on the island. They eagerly awaited each delivery from Chief Sun, which would bring tables groaning with food and plentiful alcohol. Anticipating the coming feast, they abandoned their activities and rushed to watch the dock.

Eyes fixed on the approaching ship; Katana murmured, "Father, that isn't Chief Sun."

"Who is it?" Taki Choji asked, his sight no match for his adopted son's sharp vision.

"An old man with pale skin… and no beard."

The pirate captain smiled. If it was an old man, there was

nothing to worry about. Perhaps Chief Sun was too busy today and had sent someone else to deliver tribute in his stead. His extensive seafaring knowledge told him that it couldn't be carrying more than ten people, to judge by the ship's draft. If the new arrivals had hostile intentions, he and his men would have the advantage of numbers.

"We'll board them and see what tribute they've brought," he announced.

Just then the boat docked. The gangplank had barely lowered before Taki Choji, his right-hand man and his adoptive son were mounting it before anyone on board could begin to descend. While he had set foot on Chinese soil fewer than a handful of times in previous years, he had always remained in contact with the coast and had learned to speak fluent Mandarin. It was in this language that he spoke as he arrived on the deck, bowing with hands pressed together in greeting. "May I ask what brings these honorable visitors to our island?"

The old, beardless man Katana had spied stood at the prow of the boat. He approached and bowed in turn.

"My name is Zhang, and Chief Sun sent me to offer you his tribute. Do I have the honor of speaking to Taki Choji?"

Zhang's attitude was friendly, and while his hair was already white, his clear voice was that of a young man. Putting it to the back of his mind, Taki Choji hastened to respond.

"Yes, I am. Thank you, and please convey my gratitude to Chief Sun."

Zhang did not respond and gestured at several of his crew to bring forward a large wooden box on wheels, standing as high as a man and as wide as two. Sun had previously sent meat and grain, but never anything so large as this.

"Why has the chief sent this box? Where is our livestock?" Taki Choji asked, surprised.

Still beaming, Zhang replied, "Please excuse us. Two months ago, our chickens succumbed to a fever, so all we have to offer are cured meats. We will try to make up for it with the next delivery."

While the box was large, it couldn't have been heavy as it took only two men to move it. Irritably, the pirate expressed his concern. "Each month Chief Sun is required to deliver four hundred pounds of rice and flour, and two hundred pounds of chickens and eggs. How could all that fit inside this box?"

Zhang withdrew a brass key from inside his robes.

"Mr Taki may check for himself that the promised amounts are indeed contained inside."

If he had continued to plead their difficulties or tried to get him to understand, the pirate would have soon unsheathed his tachi. But, perhaps calmed by the old man's placid countenance, he reined in his anger and handed the key to one of his men.

"Waretsuku, come check the contents of this box," he ordered. He turned towards the boat's captain. "Mr Zhang, I need to stay with you a little while if you don't mind."

Taki Choji feared that the man would flee if left unattended. He could then later dispute the bandits' count of the produce, which would force them to end this agreement to avoid losing face. Now he understood the absence of Sun, who must have hoped he could load the blame onto Zhang if the situation escalated. If the tribute was insufficient, Taki Choji wouldn't hesitate to hold the old man as a hostage until the chief delivered the missing items. But the emissary simply wore a large, fearless smile.

"Yes, yes, naturally."

The box was carefully rolled down the gangplank, held by a rope, where the pirates took it and pushed it inside one of the buildings. Greater in numbers than the crew of the boat, they handled so lightly that Taki Choji's doubts grew greater. If the correct quantities were there, it had to be magic of some kind. On closer inspection, Zhang looked like he was hiding something, his expression was almost unreadable.

A man with blond hair and blue eyes emerged from the hold of the boat.

While Taki Choji had seen foreigners many times before, he was surprised to see one there. Westerners were becoming more and more common. The man moved across the deck and spoke respectfully to Zhang. "Honored captain general, everything is in order."

The elderly man acquiesced silently, a slight smile turning up the corners of his mouth. Taki Choji struggled to understand the unusual accent but realized with surprise that the man had not called the old man by name. Fearing that the two were planning some underhanded trick, he nervously massaged the small of his back, keeping his hand close to his sword. A shout suddenly rose from behind him.

It was full of panic and terror, something not even a blade in the throat could raise from the bloodthirsty criminals under Taki Choji's command. He turned his head, twisting his neck as a thunderous roar sounded from the camp. The slam of a door echoed. A black silhouette pierced the roof of the building and sailed into the air. It looked like a man.

The roofs of the wooden houses were not solidly built, only durable enough to resist wind and rain, but it was still incredible to see them broken through so easily. The man, who had flown around twelve feet into the air, crashed to the earth partway between the camp and the dock. His bloodied, unmoving body showed no sign of life.

Taki Choji considered the dead man and took a deep breath. It was Fukuyama Waretsuku, his assistant and a swordsman skilled in a fast and precise style which belonged to no traditional school of swordsmanship. They had served under the same lord, then after his death became itinerant wanderers before finally taking to the sea so as to never serve another. Waretsuku must have weighed at least two hundred and twenty pounds. Either he had leapt through the roof with enough force to soar into the air, which seemed less than likely. Or someone had thrown him, which would have required superhuman strength. Gripped by a sense of unease, Taki Choji set his hand on the pommel of his tachi as he assumed a defensive stance.

"Who are you?" he called, smoothly unsheathing his sword to point it at the foreigner, ready to kill him if the answer didn't satisfy him.

With the situation turning against him, he needed to strike first. Using *Strike of the Buddhist monk*, a secret sword technique, he would put an end to the Westerner with the unintelligible language in no time.

Shouts rose from the camp once more, but they were less panicked, visibly disappointing the elderly man.

Taki Choji had learnt to fight in the kendo style but had refined his skill over the years at sea. Using *Strike of the Buddhist monk*, the blade moved from right to left, with its brutal power increased by the strength of the wielder – when attacking a ship, Taki Choji used it to slice opponents in two from shoulder to hip.

He attacked the foreigner without warning, yet the man already had his right hand at his left wrist, drawing a razor-sharp blade no wider than a finger. The Westerner pivoted in a flash, responding with a powerful thrust that would have pierced Taki Choji through if he had not been just half a foot out of reach.

The pirate exploited his opponent's surprise by attempting to split his skull with his tachi but was blocked by Zhang's blade with a loud clash of metal as he joined the fray. The foreigner's face had turned ashen at his narrow escape.

Zhang's was also a thin blade, in the style of those found on the central plains of China. Taki Choji expected to see these delicate weapons shatter under the power of his attacks, but they endured nonetheless, their force dissipated by Zhang's agile counters.

The pirate was amazed by the speed and talent of the seemingly frail and quiet old man, who was gradually gaining the upper hand in the fight. As if to save him from this trap, there was a growl and a shadow suddenly fell over the captain's head.

It was Katana, who had unsheathed his namesake weapon as soon as he saw his adoptive father in difficulty. Taki Choji's men were all experts in the use of the saber or sword and the young man, rather than studying any specific school, had learned from all of them and developed a composite style adapted to his speed and light frame. In his hands the short blade, only slightly longer than a dagger, was a formidable weapon which had taken the life of six men in the past.

Zhang saw the boy make a nimble leap to strike while he was busy immobilizing Taki Choji's sword, a spark of surprise in his eyes. Steel flashed in front of the old man's face, as he parried the blade at the last moment. Katana ignored the spasm that ran up his arm, but Zhang seized the short blade between two fingers, turning it and pressing the palm of his hand against the boy's heart.

The move might have seemed benign if Katana hadn't immediately felt his strength completely drain away. Zhang took control of his pressure points and gently drew the young man towards him. A little more pressure would cause his victim to cough blood and collapse, broken. He disengaged from Taki Choji's sword, and the pirate quickly leapt several steps back. Faced with the sight of his adoptive son on the brink of death, he pleaded, "Mr Zhang, please have mercy!"

The captain had not expected this reaction from the cruel and merciless pirate.

"What?"

With his hand still pressed against Katana's chest, he could end the young man at any second. The arrogant adolescent, paralyzed but still able to speak, had never imagined dying at the hands of an old man without landing even a single blow. Despite his fear, he wasn't yet ready to give in, protesting loudly as he heard his adoptive father offer his surrender.

"Father! Don't worry about me, kill him!"

Taki Choji's face was pale and drained of color. He who had never once shown emotion, had never bowed before anyone, had quickly come to realize his hopeless position during the brief exchange. If it were his life in the balance, he would rather die than surrender, but Katana's life was too precious to sacrifice for the sake of pride. How had this man been able to reduce him to such a state, incapable of even the smallest movement?

"Mr Zhang, please, let us go, and we will leave your land alone. And if you've come about the illegal goods, I can tell you where they are hidden," the bandit replied in a resigned tone.

Taki Choji had long ago lost count of how many ships he had raided. He killed indiscriminately, indifferent to the pleading of the merchants, and Katana's life was the only one that mattered to him. He assumed that Zhang must have attacked to seize control of the illicit trade he was involved in. So, even Wang wanted to get in on the business and had sent this man as his catspaw.

The old man stared at him for a moment before turning towards the foreigner, who was still pale after nearly being decapitated by the pirate's blade.

"Would this man be any use to us?"

The Westerner nodded. "He's strong. He'll be useful."

Taki Choji didn't understand what was happening, but seeing those blue eyes examining him from head to toe made his blood boil with fear and rage. Zhang let out a short laugh.

"Mr Taki, this young man is your son, is he not? Lay down your weapons, surrender, and I'll let you both live."

Taki Choji was furious. Surrendering his weapon was as good as surrendering his life. But if he didn't surrender, it would be his son who would suffer. Gritting his teeth, he cast a final glance at his tachi. He was about to let go of it just as Katana jerked into the air, driven by rage at his father's surrender. The young man had grown up among harsh, inflexible men who massacred entire crews even as they surrendered, and for whom capitulation was never an option whatever the circumstances. His lack of experience also prevented him from realizing the clear difference in skill between himself and Zhang.

Seeing his captor distracted by his father, he had taken a deep breath, contracted his chest, and hoped that it would be enough to allow him to escape the pressure of the captain's palm on his chest and make his move.

Katana thought that escaping this embrace would be enough to turn the tables, but barely had his feet left the ground than a ten-pound club crushed his throat. Before he even realized what was happening a stream of blood gushed from his mouth and his body was thrown backwards.

Taki Choji, who had been about to let go of his tachi, was heartbroken as he recognized a fatal blow. In normal circumstances his dispassionate nature was his main strength, helping to ensure the safety of his companions and thus their loyalty. The death of his son sent him into a blind rage. Without thinking, he gripped his weapon once more and twirled it to ready his attack.

He planned to execute the *Windmill*, one of his most bloody strikes. Only, to his great surprise, Zhang disappeared in front of his eyes, reappearing as if by magic as a burning pain erupted in his chest. The two men were suddenly connected, a blade planted in the pirate's heart.

Twirling his sword had not been enough to protect Taki Choji from this incredible attack, and he had fallen for the trap. Frightened and despairing, he looked at the old man, at the face where affability had fallen away to reveal extreme coldness. His thin sword had pierced the bandit's heart, but the blade lodged in the wound slowed the bleeding and kept him alive for a few more moments. Long enough for him to gasp out, "Who… are you?"

Those three words exhausted his final breath.

The captain frowned and shook his head. "What a waste."

He removed the blade from his victim's body. A jet of blood

gushed forth from the wound, mouth, and nostrils of Taki Choji as his body finally collapsed to the ground.

"I am Zhang Yong, captain general of the twelve battalions of the imperial guard," he said quietly. The dying man suddenly opened his eyes, as if shocked by an electrical charge. He knew this name: it was the name of the most powerful eunuch in the country, the head of the empire's army. He would have liked to ask why a person of such importance was wasting his time with lowly pirates. What was the reason for all this?

He would never get an answer to these questions, as his life was at an end. Zhang Yong looked at the body and muttered. "I'm sorry, Pyros, I damaged the goods."

The Westerner looked respectfully at the corpse of the pirate who had almost killed him before being swatted with a disconcerting lack of effort by the captain. He wanted to point out that the young man he had felled with the heavy blow had also been top-quality merchandise, but he was interrupted by a deafening crash.

The main gate to the camp swung open to reveal a dozen men jostling and treading on one another to get out.

The crowd of frightened, bloodthirsty pirates resembled a horde of wolves scattering like terrified cockroaches exposed to the light. The stragglers turned desperately to close the gate, and one of them, back pressed against the gate to prevent it from reopening, called out to Taki Choji, unaware of his captain's death.

"Boss! Boss! Inside, there's a–"

Bam! A huge, bloody fist shot out through broken ribs.

Built from the deck of a ship attached to whole tree trunks, the camp gate was built more solidly than the roofs of the barracks and usually required considerable effort to open. Somehow a fist had just pierced through, killing the unarmored pirate standing in front of it and shattering his ribs like mere twigs. The horrific sight sent the pirates into a panic, scattering in all directions.

Another great blow rang out, and the gate burst open as if before an unrelenting hurricane, to reveal a dark figure.

The figure was a man, not large, and dressed in blood-soaked rags as though recently bathed in it. His livid hue, blue-gray as a bruise, and soulless eyes betrayed the inhuman power that animated him. Fast as the wind, his fist collided with a fleeing pirate. He struck less powerfully than when he had pierced through the gate, but the blow was enough to send the bandit flying before him, crashing, half-dead, into the ground.

The pirates had dragged the box containing this half-monster, half-human creature to the center of the camp, and he had begun killing them as soon as he was free, uncaring of their sword strikes. Now he was out, he had claimed two further victims and seemed determined to take more as the pirates gave in to their primal fear. The island offered little hope of refuge beyond the dock and camp...

Filled with terror, one of them shouted: "We are doomed anyway, attack together!"

It was then that he saw Taki Choji lying on the ground and was torn between his duty to aid his chief and the urgent need to rid themselves of this monster. He chose the second option. Against all expectations, he discovered an ability to command, ordering the dozen men still alive to rally as they faced the enemy.

Zhang Yong was surprised by the fatalistic determination of these Japanese, who still found the strength to fight with discipline even when faced with certain death. He sighed and turned to Pyros.

"Do you think our *yuxiao* can win?"

Fingers on his wrist, the foreigner watched the scene attentively as he measured his pulse.

"I fear… not," he responded. "I think there will be two survivors."

A blood-curdling cry rose from the band of attackers. One of the pirates had sunk his axe into the shoulder of the monstrous warrior, which caught him by the leg and tore it off with bare hands, separating it as if snatching a drumstick from a roast chicken. Rather than causing them to flee, the sheer horror of this act drove the bandits to hurl themselves at their opponent with renewed ferocity.

Zhang Yong shook his head. "I think you're too ambitious, Pyros. There will be five or six left."

Only eight pirates remained, sturdy fighters who showed their best, even with their backs against the wall. The entrance to the camp was a bloody arena at the center of which the monster, an axe planted in his shoulder, seemed to reign supreme. One of the last bandits still standing somehow managed to cut off the creature's head with a daring leap – one which he could not have expected to survive. While the superhuman fighter may have been able to continue fighting despite the wound in its shoulder, this blow was its end.

The six surviving pirates regained their breath and turned towards the boat. The old man had to be even more formidable than the opponent they had just overcome for him have beaten Taki Choji, but it was clear that nothing would deter them after that terrible battle.

The captain and the foreigner were accompanied by a dozen fighters on the boat.

"Kill them!" a pirate cried harshly.

It was he who had led the remaining bandits to their victory. On his order, they moved towards the gangplank while Zhang Yong echoed, "Kill them!"

The sailors drew their guns and fired as one as the attackers tried to board the vessel. Four pirates fell, leaving only two still standing, one struck in the shoulder. Rather than leaving themselves vulnerable by reloading, the sailors drew their swords and leapt to the ground to encircle the bandits, who attempted to ward off their powerful attacks.

An impassive Zhang Yong contemplated the massacre from the prow of the boat. The blood running from Taki Choji's mouth had formed a small pool at his feet, but to the old man the body seemed much like the ropes and anchors on the ship, just part of the scenery. He didn't pay it the slightest attention. A glimmer of disappointment crossed his face.

"Tell me, Pyros, our enhanced soldier wasn't as powerful as last time, was it?"

"If the pulse is to be believed, Beelzebub's strength is much less than that of the Imperator." He paused. "We must acknowledge that we have failed once more."

The monster the foreigner had named as Beelzebub had exterminated thirteen of the twenty-one pirates before being overcome. While it had been an act of spectacular savagery, it hadn't been as invincible as the name would suggest.

"Yes," Zhang Yong replied. "Thirty valiant warriors fell to the Imperator in no time at all. We are at an impasse without the Precursor Box."

This failure was not their first. Pyros remained silent for a moment, then asked, "Venerable captain general, should we continue?"

"We will certainly not be stopping."

The corners of his mouth turned up in a small smile. "If we avoid making mistakes, the box will soon be ours."

The amazed Pyros shivered.

"Isn't it still in the possession of Ezio Auditore?"

The old man looked down at the last living pirate, whose martial prowess was certainly remarkable. While he forced two sailors to keep their distance as he parried their attacks with his long sword, another sliced his back with their blade. The pirate screamed and tried to retaliate, but the injury prevented him from moving. He staggered and fell to the floor.

"According to my latest information, the box is no longer in Ezio's hands," Zhang Yong continued.

"He no longer has it?"

Pyros trembled. His group had been unsuccessfully trying to eliminate Ezio for a long time in hope of gaining this priceless treasure, a feat which had until now seemed almost impossible.

Zhang Yong carried on. "The last person Ezio met was … the Imperial Favorite."

Pyros was even more surprised. While he came from Europe, he knew less about the events taking place there than this old Chinese man. He frowned.

"I find it hard to believe that she returned after going to so much trouble to escape to Europe!"

On land, the sailors separated the dead and those still breathing before setting fire to the pile of bodies. Soon, this pirate hideout, established over ten years before, would be nothing more than ash and no one would ever know of the massacre that had just taken place.

"Those who have escaped hell will inevitably return," Zhang Yong murmured.

As the last survivor of the Central Plain Brotherhood, Shao Jun had vowed to return and take her revenge.

Zhang Yong's smile was more mysterious than ever. Knowing this day would come, he had supported the Haijin, the new maritime policy of isolation, organized this expedition against the pirates, and even broken the previously harmonious relationship with Japan. If Shao Jun returned, she would have to take a ship from a vassal state such as Annan, Malacca, or Ryukyu, and would be immediately spotted by one of the informants stationed at their ports.

All the old man needed to do now was kill her and take the box, and the world would be his plaything.

Zhang Yong caressed his pendant, a small piece of delicately carved jade. One side showed a design of interlacing veins reminiscent of aquatic plants, while the other featured the Chinese character *Dao*, the Way.

"Accordance with this nature is called the Way."

Learned by heart as a child, he recited these words of Confucius in a low voice. A bright spark still burned in his eyes despite his twilight years. He held on to the ambitions of his youth, and his greatest dream had never been so close to becoming a reality.

"Is that really A-Qiang's childhood home?"

Shao Jun thought she could hear her friend's voice in the gloomy alley as an icy wind gusted through. While she knew it was only her imagination, she couldn't help but squeeze the bundle she held tightly against her as she scanned the surroundings.

At the top of the dilapidated walls, chipped tiles were covered with weeds and seemed to tremble with cold under the sea breeze despite the mild climate. The prefecture of Quanzhou had once been a famous port, and the maritime capital of the empire under the Songs and Yuans. It had fallen into rapid decline after the transfer of the administrative center to Fuzhou eight years earlier, and the harshness of the Haijin policies which limited the number of ships able to access the port. Within just a few years, not a single vessel would even approach its shores. The time when they had jostled hull to hull was gone, and nothing remained of the joyous bustle of the past. That Quanzhou now existed only in her memories.

Heart heavy with unfathomable bitterness, she could see that her country was no longer the same.

She recalled her years spent in the imperial harem. A-Qiang was a timid young girl when she first arrived. They had quickly become friends and confidantes in the solitude of their reclusive life in the Forbidden City, standing united among dozens of rival girls vying for the Emperor's favor without knowing exactly what it meant.

A-Qiang had often spoken of her childhood home: the sea breeze, the carp in the lake, the Indian coral trees, the Buddhist monastery. Locked away in the harem, the young Shao Jun was fascinated by these descriptions of Quanzhou, which explained why she had chosen this place for her return to the country. By visiting her friend's childhood home, she also kept the promise she had made to her friend. Unfortunately, nothing and no one here seemed able to breathe new life into her memories.

"A-Qiang, you must be an imperial consort by now, and you're probably not eager to discover the outlaw I have become."

As she was lost in her thoughts, a dark shadow fell across her and asked in a low voice, "Little sister, can you do me a favor?"

Armed with a long knife, the man stood arrogantly blocking her path. The voice of Zhu Jiuyuan reciting *The Art of War* rose in her memory: "*Do not remain on dangerous ground.*"

The alley seemed to meet this definition, so any combat would be as inescapable as it was deadly. But in a situation with no way out, you had to be certain that your skills were far superior to your opponent's if you wanted to start a fight.

She wondered if the individual barring her way was a member of the Eight Tigers, the group which had followed her to Florence and killed Master Zhu. She had hardly set foot on land and already she'd been spotted. This didn't bode well.

"And how can I help you?" she asked with feigned indifference.

The man burst into laughter.

"Little sister, you just got off a boat, with a heavy-looking bag... the Tigers of the sea have been watching you for a while. Give me your things and I'll let you live. If not... heh heh!"

He began to spin his long knife, handling it artfully in the narrow space. He'd only made the offer to spare her because he was already planning to kill her.

"You'd murder someone in broad daylight?" said Shao Jun. "You have no respect for the laws of this country!"

"What *law*?" roared the man. "I am the law!"

This vicious, cruel brigand who claimed to be a member of the Tigers thought he could attack the small Shao Jun alone.

Trained in martial arts since childhood, he had taken to robbing foreign travelers in the streets of Quanzhou where none dared provoke him. He lived alone and had no family, his life meaning little to him as he had nothing to lose. Surprised to see this supposedly easy prey standing up to him, his irritation quickly turned to anger.

With all its constraints, street fighting in alleys was his specialty. He slipped through these narrow spaces like a snake, his weapon always close to hand. His knife-fighting style had been developed by generations of fishermen to compensate for the ineffectiveness of the classic styles on small boats in constant motion. The bandit had studied the techniques closely and practiced daily until he mastered them. This environment was his favored terrain, a place where he could be certain his victim had no chance of escape.

Then the girl seemed to evaporate before his eyes just as he was about to strike.

An incredible move! Was it magic? A sudden gust of air chilled his neck, followed by a sharp pain. He staggered forwards despite himself, dropping his knife, and fell to the ground. As he lay on the earth, he thought his time had finally come before realizing that the pain was gone. He felt his neck, reassured to feel no blood, and got to his feet.

Deserted under normal circumstances, the alley seemed darker than ever. Where had the girl gone? She must have executed a dangerous jump to land behind him. He picked up his weapon and massaged his neck. It was a deadly place to be struck, and he had survived only because she'd hit him with the back of her ankle. He would have been a dead man if he had been kicked in the same place by the heel of her boot.

With a combination of excitement and bafflement, the man, who had committed more than his share of cold-blooded murder, had goosebumps as he realized that any false move could be his last.

He was lucky that the boss wasn't in Quanzhou to hear of this affair. He moved to the other end of the alley to check and reassure himself that no one had witnessed his humiliation when he heard a voice murmur behind him.

"Chen Qilang, wait there a moment."

He froze, recognizing the quiet yet clear and piercing voice. He stretched his neck, took several breaths, then slowly turned.

"Boss?"

"Did you face the person I told you about?"

Despite being unsure, he responded in the affirmative.

An independent criminal, Chen Qilang had previously only ever acted of his own volition, killing as he saw fit. Then he'd met the boss in the spring of the previous year, trying to corner him in an alley as he usually did, but his snake-like technique had been of no use. When the confrontation had rapidly turned against him, he had agreed to carry out a simple mission in exchange for his life: kill on sight a young woman whose description he had been given. Shao Jun had not been the vulnerable young child he'd expected. It was only thanks to the goddess Mazu that he still breathed – although for how much longer he didn't know, as the boss's voice was icy.

Chen Qilang hastened to explain: "Boss, the kid knew very advanced kung-fu, I–"

"I saw how it played out – you didn't even try!"

"Please understa–"

A sudden pain in his stomach cut him off mid-sentence.

When he looked down the boss was extracting a knife with a needle-like blade from his abdomen.

It was the last thing he saw before his entire body stiffened. Betraying no emotion, the boss had stabbed him using a move much faster than all his knife twirls and serpent steps could ever be, stepping over his body as if it was nothing more than a tree trunk or pile of stones.

"So, imperial whore, you escaped my hunters and managed to return."

Her time in the West had clearly improved her fighting skills. He would have to look further into it and find an opponent who could match her level of skill when the time came.

The man's mouth twisted in a rictus smile before he let out a short laugh.

"Come, Pang Chun, we're leaving!" he called to a silhouette behind him.

Pang Chun had stood by in silence as he watched him kill Chen Qilang. He responded simply, "Of course." He jerked his head. "Uncle Gao, should we tell Uncle Yu?"

"Tell him what?"

Didn't Pang Chun understand that his master wanted to deal with this personally? While the captain general had ordered him to work with Uncle Yu, he wasn't going to hand his rival such a victory. Not daring to say more, Pang Chun simply nodded.

CHAPTER 1

The prefecture of Shaoxing was once known as Kuaiji. According to legend, it was there, or more precisely in Shaoxing, that Emperor Yu the Great had gathered his feudal lords after taming the waters in the area, which until then had suffered from frequent flooding. The historical documents recorded:

> *"After containing the floods, Yu the Great gathered his feudal lords to evaluate their performance. He died and was buried in this place. And so, the town took the name of Kuaiji, meaning gathering."*

It had always been known for its grandeur and refinement. At one time, students travelled from all over the country to study at the University of Mount Wolong established by Fan Zhongyan, a great politician and man of letters of the Song dynasty. Later, the celebrated neo-Confucianist Zhu Xi led conferences there, strengthening the institution's reputation as a center of classical learning before it lost its prestige under the Yuans.

Two years earlier the prefectural magistrate of Shaoxing and the district commander had renovated the establishment, constructing the Hall of High Virtue and the Pavilion of the Great Classics. Masters and students alike gathered in great numbers, and the new Jishan University reveled in a renewed glory that was greater than ever. Each year more than four hundred scholars gathered there from as far away as the most distant southern regions and the most remote reaches of the north.

The warden was a lean old man of sixty years named Wu. His job was to maintain the building, but as he worked in the most illustrious university in the known world, he felt as though he too were invested with a scholarly duty. Thus, he studied the Four Books and the Five Classics, though he enjoyed other works for entertainment.

He was currently deep into a recent edition of the *Romance of the Three Kingdoms* by Jiang Daqi, the pages of which were almost new. Old Wu had read through to the tenth chapter, a high point in the story where Zhu Geliang foils the plot of Zhou Yu, and was so deeply engrossed that he almost didn't hear a visitor looking to make themselves known. Jishan University, a staunch proponent of universal education, opened its doors to any student as long as they identified themselves. The warden didn't even raise his head, only gesturing at the register set next to him.

"Sign here," he said simply.

The scratching of the pen on the paper reached his ear. He placed his finger on the passage "Capturing arrows with boats of straw"[1], then finally lifted his head to ask, "Which master are you looking for?"

But there was no one there. Had he imagined it? To set his mind at ease, he looked down at the register and saw several words written in a refined script: *Looking for a friend.*

Most students simply wrote their name in the register, as their handwritten signatures were complex and often illegible to prevent forgery. Wu wondered why this mysterious visitor had kept their identity from him, but he wasn't curious enough to go search inside the buildings. He cursed the sneaky children who often came to play tricks on him, then returned to delve once more into the rivalries of Zhu Geliang and Zhou Yu.

The old warden was of course unaware that it was the secret code of the Central Plain Brotherhood. Founded by Wei Yu – the man who assassinated the first emperor of China – this secular organization, whose name had changed many times, was subtle as a breeze. Its members had been so numerous and their operations so confidential that they could sometimes have been in one another's presence without knowing. To compensate for the fallibility of code names, which were too easy to unearth, an old master had had the ingenious idea of these coded signatures. People were often intrigued by these seemingly incomprehensible phrases, each of which carried a meaning learned by new members on their initiation.

It was Shao Jun who had just signed the register, but rather

---

1 A famous passage from the *Romance of the Three Kingdoms* which relates one of Zhu Geliang's ingenious strategies, where instead of making arrows to defend his devastated country, he sends straw boats before the enemy, where they absorb thousands of enemy arrows which he then collects to use in his attack. The modern expression "Capturing arrows with boats of straw" can thus mean "Use the enemy's own resources against them."

than entering the buildings she left to climb a tree on the northern side of Mount Wolong from which she could easily observe the university. In doing so, she obeyed the final instructions given to her just before her master's death.

Would the last mentor of the Brotherhood really come to find her?

After all, there was no guarantee that he had escaped the Eight Tigers. While she had made it to Europe with her master, he had been killed in Venice, and in Florence she would have been lost if hadn't been for Ezio Auditore.

The sound of wings disturbed the silent night. In the darkness she couldn't see what type of bird it was. Wrapped in her cloak, she faded into the night until she was almost invisible.

Where should she go now?

She remembered the spring day like yesterday, at the imperial harem when she had been recruited by the mentor she hoped to meet tonight. Chaos reigned in the palace following the brutal death of the Emperor, all the exits had been sealed, and the young concubine Shao Jun was completely confused. Despite being locked in the harem, she had led an easy, happy life, treated as a playmate by Zhengde, who often took her to play tricks on dignitaries or to tease the eunuchs. The conspiracy hatched by Uncle Zhang was only revealed to her later, and she too would have been exterminated if it hadn't been for the mentor's intervention. He had introduced her to the Brotherhood and given her boots with hidden daggers, then entrusted her to Zhu Jiuyuan before disappearing. She knew nothing about his identity or motivations, and even less about his current situation, supposing he was even still alive.

Master Zhu had fled to Italy to escape Zhang's growing influence, but the eunuch's seemingly limitless reach had flushed him out. In China, he had overcome all the members of the Central Plain Brotherhood… except the mentor.

When Zhu had used his final breath to tell her that the mentor was still alive, Shao Jun thought she had found hope to light the way out of the darkness in which she found herself. It would take more than a mere match to relight the embers, but with the mentor she might stand a chance of rebuilding the Brotherhood.

The foliage on her left quivered almost imperceptibly, a detail which would have escaped her if the night had not been so quiet.

"Master, it that you?" she ventured hoarsely.

A cold gleam suddenly flashed towards her, like a light. Like…

A blade!

Shao Jun drew her weapon in an instant. Anyone who was able to get this close without being noticed had to be dangerous. When he leapt, she guessed from his moves that while he was not a member of the Eight Tigers, he was at the very least one of Zhang Yong's henchmen.

His sword skimmed past her feet at incredible speed. *Crack!* The branch she was standing on suddenly snapped. She would have fallen off her perch if she hadn't already found another beneath her. Swinging from a two-fingered grip, she hurled herself in the air and grabbed a higher branch with an agile pirouette.

Shao Jun was fast, but her attacker was faster. After slicing the young woman's first perch, he quickly cut the second she had just landed on, and began sweeping the air with wide, slicing strokes. Her legs at risk, Shao Jun had no time to regain her balance.

Realizing he had the upper hand, the man sniggered. He had orders to follow Shao Jun and not to kill her, but as he had been spotted, he felt justified in injuring her. He cruelly wondered if she would survive the loss of both her legs. But while the blade flashed through the night in all directions, it cut far more bark than flesh.

Crack! Wood chips flew. The blade grazed past Shao Jun's feet to embed itself in the trunk like a knife in butter. It remained stuck there for a moment, an opening which the young woman quickly exploited to use her own sword on the man. He reacted with terrifying speed, using his middle and index fingers to draw the dagger hidden in his sleeve. She recoiled from it like a small animal, and he parried her blow at the last second with a metallic clang. His desperate defensive move, executed hastily and from unstable footing, caused him to fall from the tree.

Like a chess player who just made a mistake in a key game, he was forced to reevaluate his strategy. Deprived of his sword and with his adversary looming over him from the tree, it would have been suicide to try to reach her; better to keep his feet on firm ground and watch for the openings that would present themselves when she descended. He drew a blade from his left sleeve, ready to make good use of his two daggers. He hoped to parry the next strike with one, then immediately riposte with the second. It was his only chance of winning.

Clang! The blades clashed together. Shao Jun wielded hers with unusual strength, but the man was too busy watching for an opportunity to stab his left dagger between her ribs to dwell on it. While he had left enough space for her to jump to the ground, she didn't seem to want to leave her tree.

"Die, whore!" he managed to blurt out. While Shao Jun was more skilled than he had imagined, she had her limits: she would be unable to gain the upper hand as long as he remained on the ground and she up in the tree. Truth be told, he thought he might even be able to stab his dagger between her shoulder blades at any second.

But it was he who felt a sharp pain in his left shoulder where the young woman's sword had just been planted with unexpected speed. While the wound wasn't mortal, it prevented him from using his arm. Unable to protect himself or attack on that side, he gritted his teeth but didn't back down.

The fight had now become desperate for him. Aware that he was now defenseless on one side, he chose to put everything into one last decisive attack. As an old saying goes, "When opposing forces are equal, courage makes the difference", an idea which the furious man was fully ready to embrace. His absolute focus allowed him to ignore his wound and think of only one thing: killing his opponent. He leapt straight upwards towards Shao Jun to sink his weapon into her heart, only to strike at thin air.

Impossible! He swore. The young woman flew through the air like a supernatural spirit.

"Aah!" he cried as his right shoulder felt the kiss of steel.

Now completely incapacitated, he staggered back two steps, unable to stand properly on his feet. His face was a mix of determination and futile rage.

Shao Jun slid lightly to the bottom of the tree. While she seemed to float in the air a few seconds before, it hadn't been magic, but the rope dart given to her by former Emperor

Zhengde when he sent her to the Leopard Quarter. Several feet long, it was soft as silk and just as thin and durable, able to hold up to two hundred pounds in weight. The young woman had used it for so long that she wielded it like an extension of her own arm. When the man had moved to attack, she had already lodged it in a high branch, which had allowed her to gain the upper hand. Her formidable adversary was no longer a threat.

She hesitated to kill him. She had taken lives since Zhu Jiuyuan's death, but the vulnerability of her predator that had now become her prey made her uncomfortable. He had no such qualms and took to his heels. Shao Jun couldn't allow him to escape. She bounded forward and caught him, half-heartedly planting her sword in his back. The point of the blade ripped through the man's shoulder, causing him to trip and roll to the foot of a camphor tree. As she prepared to end him, a flash of light from the other side of the tree caught her attention.

It was a second assailant lying in wait for the right moment to strike, completely indifferent to the fate of his accomplice. He took advantage of the surprise to attack Shao Jun, forcing her to forget the man on the ground.

Despite her unusual agility it was too late to move out of reach of the attacker's sword: she could only bend her body to an almost inhuman degree to avoid being sliced in two by the sneak attack. Cold sweat soaked her back.

It wasn't the first time she'd had to deal with killers in the pay of the Eight Tigers. The one who had killed Master Zhu in Venice had followed her to Florence and would have killed her too if she hadn't been trained by Ezio Auditore. The man before her seemed even more skilled. She was finished if he reached her.

Shao Jun felt as if time slowed as the blade grazed her waist: the wind blew quieter, a leaf stood motionless in the air, a diffuse light suddenly appeared and a sword miraculously emerged as if from nowhere to intercept the strike that would have cut her in two.

The young woman didn't hear the collision of the blades, but she saw the sparks that burst forth from their meeting. She took advantage of the brief lull to take several steps back and catch her breath. The two silhouettes exchanged crashing blows for several seconds, then everything suddenly stopped.

She regained her breath, and both she and the man she had injured remained transfixed by the shadowy duel. Their faces were indiscernible in the darkness, but the one who had hidden behind the tree was the smaller of the two. In the confusion, she thought it resembled a battle between an angel and a demon.

Crash! The Eight Tigers attacker collapsed and was finished without ceremony. Shao Jun could finally breathe easily. Seized by fear, the injured man scrambled to his feet to resume his mad run. His attempt at escape was cut short by a blow almost imperceptible to the eye, and he fell to the ground. As he touched the earth, a light sparked in his hand and shot towards the sky before exploding into a thousand sparks.

A firework!

Shao Jun felt her heart stop. The man who had saved her withdrew his sword from the body under the tree, wiping it on the dead man's clothes before turning towards the young woman.

"Imperial Favorite, Gao Feng's men will soon arrive with reinforcements. Follow me!" he said quietly.

Gao Feng was one of the dead men? The questions would have to wait. A small troop of men was climbing the slope at the foot of the mountain where a string of lights twinkled. Shao Jun quickly followed the stranger in the opposite direction, into the dense forest of Mount Wolong which no paths dared traverse.

Then it hit her.

It was … it was him! The mentor! The one who had introduced her to the Brotherhood!

His voice was older, but it sounded like the one etched in her memory. And he had called her the "imperial favorite" just like the old Emperor, despite the title having officially disappeared with him. She was both emotional and excited. It was the mentor who had saved her when she was just a teenager, initiated her into the Brotherhood without ever showing her his face or revealing his identity. She hadn't seen him since and had even doubted that he still lived when she wrote the secret code on the university register. Yet he had come. Shao Jun felt like she had finally set foot on land after an eternity at sea.

Their walk led them to a clearing, at the center of which rose a large larch pine with dense branches.

"Young girl, we can rest here a moment without worry. They won't find us here," he declared in a low voice.

Shao Jun pushed through the foliage, finding a grotto formed by interlacing branches where the moonlight and stars failed to reach. She moved further in and bowed, a knee on the earth and her left hand on her chest.

"Master, please call me little sister, like before."

This was how the young recruits of the Brotherhood showed

their respect to their elders. When he had saved her from the grip of the Eight Tigers she had been little more than a child, so this nickname came naturally.

Shhh! A flame burned in the darkness as the mentor lit a small fire, by the light of which Shao Jun made out a thin face with a pointed beard. He looked at her and laughed affectionately.

"You've grown up, so I prefer to call you 'young girl'. You know, in the Brotherhood, we don't really pay much attention to official ranks, so you may simply call me Yangming."

Shao Jun quivered. Yangming? To her ears, this quite ordinary name was a veritable cataclysm.

When she lived her reclusive life in the depths of the Forbidden City she had heard talk of a Yangming. But she couldn't be sure that person had been linked to the Brotherhood, it could be nothing more than a coincidence.

It was the mentor himself who answered her silent question. "I'm also known as Wang Shouren. Young girl, the last two years must have been difficult."

The first time she saw him she was barely fourteen years old. Two years later the death of the Emperor threw the palace into complete chaos and he disappeared, leaving her in the care of Master Zhu. Over the five years that had passed since she had travelled to the other side of the world, overcoming immense challenges which had pushed her childhood to the furthest recesses of her mind. He seemed to have aged a whole decade since the night Master Zhu was assassinated, putting an end to her youthful innocence.

"Mentor, how did you join the Brotherhood?" she asked hesitantly.

If he hadn't been there in front of her, she wouldn't have

believed he still lived. But he was there now, and she was trying to answer some questions that had haunted her since their first meeting.

The fire sputtered out. In the darkness, she heard Master Yangming take several steps.

"I'll tell you everything when the time comes. First we must find a safe place to spend the night."

He looked up at the sky.

"Young girl, Zhang Yong has you in his sights now. What are you planning to do?"

"He will certainly send men after me. I need to leave as soon as possible."

Pausing for a moment, she added, "I must return to the capital."

CHAPTER 2

Yu Dayong, the governor of Nanjing, shook at the sight of the body on the table.

It was Gao Feng, supervisor of the Imperial Residence Bureau and head of the Council of Works[2]. More importantly, he had also been the disciple of the most influential man in the empire, Zhang Yong, and had climbed to this highly enviable rank despite being only thirty-four years old. The old master had much more confidence in this "Little Devil" than in Yu Dayong.

But now his fellow disciple was no more than a lifeless corpse. The governor oscillated between joy and sadness. As a member of the Eight Tigers he should cry like one of his brothers. On the other hand, the early disappearance of such a notable rival could only be in his favor, especially when he had demonstrably played no part in it. Gao Feng had chosen to act alone; against

2 Under the Ming dynasty, several thousand eunuchs governed the affairs of the Inner Palace through specialist councils under the supervision of the Imperial Residence Bureau.

the orders they had received. He had underestimated his adversary and paid for it with his life.

"Uncle Yu!" Mai Bing called from the door.

The eunuch had served him for years. Still young in mind, he immediately understood that his mercurial and opportunistic master was looking to take advantage of the situation to insinuate himself into Zhang Yong's good graces.

"What is it, Mai Bing?"

"Uncle Zhang is here," he replied in a low voice.

"Which Uncle Zhang?"

Yu Dayong had responded with shock, but Mai Bing's panicked air left no room for doubt: there was only one Uncle Zhang. Caught off guard, he rushed to open the door to a large palanquin carried by twenty-four soldiers. The governor ran and prostrated himself on the ground.

"Your humble subordinate, Yu Dayong, reverently welcomes the captain general."

China had always had eunuchs occupying positions of power, but Zhang Yong was captain general of twelve imperial guard battalions entrusted with protecting the capital. As the head of one hundred thousand soldiers in the largest national force, he was undoubtedly the most powerful man the country had ever known. His palanquin had three times as many carriers as those of high-level administrators, and for good reason: laden with beds, chaises, and tables, it was a display of luxury that was instantly recognizable wherever he went.

Not content with having an eye on everything, Uncle Zhang Yong could best anyone in the capital with a sword. The legend was born when the Tartar prince sent his best assassin to kill Zhengde when he led an expedition outside the boundaries of the empire. The man had made short work of the soldiers and the guard, but Zhang Yong had managed to stop him, his own sword against the seventy-pound iron club. During the subsequent fight he had literally dismembered the killer, cutting him apart piece by piece, removing slivers of flesh until little more than a skeleton remained.

Yu Dayong had not been present, but he had seen the huge iron club when the expedition returned to the capital, which was so large that no ordinary man could even have lifted it. He was impressed by few things in this world but knowing that his master could overcome this supernatural weapon with only a single sword sent shivers up his spine. He had vowed complete and utter obedience to him ever since Zhang Yong had removed the former leader of the Tigers and taken his place.

Qiu Ju, Zhang Yong's bodyguard, was the first to move and draw the curtain of the palanquin aside for his master to slowly emerge. The grace and elegance of his physique, relatively large for a eunuch, could have had him mistaken for an old man fond of poetry had his beard been thicker. The contrast with Yu Dayong's fierce appearance was startling. The affable governor rushed towards him with a charming smile, but the master spoke first:

"So, the Little Devil has been killed?"

"Yes, honored captain general. Most likely by the Imperial Favorite..."

Rigidly adhering to protocol, Yu Dayong continued to use Shao Jun's former honorific title despite her status as a rebel.

"How did the girl accomplish such a feat?"

"Honored captain general, Uncle... Uncle Gao did not follow the instructions we were given. He chose to track the imperial favorite on his own, and given that he ranked higher than me, I was unable to oppose his decision ...”

While Yu Dayong spun the situation to his advantage, Zhang Yong knew he would never lie. Among the five Tigers still living, excluding Qiu Ju who followed Zhang Yong like a shadow, Gao Feng had been the worthiest of trust. The captain was aware of the complex and strained relationship between his two disciples. He had hoped that a joint operation would teach them to work together, but his strategy had failed. If he had allowed Gao Feng to choose his partner, perhaps Shao Jun would now be here, bound hand and foot. After a moment of silence, he asked, “Is the body of the Little Devil inside?”

“Yes. We found him on the northern side of Mount Wolong alongside his faithful Pang Chun. The killers had been gone for a while. It was the middle of the night, and we didn’t see any sign of them.”

“Mount Wolong?”

Zhang Yong quivered.

“Let me see him.”

Yu Dayong pushed the door open and stepped aside to let the old man and his guard pass, before following and closing the door firmly behind them. The captain approached the table where the two bodies lay, and ordered in a deep voice, “Qiu Ju, remove their clothes.”

Qiu Ju was nicknamed the Demon, and Gao Feng the Devil. Zhang Yong considered them to be his left and right hands. Nonetheless, one now stood dispassionately cutting the other’s clothes with a knife, using the rough yet expert strokes of the butcher Ding carving up a cow in the fable of Zhuangzi. Their clothes now removed and exposed in all their nudity, the two men were nothing more than corpses.

Zhang Yong inspected them attentively, like a knowledgeable collector before a rare jade statue. Almost breathless, Yu Dayong wondered if the captain wasn't being a little sentimental, but he didn't dare leave. In truth as emotionless as a stone, the old man fumbled with a bamboo tube resting against his chest. It was a dark red hue from being handled over the years and contained a pair of sheepskin gloves as light and supple as a second skin. The tube's cap was lined with small slots which held glittering blades with razor-sharp edges, old but without signs of wear.

Zhang Yong put on the gloves, took out one of the bright blades, and inserted it into one of Gao Feng's wounds before removing it to measure the depth of the wound.

"His heart was pierced by a sword," he murmured.

Yu Dayong had arrived at the same conclusion. While he had never liked Gao Feng, his talent with bladed weapons had been indisputable. Shao Jun would have overcome him only if she had made phenomenal progress during her time in Europe.

"Yes, and the cut is flat at the edges and slightly convex in the center," he hurried to note. "It's an exact match for the imperial favorite's sword."

Zhang Yong said nothing in response, turning to the body of Pang Chun. He had been a low-ranking eunuch, but he was said to have been almost as skilled as Gao Feng. He had clearly taken an injury to each shoulder, fled, and then been finished with a cut to the back. Despite her progress, Yu Dayong found it surprising that the favorite had been able to catch him when she must have still been busy with Gao Feng.

He was about to express his doubts when Zhang Yong announced in a serious voice, "Dayong, the rebel Shao Jun had an accomplice!"

This fateful declaration hit the governor like a bolt of lightning. The favorite's accomplices had always been their sworn enemies. Five years earlier, during the Great Ritual controversy that followed the enthronement of Jiajing, the five representatives of the Eight Tigers threw their united forces behind Zhang Yong to exterminate the Brotherhood. Only the Favorite and Zhu Jiuyuan escaped, but the latter had been caught in Venice. If Shao Jun had been aided by an accomplice, that meant that she had found another unknown survivor to help her achieve her mad desire – to revive the dead organization. Yu Dayong refused to believe it.

Without lifting his head, Zhang Yong continued.

"The blade that pierced the Little Devil's heart was two and one third inches long and penetrated his chest at an angle of five degrees. Gao Feng was five foot three and a half inches, his sword two feet seven inches, and he could swing his blade in arcs of around three feet one inch. From this we can deduce that his killer was at least three feet three and a half inches away from him. A fighter using the correct posture holds their sword one or two inches above the navel, and judging by the wound, this person held theirs at three feet five inches from the ground. As the navel is located between six tenths and six tenths and a third of an inch of the height of the body, the killer measured at least five feet five inches and at most five foot eight inches for their sword to have entered at this angle. Three years ago, when Shao Jun left the capital, the Imperial Palace records noted her height for tailoring her clothes. At that time, she stood five feet one inch, two inches shorter than the Little Devil. Therefore, it was not she who killed him."

Zhang Yong nodded several times and continued again.

"The wounds on Pang Chun's shoulders all have an angle of

sixty-six degrees, which proves that the cuts were delivered from an elevated position. This unusual angle limits the information we can infer. But if we focus on the fatal wound in his back, it clearly results from a strike which was not delivered with great force, while the one which felled the Little Devil was so powerful that two of his ribs were broken with the violence of the impact… I thus deduce that they were not killed by the same person."

Zhang Yong used a scarf to wipe clean the small blade he had used to prod the various wounds, then continued his analysis.

"There were two killers. One measured around five feet and weighed no more than eighty pounds, which to me seems to correspond to Shao Jun… The other measures around five feet seven inches and weighs over one hundred pounds. That person is without doubt a man."

Yu Dayong held his breath. These wounds all looked alike to him and seemed to have all been dealt by the Imperial Favorite. But Zhang Yong read the injuries like an open book! Could you really deduce such detailed information from so little? Hesitantly, he ventured, "Venerable captain general…"

"Dayong, it won't be difficult. You simply need to go to Macao where my friend Pyros will take care of everything, and you will take all the glory."

Pyros? None of the Eight Tigers bore this name. Other than those present in the room, there were two more still alive: Wei Bin, known as "The Snake", and Ma Yongcheng, known as "The Butcher". The first, the former commander of the Three Great Battalions under the Mings, was an exceptional tracker who had located their enemy's headquarters in Beijing during the Great Ritual controversy, allowing them to exterminate the group. The second was known for his sadistic and bloody temperament:

all the members of the Brotherhood who had passed through his hands after their capture had ended up begging for a quick death.

Yu Dayong himself was known as "The Cruel", in homage to the last ruler of the Xia dynasty during whose reign people were exterminated with as much consideration as vermin, as demonstrated in a song from the period with a line that read *"Yet another day of funerals, why am I not dead too?"*. This cursed emperor had long been dead, but Yu Dayong seemed determined to perpetuate his bloody legacy.

It was only in the presence of Zhang Yong that he could be seen to bend and become gentle as a lamb, displaying honeyed obsequiousness. While the mention of this Pyros instantly caused an internal rush of jealousy, he betrayed none of his frustration.

Zhang Yong removed his gloves, returned them to the bamboo tube, and said bluntly, "Dayong, ensure the Little Devil and Pang Chun are get a respectful burial before you leave. They were not lucky enough to experience a natural death, but they died with honor."

A hint of emotion seemed to punctuate his last words. Gao Feng was dead and had no family, so why bother with funerals, Yu Dayong wondered, though he responded only with "Understood."

The captain turned on his heels without another word. Qiu Ju rushed to open the door, then followed him out. Yu Dayong hurried to escort his guests, who climbed back into the palanquin without paying him the slightest notice.

At that late hour, the stars twinkled in the sky and the landscape was thrown into relief by the silvery light of the moon. Inside, the two men seemed to belong to another world. Qiu Ju, who never dared to sit, stood deep in thought to one side of Zhang Yong. After a long moment, he finally said, "Qiu Ju, do you think Shao Jun is still in Shaoxing?"

Qiu Ju lowered his head for a moment, then looked back up and responded, "Venerable captain general, if Shao Jun has returned, it is most certainly to rebuild the Central Plain Brotherhood. Now she has a partner, I think she will leave the area as soon as possible."

Zhang Yong nodded.

"A fitting analysis. At least..." He hesitated briefly, then let out a cold laugh. "Supposing that the Brotherhood can only rebuild itself in the footsteps of its dead, she will either return to the capital, or remain near Mount Wolong."

Qiu Ju jerked in surprise.

"Near Mount Wolong? But there's nothing there except Jishan University. What would she be doing there?"

The rector of this scholarly institution was Master Yangming. During the rebellion of the prince of Ning, the scholar had allowed himself to be captured in an attempt to calm the ongoing unrest and had achieved his aim even before Emperor Zhengde's emissary, Zhang Yong, had set out. One of the ministers suggested that the captive must have had prior connections with the enemy to have so speedily resolved the conflict, but Zhang Yong defended him vigorously, persuading the Emperor that he was above suspicion. And while they rarely met, the two men had since developed a sincere friendship, and it was because of this that Yu Dayong had not troubled the rector when the bodies of Gao Feng and Pang Chun had been found near the university. Which was why it was so surprising that Zhang Yong now seemed to believe he could be a member of the Brotherhood.

The bodyguards of the Southern Songs had been the army's largest and finest soldiers, each wearing a belt embroidered with the words "Legs of Steel". It was after them that Zhang Yong, who hailed from an old aristocratic family, and castrated as he was, had nicknamed his porters the "legs section". All attractive and well built, they were the elite of his troops, so it could easily be argued that restricting them to this simple task was a waste of their talent. From inside the palanquin all that could be heard was the rhythmic beat of their feet on the ground as it sailed through the silent night.

"There are things we regret delegating to others," murmured Zhong.

Being illiterate, Qiu Ju didn't recognize the verse by the poet Lu You, but he understood the meaning.

"Venerable captain general, you should never have trusted anyone."

It was the watchword of the Eight Tigers. When the eunuchs founded the group, they had first taken the name of *zouwu*, named after a benevolent and vegetarian mythical creature, but their cruelty saw them quickly renamed after the tiger. At the time they were led by Liu Jin, who was hated by the people but still an influential figure for whom Zhang Yong seemed to have had boundless respect and loyalty. Who could have imagined that the captain would take advantage of the prince of Anhua's revolt to accuse his master of treason? Sentenced to death, he was subjected to the *lingchi*, the "death of a thousand cuts".

This anecdote was very characteristic of Zhang Yong: to never betray any emotion and deliver the fatal blow when it was least expected. Qiu Ju looked away to avoid looking him in the face.

The next morning Zhang Yong and Qiu Ju paid a visit to Jishan University. While they were the two most influential men in the dynasty, for this meeting they wore ordinary clothes and left the palanquin and its twenty-four porters behind at the foot of the mountain. The captain wrote their names in old Wu's register and left him a tip.

This Zhang Yong had beautiful handwriting, the warden noted as he asked, "Mr Zhang, have you come to study or to teach?"

Some pretentious travelers also visited Jishan in the hope that the prestige of the university would increase their reputation, though it would have been impolite to mention that possibility. The old Wu was slightly perplexed, as these men seemed too old to be students – the small one with light skin had to be in his sixties, and the other in his forties – neither did they have the typical scholarly air of masters. Despite not being an academic, the warden knew enough Chinese characters to read works such as the *Romance of the Three Kingdoms*, and with experience, he had become expert in the art of categorizing people. These two were difficult to pin down.

"Please can you inform Master Yangming that his old friend Zhang Yong has come to visit," asked the smaller of the two.

The request startled old Wu.

"Oh, you're a friend of Master Yangming, how wonderful! Please wait here a moment, I will let him know immediately."

It could not be denied that the university owed much of its prestige to the work of its rector. Without him, despite the efforts of the prefectural magistrate, it would have been unable to stand out from its competitors. Over the years Wu had seen many scholars come to pay their respects to the master, yet it was the first time he had seen someone claiming his friendship. It would have unacceptable to disrespect this imposing man, under whose gaze he had to restrain his tremors. He had barely taken several steps before he encountered Wang Ji, Yangming's favored disciple, reading a document as he walked.

"Hey! Wang Ji!" the warden called.

The twenty-eight year-old Shaoxing native had failed the entrance exam at the ministry of rites three years earlier and returned to the country to continue studying under the rector. Since then, he had single-mindedly dedicated himself to preparing for this year's session.

"Old Wu, what is it?"

"Wang Ji, please can you find Master Yangming and tell him that his old friend Zhang Yong is here?" the warden asked quietly.

While he was trying to avoid saying the visitor's name with any emphasis, Wang Ji, was a well-informed young man, and so was seized with a sudden shiver. Mind racing, he began to think aloud.

"Uncle Zhang! What is he doing here? I didn't know he and my master were close..."

Of course, the most powerful man in the empire would never come here simply to study, but then it seemed just as unlikely that he knew the rector personally. "Very well, old Wu, I will accompany him."

In *The Great Learning,* Confucius wrote that "*the principle of higher learning lies in high virtue*". This text and this quote had greatly inspired the precepts of the university. Wang Ji guided the visitors to the room of Great Learning and stopped before the

Hall of High Virtue where Master Yangming gave his lectures. The vast room was divided into two sections, the first dedicated to Confucius, the second to canonical texts. Once, this library had been known as the Reading Room, but when the old academy had given way to the beautiful new buildings it had been renamed the Chamber of Canonical Texts in a fit of enthusiasm.

Wang Ji turned towards his guests. "Please wait here, I will inform my master immediately."

Qiu Ju, who found it unacceptable that anyone would dare make anyone of their importance wait, felt his anger build. If Zhang Yong had not been there, he would already have become enraged.

He complained despite himself. "Venerable captain general, these petty intellectuals overstep themselves."

"The rector of this university is the most learned man in the empire," Zhang Yong smiled. "You don't want to skip the courtesies, is that not right, Qiu Ju?"

"Of course not, venerable captain general."

The bodyguard examined their surroundings to distract himself from his frustration. The Hall of High Virtue was a large, spacious construction with a very high ceiling, in the corner of which stood a statue of an eagle ferociously tearing its prey to pieces. The bird was not large, perched arrogantly on a protruding beam, its eyes flashing in the light. That bird of prey looks down on us, just like these damned intellectuals, Qiu Ju grumbled to himself.

A man strode towards them, calling out before he reached them, "Uncle Zhang, how shameful! My warden did not recognize you, and my disciple left you waiting here, it's inexcusable!"

At the age of fifty-four, Master Yangming was no longer a young man but his elegance and the spontaneous openness on his face charmed even the impatient Qiu Ju, his anger dissipating like smoke blown by an auspicious wind. Zhang Yong moved to greet the newcomer.

"Brother Yangming, I see the years have treated you kindly, congratulations!"

Anyone who didn't recognize the most influential man in the country would have thought that this was an everyday meeting between old friends. When Master Yangming gave lectures from his platform in the Hall of High Virtue, the crowd of students gathered there to listen exceeded the room's capacity and flowed out onto the steps. When they saw him enter, the young people studying there prostrated themselves, pressing their foreheads to the ground and welcoming him with the formal greeting of "Honor to our esteemed master", as required by the strict rules. The rector led his two guests to the platform and asked a servant to bring some tea.

"Brother Yangming," said Zhang Yong, "you returned to the region of your birth to continue your glorious teachings. I am humbled by your success."

"You flatter me," the rector responded with a small laugh, "I am but a simple teacher who gives instruction to these young students, nothing more."

"Have you seen Brother Ning recently?"

"The prince of Ning is a vigorous old man, the brave always last the longest. But I haven't seen him for a while. You haven't seen him in the capital, Uncle Zhang?"

"Brother Ning is over seventy years old now, and while he is as hardy as an ancient tree, he is no longer of an age to make merry in the city. The Emperor still needs him on the border, so he has not been to the capital for two years."

These nostalgic platitudes annoyed Qiu Ju, who was keen to find out more about the death of Gao Feng. Nonetheless, he suspected that Zhang Yong, cunning tactician that he was, was surely taking the most direct route to achieve his ends. With the congratulations and reminiscing over the pacification of the rebellion finished, the captain mentioned news from the capital, then turned to the banners displayed on the walls of the Hall of High Virtue over the platform. They read: *The mind itself is neither good nor evil. Good and evil are born of intention. Discerning good and evil is an essential knowledge. Studying the ten thousand things enables one to work for good and eliminate evil.*

These words, which summarized the philosophy of the institution, were now known as the "four principles of Master Wang Yangming", and all his students knew them by heart.

"Are these the four principles of the School of Mind?"[3] asked the captain.

"Exactly, but don't laugh, Uncle Zhang!"

Zhang Yong read the sentences aloud before saying:

"Brother Yangming, if the mind is neither good nor evil, then the universe is my mind, and my mind is the universe. In this case, intention, knowledge, and the ten thousand things are also the universe. How then could there be good and evil in them?"

"You ask a very pertinent question, Uncle Zhang. While good and evil didn't exist in the beginning, they appeared alongside intention, which is why we have an innate understanding

3 Wang Yangming, also known by the name Wang Shouren, was the famous representative of the School of Mind which revolutionized Confucianism under the Mings.

of them. However, as knowledge governs behavior, it is by studying, by examining the fundamental principles, that we cultivate good and reject evil."

Growing more confused with every word, Qiu Ju was a man who rejected wholesale anything he didn't immediately understand. What an old bookworm! He grumbled inwardly. Zhang Yong on the other hand was bursting with joy.

"Yes, yes, what clarity!"

The two men exchanged several more pleasantries before the captain finally said, "The hour grows late, we should go. Brother Yangming, you are a philosophical genius. If I didn't have so many duties to perform for the Emperor, I'd stay here to benefit further from your knowledge."

The rector offered his guests one last cup of tea before entrusting them to Wang Ji. The student, who worshipped his master like one of China's sacred mountains, had never noticed that the first of the principles seemed to contradict the other three, and admired Zhang Yong for the unexpected pertinence of his remark. Never had he imagined that a man with such political power could also be a scholar! And even more admirable, he'd had the courtesy to address the rector with respect despite his elder years.

After leaving the building and returning down the mountain, the visitors climbed back into their palanquin.

"Qiu Ju," ordered the captain, "return to the university with several of our most competent agents and identify all the men, young and old, standing five feet five inches and taller and examine their comings and goings over the last three days. I want a thorough investigation and a full report."

Qiu Ju was relieved to finally have concrete instructions.

Barely able to recognize even a few Chinese characters, he hadn't understood a single word of the exchange he had heard. Among the Eight Tigers, Wei Bin and Zhang Yong were the ones who had received the best education, but disparities within the group could be significant…

"Yes, venerable captain general!" he responded enthusiastically.

Between the masters, their disciples, and travelling scholars, Jishan University could hold around a thousand people, with almost two hundred standing over five feet five inches tall. The operation was simple in principle, but long and tiresome in its execution.

"Must Master Yangming also be questioned?"

Qiu Ju wondered if Zhang Yong had forgotten that his old friend also measured over five feet five inches. The rector was undoubtedly a special case, so perhaps it was better he himself asked the question. Would it be overstepping the mark to trouble a person of such stature?

Zhang Yong considered his answer for a moment. The reason he had discussed the four principles with his old friend was to better understand his philosophical beliefs and confirm, as he believed, that their thoughts had diverged since their younger years.

For Master Yangming, the mind was neither good nor evil, and one must examine the nature of good and evil to eliminate the latter. Was this world view compatible with his own? It was a dilemma but returning to the university to resolve it was out of the question.

"Yes, question him the same as the others," he answered coldly.

"You don't completely trust him, venerable captain general?"

"Of course I do, but everyone must be treated equally, that is the principle of acquiring information. Thanks to Yu Dayong and Ma Yongcheng, the prostitute Shao Jun will be caught in our net whether she travels north or south. It will of course be her accomplice who chooses their destination. And if she chooses to go south..."

He chose not to continue, aware that his subordinate was as weak in mind as he was physically powerful. He felt like a general of old, playing out his war like a game of chess. Now his pawns were in place, the game could really begin. Shao Jun had gained the upper hand for now, but neither she nor her companion could have suspected that they were actually heading into a trap set by Zhang Yong. Yu Dayong, waiting in the south, was slightly weaker than Ma Yongcheng. Zhang Yong deduced that he would be correct about her guide's identity if she chose to travel in that direction.

He smirked and let out an evil laugh. His master's opaque humor irritated Qiu Ju. Why had he not finished his thought? What did it matter if the prostitute went south?

Zhang Yong had nonetheless felt pained on realizing that his old friend had become distant from him, despite his courtesy. While their goals remained the same, their paths to reach it were radically different. Far from the assured façade he displayed to Qiu Ju, in his heart he prayed that Master Yangming was not his mysterious adversary.

CHAPTER 3

Zhang Qiang couldn't help looking in the direction of the Palace of Earthly Tranquility as the setting sun reflected off the glossy varnished tiles. She took a deep breath and pushed open the doors of the imperial palace.

"Let's go in," she said to her servant.

The concubine hierarchy had seven ranks: the pure, the beauteous, the worthy, the respectful, the favored, the clear, and the serene. Just a few years earlier Zhang Qiang had been in the fifth rank and lived in the sixth pavilion to the east, in the coldest and most miserable corner of the palace complex.

Now she lived in the imperial palace, a huge building that was still freezing due to the small number of people who lived there. Once in her apartments she washed, then her servant lit a candle, bid her goodnight and left. Alone in her room, the concubine watched the play of light and shadow caused by the flame, remembering with a smile how she had reprimanded the Empress that day – she couldn't bear to see a mere favored named as an imperial consort.

Zhang Qiang recalled her trepidation as she waited to discover her rank on arriving at the harem, and her jealousy when Jun was named the imperial favorite. It all seemed so distant that it felt like another life.

She wished she could see Jun again…

"A-Qiang…" someone whispered.

She leapt up, heart thudding in her chest.

Had her prayers been answered? Perhaps she was going mad, the result of living like a recluse for so long in the palace. She almost screamed when a hooded shadow appeared in front of her, but stopped as she recognized a familiar face. The intruder removed their dark cloak and stepped into the light, and Zhang Qiang had to hold back another exclamation, this time of joy. The person standing before her was none other than the only friend she had ever had in the palace. The concubine had to control the urge to jump forward and envelop her in a hug, as her bound feet made any sudden physical movement painful. Full of emotion, she lost her balance and was caught by a hand whose warm contact finally convinced her that it wasn't a ghost. No, it was really her. She seemed to have been marked by the challenges of recent years, but there was no doubt…

"Jun! Is it really you?"

"Yes," her friend answered before glancing around the room. "A-Qiang, how long have you lived in the imperial palace?"

"Three years. I moved here after you left."

The imperial consort's voice trembled. She cast a suspicious look at her friend, and asked, "Jun, how did you get in here?"

Jun gave a small smile. They were so different. When Emperor Zhengde had chosen her as favorite, he had entrusted her with the task of spying on the eunuchs. She had come to know the

Forbidden City like the back of her hand and was certainly more familiar with the topography than A-Qiang. Nonetheless, while she had easily entered on this occasion, it was only thanks to Master Yangming, who still maintained a solid network of contacts in Beijing despite the fall of the Brotherhood. People everywhere still treated him with deference – in the roads, the shops, and even within the palace complex. Under these conditions, avoiding the surveillance of the Hidden City was not as impossible a task as Zhang Qiang seemed to imagine.

"Don't worry," Shao Jun responded quietly. "No one saw me. I just came to see you; I'll leave again soon."

The imperial consort's face was beautiful, but she seemed to lack vitality as she gazed blankly into the distance.

"Jun, have you come t-t-to collect it?" she stammered, very unlike herself.

The Emperor had been seduced by her dancing and singing talent. Seeing the young woman, who always spoke with such clarity and confidence, expressing herself in such an uncertain way didn't bode well. Hesitating a moment, she continued.

"Jun, I'm really sorry but I… lost it."

Shao Jun's eyebrows twitched slightly, but she simply rested a hand on her friend's shoulder to reassure her.

"Do you remember where you were when you lost it?"

"The day you left and I performed the mulberry tree dance for the Dowager Empress, I left it in the Palace of Benevolent Longevity…"

It had been the third year of Jiajing's reign. As an imperial concubine, Shao Jun had lived with the Dowager Empress in the Palace of Benevolent Tranquility and been subject to a strict regime which forbade her from going out without permission. As a result, she had needed to disguise herself to flee when Zhang Yong had begun to eradicate the Brotherhood in Beijing. Urgently needing to leave and avoid being caught up in it, she had entrusted her most precious possession to Zhang Qiang, who had been free to move around. She had hidden it in a decorative vase in the Palace of Benevolent Longevity, a relatively safe place due to the small number of people who lived in the residence. Who could have known that two years and three months later the palace would be devastated by a fire which ravaged the building down to the last tile? Now it was nothing more than a pile of ashes, vases included.

Shao Jun listened to this tearful account without betraying the slightest emotion.

"It must have been fate," she eventually sighed.

She had noticed when she entered the Forbidden City that the Palace of Benevolent Longevity had been destroyed and replaced with a new building, but she had never imagined that a fire was to blame.

The gift from former Emperor Zhengde had thus disappeared forever. The young woman almost felt like she was grieving a second time over.

The life she had led in the Forbidden City had been sad and lonely, but she had least had her freedom thanks to Zhengde. He had granted her the right to move around as she pleased, a privilege no other concubine had ever received. In the beginning he had asked her to spy on the nobles, dignitaries, and eunuchs, but shortly before his death when she was thirteen, he had given her an object and asked her to keep it safe. This mark of absolute trust had made her cry for the first time in her life. The item in question had become a symbol of her relationship with her deceased spouse.

With the fire, the last vestige of a bygone era had gone up in smoke.

"There is nothing to be done, A-Qiang, what is past is past. Is Uncle Chen still in the palace?"

"Which Uncle Chen?" asked the imperial consort, relieved at the change of subject.

The name was so common that at least five or six eunuchs bore it. One of them was in her retinue, but he was unlikely to know Shao Jun.

"Uncle Chen Xijian."

"Oh, that Chen! His reputation was in tatters when he was no longer wanted in the Leopard Quarter and he was asked to leave the capital. I don't know what happened to him after."

Chen Xijian had been the eunuch attending the Leopard Quarter and a loyal servant of Emperor Zhengde, which was why he was removed from the capital following the Emperor's death. Shao Jun remembered him as a courteous man, and importantly, one with no links to Zhang Yong. She tried to look detached.

"Oh really? Then there's no one else for me to see here… I should go."

The imperial consort dried her tears.

"Where will you go, Jun?" she asked with a surprised expression that amused her friend.

"Much has changed, A-Qiang. The less you know, the better."

Zhang Qiang had been unable to hide her jealousy when Shao Jun was named the imperial favorite, first among the imperial consorts, because she had always aspired to a similar position. Now that she had achieved her dream under the reign of Emperor Jiajing, she was worried it might evaporate.

The time had come for the two friends to say their goodbyes, but they stood for a moment, plainly measuring the depth of the gulf that existed between them.

The trespasser almost faded into the dark night with her dark clothing, invisible as long as she avoided the moonlight. She pulled up her hood.

"Jun, go quickly," breathed an increasingly alarmed Zhang Qiang. The imperial palace seemed to be deserted, but a patrol could appear at any minute, and if they found her there…

The hour was late, but between the porters, escorts, bodyguards, and administrators assigned to posts and patrols, over a hundred people were still coming and going within the Forbidden City. Shao Jun had made it to her friend without being seen and she trusted her ability to leave just as discreetly, but it would be disastrous if she were discovered.

"Very well, I'm going," she said quietly before opening the window.

Zhang Qiang sighed. As she left, her friend turned to add:

"A-Qiang, when I returned from Europe, I arrived at the port in the city with the Indian coral trees."

"Is it still the same as I described?"

"Hmm."

Shao Jun didn't say more, fearing that her friend would hear the catch in her voice. Despite all the years spent like sisters in the harem, they had become strangers to one another.

A gust of wind caused Zhang Qiang to shiver, then she was suddenly alone, as if she had been visited by a ghost. Nothing moved in the dark night beyond the half-open window.

"Take care, Jun," she whispered.

The Chinese Emperor's highest-ranking concubine felt tears roll down her cheeks, her face pale as the whitest jade.

She knew it was the last time she would see the only person to ever inspire tenderness and friendship in her, and regretted losing the object entrusted to her friend by the dead Emperor.

Before Italy, Shao Jun would never have seen things in the same way. But after all the years of being hunted, plotting, and lying she was no longer the carefree girl she had once been. She'd remembered a detail from Ezio Auditore's teaching on the subject of loyalty and treason: if the pupils of the person you are speaking to dilate and their pulse increases, they are hiding something. This was why she had moved close to Zhang Qiang and put her hand on her shoulder. Looking into her friend's eyes, she hadn't seen joy at the sight of an old friend, only fear of the consequences of this unexpected return.

The woman she had seen tonight was no longer her childhood friend.

Her heart shattered into a thousand pieces; Shao Jun stood deep in thought. Memories of their friendship had helped her though the difficult years overseas, but now she had to face the truth: their friendship was dead.

Who were her parents? Why had they left her in the palace at such a young age? Her earliest memories were of growing up in the walls of the harem, constantly terrified of the older concubines who never treated her as one of their own. Zhang Qiang had been the only one to open her heart to her. She had thought the connection between them infallible, everlasting. She'd been wrong. How could she blame her friend? People changed; it was as simple as that. At least she hadn't alerted the guard.

"Perhaps I'm cursed…" Shao Jun whispered to herself.

Before the Emperor chose her as his favorite, the only person who didn't avoid her was an ancient palace worker who sometimes gave her fruit when there was no one around. One day the young Shao Jun asked her why the others weren't nice to her, and the servant responded by stroking her head, simply answering that she must have been born under an unlucky star.

It was the first time she ever heard someone speak of fate, and at the time she hadn't understood what it was. The old woman's words took on greater meaning now her life was nothing but misfortune.

The old woman had been killed after discovering the plot of the Eight Tigers, but the mentor had saved Shao Jun and welcomed her to the Brotherhood, where she had been doted upon by novices and masters alike. Despite being the youngest member, she had finally felt like she belonged to a family. Her good luck had been short lived however, as her new world was soon torn apart during the events unleashed by the plot. The Emperor's favorites had perished with him and her friendship with A-Qiang was gone… Shao Jun could no longer believe in anything except her ill-starred fate.

The Emperor may have changed but the guards' rounds were the same as ever. Shao Jun knew their routes like the back of her hand and moved through the Forbidden City like a shadow. She crept around blind corners, pressed herself against walls to allow guards to pass at intersections, and melted into the shadows with her cloak. But though she swam through the night like a fish through water, she was gripped by unease.

The Six Eastern Palaces stood to the west. She passed through the rear galleries, then came out into the new Palace of

Benevolent Longevity, built on the ruins of the old palace and surrounded by a high wall. The guards never went this far, so she could finally relax a little. The ground was still blackened by the fire that had destroyed the old building.

Beyond the protective wall and its moat lay one of a dozen imperial warehouses, used to store various unique items and tools created by a range of artisans. Former Emperor Zhengde had been interested in these types of strange curiosities, and had often taken Shao Jun to see them. But the young woman's attention had always been drawn to Xiyuan, the small landscaped islet between the southern lake and the central lake of Lake Taiye which was the imperial city's weakest point.

One of the iron beams which passed underneath the wall was removable: once taken out, she could easily come and go without being observed. The secret passage was Zhengde's idea, executed when he had the Leopard Quarter built in Xiyuan park. He liked the building much more than his palace apartments; he had even received the Portuguese delegation from Perez there. Shao Jun lived there for two years before the old Emperor noticed her, and seduced by her graceful figure, had made her his favorite to more easily assign her spying missions both inside and outside the City. He had sometimes taken this secret passage himself when his life of confinement weighed on him too heavily, but now she was probably the only one who still know of its existence. Nonetheless, she wanted to visit the ruins of the Leopard residence before leaving, particularly the Xifan pavilion.

A cool breeze blew across Shao Jun's face. She had passed the imperial warehouse without realizing and was now on the large bridge with arches that marked the boundary between the central and southern sections of Lake Taiye. She had gone halfway across before stopping, chilled by a freezing blast of wind that cut through the air like a knife. A light blue mist floated above water that was probably frozen at this late hour.

A blurred silhouette began to appear at the end of the lake.

The Leopard Quarter had been left to rot since Emperor Zhengde's death and no one visited Xiyuan park any more. Even the guards no longer made the effort to include this deserted place in their rounds. Shao Jun would never have expected to see anyone there in the middle of the night. The silhouette also froze, just as surprised as she. It would have been easy to believe time had stopped if the fog had not continued its malicious swirl. The unknown figure seemed to wear a guard's uniform, but the fact that they hadn't immediately alerted the others was suspicious. Perhaps it was someone else who had also crept quietly into the Forbidden City? But what were they be doing there?

Tching! The characteristic sound of a blade being drawn from its sheath. The silhouette leapt forward and hurled itself at Shao Jun.

Less muscular than a man, the young woman had trained hard to compensate for her lack of strength. Refusing to flee the confrontation, she ran to meet her adversary, reaching them in seconds. Even from several feet away she still couldn't see their face, hidden as it was in the shadows. She noticed that it was a small man, armed with a saber longer than those carried by the palace guards.

The bridge was barely wide enough for five or six people to walk side by side, a constraint which could determine the outcome of this fight.

Shao Jun drew her weapon and immediately attempted a thrust, which was easily parried by her opponent. The response came fast but was quickly intercepted with a clang. The sabre instantly swept underneath the young woman's blade as she once again avoided injury. In a heartbeat the man transferred his weapon to his left hand and sliced the air with an unexpectedly wide blow. Shao Jun should have no choice but to jump into the icy water of the lake to escape the kiss of steel. But somehow she reacted quickly enough to counter. *Clang!*

The two combatants seemed equally surprised by the other's skill. They moved almost soundlessly across the stones of the bridge, crossing their weapons in a flurry of strikes, each more dangerous than the last. The smallest mistake could be fatal in such an exchange. The man switched the blade between his hands once more as he bent low. This time he tried to reach Shao Jun's legs, sending her leaping into the air, arms outspread like the wings of an eagle as she jumped to avoid the blow.

The knife-edge combat was a nightmare. She had not expected a fight during her furtive visit to the Forbidden City, and certainly not to fight such a powerful opponent. Fortunately, she wore the cloak given to her by Ezio Auditore which cushioned the sword strikes and made her moves harder to predict without constricting her movement. The accessory was typical of the Western brotherhoods, which compensated for their lesser kung-fu skills by using creative tools. To increase her chance of survival, Shao Jun decided to fight with her sword in her right hand and her rope dart in the other.

She thought she would be sliced open like a sacrificial lamb when her adversary switched hands for the third time. She tugged sharply on the rope that she had quietly hooked over the bridge's opposing guardrail, sending herself flying to land behind the man. Her leg would have been cut off without her cloak to soften the blows from her opponent's saber.

The two combatants had changed positions again, switching from east to west. Shao Jun tightened her sweaty grip on her weapons as they threated to slip from her hands. Her trusty dart was of no use during the next flurry of blows. Gritting her teeth, she emptied her mind and prepared to receive the next attack. But the man had left the bridge and disappeared into the black night.

Was he preparing an ambush? The location wasn't ideal. Suddenly, the young woman realized that the dark night was brighter, and a thunderous sound echoed behind her.

The Leopard Quarter was on fire!

She couldn't believe her eyes. This was why the other intruder, who was clearly responsible, had chosen to flee instead of continuing the fight. A fire of this size would soon attract the attention of the guards. But why destroy a building which hadn't been used since the death of the old Emperor?

These questions would have to wait until later. Shao Jun jumped from the bridge and glanced behind her before moving to her secret passage. It was better not to linger.

The building of the Leopard Quarter began in the third year of the Emperor's reign, when he had been seventeen, and she at least fourteen. The construction had taken four years and cost two hundred and forty thousand two hundred silver taels. The young woman was sufficiently familiar with the place to identify the section where the fire had begun: the Xifan pavilion.

It was the largest of the almost two hundred buildings

which formed the residence, and Shao Jun had not been allowed to go near it, on Zhengde's orders. She once heard that someone who made it inside had seen dismembered bodies hung on the wall, their stomachs sliced open and intestines on view. The description had terrified her, but curiosity won out and she had often tried to spy through the windows, though she never saw anything more than vague shapes. A few chairs and tables, as well as a huge iron cage that might hold a ferocious animal, were the only solid elements she had made out, but she had been certain that the walls were stained with splashes of blood.

What had been the purpose of the Xifan pavilion? Perhaps the Emperor had given her the answers to her questions on the day of his death, when he had entrusted her with the sealed metal tube that must contain a scroll. She remembered its smooth surface had been engraved with the characters Dai Yu, which she had also seen on a tablet hanging inside the Xifan pavilion. They referred to one of the sacred mountains at the edge of the East China Sea. If A-Qiang was to be believed, the answers she sought had been lost forever along with the case.

Struck down by a devastating illness, at the time of his death Zhengde had suspicions about the last man he still trusted, Zhang Yong. It was why he told Shao Jun to prevent the scroll he entrusted her with from ever falling into his hands.

Filled with nostalgia and regret, the young woman shivered in the cold night air. As she reminisced, she suddenly realized the identity of the man she had just fought.

Wei Bin, a member of the Eight Tigers!

And the most powerful, according to Zhu Jiuyuan. He could

only have been there on Zhang Yong's orders. But why risk coming here just to burn these dilapidated old buildings?

The leader of the Tigers must have got his hands on the scroll. But it was strange that he had waited for Shao Jun to return before he acted, if he'd had it in his possession since the destruction of the Palace of Benevolent Longevity. She was missing a piece of the puzzle.

The young woman was illuminated by a sudden burst of flames.

A-Qiang had been lying when she said that the scroll had been burned. That was the real reason for her nervousness. She'd been worried that her betrayal would be discovered! There was only one explanation: the imperial consort had given the scroll to Zhang Yong herself.

Shao Jun felt her heart sink.

A-Qiang must have been supported by a high-ranking dignitary to become an imperial concubine on the new Emperor's accession to the throne, and Zhang Yong was the only one who could have helped her climb the ranks at such speed. It was easy to imagine what she might have offered in exchange. After all, she had said that she had hidden the scroll in the palace after Shao Jun's departure, almost a year before the fire. At the time, A-Qiang had simply been one concubine among many at the imperial residence and had many opportunities to visit the Palace of Benevolent Longevity despite not living there. In addition, her rank was not far above that of a servant, allowing her to come and go without being watched. She would have easily been able to move the scroll.

It was impossible to ignore the evidence. Despite the trust placed in her by her old friend, all Zhang Yong had needed to

do was promise A-Qiang the title of consort in exchange for the object of his desire. Anything could be sacrificed if it achieved her goal to ascend the social ranks. It wasn't surprising that Shao Jun's arrival had terrified her.

A single tear rolled down her face as she squatted in front of the secret passage, looking back as the flames rose from Xiyuan park.

CHAPTER 4

"There were such horrors in the Leopard Quarter?"

Eyebrows furrowed, Master Yangming drank a mouthful of his tea as he contemplated the blanket of snow covering Lake Bixia[4]. Its surface was entirely frozen, but the shoreline was fortunately still visible to passersby.

Master Yangming himself had written the words *Emerald Clouds,* the translation of "Bixia", on the front of his home facing the lake. The manor had been gifted to him by the prefect of Shaoxing as thanks for his help in ending the revolt of the prince of Ning.

"It must have been A-Qiang who gave the scroll to Zhang Yong," Shao Jun said quietly.

After considering for a moment, Wang Yangming put down his cup and picked up two bamboo canes resting near the back door.

---

4 Lake Bixia was originally located opposite the philosopher's home in Shaoxing, Zhejiang, China.

"Come, let's go break a little ice!"

The young woman wondered why the mentor changed the subject so suddenly, but, knowing there was always purpose behind his actions, she followed and took the proffered cane without asking any further questions. One of its ends had turned brown with use, while the other was rough and worn. Wang Yangming made towards the snow-covered Tianquan bridge and once there he hit the frozen lake with a loud bang. Despite his frail appearance, his firm posture added strength to his blow: the cane slid smoothly through the powdery snow, then into the ice with enough power to break it. A large, gurgling crack opened in the ice, a gaping wound on the pristine expanse.

"Now no one will accidentally venture onto the lake tonight," he explained.

This part of the lake, which was its smallest and least frequented area, was part of the prefectural district. The snow there was deeper and more tenacious, and its surroundings easily flooded, but its water was much clearer.

Finally, Wang Yangming said, "I started secretly investigating Zhang Yong when he started acting strangely after the investiture of the new Emperor… I later discovered he was diverting a large portion of funds for the imperial guard towards Canton instead."

"Canton? Why Canton?"

Headquarters of the provincial government and capital of the province of Guangdong, this important city was a trading center between land and sea, despite being some distance from the coast. It was also a long way from the empire's capital, so it was easy to imagine it as a good place for discreetly carrying out shady operations.

"I was just as surprised as you," said Yangming. "I later learned he was communicating secretly with the Portuguese and managing a small island in the South China Sea from this base."

He hit the ice again and a pool of water formed on the surface.

"I think it's connected with what you just told me," he murmured.

"I still don't understand what that scroll was supposed to be…"

"No one seems to know, to tell the truth. But our former Emperor gave it to you on his deathbed, prophesying that the person who opened it would control the world, so it must be an incredibly important document. It's no surprise that Zhang Yong is so eager to get his hands on it."

The mentor hesitated for a moment, then suddenly raised his head.

"I'll worry about that later. For now, I have ice to break."

They moved around the lake, breaking the frozen surface along the banks to reveal pure, clear water. Master Yangming noticed Shao Jun's reddened hands.

"Are you cold, young girl?" he asked with a small laugh.

"No, no."

While the beginning of this spring[5] was not the most clement, as evidenced by the persistence of the snow, the young woman had warmed up as she walked.

"The universe is my mind and my mind is the universe," declared Wang Yangming. "Warmth and cold exist only in my mind. The ten thousand things of this world are nothing and my mind alone gives birth to them. The weather is what it is, and if you are cold, it is only in your mind."

---

5 According to the lunar calendar, spring begins after Chinese New Year (end of January or the beginning of February).

The first phrase of this declaration was a quote from Liu Jiuyuan, one of the great philosophers of the Song dynasty. It was based on these words that the Beijing Brotherhood had been named the Society of the Mind, that the mentor had named his school of thought the School of Mind, and why Master Zhu had become Zhu Jiuyuan, in homage to the philosopher. When Wang Yangming had welcomed the young girl into the organization, he had never revealed his name to her and had limited himself to teaching her only the basics of martial arts due to her age, entrusting Zhu Jiuyuan with her intellectual education. A task which he was able to undertake in only a very limited way due to the limitations imposed by their flight to the West. Intrigued by these words, Shao Jun asked, "Master, if the ten thousand things are born from my mind, then they have no existence of their own… Does that mean that neither good nor evil truly exist?"

"In the beginning there was neither good nor evil," the mentor responded with a short laugh. "Just like the beauty and strength of a new carriage are put to the test when travelling, the natural balance of our mind is threatened by the appearance of emotion. Therefore we must endeavor to harmonize them through knowledge and exercise, which allow us to 'drive' our spiritual carriage safely for thousands of lis."[6]

This analogy was the basis of the School of Mind, whose basic principles were written on the great scroll hung in the Hall of High Virtue. Although it was up to individuals to combine knowledge with practice, few used it to distinguish good from evil. After successfully exploring all the subtleties of his

6 A Chinese measure of distance. One li measures around 500m.

thoughts, Wang Yangming had passed it and its accompanying military applications on to his disciples in Wang Ji's generation. Zhu Jiuyuan was a military expert, but despite his best intentions he was far from the most learned scholar and was unable to be the teacher Shao Jun needed to fully embrace the School of Mind. Hardened by her years of wandering and the massacre of her loved ones by the Eight Tigers, the young girl's heart had filled with anger. It was possible she might succumb to the demons that haunted her soul, and her crimes lead her to certain death. At this crossroads in her life, she had thus become the living embodiment of the principle by which "good and evil are born of intention". And it was Wang Yangming's duty to teach her how to work for good and to eliminate evil. Fortunately for her, the wise old man was a kind and patient master who communicated his philosophy in clear and simple terms.

"Thank you for your teaching, master," she said without understanding that it was the turbulence of her mind which had made her insensible to the cold.

Wang Yangming struck the surface of the lake once more with his cane, but the ice was already broken, and the bamboo only stirred small pieces of it which collided with a quiet thud.

"What secret hides this ice which is sharp as a blade?" he asked.

The School of Mind was based on Confucianism, but it also owed some of its foundation to Zen Buddhism. Its four principles were styled on the enigmatic format of the verses in canonical texts. Wang Yangming's disciples thus argued in the Zen style, beginning with an opaque statement and then arriving at a clear philosophical conclusion. Despite her low

level of instruction and the fact that she was unused to this type of thinking, Shao Jun had an epiphany:

"Even the sharpest ice returns to water in the spring."

The master let out a sincere laugh, then quickly lifted his cane to point it at the young woman's chest like a sword, which she parried with a loud *crack*! The bamboo seemed like it could fell an army when in the hands of such a talented fighter.

If one breaks the ice and waves emerge, the solid and liquid coexist under our gaze. But when this broken pellicle melts as spring arrives, who then can still separate it from the lake? At its height, the art of the sword does not imitate the stiff inflexibility of ice, but the liquid properties of water: the blade is no longer hard and slicing, but fluid, ephemeral... and thus impossible to counter.

Shao Jun's style was derived from Master Wang's, and she already had a high level of skill when Ezio Auditore stepped in to continue her training. Despite her efforts, her basic technique had mingled with that of her Italian mentor, but she had been unable to successfully compensate for the fundamental differences that existed between the Western school and the Chinese school. Noting her martial uncertainties, Wang Yangming had brought her to break the ice in the hope that she would understand the absurdity of setting the Western art of the sword against the Chinese because, like ice and water, they were simply two forms of the same basic element.

To counterattack and defend against the cane pointed at her, the young woman had been forced to use Zhu Jiuyuan's and Ezio Auditore's teachings together at the same time. She had parried the strike with speed rather than dodging but had rounded off her riposte instead of thrusting, a very natural and thus more effective move. She had just assimilated Wang Yangming's complex precepts with complete clarity through the instinctive language of her body, and now exchanged high-speed strikes with him without the slightest effort.

"Oh thank you, master!" she exulted.

"Martial arts and philosophy are different, but their foundations are identical. I studied the Six Classics[7] fervently, and the Six Classics shaped my thinking."

This mention of the Six Classics was actually a quote from Liu Jiuyuan, who had given this exact answer when asked why he no longer studied. He had also been an eminent teacher, as accomplished in martial arts as he was in philosophical study.

Shao Jun had not studied these texts, but she had been trained by two great masters whose teachings she had blended to shape her mind, without which she would not have had the confidence to face opponents such as Gao Feng or Wei Bin. Wang Yangming's analogies had been the alchemy she needed to transform the lead of her bastard style into gold. Pleased with her success, he smiled at his pupil.

"Young girl, you have not studied long, but you understand the greatness of the mind, which is not something everyone can achieve. I have taught many students the philosophy of my school, but you are the only one who has ever received my teachings in the martial arts."

Seeing the sadness in his eyes, Shao Jun realized he was thinking of the almost entirely destroyed Society of the Mind. While the master certainly had many able students of his

---

7 Foundational books of Chinese philosophy, including the Books of Rites, Odes, Changes, and the Spring and Autumn Annals compiled by Confucius.

philosophy at the university, very few were equally competent in martial arts. Now she was the only one left to take over and continue his teachings.

"Master, you will find peace again when the Society of the Mind is restored."

She managed to draw a smile from him, and he resumed his role as teacher.

"To continue your path towards the law of mind, you must have complete understanding of the principle of developing knowledge through practice, because unfortunately our road inevitably leads to Uncle Zhang."

Shao Jun remained silent as she considered Master Yangming's words. She had begun on the path to the law of mind several years before. With the death of Gao Feng, only six of the Eight Tigers remained, with Yu Dayong the Cruel and Ma Yongcheng the Butcher both being less skilled in the use of swords – though this did not mean they lacked talent. Qiu Ju the Demon and Wei Bin the Snake were both quite accomplished. When she faced the latter on the bridge leading to the Leopard Quarter, she had observed the yawning gap that still existed between her and these dangerous martial arts experts. Wang Yangming believed himself to be of a similar level, but knew he was far from being a match for Zhang Yong.

Yet she refused to give up.

"Master, even a three-foot layer of ice must melt eventually."

"Excellent!" Wang Yangming replied, breaking into laughter. "The treasures of the greatest army can be taken, but the ideals of the most ordinary men are inviolable. Your determination does you credit, young girl."

But the mentor's pride was very real.

"Zhang Yong doesn't seem to scare you, master. How is this possible?"

She noticed that he called the leader of the Tigers "Uncle Zhang", and spoke of him with something close to respect despite the fact that the man had reduced the Society of the Mind to nothing. Her question was bold and perhaps lacked deference, but she needed to understand.

Wang Yangming swallowed and took a deep breath before replying.

"I sometimes wonder if Uncle Zhang and I are not two sides of the same coin."

Shao Jun was speechless.

"Once," the master muttered, "when I helped quell the rebellion of the prince of Ning, Zhang Yong came as Emperor Zhengde's representative, and we had a long discussion..."

Master Yang Yiqing, who they both respected, and this conversation had remained etched into both their memories. Despite the difference in their age and status, that evening the three men realized they shared the same ideals and regretted not meeting one another sooner. While normally a reserved character, the master seemed emotional as he reminisced. He turned his head to hide his face from Shao Jun and said, "About that box you left here last time... I've got a few leads..."

She had left it with him as a safety measure before departing for Beijing. The object had previously been given to her by Ezio Auditore when they parted. He had explained to her that it was a treasure that members of the European Brotherhood passed from generation to generation, and that she could open it to use its secrets if she was ever faced with insurmountable difficulty. Not knowing where to start to revive the Society of the Mind, she had opened it in Master Yangming's company. Instead of the magical object she had expected, the box was completely empty. Even the wise mentor was at a loss to explain what this meant.

"Why was the box empty, master?"

"I remember a book I read a long time ago. It mentioned scant detail but spoke of an object known as the 'Precursor Box'. All the author knew was that it dated from ancient times, and that its purpose was a mystery."

"Do you remember the name of the book?"

"It was called the *Record of Blood Spilt for a Righteous Cause* and was written under the reign of the Songs, but I don't know the author. According to my notes, it was an account of the siege of Diaoyu fortress in 1259, and the box is only briefly mentioned."

That was disappointing. Wang Yangming was amused by the young woman's crestfallen expression.

"I have learned something else, however."

"What?"

"The Tao priest Yan of the Imperial Academy also writes of a box."

"What is the Imperial Academy?" asked Shao Jun, frowning.

It was the most prestigious institute of higher learning in the capital. The Classical Academy was administered and led by Shan, and the imperial academy by Priest Yan.

"His full name is Yan Song. He held an insignificant position at Hanlin academy in Nanjing until last year, when suddenly he was promoted on Uncle Zhang's recommendation.

"Does that mean the Tigers are after the box?"

Master Yangming nodded.

"The other night on Mount Wolong, Gao Feng remained hidden while you fought his accomplice not only because he wanted to see who you were meeting, but also to ensure that the box was in your possession. It also explains why you were able to avoid the killing blow… because he hesitated at the last second."

Shao Jun had initially underestimated Gao Feng due to the clumsy attack that she had avoided despite the element of surprise. But she now knew that it had been at least as dangerous as her encounter with Wei Bin on the bridge in Xiyuan park. She also understood why the Tiger had hesitated.

"He saw the box at my waist!"

The young woman had kept it with her ever since leaving Europe, and had attached it to her belt that night. Gao Feng hadn't seen it until he was close, at the very moment he made to attack. He had been forced to change his attack at the last second to avoid damaging the precious object.

Master Yangming nodded slightly.

"He missed his target, but not by much!" he said.

Shao Jun remained silent. She still didn't know the purpose of the box, but she had at least learnt that Zhang Yong sought it. It was now clear that the Society of the Mind could only be rebuilt if the Eight Tigers were defeated first. Although two were already dead, the survivors had immense political power and each was a master of the art of kung-fu; vanquishing them would be no mean feat. Gao Feng had fallen to Wang Yangming's blade because he hadn't expected him to be there, and without that timely intervention Shao Jun would most certainly have perished. And Zhang Yong would continue to hunt them while he remained determined to have the box…

Master Yangming stroked his beard with a mischievous twinkle in his eye.

"Young girl, what do you think of using the box to lure and trap one Tiger after another?" he asked.

"It's a brilliant idea, master."

"This plan will put you in great danger."

"I will do whatever it takes to destroy the Eight Tigers and rebuild the Society of the Mind."

"Good," stated the mentor after thinking for a moment. "Other than Uncle Zhang, Qiu the Demon and Wei the Snake will be the most troublesome. The first is cruel, unable to think on his own, and follows his master like a shadow; the second is not as skilled, but we will need to get him out of the way quickly before he becomes a problem. The original chess players, whose style defied convention, were the most unpredictable as their opponents could only react to their moves and not anticipate them. That is how we must plan our strategy: in assuming your next move, Uncle Zhang will surely send Ma the Butcher or Yu the Cruel against you ... But we will take the initiative and attack Wei Bin, which neither he nor his master will expect. Our only alternative would have been Luo Ziang, the last of the Tigers, but we don't know where he is or when he will reappear."

Shao Jun was suddenly overcome with doubt. Was she up to the task? Perhaps there was still time to avoid the worst and change things. Once the first Tiger was down, the others would quickly realize that they were also potential targets and would become much more difficult to fool.

"Do you lack confidence, young girl?" teased Wang Yangming.

"Master, I worry that the task exceeds my abilities. When I fought Wei Bin the other night, it was clear that his level of skill far exceeded mine."

"The Tigers all have their own strengths and weaknesses. Wei Bin, the former head of the imperial guard, is very close to Ma Yongcheng, but Qiu has never seen him fight and knows nothing about his favorite weapons. He always gives off a disinterested air, but really he seeks to excel above all others, and is thus very easy to provoke. He won't be able to resist the temptation, we simply need to him to believe he has an opportunity to flaunt his skills."

Master Yangming spoke of the Eight Tigers as if they were close acquaintances. And for good reason. He had waited to rebuild his Society of the Mind for years and had had time to study them down to the smallest detail, but Shao Jun still had trouble believing that Wei Bin would be easy to beat.

"So, master, how should we proceed?" she asked.

"A contest of strength does not equal a contest of minds," he responded with a smile.

A gust of wind caused the thick layer of snow on the roof to fall with a soft thud.

"When Two arrives, Six is not far behind," said Master Yangming in a low voice. "It grows late, young girl, let us discuss the details over a drink, it will give you the strength to cut off the head of Wei the Snake."

In his *Book of Strange and Incredible Things,* Niu Shengru of the Tang dynasty called the god of the wind Two and the god of snow Six. It amused Shao Jun that this scholarly commentary could also be applied to their current plan to kill Wei Bin. She bowed her head.

"I will follow your instruction, master."

While Shao Jun and Wang Yangming discussed how they would cut off the head of Wei Bin, the latter was himself drinking in his home, looking out at the winter-flowering plums sagging under a thick layer of snow. Despite the wide variety of vegetation surrounding his elegant manor, those plants, which formed their buds in winter, were his favorites. Most were not very popular, with their flowers sometimes referred to as looking like "ticks on a dog", but this variety was an exception. *The Village of Flowering Plums,* a work from the Song dynasty, described it in these terms: "Its wood is light yellow, its ochre flowers small and perfumed. It is very beautiful."

Wei Bin considered himself to be refined and elegant despite his military experience. He drank alcohol only in moderation, ate only the finest foods, and avoided sumptuous banquets. If one didn't know his identity, one might mistake this middle-aged man with clear, hairless skin for a scholar rather than the military man that he was. He felt that he was like the wintersweet, an exceptional being among a sea of vulgarity. He had blindly obeyed his orders from Uncle Liu, then when Zhang Yong betrayed him, he had immediately sworn allegiance to his new master. He had never been motivated by ambition, but the years had begun to weigh on him and he felt like he was growing old alone with "a pitcher of wine among the flowers".[8]

The alcohol was cool and sweet, and Wei Bin savored it, and was far from being drunk as he thought back to the events at the palace.

8 From the famous poem by Li Po, *Drinking alone by moonlight,* expressing the author's solitude.

He had grudgingly visited the Leopard Quarter on Uncle Zhang's orders and had not succeeded in completing the mission. He had encountered that person in strange clothing as he left Xiyuan park, initially mistaking them for a lost guard. Initially he had planned to kill them quickly and throw the body into the lake, but as they fought he had soon realized that his opponent was far too skilled for a mere soldier. Now he thought about it, he had been wrong to slip away, because that person must have been connected to the old Brotherhood …

Wei Bin didn't dare believe that it could have been Shao Jun; that would have been too great a coincidence. But it was the only possibility. While several members had escaped the eradication of the Central Plain Brotherhood during the Great Ritual controversy, they had only been insignificant people who would never dare involve themselves in palace affairs. The only person with the motivation and ability to do so was the former imperial favorite. He had missed a golden opportunity to get rid of her once and for all!

He calmed himself with a mouthful of wine, then suddenly stood and turned as he heard quiet footsteps on the stairs behind him.

He always said that he was not to be disturbed when he drank alone in front of the window overlooking the tree-lined courtyard. He knew of only one person who would consider themselves sufficiently important to ignore these instructions, and it was indeed he who calmly glided up the steps. Irritated, Wei Bin tugged his right sleeve with his left hand. Taking a deep breath, he leaned over the railing.

"Venerable captain general?" he called.

It did indeed appear to be him, dressed in a simple coat despite the cold weather.

He quietly protested as Wei Bin prostrated himself before him, and noting the jug of wine that was warming on a stove near the window, commented mischievously, "How elegant, drinking in the company of plum blossom."

Despite the warm tone, Wei Bin felt an icy chill run down his back. He invited Zhang Yong to join him, sitting down only after his guest.

"Venerable captain general, your humble servant has completed the mission you entrusted him with last month."

"That's what I wanted to hear. And you left no evidence, it's perfect."

The month before, the leader of the Tigers had ordered Wei Bin to enter Xiyuan park to set fire to the Leopard Quarter. The place had been abandoned and emptied of any items of value long ago, but having lived there for two years Shao Jun may have known hidden nooks that only complete destruction of the building would prevent her from reaching. By the time the guards discovered there had been a fire the following morning, Xiyuan park had been reduced to ashes. Fortunately, while the fire had been fierce, there had been no victims as most of the leopards once raised in the park had been moved on Emperor Zhengde's death, and Lake Taiye had prevented the fire from spreading.

Dreading his master's reaction, Wei Bin was careful as he broached the sensitive subject of Shao Jun.

"I don't have any leads on Shao Jun for the moment."

He felt the chill as Zhang Yong glared at him, keeping his thoughts to himself. While both were members of the Eight

Tigers and occupied positions of similar rank in the palace, moments like this clearly reinforced the balance of power that governed their relationship. Having no desire to follow in Liu Juin's footsteps, Wei Bin maintained a respectful and docile attitude.

"Wei Bin, the whore Shao Jun is certainly already in Beijing."

"Does the honored captain general have new information?"

"No."

Wei Bin shivered again. Why the sharp tone if they had received no information? Zhang Yong answered his unspoken question.

"I find this lack of news increasingly strange. It's almost as if she vanished into thin air after Geo Feng's death. Someone has to be protecting her."

"I also wondered who would dare such a thing, venerable captain general…"

"Tell me, Wei Bin. Three years ago, you executed all the leaders of the Brotherhood with your own hands, did you not?"

Following the Great Rites controversy, Wei Bin had used his exceptional tracking skills to unearth the location of the Brotherhood's secret meeting place, putting to the sword all those he found there. He remembered finishing off their leader, who had resisted until the very last second.

"Yes, captain. The last one was Hong Liwei…"

"Hong Liwei was merely a fighter, not a visionary. Someone else must have been pulling the strings from the shadows."

The war between the Eight Tigers and the Brotherhood had lasted for centuries. Even during the Warring States period, the predecessors to the Tigers had helped Emperor Qin Shihuang annihilate the six rival kingdoms while their opponents fought against the Qin empire.

In the world of the ten thousand things, each must remain in their place and avoid disturbing the natural order. It was a vision of existence that the Eight Tigers defended without any compunctions on the use of force. For the Brotherhood, everything was permitted, it being up to individuals to decide their place in the world. Thus, when Wei Yu assassinated Emperor Qin Shihuang in 210 BC, Zhang Yong's predecessors declared themselves the sworn enemies of the Brotherhood. Their philosophies being completely at odds, the two factions had been at war ever since. Their feud had continued from dynasty to dynasty, from generation to generation, with each side taking the upper hand in turn but never succeeding in annihilating the other… until 1524. The almost complete destruction of the Brotherhood by the Eight Tigers was unprecedented.

The thought of it made Zhang Yong emotional, but he was very aware that the Brotherhoods of Europe could not be considered defeated while they still had a mentor at their head. Pyros had explained to him that the mentors were hard to identify because they were not necessarily the Brotherhood's best fighters. Hong Liwei had been powerful and influential, but Zhu Jiuyuan, for example, had been much more so. And so, Zhang Yong had growing doubts over their victory, which did not seem as complete as they had hoped.

Leading such an organization required extraordinary charisma and intelligence. Wei Bin allowed no one to attend his executions, but when Zhang Yong saw Hong Liwei's body, it was nothing more than a corpse punctured by a thousand sword cuts. A brave man for sure, but he was no leader. The attempts by the head of the Eight Tigers to unmask the last remaining members of the Chinese Brotherhood had been so unsuccessful that he sometimes wondered if it was indeed possible that they had been well and truly destroyed. But Shao Jun's return suggested otherwise, and the fact that she had an accomplice indicated that they had failed to kill the important target during the Great Rites controversy.

Wei Bin nodded.

"You speak the truth, venerable captain general. I have always believed the same."

He instantly regretted these words. He had betrayed himself by confessing his suspicions, as they implied he had always known he hadn't killed the right person, and that he had failed to inform his master. He was normally a cautious man but had just exposed himself to accusations of treason. He hastened to redeem himself.

"But as we never had any evidence, I told myself that I must be mistaken. I only saw it clearly as I listened to you just now."

Zhang Yong didn't really care about these considerations, being at that moment intrigued by the winter-flowering plum in the center of the courtyard.

"Regardless of their identity," he said, "we will find them eventually. Yu Dayong will soon have everything ready, and the Precursor Box is the last item we need to bring the Dai Yu project to fruition. When do you think you will finally be able to get it?"

While the captain's tone betrayed no animosity, Wei Bin felt an icy chill run through his body as he struggled to hide his anxiety. He thought of the death of Uncle Liu, who he subjected to the torture of a thousand cuts – not out of compassion for the torture he had gone through, but thinking back to the faithful and loyal demeanor Zhang Yong had shown before his former ally. The man was truly incomprehensible. He had given him two missions: burn the Xifan pavilion, and find Shao Jun and seize the Precursor Box. However, he had no leads to begin this second task.

Choosing his words carefully, he asked, "Your humble servant wishes only to complete his missions, but are you sure Shao Jun has the Precursor Box?"

"According to Pyros, it was in Ezio Auditore's possession before it disappeared, and the whore was the last person to see him alive. Only..."

Zhang Yong blinked. The clarity of his vision and thoughts were closely linked. He continued.

"The box isn't large, but it's impractical to carry all the time. Shao Jun will almost certainly have left it with her compatriot, so she mustn't be killed before she reveals its location."

With that he decided to take his leave, but stopped after several steps and added, "You remember how we kill theirs, do you not?"

"How could I forget, venerable captain general?"

"Of course, it is not something to be forgotten easily."

Full of fear, Wei Bin bowed his head in deference to the figure facing away from him.

"Your instructions will be obeyed, venerable captain general."

Outside the snow was as thick as in winter, but spring made it almost as warm and soft as willow catkins. As Zhang Yong left the manor with Qiu Ju at his heels, he looked up to admire the pleasant sight.

"February," he said. "Next month, old Xie will return in the new ministerial cabinet."

Alongside Minister Li and Minister Liu, Xie Qian had been one of the three wisest advisors to Emperor Hongzhi, Zhengde's father. At the time there was even a saying that went, "Minister Li suggests, Minister Liu decides, and Minister Xie carries it out". But Emperor Zhengde made Liu Jin, the eunuch at the head of the Eight Tigers, his most trusted confidante, and Xie Qian was quickly relieved of his duties when he dared criticize this choice. He was recalled to government when Jiajing took the throne, and the minister would have to return in March to form a new cabinet despite his protestations.

The Great Rites controversy began in the sixteenth year of Zhengde's reign and remained unresolved to that day, as the Eight Tigers still had opponents in high places. Zhang Yong had taken advantage of this turbulent period to attack the Brotherhood. He knew that certain officials such as Xie Qian, who had always been opposed to him and disapproved of his acts, had constantly drawn the Emperor's attention to his schemes. His high rank and status as a veteran minister made him almost untouchable, and after his return to the cabinet it would be almost impossible to accuse him of some crime to remove him. He might become a problem at least as urgent as that of Shao Jun. Some way must be found to force him to resign and finally turn the page. Meanwhile, the captain had to trust Wei Bin to find the Precursor Box, upon which the success of the Dai Yu project depended.

Xie Qian was cunning as a fox and could count on much more support than Zhang Yong, who shuddered at the thought of this threat. He had trampled over the body of Liu Jin to become the leader of the Eight Tigers and had no intention of ceding his position, despite his advanced age.

"I have always believed the same", Wei Bin had said. So, he too had long suspected that Hong Liwei had not been the leader of the Brotherhood but had never said anything. Why had he withheld such a significant doubt? Ulterior motives as unfathomable as a bottomless lake might make this man even more dangerous than Shao Jun.

"He who would take must give," the captain murmured.

Thinking his master was addressing him, Qiu Ju heard these words without recognizing the quote from Laozi.

"Venerable captain general, did you give me an order?" he asked.

"No, nothing. Where is Ma Yongcheng right now?"

"He is on his way back to the capital in accordance with your instructions. He should arrive in several days."

"Tell him to search for Shao Jun for another five days before returning."

Qiu Ju failed to hide his surprise.

"May I ask why, venerable captain general?"

United by their common interests, the Eight Tigers were not necessarily linked to one another by personal relationships. Liu Jin had been executed as the result of a plot led by Zhang Yong, and Gao Feng did not get along with Yu Dayong. But Ma Yongcheng and Wei Bun had cordial relations that made them an effective team, with one excelling in tracking their enemies, and the other in executing them.

The slow-witted Qiu Ju was unable to understand why the captain wanted to keep Ma Yongcheng away from the capital for several more days. But he was a bodyguard; no one expected him to think.

As night fell the two men walked up a wide avenue as the snow grew thicker, almost seeming to dare the spring to stop it as it blanketed the roofs of the capital.

CHAPTER 5

The empire had two capitals for a large part of the Ming dynasty: Nanjing in the south, and Beijing in the north. Each had its own Imperial Academy.

They offered no lucrative careers, but the position of libationer, while a ceremonial role with no political power, conferred a certain level of prestige.

Wei Bin had a talent for reading people, so he was surprised that the man he visited seemed more like an austere scholar than a collector of titles and flatteries. On the contrary, Libationer Yan was commonly acknowledged to be a methodical and competent individual. Wei Bin was impressed as he leafed through the documents the scholar had handed him.

"How did you locate the box so quickly?" he asked.

"I would be delighted to answer all of Uncle Wei's questions. Do you know the *Yongle Encyclopedia*?"

The Tiger was offended by the question. Of course, everyone

knew of this famous book, but those who had read it could be counted on the fingers of one hand.

"Master Yan, I may just be a mere servant of the Emperor, but I do have some education."

"Of course, of course, Uncle Wei is an important man before whom I humbly prostrate myself. The nineteen thousand six hundred and sixty-third scroll of the *Yongle Encyclopedia* includes the two tomes of the *Record of Blood Spilt for a Righteous Cause,* author unknown. However, in the nineteenth chapter of this manuscript, it mentions a 'Precursor Box' located somewhere in the West. This must be the object you search for."

"Really? That's incredible!"

Wei Bin occupied the third rank of the official hierarchy. As Libationer was as close a rank – the fourth – in reality nothing obliged him to agree to his visitor's requests. But he was the second-most important person in the Eight Tigers, and in this respect it was difficult to refuse him anything. The scholar had thus spent over a month examining his collection of old books, over a hundred of them, searching for references to the Precursor Box.

Zhang Yong had prioritized the search for the object ever since the Portuguese man Pyros had told him of it. Wei Bin had only asked Libationer Yan to search the archives simply to look like he was doing something; he had never dreamed that he would find anything of use. He had focused on tracking Shao Jun, but as that was currently at an impasse, the scholar's unexpected discovery had come at just the right time.

Seeing Wei Bin's excitement, the libationer couldn't help but feel a huge wave of pride. Coming from a poor background, he had toiled throughout his youth to study without compromising the righteousness of his ideals. But his ascension had been hampered by the excessive pride of Liu Jin, and the previous year he had finally been forced to renounce his integrity to gain this position through Zhang Yong's connections and influence. As a result he had needed to redouble his sycophancy towards the latter, contrary to his beliefs. Since then, he had departed from the Confucian maxim that instructed "*govern your morality to govern the country*", which he had followed his entire life up to that point. He was tired of being the last in line, so if he had to devote himself body and soul to the Eight Tigers in order to fulfil his ambitions, then he would do so. Truthfully, he was even slightly flattered that Wei Bin had entrusted him with this task; he saw it as a mark of trust on his part, and would never have dreamed of lying to him.

"Uncle Wei," he said quietly, "in reality, the *Record of Blood Spilt for a Righteous Cause* contains only fragments of information, but there is something else which may interest you."

"Master Yan, get to the point, please!"

"Someone came to look at that book the day before yesterday, and he specifically requested a copy of scroll nineteen thousand six hundred and sixty-three of the *Yongle Encyclopedia*."

This encyclopedia contained all of the knowledge acquired since the time of Emperor Qin Shihuang through to the reign of Emperor Yongle. It was the largest book in the world, composed of over six thousand volumes in some twenty-two thousand scrolls. Alone, it could fill an entire building, and contained more text than a single person could read in a lifetime. When it was complete, it was stored in a pavilion at the Imperial Academy in Nanjing, then transferred to Beijing when the building was destroyed in a fire. There it was stored in the Pavilion of Literature in the Forbidden City, not far from the Palace of Splendid Literature. Entry was forbidden to commoners, and anyone wishing to consult the *Yongle Encyclopedia* had to undergo a significant application process. This applied even to Libationer Yan, who had free access all other parts of the collection of rare and ancient books.

"The person who consulted the encyclopedia was not a civil servant, but they had been granted access," he clarified.

The copyist eunuchs of the academies and pavilions used to secretly engage in reproducing the secret and rare works in their care. At the beginning of the Ming dynasty, Emperor Hongwu tried to curb their efforts by forbidding them from learning to read, but his successor, Xuanzong, repealed this measure and even established an academy in the palace dedicated to teaching them. Having given lessons in the establishments, Libationer Yan was well aware that most could now read, and that among them there were some excellent calligraphers whose talent was wasted on merely reproducing texts. The training of these qualified staff was a necessity, but over time, the eunuchs began to charge higher and higher prices for copies of rare books, and to maximize their profits, they broke the rules and accepted commissions from anyone willing to pay the price, regardless of whether they had the correct permissions.

Identifying an old book that mentioned the Precursor Box was like looking for a needle in a haystack, and the libationer had been lucky to be informed by one of his contacts that another visitor had asked to consult the *Record of Blood Spilt for a Righteous Cause* in scroll nineteen thousand six hundred and sixty-three of the *Yongle Encyclopedia*. He was filled with joy and had immediately informed Uncle Wei of his good fortune.

For his part, the Tiger gave nothing away, but his heart was pounding in his chest as he listened to the libationer's account. While it hadn't been Shao Jun herself who had accessed the text, it had to have been a member of the Central Plain Brotherhood, most likely the disappeared mentor himself. The situation, which had until that point seemed insoluble, had taken a new turn.

"Who was the permission to consult the text issued to?" he asked.

"See for yourself," responded Libationer Yan, handing him a piece of paper drawn from his sleeve.

Wei Bin did not like what he saw.

"This form has no name on it!"

"It's because… Uncle Wei, it's because… according to the Confucian precept of 'education for all', the Imperial Academy is open to everyone, so the administrators cannot refuse entry to anyone…"

"All you need to do is pay to enter," the Tiger finished. He suddenly realized that the very respectable Imperial Academy had become a source of dishonest income for swindlers like Yan. However, he did not have any desire to reprimand the libationer for his greed, for he would never have found Shao Jun's trail without it. How ironic!

"When was the copy collected?"

"It will be collected tomorrow!"

"Tomorrow?"

Was it possible? In that case, Wei Bin simply needed to wait at the Academy to catch Shao Jun. He would never have thought that the problem that had caused him such a headache for days could be resolved so easily. Struggling to hide his eagerness, he simply said, “Very well. I will return tomorrow, and I will capture this individual when they arrive.”

Unenthusiastic about the idea of an altercation in the Imperial Academy, Libationer Yan shuddered.

“That is to say that… Master Bin, this situation should be considered carefully… If you were to come to blows in our institution…”

Indeed, if the Academy was the backdrop to a scuffle, the juicy illicit trade that took place there would risk being dealt a terrible blow. Deciding that it would be unwise to cause problems for the person who had metaphorically pulled the thorn from his paw, Wei Bin agreed to make a concession.

“I will only attack them once they are outside your walls.”

Sighing with relief, Libationer Yan bowed deeply.

“Thank you for your generosity, Uncle Wei!”

The following day was wet, and in the cold and wet climate of the beginning of the decidedly inclement spring, the Academy building seemed even gloomier and more desolate than ever to Wei Bin. He waited in a room upstairs from which he could observe the main entrance, and his day had been terribly boring, interrupted only by the meal sent to him by Libationer Yan near midday. The institution housed around a thousand students and disciples, but generally had very few visitors. Only two had presented themselves, and neither collected a copy of the *Record of Blood Spilt for a Righteous Cause*. When twilight arrived, just as he was ready to give up, his disciple, who he had nicknamed “Left paw”, whispered, “Master, they’re here!”

Wei Bin liked to see himself as an incarnation of the Great Bear, as legend attributed it with the power to decide who lived and who died. He had decided to rename his assistants after the faintest stars in the constellation: "Right paw" and "Left paw". Several days earlier, he had sent the first to kill an enemy, and today was accompanied only by the second, who had excellent kung-fu skills.

Stirred from his reverie, Wei Bin immediately looked out of the window, from which he could only see a shadow sheltered by an umbrella as they walked slowly through the *hutong*[9] towards the entrance. It was impossible to identify them from this vantage point.

Could it be the imperial favorite? He didn't remember how tall she was. Arriving at the door, the visitor exchanged several words with the concierge, who rang the small bell hanging in the entrance. *Ding!*

That was the signal! Left Paw jumped to his feet. "Master, do we attack now?" he asked.

If it was Shao Jun, Wei Bin was ready to break the promise he made to the libationer and immediately engage her in combat. Some caution was nonetheless necessary.

"Let us wait a while longer."

He was too far away to distinguish the words, but he could hear the timbre of his target's voice, and it couldn't be a woman. Shao Jun must have sent someone in her stead, one of the beggars who would do your shopping for several measly coins. In that case, attacking now would only raise the alarm... Better to let this one go for now and follow this person to their real target.

9 *A small neighborhood composed of traditional houses and narrow lanes.*

"Assistant," said Wei Bin, "you will stay behind. We mustn't be seen."

"Understood!"

The Tiger knew his disciple was a good tracker, having trained him himself, but preferred to leave nothing to chance on this occasion. He collected his umbrella from the wall and descended the stairs alone.

When he arrived on the floor below, the unknown visitor has already collected their reservation and left the building. Wei Bin waited for them to take a dozen steps before beginning to follow. The art of tailing someone relied on estimating the correct distance to leave between the hunter and their prey. Too close, and you risked being spotted; too far, and you risked losing them. The best distance is normally between ten and twenty steps for a good balance between discretion and visibility. After years spent in the imperial guard, Wei Bin applied these principles instinctively.

The Imperial Academy, overlooked by the temple of Confucius, was located on the Street of Venerable Learning, in the Dongcheng district. The unknown figure entered the *hutong* by the Lane of Virtuous Success, heading west to cross Andingmen Street, then joining Imperial Carriage Way via Street of the Tree of Mind.

Wei Bin was pleased to see his mark heading towards a district that was just as desolate and more importantly, devoid of people due to the bad weather. Perhaps by following the vine to reach the melon, he would not only find Shao Jun's hiding place, but also that of the mentor. As Zhang Yong seemed more concerned about this mysterious adversary than the imperial favorite, Wei Bin was certain to return to his good graces if he succeeded in flushing them out.

Clearly unaware of the danger stalking him, the person walked at a steady pace and whistled popular tunes. At the end of Imperial Carriage Way, he turned onto the Lane of Drums and Gongs, on the edge of the Jintai district and at the entrance to a *hutong* bounded by a yellow wall, a color reserved for imperial palaces and temples. It was a peaceful neighborhood full of luxurious villas, where the motley crowd of the center never ventured. Its temple was the Temple of the Understanding of Law, built during the reign of the last Yuan emperor, with three rooms added fifty years ago. It had since fallen into relative abandonment; now all that frequented the temple were several monks who placed prayer stones every day and sometimes burned incense.

That was where Wei Bin's prey was going.

He chuckled as he saw the figure steal into the building. No one could have imagined that the imperial concubine, a girl of ill repute mixed up in powerful intrigues, would set foot in a Buddhist temple… She must have asked the man with the umbrella to leave the book in a safe place so she could come to collect it later.

The Tiger couldn't help but have some admiration for this young girl of the court who had now transformed into a rebel adept in the use of cunning tricks. But her talents and spirit would not help her here: she would soon be just another anonymous body dumped in the slums.

"*One who prospers in calamity perishes in comfort*", Mencius said. Wei Bin might not be a scholar on the level of Zhang Yong, but he at least remembered this quote. It had not been so long ago, during the previous dynasty, that he had taken the oath to be an upstanding and respected mandarin; as he remembered this, his smile faded and he was overcome by a feeling of shame.

"Future generations may judge me as they will, there was but one path leading to where I am today," he thought to himself.

When the figure exited the temple and returned to Imperial Carriage Way, he turned and blocked its way. After all, although this person may not know all the details, they could at least reveal who had employed them.

"Little brother..." he whispered.

The unknown man lowered his umbrella to hide his movements as he drew a knife from his belt, then began a strike towards Wei Bin's throat, all before he had even had the chance to finish his sentence.

The Tiger had not expected for one moment that he would be attacked by this insignificant creature. But he suddenly recognized the style of these fast and precise moves, and realized who he was dealing with–

"Shao Jun!"

Blinded by his prejudices, he had fallen right into her trap.

Nonetheless, he still believed that she couldn't be the one behind these strategies. But who could her mysterious ally be? It had to be the mentor, and if he had escaped the careful searching during the Great Rites controversy, he clearly deserved the title. Having an adversary of this caliber was as troubling as it was exhilarating.

But first he had to take care of the most immediate threat, the blade aimed at his throat. With extraordinary reflexes, he raised his left arm and the blade clanged against his protective metal bracer. While legends spoke of the *Golden Mask*, the *Iron Shirt*, and the *Thirteen magical movements* to protect against all attacks, this type of kung-fu required extremely demanding training and magical knowledge. Having parried the blade, he grabbed the knife handle in the other hand and snatched it from the young woman. This highly skilled move known as *The guest acts as host* allowed him to turn the tables.

The brief moment of frenzy passed, he calmed himself once more. Now he had his assailant's weapon, he was back in control. He let out a cold laugh.

"You see, little imperial favorite, I now have three weapons..."

After Zhang Yong, Wei Bin was the most highly trained of the Eight Tigers, and he had mastered the dao of combat down to the finest detail, one of the precepts of which is knowing your opponent. As a student he had been very taken with the *Romance of the Three Kingdoms*. He would have liked to see Masu make Zhu Geliang's ambition – to face the Wei and Wu kingdoms – his own, after successfully thwarting the latter's plans for a punitive expedition to the south. He had subsequently been very disappointed when his favorite character, the one he most identified with, was killed following his defeat at the battle of Jieting! Over time, he had come to realize that Masu, while he had commanded three thousand battalions, had never experienced the reality of the battlefield, his ingenuity had been merely theoretical, and his strategies too focused on the attack to be effective. In a real fight, taking control of mistakes was the key to victory: thanks to his original riposte, Wei Bin was sure to have a decisive advantage over Shao Jun. But against all expectations, she did not allow herself to be thrown, and instead of fighting to recover her knife, she fled towards the Temple of the Understanding of Law.

What was she playing at?

As the several remaining monks were still in the meditation room of Western Paradise, the main building seemed completely deserted when Wei Bin entered. He saw the former imperial favorite slip into a side room, and for a moment wondered if she planned to ambush him, but quickly rejected the idea. Still, he would have no trouble extricating himself from any predicament, and at worst, Left Paw would soon be joining him.

While most eunuchs were Buddhist, Wei Bin was a follower of *yelikewen*, a form of Christianity imported under the Mongol dynasty of the Yuans, and thus paid little attention to the fact that the pediment of the room he ventured into bore the title "Buddha of Healing". This was the name of the human-sized statue that occupied the center of the small, faded, empty room, where no incense had been burnt for years. Shao Jun stood in front of the deity, with no exit and no one to help her.

She had probably taken a wrong turn, and now here she was, trapped in a dead end! And because the Tiger now had her knife, there was a good chance she was completely disarmed.

He let out a short laugh.

"It's over! The imperial concubine would be wise to avoid upsetting this imperial slave…"

While the Tiger was indeed an imperial slave – a term used to refer to the eunuchs who occupied posts at the palace – as a traitor with a warrant for her arrest, Shao Jun was no longer officially a concubine and even less so an imperial favorite. He had used these terms mockingly, to highlight the difference in their positions.

"Slave Wei, are you loyal to His Majesty the former Emperor?"

"The old Emperor can no longer protect his dear concubine from where he is now. You'll be better off if you come without causing trouble."

"You want to see me dead whether I come quietly or not."

"Give me the Precursor Box, a-and I promise that… your life will be spared."

In reality, Zhang Yong would never let her go. He would imprison her, torture her, and then take great pleasure in watching her suffer as she died. Why had Wei Bin hesitated so much as he uttered his lie?

Cursing himself for this mistake, he remembered the first time he saw Shao Jun, at an audience with the old Emperor Zhengde. Even then, the young concubine, the only one not to have her feet bound, stood out for her determination and her proud expression, the complete antithesis of the delicate façade projected by the other women and girls in the harem. He had been fascinated by her individuality, not because he was attracted to her, but because he envied her. And today, while her experiences had marked the young woman's face as much as they had built her character, the eunuch's feelings were amplified: free and indomitable, Shao Jun was everything he wished he could be. Worse, she was young and her whole future lay ahead of her, while he had begun to decline and was nothing more than an old man in waiting. He was enraged.

"What do you want with the Precursor Box?" she asked him.

"You remember the scroll you entrusted to your friend, the imperial consort Zhang?"

"So, she did give it to you… Is it connected to the box?"

"Of course…"

Wei Bin had said too much. He must be growing soft in his

old age. But this confession could be turned to his advantage, as the former imperial favorite had been close to Zhang Qiang, and learning that her childhood friend had betrayed her had to have shaken her. But she showed neither surprise nor sadness.

Now in his fifties, Wei Bin guessed it had been some twenty years at least since he had last felt compassion. Killing affected him so little that he couldn't say how many people he had executed during the Great Rites Controversy. He had simply obeyed Zhang Yong's orders as he always did, helping him achieve his dream without receiving a great deal in return. His mission had been to bring back Shao Jun alive, but he decided to have fun, just this once.

The first of his three weapons was his ability to throw his enemies off balance, which seemed to have failed this evening. Fortunately, the second was more reliable, consisting of a flexible sword wrapped around his waist, durable enough to counter the most dangerous strikes, and sharp enough to slice through iron like butter. He unsheathed it and wielded it with such speed that many of his victims were dead before they even had time to see it. The third and final weapon was the trio of poisoned needles that he could release from his left bracer when he pressed a specific point. Using his sword and needles simultaneously made him a deadly opponent.

Shao Jun had been saved by her cloak when they fought in Xiyuan park, Wei Bin having underestimated its usefulness. It served to give her a majestic air while also protecting her from any blades that tried to reach her. But she wasn't wearing it tonight, here in the temple. There was nothing that could offer her unexpected salvation.

As the Tiger unsheathed his sword and discreetly removed the needles from his bracer ready to throw, Shao Jun stepped back a pace and grabbed a golden-bladed dagger from behind the statue. Gold made for a good weapon, as it was more flexible, but was also twice as heavy as an equal quantity of iron.

Except that... the imperial favorite's weapon was not gold, but simple copper, a material which had no specific advantage. This incongruity made Wei Bin nervous. It proved something unforeseen was happening. A trap.

Deciding to put an end to this scheming once and for all, he threw his needles with a sudden gesture and rushed toward the young woman. At this distance, and with his experience, she made an unmissable target; she would soon be unable to move, and he would simply need to drive his blade into her body. But against all expectations, the metal needles deflected from their course to bury themselves in the Buddha's left palm with a sound – *fip! fip! fip!* – that echoed in the empty room like a mocking laugh.

At the same instant, from his first step towards his opponent, he felt his sword become abnormally light at the end of his arm, as if drawn by an invisible hand. He had mastered the subtleties of this difficult weapon like no other, able to soften or stiffen the blade as he pleased, but he had never seen it react in such a way before. And the closer he got to the imperial favorite, the worse the phenomenon became.

Panic overcame him. He had thought he was pinning his prey down, but in reality it had been she who had led him by the nose to the terrain she had prepared for her attack. His two favorite weapons now unusable, he had little room to maneuver.

Tcha! He felt a sudden pain through his chest. Shao Jun had plunged her common, copper dagger through his ribs.

His strength left him. He staggered and fell to the floor. Having killed so many himself, he knew what to expect. A rush of blood would fill his chest until it flooded out from his nose and mouth.

Ah, so this was what death felt like? He suddenly felt like laughing. He had had himself castrated several decades before to escape poverty and to enter the palace, where he devoted himself to studying to become a great eunuch, benevolent and highly respected.

He never left any opponent alive, so no one was supposed to know his fighting techniques. And despite her skill, Shao Jun was far below his level. If he died now, it was only because the trap had been designed specifically for him, so finely crafted that there had never been any chance of escape. The person who conceived it must be exceptional.

"Here I am, about to die like a mere pawn in the service of Uncle Zhang," he thought to himself.

He who had so desired not to be used by anyone… What a waste.

But his defeat would also be the defeat of the leader of the Eight Tigers. Was it possible?

In the end he had no time to consider this further. A voice called him from outside the room.

"Uncle Wei!"

It was Left Paw, standing in the doorway. Wei Bin had told him to keep his distance, and he had obeyed the instructions. When he had seen his master, who he considered to be almost a demi-god, fighting then collapsing inside the temple, he hadn't believed his eyes, and had been paralyzed by shock.

Shao Jun was as stunned as she was amazed. Her heart beat fit to burst as her body, until that point strung tight as a bow, suddenly relaxed. Even though Master Yangming had reassured her that Wei Bin would not escape their trap, any unexpected detail could have derailed their plan. She hadn't dared believe that one of the legendary Eight Tigers, who had seemed invincible during their encounter on the bridge in Xiyuan park, would fall for their trap so easily.

"A contest of strength does not equal a contest of minds", Master Yangming had rightly said... She did however regret not having been able to draw explanations out of Wei Bin concerning the scroll and the words *Dai Yu* written on its case. He had at least confirmed that there was a close link between the Precursor Box and that his group was urgently looking for it. What could possibly link these two apparently unrelated objects? She would have to think about it later.

Catching sight of the young eunuch in the doorway, she leapt towards him, pulling her dagger out of Wei Bin's chest as she did so.

"Do you want to die alongside your master?"

Left Paw jumped in fear, and set off running as fast as he could.

Should she kill him too? Given his age, his kung-fu wouldn't be a threat, particularly as he seemed completely bewildered by his master's death. But he might cause them problems in the future if he was allowed to live. Instead of taking action, Shao Jun wasted time considering the advantages and disadvantages.

The mind itself is neither good nor evil. Good and evil are born of intention. Discerning good and evil is an essential knowledge. Studying the ten thousand things enables one to work for good and eliminate evil. Master Yangming's four precepts came back to her. What knowledge could really come from cold-blooded slaughter? If she gave up on mercy, the Society of Mind would not deserve its name.

Shao Jun decided to listen to her heart, and it told her to stop there. She was however aware that the path she trod would be bloody, and that it was too late to turn back now.

CHAPTER 6

"Venerable captain of the imperial guard!"

Ma Yongcheng greeted Zhang Yong, then went to stand at his side. He should have returned to the capital five days earlier, but had been delayed en route. When he learned of the death of Wei Bin, which had occurred while he was away, he immediately volunteered to personally take care of Shao Jun, once and for all.

True to his nickname, the "Butcher", Ma Yongcheng killed mercilessly at every opportunity. Yet despite this, he had shared a steadfast friendship with Wei Bin which no disagreement had ever managed to break. When Wei Bin had returned covered in glory from the war in Ningxia, he had been unable to accept the noble titles he had earned for his service due to his status as a eunuch, but had instead offered them to his own brother, who had since become the Count of Zhenan, and to Ma Yongcheng's brother, who now administered Pingliang. Such was the strength of the bond between them.

"My vigorous Ma Yongcheng," announced the captain, "I must leave for some time. I leave it to you to put an end to this situation, but remember to bring her back to me alive!"

"Uncle Zhang, you can be sure that she will not be allowed to die before she is held accountable before the law."

At first glance, the term "vigorous" would not be the first word to apply to this man with the pale face and arrogant, high-pitched voice, but seeing him fight quickly demonstrated the aptness of the term. He licked his lips with his tongue that was rough as a cat's, giving him the air of a wild beast. Yes, the Butcher was decidedly the most cat-like of the Eight Tigers.

A sly smile on his face, Zhang Yong sniffed the air, savoring the subtle scents of plum blossom that heralded the beginning of an idyllic spring.

"Tell me, Uncle Ma, how do you plan to stop Shao Jun if the whore has already left the capital?"

"I don't know, Uncle Zhang. Please, enlighten me."

"She succeeded in killing Wei Bin. Such an extraordinary man could not have been overcome by ordinary means. You must be more cautious!"

More a man of action than of thought, Ma Yongcheng was not one of those who spent hours crafting complex military strategies in a tent in the company of other officers. No, he preferred to be on the front line, in the middle of the fight. And when even a fighter as careful and accomplished as Wei Bin had fallen to Shao Jun, Zhang Yong doubted that the Butcher would succeed where his comrade had failed, particularly if he allowed himself to be overcome with anger. And so the captain harbored little hope for the success of this enterprise. He sought the opinion of Qiu

Ju, whose views he respected despite the man's lack of education.

The unlikely friendship that had united Wei Bin and Ma Yongcheng had been their strength when they were together. There would have been no doubt that they could have captured Shao Jun if they had worked as a team. But now one of the two had fallen, it was important that the remaining Tigers pooled their strengths. But Zhang Yong apparently wanted to visit the island of Dai Yu while delegating the matter of the young woman to someone else… What could really be behind such an irrational decision?

Of course, Qiu Ju refrained from mentioning these concerns, but his master seemed deep in thought, almost lost as he meditated on some problem.

"Qiu Ju," he asked suddenly, "do you remember Wei Bin's wound?"

"It was three point one inches deep. The left lung and heart were pierced through simultaneously."

"Precisely. There were no other marks on the body, as if it took Shao Jun only one blow to win the fight. How many would it have taken you?"

"It's hard to say… But has the whore really attained such an extraordinary level of skill?"

Qiu Ju's unusually sharp memory had allowed him to immediately recall the details of the autopsy, and he also remembered Wei Bini's incomparable martial techniques with equal clarity. He fought with a unique sword, a flexible blade that he could wrap around his waist, which he alone knew how to exploit to its full capabilities. He was undeniably one of the greatest fighters among the Eight Tigers, and despite his arrogance, Qiu Ju was forced to admit that he would have been unable to overcome him without outside help. And yet, this formidable swordsman had been vanquished by Shao Jun, and his assistant had seen everything!

"I'd like to believe that the slattern had improved her kung-fu," growled Zhang Yong, "but there is no way she could have raised herself to Wei Bin's level in such a short period of time. That means that he was not felled by the sword, but by some trick. Cunning is a key part of kung-fu, and he lost his life because he forgot this fundamental truth."

"But venerable captain, there are only four toothless monks left in the Temple of the Understanding of Law... Do you think they are all part of her group?"

"Monks who fight? Ha ha! Don't make me laugh! You clearly don't know the history of the meditation room."

"No, I don't."

"It was fifty years ago... At the time, the temple had just been gifted the Buddha of Healing by its leader, a monk named Blinding Light, a statue that was said to have supernatural powers. It was apparently able to heal its worshippers when medicine failed, and quickly became a local celebrity. Among the mass of believers who crowded to benefit from its miracles was the head of the imperial cavalry, Liu Xan, and the supervisor of the imperial apartments, Ma Hua. Both donated towards the temple renovation, and it was thanks to their funds that the mediation room of the Western Paradise was built."

"Does it really exist? I mean, is this statue really supernatural?"

"Blinding Light arranged it so that people believed that. One day, he placed a small bowl of pills before the statue, and begged it to take them from him, saying that he relied only on faith to heal him. The tablets rose into the air to the statue's hand on their own in front of the stunned crowd, and new of the miracle quickly spread."

The story was interesting, but Qiu Ju didn't see how it was connected with the murder of Wei Bin. As if reading his mind, Zhang Yong continued.

"But in reality, there was no divine intervention at work. The statue's palm had been magnetized, and Blinding Light had filled his pills with metal powder. When the deception was discovered, the temple fell into disgrace, the faithful stopped visiting and the monk was chased out, but the Buddha remained where it was. Shao Jun must have known of this statue, and knew that if she drew Wei Bin near to it, his poisoned needles and his light, flexible sword would be attracted towards its magnetic palm… unlike the whore's copper dagger! After that, all she had to do was strike at her disarmed enemy."

"What ingenious sorcery!"

The trick had been designed specifically for Wei Bin, Qiu Ju realized with admiration, because any other sword – his own, for example – would have been too heavy to be drawn towards the Buddha's hand.

"While I sent Ma Yongcheng after her, she deprived me of Wei Bin, my best man," said Zhang Yong. "This time, I will make it seem as if I am setting a trap for her with Ma Yongcheng, so she will be blind to my real plan." He smiled secretively. "I must get to Dai Yu island without further delay."

Qi Jiu shivered. This destination was unexpected.

"Venerable captain, does that mean you're going to use…?"

"According to my information, it will soon be operational. The man in the shadows will be forced to come out into the light of day!"

By this he could only mean Shao Jun's mysterious ally, Qiu Ju thought to himself.

Because it was this unknown mentor that Zhang Yong had really feared ever since his existence was confirmed. A girl barely twenty years old, of little education and who had spent most of her life shut away in a harem, could never have known the history of the statue of the Buddha of Healing, a story fifty years old and known only to a few. Furthermore, the plan which had cost Wei Bin his life had been of rare meticulousness and ingenuity. The shadowy figure behind Shao Jun had to have an intellect at least as exceptional as Zhang Yong himself, which significantly reduced the list of suspects. While he most certainly had the Precursor Box in his possession, he had left some clues in the process, such as during his visit to the Imperial Academy, which would lead the captain to him as inevitably as a length of yarn leads to a ball of wool. That day would soon come. And to be ready to confront his when his identity was revealed, the leader of the Tigers must visit Dai Yu island…

It would kill two birds with one stone, as Pyros would say, but Zhang Yong refrained from disclosing the full scope of his plan to Qiu Ju. He was already halfway to winning anyway. Whatever happened to the deadweight Ma Yongcheng, the captain knew that his victory over his inscrutable adversary would be magnificent if all went as planned on the island.

But it was a question of balance, and the tables could always turn. Zhang Yong's eyes still burned with youth despite his six decades of existence.

As Ma Yongcheng reached the capital on the fifteenth day of the third month, Shao Jun took the road to Baoji tea house to the west of the city.

The establishment was next to Miaoying temple, known locally as the Temple of the White Pagoda due to its unusual architecture. Built by Kublai Khan during the Mongol dynasty of the Yuans, it was originally huge and taller than anything else in the area, making it an ideal spot for archers in times of conflict. Later ravaged by a fire, it had been destroyed and then rebuilt to more modest dimensions by Emperor Ming Xuanzong. Its local festival had a lively atmosphere, drawing crowds from all over the province come to pray and trade. Paradoxically, during this event, prayers and incense sticks were relegated to the background, far behind the hundreds of rich and varied goods displayed on the stalls. When their business was concluded or their walk finished, visitors and traders would then sit and quench their thirst at the tea house, which was almost as animated as the market itself, despite the fact that establishments of this type were generally quiet and peaceful places where one could escape the hustle and bustle of the outside world.

To accommodate the tastes of the foreign monks who officiated at the Temple of the White Pagoda, the manager served butter tea, which they loved, in addition to the more usual jasmine and long jing teas. And to add a local touch to the establishment, he had also named the various rooms after the six syllables of the mantra *om mani padme hum*, which he heard throughout the day. Unfortunately, he wasn't himself a Buddhist and so his pronunciation was rough to say the least… So, he welcomed customers to the tea house by asking them which of the "*Oh money pa ni hom*" rooms they preferred.

Shao Jun couldn't help laughing when she heard the Buddhist

prayer so mangled. She understood why the sender of the anonymous letter that had sent her here had asked her to sit in the "money" room.

The missive, which appeared to be a banal exchange of courtesies ending in a large flourished signature, was encoded using the methods of the Society of the Mind, of which only the most eminent members, such as Zhu Jiuyuan, Hong Liwei, and Wang Yangming, had knowledge – and the first two were no longer in this world. Shao Jun was also able to decipher this type of message, and so it was in this style that the mentor had written her instructions to ensnare Wei Bin. The young woman was grateful to have this new letter to tell her what to do, because, stunned by her own victory, she would have unable to decide what to do next on her own. The orders in the letter were nonetheless strange: they told her to visit Baoji tea house to meet someone.

Who could have sent it her? Only Master Yangming knew she was in Beijing, where the former headquarters of the Society of the Mind had been located. Was it possible that another member of the Brotherhood had escaped and was here still?

Like all the others in the tea house, the "Mani" room was only separated from the main room by a thin wall, making it difficult to ignore the surrounding hubbub. Through the crack in the curtain that hid the entrance, Shao Jun could see the back of a man sitting at the table in front of the window.

Who was it? Could it be a trap? To her knowledge, she and the mentor were the last remaining members to know the Brotherhood's code, but she couldn't imagine him setting up a meeting right in the middle of the capital.

Of course, he could have sent someone else in his place, but who would he trust enough to do so?

The man inside must have seen her as she hesitated before the curtain.

"Young girl!" he called.

It was Master Yangming's voice! Despite her surprise, she entered and sat at the table.

"Master..." she began to whisper before suddenly stopping.

While she was known to the Eight Tigers, Master Yangming's identity was still unknown to them, so she preferred to avoid saying his name. Yet she found it very unwise to meet in such a busy location. What if one of their enemy's informers found them?

"Young girl," the mentor said in a low voice, "there is no need to be so concerned. We are not in Shaoxing, where everyone watches everyone else. Do not fear, this place is safe."

He must have thought that her paranoia resulted from the surprise attack on Mount Wolong that could have cost her life, when Gao Feng and his accomplice had failed to kill her.

"Master, don't make fun of me," she laughed. "How was I to know that you would ask me to meet in a place like this?"

"That is entirely the point. Who would think to find us here? The truly wise do not live as hermits in the mountains, but in contact with human trepidations."

She had already heard this sentence several times before, but it was certainly the first time she saw it applied so scrupulously. Knowing that the mentor would answer her questions in due course, she simply asked, "Master, how did you reach Beijing?"

Wang Yangming spent most of his time at Jishan University since he retired from his government post. The situation must be serious if he felt the need to come to the capital. But the calmness with which he sipped his tea belied this supposition.

"The Emperor called me to Beijing because an uprising has broken out in Tianzhou. As I arrived yesterday and depart tomorrow, I could only see you today. So, did you manage to kill Wei the Snake?"

Tianzhou prefecture in Guangxi had been unstable since Lu Su, a local tribal chief, had rebelled in the fourth year of Jiajing's reign, and Viceroy Yao Mo and the deputy Chen Xi had to unite to reestablish order. But Lu Su had once again begun to cause trouble. The central government had chosen to send Wang Yangming in response to the viceroy's request for aid, who was to take part in the military expedition despite no longer being in post. He surely owed this dubious privilege due to the role he had played in the revolt of the prince of Ning.

"Yes, master. I followed your instructions and Wei the Snake is dead."

The mentor's expression grew more serious as she recounted the events, which intrigued the young woman.

"Ma the Butcher has not appeared?" he asked after she had finished her story.

"No, not yet. Why?"

"How strange..."

Based on his strategy, Wang Yangming was not surprised that Shao Jun had succeeded in killing Wei Bin, but he did find it strange that Ma Yongcheng, from whom he was normally inseparable, had not yet appeared. He had even concocted a trick to separate them from one another, because they were practically invincible when they were together.

It was possible that the Snake didn't always accompany the Butcher on his missions, but the two both answered to the same superior: Zhang Yong. And the fact that he had not yet retaliated must mean he was planning something unexpected. Wang Yangming had hoped to get rid of Wei Bin and find out the secret of his old friend and rival, but clearly only the first part of his plan had worked.

Unaware of these inner thoughts, Shao Jun waited for the mentor to sit up and drink a mouthful of tea, before asking, "So, is Ma the Butcher next on my list?"

Many members of the Brotherhood who had fallen into his clutches had begged him to allow them to die quickly. Of all the Tigers, he was the most inhuman, and it was he who the young woman hated the most. Once again, the master ignored her question and continued to sip his tea, which only increased her nervousness.

After a long moment he looked up at her. "Young girl, what do you think of the mind?"

Confused, she wondered why he asked this question. Convinced that she must be missing something, she only dared answer after thinking for a time.

"It's the universe."

"*The universe is my mind and my mind is the universe*", Zhu Jiuyuan had often said, himself citing the teachings of Master Yangming.

The latter smiled.

"Yes, the universe. It extends above, below, and in all four directions, since time immemorial through to the present day. The universe is all, limitless, in time and space."

Shao Jun was not in the mood to learn patience. The Society of the Mind could only be rebuilt once the Eight Tigers had been eliminated. They had already killed two since her return to China, and it was time to attack the others. But for now, she just nodded politely.

"Now Wei Bin is dead," the master continued, "I think the rest of the operation can wait. The trouble in Tianzhou should stabilize within a year, and we can return to our mission when I return. I recommend you leave Beijing until then."

"Leave Beijing?"

"You did kill Wei Bin after all. I doubt that Zhang Yong is pleased!"

The young woman was lost for words. When she came out of her reverie, she asked, "But what will he do?"

"I don't know what he has in mind, but the most likely is that he will send Ma the Butcher after you. His attack will be meticulously planned, and I am afraid you will be in deep trouble without me."

As captain of the Eastern Bureau, the empire's secret police, Ma Yongcheng had numerous spies at his disposal, which made him difficult to trap and a dangerous adversary. And so, despite her annoyance, Shao Jun was forced to admit that she had no chance of winning against him without Master Yangming's help, just like she would never have triumphed over Wei Bin. While he worked to pacify the rebellion, she would lie low for a time. She was ready to accept this, but would have liked to know when exactly the fight could recommence.

As if he was reading her mind, the mentor continued. "Don't worry, young girl. You won't be bored while I am away in Tianzhou."

"Hm? What do you want me to do?"

"It's about that scroll..."

"What does it contain exactly?"

When the former Emperor had given this mysterious object to his favorite just before his death, he had asked her to give it to one man: Wang Yangming. But at the time, the young woman had no idea he was the mentor of the Society of the Mind, and so she had missed her opportunity.

Zhang Yong had then turned the palace upside down looking for it, and finally had it in his possession.

"While we still don't know what they want it for," said the mentor, "we now know that the scroll and the box are connected, and that Zhang Yong is determined to have them both, badly enough even to set fire to the Leopard Quarter. Your task will be to investigate this matter. If Wei Bin was prepared to let you live in exchange for the box, it must be of the utmost importance."

"Certainly, master. But do you know the meaning of the characters *Dai Yu* engraved on the scroll case?"

"According to the writings of the philosopher Lie Tzu, it was the place the old Emperor named, by imperial edict, one of the five sacred mountains in the east of the Bohai Sea, into which the Sky River flows near the gulf of Guixiu, 'the place of return.'"

"The sacred mountains?" Shao Jun repeated with a shiver.

Old Emperor Zhengde had received a number of Tao monks and magicians from various places into the court, and had himself practiced their art, "the way of enlightenment, wisdom, and plenty which leads to eternal life", as it was known then. But the Emperor died at the age of thirty-one, and all the masters who had predicted a long life were ridiculed.

"Lie Tzu says that the giants of the dragon kingdom once fished the two turtles which carried Dai Yu and Yuan Jiao on their backs, and that the mountains then drifted towards the north pole. That is why now only three remain."

Shao Jun had long ago heard of these three mountainous islands from the supervisor of the harem.

"But why did the old Emperor insist on naming the island?"

"He was a wise man, so there must have been a reason."

Wang Yangming put down his tea cup and gazed out of the window. The individual rooms in Baoji tea house looked over a small garden planted with gingkos, a tree which grows so slowly that it takes two generations to produce fruit, earning it the nickname of "the grandchildren tree". The ones near the temple, planted under the Yuans over two hundred years before, bore small buds in the early spring weather. In just a few weeks they would be covered in luxuriant leaves. Contemplating this unmoving spectacle, the mentor spoke again.

"You said you knew Chen Xijian, the old eunuch who attended the Leopard Quarter, is that right?"

"Yes! Do you know if he is still alive?"

"Yes, he now oversees the Xiaoling tomb in Nanjing,"

Although the tomb was the burial place of the founder of the Ming dynasty, Emperor Hongwu, the position was not that prestigious. After the capital was moved, the emperors had their mausoleums built in Beijing, so a move to Xiaoling was a lackluster end to any career.

"He was transferred there in the third year of Jiajing's reign," the mentor explained, "after taking part in the mutiny against Zhang Yong. But as a former attendant of the Leopard Quarter, he must know the scroll's secret."

"That's true, he was present when Emperor Zhengde gave it to me."

"That said, he won't necessarily agree to help you just because he was demoted. Who knows, he may have been the one who told Zhang Yong about the scroll…"

Shao Jun's heart sank. She couldn't bring herself to tell Master Yangming about A-Qiang. Her friend had betrayed her. She didn't want to think about it anymore.

"Master," she responded quietly, "Uncle Chen can be trusted."

The mentor remained silent for a moment, then suddenly declared, "Young girl, trusting too easily will get us into serious trouble. Perhaps Uncle Chen has been corrupted, in which case you will need to take drastic measures."

If Uncle Chen tried to denounce her, she would be forced to kill him, but the idea seemed inconceivable when she thought of the kindly old septuagenarian. As if reading her mind, the mentor added, "Distinguishing good from evil is an essential knowledge, and true knowledge allows evil to be transformed into good. If this man has broken faith, you place your life in his hands simply by visiting him, and if his heart is still treacherous, then he will be beyond all redemption. Young girl, you have a good heart but you are too indecisive: you consider your smallest actions a thousand times instead of acting decisively in the midst of chaos. I must warn you that this attitude could be your downfall. Remember it well."

Shao Jun's thoughts suddenly cleared.

"Master, is it not true that, great or small, good is good, and likewise for evil?"

"The general who spends his life killing in cold blood could become a great buddha at the time of his death," Wang Yangming laughed.

Good and evil are not so opposed as they may seem. As Confucius said, "The father conceals the misconduct of the son, and the son conceals the misconduct of the father": they each evolve in a constant relationship of equivalence and interdependence, their edges often blurred by the complexity of their entwinement. And yet, it is precisely because they are inseparable that Master Yangming's philosophy aspired to distinguish them in order to act with an enlightened mind.

There is a tale of a king who, after spending his life killing at every opportunity, on his deathbed regretted his actions and had a Buddhist priestess called to his bedside. She burned incense and told him that under the Song dynasty, the monks of her faith preached that "one who spends their life committing the greatest crimes is not necessarily devoid of compassion, just as one who never steps on an ant is not necessarily a model of altruism". By this, she meant that his crimes were no longer sins as his heart had already begun on the path to enlightenment.

Master Yangming's philosophy was inspired by Confucianism, Taoism, and Buddhism, and he would use all of their secrets to help Shao Jun find her peace. Drawing a small piece of jade from his pocket, he said, "Keep this with you, young girl. When you reach Nanjing, if you are in dire straits, present this pendant to the master of the Temple of the Jade of the Five Virtues, and he will protect you. His influence is such that not even Zhang Yong will be able to find your trail." He was silent for a moment, then continued. "But please, only go to him as a last resort."

The jade was small but of excellent quality. On one side it featured the sculpted character for teaching in seal script, and plants and waves on the other. Wang Yangming had complete trust in his friend, but did not wish to trouble him unless the need was extreme.

Hands pressed together, Shao Jun bowed as a sign of respect.

"Thank you, master!"

When she lifted her head, the mentor had disappeared, but his smile was engraved in her memory. She was happy that he had indicated the path to follow. When Ezio Auditore and she had parted ways, he had given her the Precursor Box to guide her in the case of uncertainty, but the box was empty, and she had found no hint or guide within.

Wang Yangming was on his guard against the unlikely possibility that he was being watched by a spy, but he passed as unnoticed as a drop of water in the ocean when he merged into the crowd of visitors and pilgrims exiting the tea house.

He must immediately depart for Tianzhou prefecture. While the rebellion was smaller than that of the prince of Ning, he did not know how long it would last. As minister of state, he willingly agreed to put his talents at his country's service, but he was nevertheless concerned that he had been recommended for this task by… Zhang Yong!

Wang Yangming was not convinced that it was a simple political favor from an old friend, and his unease had continued ever since the leader of the Eight Tigers had visited him at the university. Yes, he must be suspicious. But more than anything, the mentor was worried about Shao Jun, whose impatience and youth led her to underestimate her enemies. And it had been far too easy to trap Wei Bin… Zhang Yong was not a man to make this kind of mistake.

The leader of the Tigers maintained that the reform of the empire must come through conquest, which required radical decisions and careful study of past mistakes to avoid repeating them. But he must know that control on this scale was an illusion. His power was certainly considerable, but he did not have the time to lead the citizens and military of the empire. Did he really think that the scroll would allow him to control the world? If so, how? With devastating artillery? Some kind of firearm which didn't need to be reloaded? Whatever it was, weapons alone were not enough to control the world. And what Shao Jun saw at the Leopard Quarter didn't look like research for military equipment.

Before he died, Wei Bin had revealed a link between the scroll and the box, but too many details were still unknown. It was however certain that Zhang Yong was determined to acquire the box then kill Shao Jun, and it was probably why he had sent her protector to Tianzhou, evidence that he suspected a connection between them. Wang Yangming congratulated himself on having kept the item with him, it was safer that way. It had also been wise of him to advise the former imperial favorite to leave the capital, as unlike her, the mentor felt the cold jaws of the trap beginning to close around them. Their enemy would probably try to use Wei Bin's death to his advantage.

Like any cautious chess player, Wang Yangming preferred to avoid reckless risks and to move the fewest pieces as possible while he tried to read his opponent's strategy. But his adversary wasn't afraid to break the rules completely, and his disregard for human lives, including those close to him, appeared to give him a certain advantage. Unable to do anything but wait for the other's move, the mentor knew he was in a weak position, despite his secret weapon. For the moment, the key was finding out if this Chen Xijian was reliable or if he was nothing more than bait …

The old master suddenly broke into laughter.

He was overthinking things, that was it. The more he thought, the more problems he would find. Perhaps it was he who was blind to Shao Jun's potential. After all, she had lured Wei Bin into the trap and killed him, which was far beyond the skills of any ordinary girl. So, if she trusted Uncle Chen, she must have good reason, and the rest didn't matter. It would be good for her to develop her own plans and carry them out without his help. And if it went badly, he had told her of the safe haven in Nanjing…

Wang Yangming was not pleased with the turn in this latest chapter of his friendship with Zhang Yong, the conclusion of which would not be long in coming. Whether it pleased him or not, they may soon face one another in a final duel from which only one of them would emerge alive.

The jade pendant he had just given away had symbolized the affection and respect between Zhang Yong and Yang Yiqing. He had never imagined he would use it so, but he was relieved to hand it over to Shao Jun, as recently he had felt as if it were burning against his chest.

An ironic smile stayed on Wang Yangming's face as he went on his way.

CHAPTER 7

The Xiaoling tomb in Nanjing covered an area of over two thousand five hundred *mous*[10] and encompassed almost all of Zhongshan. It had taken almost twenty-five years to complete the final resting place of the founder of the Ming dynasty, Emperor Hongwu.

While Nanjing was officially one of the two capitals of the empire, it was solely in name , and only disgraced civil servants or those at the end of their careers were sent there. Nonetheless, Chen Xijian carried out his duties as keeper of the tomb with exemplary professionalism, despite the increasing desertification of the area. The region's inhabitants worried about inadvertently breaking one of the numerous laws governing the place, as the punishments inflicted were terrible: twenty-four strikes with a stick for cutting wood, disturbing the soil or bringing a herd to graze on the grounds

10 *An old unit of measure equivalent to a fifteenth of a hectare.*

of the mausoleum; twenty-five strikes with a stick for those who entered the building or approached the tumulus without permission; and the death of a thousand cuts for any who broke anything within the tomb, and banishment for their entire family. And any who witnessed a violation but failed to report it could face one hundred strikes with a stick and exile to a location at least three thousand lis distant.

And so it was frequented only by the stooped old eunuchs sweeping the grounds in the vain hope that a ritual feast might one day deign to be held there. Yet Chen Xijian was not lazy: wind or snow, every morning and evening he inspected the five lis between the Golden Water Bridge and the arch where visitors dismounted their horses, a not insignificant task for a septuagenarian like himself, and it took him some considerable time. He knew that, despite his hopes to the contrary, this post would undoubtedly be his last and that it could have been worse, one way or another. His companion on the other hand did not share this opinion. That said, at his age, it was quite normal that Xiao Dezi – as he was named – who was just twenty years old and had been a eunuch only for several seasons, complained of having to work in such a dreary place…

Even when Xijian complained, he still had an authoritarian air, as if to remind those around him that he was a member of Uncle Zhang's family and deserved better than this position as head attendant of the mausoleum. But he had lost all his influence at court when the emperor changed and unlike the leader of the Tigers, he was not a follower of the yelikewen faith, which did not count in his favor.

"I've become a worthless old machine," he sighed as night fell. From the great golden gate, he could see the arch where visitors were required to dismount from their horses, with the inscription ordering visitors to do so seeming to dissolve into the gloom.

As he remained standing still, Xiao Dezi asked him, "Uncle Chen, you're not going as far as the arch today?"

"That will do for tonight. Write that nothing has happened today."

His companion nodded while thinking that nothing ever happened anyway. He couldn't stand his master any more. "Pretentious old fool," he thought to himself, "you'll get yourself killed eventually if you continue with your grand airs. You will regret it one day."

Seeing the annoyance in his eyes, Xijian fingered the silver coins he carried against his chest.

"Dezi," he said, "given that the last two days have been difficult, you can have the day off tomorrow. Would you like to take advantage of us being near the town and clear your head there this evening? I have a little money for you."

This generous offer was so unexpected coming from his miserly master, who had never offered him the smallest bonus, that the young man almost couldn't believe his ears. But his eyes were already fixed on the five or six taels on Chen Xijian's open palm. The master knew that his assistant was going to get drunk, because after all, no man in this world could live without women and wine, he thought, and as a eunuch, Xiao Dezi could only enjoy the pleasures of drink. Of course, he was not allowed to buy wine in Zhongshan, and certainly not to consume it at the Xiaoling tomb, but this money would allow him to purchase a good meal and several pitchers of wine in the city. He was already imagining the hustle and bustle of the city and the boats floating like clouds on the river Qinhuai like in a traditional painting, as well as the salted duck he would buy in Nanjing, accompanied by stuffed donuts… His mouth watered.

"But, Uncle Chen, how can I…"

"You have served me well for several years, it's the least I can do. Take this money and go to the Spring River Pavilion, you can bring me half a duck on your way back."

Famous for its duck and its wines and liquors, the Spring River Pavilion was Dezi's favorite restaurant when he went searching for a drink. Even better, the place had applied a ten-percent discount for attendants at the mausoleum ever since it was founded, partly funded by a eunuch. Five or six taels was more than enough for a feast, even after buying the half-duck for the old man.

"Uncle Chen, I will get you a wonderful fatty half-duck," Dezi promised before his master changed his mind.

"Perfect. Make sure you say the duck is for me, and that I would like it prepared by Master Yao and no one else."

"How does a crusty old man like him know the managers at Spring River Pavilion? Never mind, knowing the name of the boss might get me preferential treatment," thought the young man as he reached to take the coins.

"Thank you, Uncle Chen, I will go immediately."

While he normally failed to bow and generally cut short his courtesies, this time he bowed without being reminded, before following the path down the hill towards the city. Chen Xijian walked up the hill, hands pressed to his back.

Arriving at the Square Tower, he brushed the base of the stele that stood there – he would have no peace of mind if even a single dead leaf lay there. Erected in the eleventh year of Yongle's reign, it bore the inscription *Stele to the miraculous benevolence of the Xiaoling mausoleum of the Ming dynasty,* and it was rumored to perform miracles. Looking up as he contemplated it, the official looked as if he were about to be crushed by the monument, which was tall as six or seven men and casting a long shadow as it was silhouetted against the setting sun.

The stele stood on the back of a sculpture representing Bixi – a tortoise – one of the nine sons of the dragon king, given the role of carrying stelae due to his strength. The statue itself was so tall that Chen Xijian looked like a stalk of mustard in comparison.

Night fell quickly during this season, particularly around the mausoleum where tree cutting was prohibited. The faint light remaining around the Great Gate suddenly disappeared, absorbed by the walls of the Square Tower. As his shadow faded into the gloom, the old official suddenly had the feeling he was no longer alone. He seized the brass vajra resting next to a ritual bell at the foot of the stele and rushed to the other side, where to his astonishment and anguish he discovered a silhouette dressed in a dark cape which faded into the growing darkness so as to be almost invisible.

He pointed his weapon at it, ready to stab it through the heart.

"Did Uncle Zhang send you to kill me?" he asked in a deep voice.

The vajra had been given to him by a great tantric master named Singgibandan. This important figure in mizong, esoteric Buddhism, was an expert in the use of kundalini, a latent human energy he had trained Chen Xijian to use. He had reached levels five and six in his practice.

Singgibandan viewed progression in the use of kundalini as a scale with five stages – smoke, yang flame, campfire, lantern, and cloudless sky – and eight virtues – contained vitality, humidity, abundant heat, peace, lack of envy, purity, invisibility, and unfettered.

The martial artist who attained the seventh virtue could move without being seen by anyone; past the eighth, they would be able to pass through a mountain, free themselves of all constraints, achieve complete freedom. For the master who also attained the five stages, nothing was impossible.

Despite training for a long time, Chen Xijian had only achieved the yang flame and the virtue of peace. Though he might never achieve a high level, his skill conferred upon him an above-average level of agility and vitality. Sometimes Xiao Dezi had trouble keeping up with him on their daily travels, despite his age. When he drew on his inner heat through his tantric mastery, it was as if he were filled with an incredible strength.

The troubling visitor seemed surprised by this show of vitality, but still rushed to the front of the stele and adopted a defensive posture, stepping back each time the old man advanced. Chen Xijian had the upper hand, but if this dance continued for too long, he would undoubtedly tire before his adversary. He took a deep breath and was readying himself to launch an attack when the silhouette suddenly spoke.

"Uncle Chen, don't you recognize me?" it asked.

The voice hit him with a wave of familiarity. He almost choked with sobs of relief and joy.

"Miss… The imperial… favorite!"

Shao Jun was reassured by this reaction. She didn't need any more proof to convince her that the old man was not in the pay of Zhang Yong.

"Yes, it's really me… but I no longer bear that title."

"Miss, you will always be the imperial favorite in my eyes. But why have you come to visit an old imperial slave like me?"

The first time he had seen her, she had just been promoted concubine, and Emperor Zhengde had taken her to the Leopard Quarter to show her the tame hawks he had recently acquired. The other eunuchs had shown her little respect, but Chen Xijian, always irreproachable in his manners and greeting, had bowed deeply and sincerely before her. Later, when he had surprised her when she spied on the shadowy operations taking place in the Leopard Quarter, he had hidden her so she could return safely instead of reporting her offense, despite its seriousness. He had also remained at the Emperor's deathbed to his very last breath when he had succumbed to an illness after falling into water, and had thus been present on the day Zhengde gave the scroll to Shao Jun. His own life had been turned upside down when Zhang Yong had sent him to Nanjing to attend the Xiaoling mausoleum and keep him away from official business.

The years had passed and the young woman had matured as the old man had weakened, but her voice was the same. The former imperial favorite felt a wave of nostalgia.

"Uncle Chen, do you know my current status?" she asked.

"Of course. But even though I already have one foot in the grave, I could never see you as a criminal as long as I walk this earth. You will always be the imperial favorite to me."

The steward's caution set the young woman a little on edge, but his complete lack of hostility was encouraging.

"Uncle Chen, you thought I'd been sent by Zhang Yong… Why would he want to kill you?"

He lowered his head and was silent for a moment.

"Miss Favorite, that does not concern you. But if I may give you some advice, you should go. This humble imperial slave will not tell anyone of your visit."

She realized he feared more for her life than he did his own.

"You fear that Zhang Yong will come after you if he learns I visited you."

After a febrile silence, he responded, "This is not the place to have this discussion. Follow me!"

Beyond the Square Tower, the Spirit Way ran straight for several lis before veering towards Plum Blossom Hill, which housed the tomb of Sun Quan, the first of the Wu emperors. The commander in chief of the works on the Xiaoling mausoleum had suggested to Emperor Hongwu that it could be moved, but he had been firmly opposed to disturbing the proud warrior's eternal rest. And so, the Spirit Way took its current path, resembling that of the Great Bear.

In one of the curves the road made to avoid the hill lay a small pavilion surrounded by trees, usually serving as a lodge on wet or snowy days for the eunuchs who normally lived in buildings on either side of the Golden Waters. As it was currently unoccupied, Chen Xijian invited the young woman to enter.

While she remained on her guard as a precaution, she didn't feel in danger, partly because she was convinced that the old man still bore an unyielding loyalty to the dead Emperor, and partly because she knew her martial skills were of a higher level than his, having seen them demonstrated near the stele. What's more, she had arrived suddenly and it was therefore impossible for him to have prepared an ambush, particularly with so few people around.

"Uncle Chen..." she whispered.

He struck his flint to light a candle on a candleholder resting on the central table.

"Here we are safe from eavesdroppers, Miss Favorite. Please, sit."

The pavilion's location had been chosen to ensure that it was not visible from the Spirit Way, as it had once housed high-ranking officials come to pay homage to the deceased emperors. Like all the buildings within the Xiaoling mausoleum, its red walls were topped with splendid varnished tiles, but the interior was much more basic, featuring only a table, a bench, several bamboo chairs and clothing hooks on the wall. No visitors used it any more.

Seeing the austerity of the room, Shao Jun thought that the old man's demotion could not have been easy to bear; his living conditions at the palace had been much more comfortable.

"Uncle Chen, I'm sorry you were sent here."

"It's nothing," he responded with a bitter smile. "Tell me what brings you here."

She hesitated for a moment, then made her decision.

"Can you tell me more about what happened at the Xifan pavilion?"

Chen Xijian's hand, which had been in the process of lighting a second candle, began to shake.

"Ah, so that's it."

"What are you saying?"

He gave her a rueful smile.

"We had only met on a few occasions at the time."

"Yes, three times."

"I saw you four times," he said with a small smile. "But you didn't notice me when I caught you spying on the pavilion."

"Of course," she responded impassively.

He regarded the young woman almost half a century his junior with admiration. She must be talented indeed to have caught the Emperor's attention and elevated herself to the rank of imperial favorite, and have extraordinary strength of character to overcome the collapse of her dreams and former life.

"When Zhang Yong sacked the palace to find all the objects left by the deceased Emperor, I knew it must have something to do with your disappearance."

"But what was happening in the Xifan pavilion?" Shao Jun pushed, frowning.

A gust of wind rushed in through one of the torn paper windows, blowing out the candles. Chen Xijian hurried to re-light them.

"Are you sure you want to know?" he asked, his face marked with pain and sadness. "I-I've tried to make myself forget."

"Yes, I need to know the truth."

"Do you still have the scroll our deceased Emperor gave you before his death?"

"In the confusion and with Zhang Yong on my tail, I didn't have time to open it. But it wasn't for me anyway, I was told to give it to someone."

"Was that person Yang Tinghe?"

Yang Tinghe had been the head secretary responsible for the constitution, rites, and military affairs for twenty-seven years. Traditionally, therefore, he was considered to be the first to have served as prime minister. But during the succession, Zhang

Yong had sent him back to his home village.

"No," Shao Jun answered, "it wasn't him. Do you know what the scroll contained?"

"Ah, miss, that was seventeen years ago..."

At the time Shao Jun hadn't yet celebrated her sixth birthday and had no inkling of the future that awaited her, when the young Emperor Zhengde, an irreverent, impatient, and unpredictable youth who cared little for the affairs of the country, had just ascended to the throne. During the first years of his reign, he invited Master Singgibandan from the Huguo monastery to visit and teach his faith at the palace, and was so captivated by it that he proclaimed himself the "great Buddha of Wisdom – the enlightened Sakyamuni". One of his predecessors, Liang Wudi, had attempted to take his life three times in an attempt to hasten his reincarnation as a buddha, but Zhengde was the first in China to claim this title while still living. As ever, a crowd of extravagant individuals presented themselves at court to offer gifts to the Emperor to gain his favor. One of these presents, sent from Guangdong, was an incomplete page of a Western manuscript, covered in plans and designs and written in a language that resembled no known tongue.

The official who had brought it claimed that it came from a volume in which a mysterious Western soldier had recorded the discoveries of an entire life dedicated to studying the occult. He wrote it in an incomprehensible language to protect its dangerous secrets, which he still shared with a Western king of the time to help him achieve dominance. The book could only be deciphered using an antique box whose location had been lost to time. The official had himself come into possession of this extract through a traveler from the West.

Having always been intrigued by the unusual, Emperor Zhengde immediately charged his best magicians to work on this mysterious document, hoping that even if they were unable to translate it, they could at least obtain some small pieces of information. However, while the group of imperial magicians was largely composed of charlatans, some were true scholars. Through discussion and with the talents of some compensating for the weaknesses of others, they were able to identify within it the alchemical process needed to create a pill that grants immortality.

"Does such a thing really exist?" gaped Shao Jun.

Chen Xijian let out a forced laugh.

"Young lady, a humble imperial slave such as myself could never answer that. But I heard rumors that a caliph had made it, and Emperor Zhengde walked in his footsteps, put his specialists to work to accomplish the same miracle… They worked in the Xifan pavilion in the Leopard Quarter, until they all suddenly died in the fifteenth year of His Majesty's reign. I heard that they devoured one another, sent mad by a poison used to make the pill. The only positive outcome of this was to help the Emperor see reason. He saw that he was on the path to repeating the mistakes of the illustrious Win Shihuang who wasted his life in a vain quest for immortality, and decided to close the pavilion and seal the scroll forever."

Shao Jun remembered Zhengde as a curious and stubborn man, who had repeatedly told her of his interest in immortality. And to think he had then been taken by death at the age of thirty-one… How ironic.

She felt strangely disappointed now the mystery had been revealed. So, now Zhang Yong wanted to make the pill of immortality for himself. It was obvious that in the end, even the most powerful man in the empire was just another sixty year-old who feared his own demise. After the terrible events in the Xifan pavilion, he had to have been aware of the instability of the recipe, which explained why he sought the means to decipher the mysterious Western document. And Shao Jun now had no doubt that this means was the object Ezio Auditore had given her: the Precursor Box.

Chen Xijian blew out the candles. Illuminated by the light of the moon at its zenith, the night outside was much lighter than inside the pavilion.

"Did you ensure no one followed you?" he asked quietly.

Shao Jun was embarrassed to have been caught in Gao Feng's net on her return to China despite having taken what she thought were all the necessary precautions. She had since redoubled her efforts, particularly at the Temple of the White Pagoda and on her way to the Xiaoling mausoleum – Chen Xijian had only seen her because she had wanted him to. Master Yangming had taught her the *Heart of the mountain* technique, thanks to which she was able to notice the slightest unusual movement around her. Shao Jun was nowhere near the level of the mentor, who had attained *The eye pierces the sky*, one of the six stages of Buddhist extra lucid perception, but her sight and hearing were much sharper than the average person. However, it was Chen Xijian who was first to worry when he heard a suspicious sound.

"Someone comes!" He was immediately alert. "Miss Favorite, please stay hidden here. I will take care of it. I will create a distraction if things go badly. Take the opportunity and leave by the back entrance, avoiding the mausoleum."

He spoke so quietly that the young woman had to strain her ears to hear him. But barely had he finished his sentence than a high, piercing voice rang out.

"Uncle Chen!"

CHAPTER 8

Chen Xijian, pale as chalk, gestured to Shao Jun not to move as he left the building.

"Ah!" he exclaimed sufficiently loudly to be heard from inside. "Uncle Ma honors me with his visit!"

How was it possible? Master Yangming had predicted that Ma Yongcheng would stay in the capital vainly searching for any trace of the former imperial favorite, and yet here he was in Nanjing! The mentor had been wrong this time. No one was infallible, as she well knew, but until now his miraculous plans had always been a success, and she had begun to forget that he was still just a man. Unless Ma Yongcheng's visit to the mausoleum was just a coincidence… How could she know?

She was paralyzed by indecision. Should she flee? If the Tiger had company, she would be exposed. Should she confront him then? Master Yangming had told her that she could beat him in single combat, but once again, she would lose if he wasn't alone. The more she thought, the harder it was to make a decision. It was fortunate that Chen Xijian didn't seem like he wanted to denounce her.

Through the open door she could see the imposing silhouette of the Tiger, towering over the old man. Every time Shao Jun met him, she had been struck by the contrast between his colossal physique – all he lacked was a beard and he would have resembled a legendary warrior – and his high-pitched castrato voice. The disparity would have been comical if he hadn't been so terrifying.

"Uncle Ma," said the old man as he approached, "we haven't seen one another for years. What brings you here?"

Under Zhengde's reign Ma Yongcheng had been head of the East Factory, and Chen Xijian of the Leopard Quarter, and while one now flew high as the other wallowed in the mud, the mausoleum steward was not required to show excessive deference to his guest, who laughed at this relative impertinence.

"Come, Uncle Chen, you should have expected our visit, given what you shelter here…"

Shao Jun was surprised that the Tiger had managed to follow her trail here, though he may perhaps not have suspected that she was in the pavilion. After all, Wei Bin had supposedly been the best tracker in their group, someone from whom no one could escape via land or sea, or even the air. Ma Yongcheng's skill was not equal to that of his fallen comrade, and the young woman's slim figure made her a difficult target.

"Uncle Ma," Chen Xijian responded calmly and confidently, "I feel old, miserable, and ashamed in the face of your nobility and wealth. I would be delighted to help you, but I have no idea which of my possessions you could possibly desire."

"Ha ha ha, I'm not surprised that Captain Zhang sent an

incompetent like you to sweep the tombs. He should have planned a much worse fate! But if, by any chance, the traitor Shao Jun is in the pavilion and you were to hand her over to me…"

The old man's face lit up. He suddenly rushed forwards to cover the six or seven feet between them, and struck Ma Yongcheng's chest with his palm while the man was too surprised to react. Thanks to the teachings of the great Master Singgibandan, Chen Xijian had developed solid kung-fu skills that he maintained through regular practice. And so, despite his old age, he was more than able to deliver a fatal blow to an adversary who seemed physically superior.

Shao Jun knew that he had been the disciple of an expert in tantric Buddhism, but she had never expected to see him attack so quicky. When they travelled together, Zhu Jiuyuan had summarized the esoteric martial philosophy of Singgibandan, who had infused his kung-fu with his own spiritual doctrines. But the sound produced by the blow that had just struck was enough to convince her that she had just witnessed a devastating attack. And for good reason: Ma Yongcheng's huge mass sagged, then tumbled to the ground. When the young woman came out of the pavilion, his head swam in the blood flowing from his mouth. But as she turned towards Chen Xijian, she saw with horror that the Tiger had managed to plant his dagger in the old man's chest before he fell.

She moved towards him to offer support.

"Uncle Chen…"

"Miss, you are safe, don't worry about me."

"But you're hurt!"

"I'm still standing, see? The wound isn't deep."

True to his words, he seized the handle, removed the weapon from his wound and dropped it on the ground. Judging by the blood on the blade, the blow should have been fatal. And yet, the old man's face expressed only pain, not the agony that would have been expected. He clarified answered her silent question himself.

"Your humble servant was born with his heart on the right. If I had a normal constitution I would have died before your very eyes. But time is running out: Ma the Butcher certainly did not come alone; he must have men at the foot of the mountain. Miss, you must leave, immediately."

Shao Jun felt responsible for having stayed hidden; perhaps if she had come out of hiding immediately and fought the Tiger herself, then Chen Xijian would not have been injured. While his unique physiology had saved him from immediate death, his life would be at risk if his injury wasn't treated soon.

"What are you going to do?" she asked him.

"At my age," he answered with a tight smile, "I don't have much to hope for. But, miss, I didn't tell you everything: Uncle Zhang was certain that you would come to find me, and so ordered me to arrest you as soon as you appeared. However, I do not know how Ma Yongcheng came here so quickly, but you should consider that your presence here is now known. Please, don't trust anyone."

He was right, she must go. The Tiger must have come to the pavilion alone out of an abundance of confidence, but his followers would quickly grow concerned when he didn't return. However, she couldn't possibly leave the old steward to his fate.

"Uncle Chen, what are you going to do? I can't just leave you."

"Humble imperial slave that I am, I would rather die than suffer the reprisals of Uncle Ma's men."

"Do not despair, your wound isn't mortal. All is not lost…"

"Miss, I have neither friends nor family in Nanjing, where could I find refuge? And even if I could escape them for a time, it wouldn't last… The world is vast, but the Eight Tigers always find their enemies. Death awaits me, one way or another, but I beg you, please don't be sad."

Master Yangming often told Shao Jun that she must make a decision after considering her question three times, but she couldn't make up her mind. As she held him, she noticed Chen Xijian's pulse weakening. Despairing, she pressed her hand against the old man's chest.

"Uncle Chen, can you walk?" she asked.

"Yes, but I won't get far, and I have nowhere to hide."

"I know where we can go."

The old man stood back up, hope and surprise flaring in his eyes.

"But where? If you tell me where, I will get there on my own somewhere, don't let me slow you down."

"You won't find it without me. Come, Uncle Chen. Let's go!"

Master Yangming had told his protegee to use the jade plaque only as a last resort. While she personally was not at an impasse, this pendant was the key to the survival of an injured old man who had no one but her to come to his aid. One of the principles of the Society of the Mind was to work for good and to eliminate evil, and so it was her duty to use all means possible to save Chen Xijian. Besides, Ma Yongcheng's men would soon arrive, and she had no time to continue thinking about the issue.

The steward leaning against her, they moved away from the Butcher's body as it lay in a pool of blood that was already beginning to dry in the wind. She was pleased that the bloodthirsty man, who had killed so many of her peers in the Society of the Mind, was no longer a threat. But from their first steps she thought she felt an unpleasant chill sink into her bones.

They were coming!

Naturally slim and agile, she had developed her skill for dissimulation thanks to Wang Yangming, and the cloak given to her by Master Auditore allowed her to easily hide from anyone whenever she wished. So, she stepped aside to blend into the shadows at the edge of the path, Chen Xijian hidden behind her. As soon as their pursuer arrived, she unsheathed and executed *Sword cutting as the crescent moon.*

But before the blow could hit, her sword suddenly seemed to grow heavier in her hand and she was seized with a sudden malaise. A strange warmth spread through her from the bottom of her back, completely incapacitating her. It was the work of the old steward, who had used the *Great Imprint,* a tantric Buddhism technique, to block her vital essence from her lower back, triple burner, and life gate. This powerful neutralizing move required perfect knowledge of acupuncture points, without which touching it could have unexpected consequences, often dramatic and irreparable. The special feature of the *Great Imprint* in relation to the dim mak[11] of the central plain was that it trapped energy using the palm. This is what had just happened to Shao Jun.

Deprived of her strength, the young woman felt her lower

---

11 *A group of martial arts techniques that use energy points.*

body begin to turn numb. By the time she was kneeling on the ground, she had no strength left to lift her sword, which fell to the ground with a loud clang. Still able to move her left arm, she tried to pick up, but she had barely touched when three of the energy points in her back – zhiyang, lingtai, and shendao – were blocked. She collapsed to the ground wondering who had done it. Part of her still couldn't accept the painful truth: Chen Xijian had betrayed her. She heard him murmur into her back, "Excuse me, Miss Favorite, this humble imperial slave has disrespected you."

This time his respectful deference was tinged with mockery. Shao Jun had taken extra care at each stage of her journey to the mausoleum, but she had been unable to believe that the benevolent old man in her memories was to be distrusted. He had been the eunuch closest to Emperor Zhengde … How could he have fallen to Zhang Yong's influence in just a few years?

Chen Xijian kicked the young woman's sword, then leaned down to touch her neck – at court he would never have been allowed to show such a lack of respect – and take the jade pendant, inspecting it with a satisfied smile.

It was then Shao Jun saw the face of the man who had followed them, the one she had been about to attack before collapsing. She couldn't believe her eyes. It was …

Ma Yongcheng!

He had pretended to be dead to avoid risking a direct confrontation with the former imperial favorite; after all, the Butcher had a reputation for never having been injured by an opponent. The plan must have been prepared in advance, as he would have needed to carry a pouch of blood to perfect the illusion. If he had been so keen to win without a fight, it must be because he considered Shao Jun to an opponent at least equal to his own level. But how had he reached this conclusion?

Standing next to the young woman, Chen Xijian felt his anger grow. He would never have put the young favorite's life in danger if it hadn't been a direct order from Zhang Yong. And now, Ma Yongcheng was undoubtedly going to unceremoniously slice her throat as she lay helpless on the ground. The old man hated everything about this situation.

"Chen Xijian, what did you take from the whore?" asked the Tiger, who had seen him take the pendant.

The Butcher was far from showing his elder the respect due by convention, but the latter did not take offence, bowing as he responded, "Uncle Ma, the imperial favorite mentioned a place where she could have hidden us. I noticed that she touched her chest as she spoke, so I thought that she might have an important item hidden there. And I wasn't wrong..."

"Really? Show me?"

Ma Yongcheng sheathed his short sword, that he had kept in hand until then, fully aware that if she had not been stopped by his accomplice, Shao Jun could have sliced him in half several seconds earlier. He took the jade pendant from the old eunuch, appreciating as a connoisseur the exceptional soft sheen of the high quality "mutton fat" jade. Such a stone, if it had been the size of a child's palm, would certainly be worthy of joining the finest pieces in the imperial collection.

"Uncle Ma," Chen Xijian continued, "if my suspicions are correct, this item should help you find the man who hides behind Shao Jun."

He was right: if this precious object fell into Zhang Yong's hands, he would quickly realize his adversary was Master

Yangming. Shao Jun focused on trying to free herself, but the technique that had blocked her energy flows was different from the dim mak of the Central Plain, her acupuncture points had been captured as if caught in a tightening web. And so, it was impossible for her to unblock them one by one.

Ma Yongcheng lifted the jade up in the moonlight to take a better look.

"Excellent. The imperial apartments do not have much of this variety, so it won't be hard to find where it comes from. The venerable captain has led straight to Shao Jun without even leaving his apartments … What an exceptional man!"

Zhang Yong had predicted that Shao Jun would leave Beijing after the murder of Wei Bin, and that they could then deduce where she would reappear. The Xiaoling mausoleum was certainly not the top of the list of possibilities, but the Butcher had wanted to take a look regardless. Arriving in Nanjing the day before, he had paid Chen Xijian a brief visit and had prepared to continue on his way south the following day. What a happy surprise it had been to learn so shortly before his departure that the young woman had been to see the steward!

"Uncle Ma, should I unblock her energy points?" the old man asked.

Busy examining the tangled engravings on the pendant in the moonlight, the Tiger had little interest in the elderly official's questions.

"What?"

"My dim mak is not the best, and the favorite is not an ordinary young woman. I have just had to block three additional points because her pulse was already speeding up. Even invoking the power of the Buddha of Light to close the four chakras in the back, I fear that she will soon find the strength to free herself. She will soon be a problem."

Being a disciple of yelikewen, Ma Yongcheng had not followed the esoteric Buddhist teachings of Master Singgibandan, but he had learnt a kundalini technique that allowed him to control a person's pulse. It was by applying it to himself that he had been able to simulate his own death a few moments earlier. At the highest level, experts could slow their heartbeats to make themselves completely imperceptible, then return to life after several days underground as if nothing had happened.

But while the results were similar, in reality there were few similarities between the physiological mechanisms of the Central Plain dim mak and the *Great Imprint* technique, as the former was based on activating very precise points, while the latter was the result of a blockage caused by applying the palm, where the attacker's energy had previously been concentrated – and so was more a manipulation of a zone. As a result, blockages caused by kundalini could potentially be broken, but only by those with a very high level of kung-fu. It was therefore very worrying that Shao Jun was able to overcome such a powerful technique.

"Yes, we should avoid taking risks if her kung-fu is that powerful."

He'd had no regard for her when she had been Emperor Zhengde's favorite, but she must have made phenomenal progress in her mastery of martial arts in order to kill Wei Bin. And if Chen Xijian thought her capable of breaking free of his dim mak, that possibility had to be taken seriously. Ma Yongcheng wouldn't dare tell Zhang Yong the news if she escaped and disappeared again.

"I will complete her incapacitation myself," he said as he advanced towards Shao Jun.

"Would it perhaps be more prudent for me to hold the precious jade while you perform the manipulation?"

With the way the old man's eyes remained fixed on the pendant, the Tiger imagined that the old man worried he would not be rewarded for his loyalty. Pleased by the turn events had taken, he was in such a generous mood that he was ready to make a gesture of goodwill to this deposed official who undoubtedly dreamed of leaving the frugality of his present situation to return to the comfort of the imperial palace. He handed the jade plaque back to him.

"Uncle Chen, keep it in a safe place."

Ma Yongcheng was not a specialist in tantric techniques, but his high level of kung-fu had allowed him to skip enough steps in his training to reach the meditative state that esoteric Buddhism named as Samadhi – he was thus at a higher level than Chen Xijian. When he applied his palm to Shao Jun's back to penetrate her energy points, he was surprised to note that her pulse was quite weak, despite what the old steward had said. And for good reason: under the effect of the *Great Imprint*, the blood could no longer circulate freely throughout the body, which prevented the victim from walking or even standing. One more blockage and the former imperial favorite would be reduced to a vegetative state for a day or two.

He confusion was violently interrupted by an agonizing pain in his lower back. Paralyzed with agony and surprise, he looked down and saw Shao Jun's sword planted in his side.

The master of conspiracy and scheming could never have imagined ever falling for such an ingenious trap even in his worst nightmares. He reached out, but his hand that was once so powerful, so agile, brushed only air; the sword had already been removed, and his kung-fu would no longer be of any use. When he turned, he saw that it was Chen Xijian who had betrayed him. He glared at him with deadly hatred in his eyes, hatred that was only strengthened by his complete powerlessness. "You..." he groaned before coughing up a stream of very real blood. He knew the wound would be fatal.

"Uncle Ma," said the old man, "which is greater, to enjoy oneself alone or with others? I would say that one is never better than when one is alone!"

Completely devoid of culture, Ma Yongcheng couldn't have recognized this quote from Mengzi, but understood that his killed had no desire to share the triumph of capturing Shao Jun. He had killed enough men to know that his agony would doubtless be long and solitary, but this pain was nothing compared to that inflicted by his regret. How could he have lowered his guard before this affable old man? Chen Xijian on the other hand drew sadistic satisfaction from the Tiger's suffering.

"Uncle Ma," he said warmly, "you'll die at the same time as the imperial favorite because you rushed in without thinking. But don't worry, I will sing your praises before the venerable captain, and we will honor your memory."

Ma Yongcheng's hatred deepened: "This pathetic old husk was planning this from the start!" he thought.

It was true. As soon as he learned that Shao Jun may come to see him, the old steward had decided to take advantage of the situation to recover the honors that had been stripped from him. And the Tiger, whom he had absolutely not trusted to reward him, was nothing more than an obstacle to be overcome. The two men had agreed a signal: if Dezi, Chen Xijian's assistant, visited the city to buy a salted duck prepared by Master Yao, that would mean that the former imperial favorite had appeared, and that Ma Yongcheng should hurry to the pavilion at the edge of the Spirit Way. He had never suspected that the trap had instead been laid for him.

His hatred increased as his body weakened. It was so palpable that Chen Xijian stood a few steps away to be sure that his victim, collapsed on top of Shao Jun, had finally succumbed. He would then finish off the young woman, something in which he took no pleasure, and set it up to appear as if the two dead fighters had killed one another.

"Uncle Ma," he whispered, "you have tasted enough of the pleasures of this world. It is time that the humble Xijian takes what he is owed."

But as he moved to take his dagger, the Tiger's body stirred. The old man jumped back, as the Butcher was no ordinary man, and even his final death throes, if that is what they were, could prove fatal. Unless he was pretending to be dead?

"Uncle Chen, you torture me!"

It was Shao Jun! The young woman stood with unreal slowness, pushing off the heavy body that lay on top of her. Struck with terror, Chen Xijian retreated without even realizing.

"Ma Yongcheng wanted to drag me down with him!" he growled as he understood what had happened.

In the last seconds of his life, the Tiger had freed the former imperial favorite from her chains of ki so he could have his revenge, albeit indirectly. The very fact that she had been saved by the assassin who had killed dozens of members of the

Society of the Mind, a man who disgusted her more than any other, filled her with rage. And she knew where to direct that anger: toward the old eunuch who had tricked her so but whose greed had finally led him to defeat.

She had to retrieve the jade pendant, the irrefutable proof of Master Yangming's involvement in the murder of the Tigers. The task wouldn't prove easy, because the Butcher hadn't been able to remove all the energy blocks – both her arms were free but her legs were still numb – but she had to give it her all. Nothing else mattered.

Chen Xijian thought he had a chance of beating her if he took advantage of her partial weakness. His age was against him, but he had managed to trick both her and Ma Yongcheng after all, which gave him confidence in his strategic capabilities. Raising his vajra to her heart as he moved forward, he attempted a tone of assured indifference as he spoke.

"If Miss Favorite would do me this honor..."

According to Buddhist canons, the vajra – which could have one, three, or even nine spokes – was used to destroy ignorance, and those who wield it seek enlightenment. But Chen Xijian used it only for combat, seeking a victory that had nothing to do with the spiritual. His opponent was weakened; all he needed to overcome her was a single, effective strike that her clumsy legs would be unable to help her avoid. He prepared to use *Garuda's Flame* and was already savoring his victory... when he felt a breath of wind across his left shoulder, followed by violent pain.

He let out a tragic cry and quickly pivoted to the right to avoid having his arm severed. Nevertheless, blood sprayed from his wound, testifying to the severity of the injury. His eyes had been on her feet the whole time, ensuring that her handicap was not feigned… How had the favorite avoided his attack with her legs so weakened? There! A flash of moonlight gave him the answer. He saw his adversary throw her rope dart at a tree branch. So that was how she had overcome the partial blockage of her legs! But this discovery was of no use to him: he'd lost his advantage now he was injured, and his kung-fu was too weak for him to win this fight.

"Hide your strengths as well as your weaknesses," the master had said. It was exactly what the former concubine had done, using her rope dart to make the old man believe she was still able to move at full speed – she had no idea her subterfuge had been discovered. But it was only a stopgap, because every time she wanted to move, she had to reel in her dart and throw it around another branch. Now correctly positioned above Chen Xijian, she launched her attack, but he dodged and instead of trying to retaliate, he fled down the path.

The old man's injury had already smeared blood all over the top of his clothing. He felt the situation getting out of his control, but his legs still worked so perhaps not all was yet lost. Shao Jun grew angry as she saw him run. Rebuilding the Brotherhood would be irredeemably compromised if he escaped with the jade pendant. Driven by anger and determination, she sheathed her sword, threw her rope and pulled upwards with all her strength. Her powerful muscles, forged through intensive martial arts practice, allowed her to fly through the air past Chen Xijian and land just in front of him, near a statue of a horse. She gripped her weapon. It was time to end this.

But the old eunuch leapt over her using the statue before she could strike, high enough to be out of reach of her blade, and continued to run. He knew that the young woman would soon be entirely free of the effects of the *Great Imprint*, and she would make short work of him as soon as her blood was circulating normally. He had to lose her, and fast!

But how? Heart pumping, he prayed for an open space without branches his pursuer could latch onto with her rope, but he well knew that the entire area was densely wooded due to the prohibition on logging within the vicinity of the mausoleum. They passed before the Square Tower, then Golden Waters Bridge, and soon arrived before the horse-dismounting arch. Past this point, the great avenue left the mountain and the landscape was more open. Knowing that this was probably her last opportunity, Shao Jun threw her rope once more and propelled herself forwards.

Woven from natural silk and deer sinew, the rope dart given to her by the former Emperor had more than once been her closest ally in sticky situations. Its elasticity and durability allowed her to sail through the air at a height that risked breaking her bones on landing. But hesitation was a luxury she could no longer afford: she must bar Chen Xijian's way. She would have caught him within a few strides if she hadn't been so incapacitated…

Fortunately, she had her cloak. She deployed it at the height of her leap, allowing her to glide through the air like an eagle for a moment, a sight which drew a scream of terror from her prey. Arriving at the bottom of the mountain, there was a wide moat formed by a tributary of the River Qinhuai which then ran into Black Tortoise Lake. He tried to speed up, though it was never going to be enough to escape Shao Jun. Consumed by panic as she landed in front of him, he rushed forwards and threw himself into the water.

Shao Jun was only just recovering from her miraculous

landing. Her momentum obliged her to take a dozen steps to soften the force of the impact as she landed, without which her legs would have undoubtedly broken. The shock had been beneficial for her circulation as her numbed legs, while painful, could now feel again, as if the energy block had finally lifted. When she came to a halt, she heard a splash as Chen Xijian jumped into the moat a short distance away.

She couldn't fail, not so close to her goal! Though her body hadn't yet fully recovered, she followed him into the black waters of the moat. But barely had she entered the water when she felt a sharp pain pierce through her: Chen Xijian had stabbed his vajra into her right shoulder.

Instead of trying to escape, he had kept still in the water waiting to strike. It was a dangerous gamble, because his strength was reduced by the resistance of the water, and the young woman's cloak could have stopped the blow from landing, but luck was on his side this time.

Despite the intense pain, Shao Jun grabbed the vajra in her left hand, opening her palm over its blades. She ignored the pain as she pulled it out of her wound before planting it in Chen Xijian's chest. She didn't reach his heart, which contrary to his claims was on the left, but the weapon pierced through the old man like the tenderest meat. Blood bubbled out, and the steward knew he was in a situation he would be unable to get out of on his own. Even injured and drained by the energy blocks she had suffered, the former imperial favorite still had more than enough reserves to end him. But a cold breeze swept across the surface of the river, carrying the lines of a song:

Thick coat flying in the wind, showers of petals raised by the horse's hooves, the air is cold in the early morning…

They were taken from *Tale of the Pipa*, a theatrical opera that was popular south of the Yangxi and with fishermen on the River Qinhuai. "I'm saved!" Chen Xijian thought to himself, beginning to swim in the direction of the voice with such vigor that Shao Jun could do nothing to prevent him putting dozens of meters between them. Despair had only increased his strength.

The young woman was in agony. Gritting her teeth against the pain, she heard the song as the singer began the last verse:

Country of rivers and mountains, I must go. Turn my back on my beloved parents and leave. Wounded love, the cuckoo sings and the collar of my jacket is wet with tears.

It was a young and charming voice, certainly that of a young noble who had come to sing in the silence of the night to escape the din of the city.

Chen Xijian saw the gleam of the lanterns illuminating the barge, and as he turned his head, saw that his pursuer had redoubled her efforts to cover the distance between them. Filled with panic, he called for help at the top of his lungs.

At first the five or six occupants of the boat were frightened by the shout coming out of the darkness, but they stood to hold their lights as they searched the night. It was a small group of young lords dressed in brocade, accompanied by a beautiful young woman – the singer – who held a pipa[12] against her. Chen Xijian soon appeared in the lamplight and tried to grab the front of the boat like a demon surging out of the water. With his bloody wounds and soaked clothes clinging to his body, he was a terrifying sight.

---

12 *A lute-type instrument.*

"I am the steward of the Xiaoling mausoleum, and someone is trying to kill me!" he cried.

The men hurried to help him onto their boat, and were surprised to see Shao Jun, who looked equally terrifying, climbing onto the boat and drawing her sword, ready to stab the old man through the heart and ensure that the jade pendant would never fall into Zhang Yong's hands.

Sensing that his last minutes drew near, the old man let out a scream of fear as the blade rushed towards him, only to be parried with a clang by a wooden stick. A baby-faced young lord, whose fighting skills were doubtful if based on appearance alone, had stepped in to save his life.

He wielded his ash club like a fighting stick, with speed and precision. After repelling Shao Jun's sword, he lifted his makeshift weapon over his head and hit the shoulder of the injured young woman, who was too exhausted and weighed down by her wet clothes to react in time. *Pah!* She felt the full impact of the blow, pain shooting through her like a knife.

"Master, please forgive me…" was her final thought as she blacked out.

CHAPTER 9

Shao Jun woke to the sound of singing. She didn't know how much time had passed.

The flower twirls in circles in the wind; my wandering life has led me to the bars of a prison…

She couldn't hear all the words clearly, but the voice was charming.

In her dazed state, the young woman believed she was once more in the Leopard Quarter, where Emperor Zhengde often held his operas. He had been so passionate about them that he never missed a single one, and when Shao Jun became his favorite, he had even disguised her and taken her to a performance at the Great Gate of the Forbidden City. It was there she had first heard the melody that woke her now, though she had never paid much attention to the words at the time. The melody she was currently listening to had several incorrect notes, but comparing it with the country's greatest singers seemed unfair. Confused, she slowly opened her eyes only to quickly close them again, dazzled by the bright light of the room she found herself in.

Lying down, she began to return to her full senses. The singer had to be very young, and during the line "The beauty was surprised and frightened by her dream so sweet, fearing to blush as if the east wind would sweep away her emotion. Three or four steps below…", her voice broke on "three or four steps below" and if she had tripped on a step herself. She repeated the verse over and over to perfect it, but to no avail.

When she opened her eyes properly, Shao Jun saw that she was on a bed, covered by a thick comforter, in a finely decorated office. The light which had blinded her before came from candles as thick as her arm, standing on thick red candleholders that sat on a nightstand next to her. The room also had a table, and a bench on which sat the young singer, who looked to be at most twelve or thirteen years old. Her hair was divided into two buns either side of her ears, and she swung her feet back and forth as she continued to fumble the lines of the song.

Although she was relieved not to be in a cell, Shao Jun wanted to know more about her situation. She rested a hand on the edge of the bed to sit up, but even that simple movement triggered a wave of pain through the muscles and nerves of her battered body. Hearing her groan, the young girl stopped singing and rushed to the bedside, sliding cushions behind her back to help her sit up.

"Oh no, miss, it looks like the sedatives have worn off. Don't move, I'll get you a cup of ginseng tea."

Here memories began to return: the day before, on board a boat, a young noble had struck her hard with a wooden stick… Everything after that was a blank. When she touched her shoulder, she found it numb and covered in thick bandages. So, they had treated her wound. Leaning against the cushions, she looked at the young girl stand on tiptoe to reach a large cup on the table and carefully bring it to the bedside.

"Here," she said, "it'll do you good."

As a concubine she had often drunk the Emperor's tea to ensure it wasn't poisoned, and over time she had developed a good knowledge of this beverage. She could tell from the smell alone that it was the best quality Himalayan ginseng, and each sip restored a little more energy as she drank. Still unable to shake her disquiet, she looked around and asked, "Little sister, where am I?"

"Oh, you can call me Yanfei, miss! 'Little sister' is too great an honor!"

It was surprising that she bore this name, which meant "snow mist", when most slaves were usually named after flowers and the seasons, such as "Orchid of Spring" or "Fall Chrysanthemum". Seeing Shao Jun's surprise, the young girl gestured at the wall and quickly explained.

"The master chose my name from this poem. Can you read, miss? Please tell me the master isn't making fun of me!"

Seeing how this slave was treated and hearing her speak of her master, the young woman had the feeling that he was a good man, which only confused her more. Who could he be? Why had he saved her life?

As Shao Jun pondered, the young slave grew impatient, worried that she would be told her name was not in the poem after all.

"I know," she grumbled, "the master is teasing me again, as usual!"

The young woman started out of her reverie and focused on Su Shi's poem, written in a neat, careful script on the wall scroll:

A range in panorama, peaks if viewed from the side. The true face of Mount Lu is unknowable; in its mist of snow, we are lost in the heart of the place itself.

"There it is!" she exclaimed. "Your name really is in the poem!"

"Really? So, the master didn't lie to me! So that means the names of Duojin 'Brocade button', Xunfang 'Fragrant quest', and Yaoqin 'Jade zither' must also have come from poems. The master knows so many things!"

Shao Jun couldn't hold back a small laugh. You didn't need to be a great scholar to read a few characters here and there… But in her innocent naiveté, the young girl was full of excitement.

"Miss, please, can you show me where Xunfang's name is written?"

The four walls were covered in calligraphy, all written in an extremely definite, regular script with no emphasis or strange cursive sections. The former imperial favorite followed the young slave's finger towards a four-verse poem:

After all these years my soldier's uniform lies covered in dust; I now climb the blue mountain driven by a fragrant quest; never do I allow myself to contemplate the waters and peaks; urging my horse on, the moon lights my return.

Most of these scrolls had no title. But this one read: Drunk under the moon, Hermit Who Touches the Clouds wrote these lines in memory of General Yue Fei.

"Oh! So, your master is nicknamed 'Hermit Who Touches the Clouds'?"

"I don't know, but he wrote these calligraphies. The characters on this scroll are drafts, I prefer the ones with cleaner edges."

Shao Jun hadn't studied the classics, but she had read some passages; her masters had represented the elite of their time, particularly Wang Yangming, who was a Confucian scholar of the highest rank. She had therefore heard of General Yue Fei of the Song dynasty, who had fought for his emperor with such loyalty that a temple had been erected in his honor after his death. But the story had been somewhat forgotten, and poems in his honor were rare. So, it seemed strange to name a slave based on one of them.

Except for this scroll, written in a drunken state with a light and loose hand, all the works displayed in this office, which seemed to be study drafts, had been written carefully and definitely. This Hermit Who Touches the Clouds had to be some kind of great ascetic to produce such invariably neat work. Shao Jun would have liked to know what he was thinking, supposing that he was her host.

"Yanfei, why did your master name you after a poem honoring General Yue Fei?"

"Oh, you know Yue Fei? You are so cultured, miss! The master displayed his poems here because he holds him in such esteem."

Shao Jun was stunned. She had been completely unaware that General Yue Fei, known for his martial prowess, had also composed poetry. As her education had been managed by Zhu Jiuyuan and he didn't like to read aloud, she had considerable gaps in the areas of literature and poetry.

This Hermit Who Touches the Clouds must be a very refined man, Shao Jun thought as she looked at the white walls covered in his calligraphy. She could see a large flowering pagoda tree through the large windows that were partly open to reduce the ambient heat.

"Yanfei," she frowned, "what is your master's name?"

"Oh, I don't know, miss! I thought that y- you knew it."

"You don't know your master's name?"

"No, I just call him 'master.'"

Yanfei reminded Shao Jun of her years spent in the palace, where it was greatly frowned upon to speak or ask the Emperor's name, instead simply referring to him as "His Majesty". Even when she became an imperial concubine the young woman had never known his real name, Zhu Houzhao, only the name he had taken for his reign: Zhengde.

"In that case, could you take me to him?"

The young girl's eyes grew round. "But, miss, aren't you hurt?"

"No, I'm better now!"

To support her affirmation, she got up and moved her limbs, surprised that even her shoulder, despite being stabbed then hit with a club, didn't cause her pain – it just felt cold. While running and jumping were out of the question, the ginseng tea had returned her strength. For Yanfei, who had seen her arrive unconscious several days before, her rapid recovery was incredible.

"When you arrived here two days ago, the master asked for you to be left alone to rest. He said that your injury was serious and that he would see you when you were better."

"I've been here for two days?"

"Yes. The master brought you here the night before yesterday, and you slept all day yesterday."

Two days! So much must have happened while she was unconscious. Where could she find Chen Xijian? Did he still have the jade pendant? She couldn't lie around here and do nothing any longer.

"I need to speak to your master straight away," she said. "It can't wait. Where is he?"

"He spends the day in the shade on the Greenfinch terrace."

"How do I find him?"

"Just go down and follow the path until the Prince's Pond. From there you'll see the Greenfinch, it's a stone boat. But it's late, you should rest..."

The young girl hadn't expected that Shao Jun would really go, so she panicked when she saw the older woman heading for the door before she'd even finished speaking. Desperate, she grabbed her sleeve, then stood in front of the door to block the way. It was useless of course, as the former imperial favorite passed her in the blink of an eye despite her injured shoulder, and was soon down the stairs and out of the building. When she reached the outer door, she saw that the residence was surrounded enchanting gardens full of trees and flowers. As night had already fallen, she hesitated for a moment before walking up the winding narrow path through the garden, but quickly made her decision. She'd already lost two days. Behind her, the small slave, unable to keep up with her strides, begged her not to go.

If Zhang Yong got hold of the pendant that Chen Xijian had managed to steal, he would send his men to the Temple of the Jade of the Five Virtues and extinguish the last hope of ever seeing the Brotherhood rise from the ashes. Shao Jun had to find the master of this place as quickly as possible to find out more about her current situation, then take urgent action without any further delay, regardless of the risks.

Residential gardens usually only covered several acres, but the path was so winding that Shao Jun, slowed even further by the darkness, felt like she was walking a significant distance. Then, after yet another bend, the sparkling surface of a body of water covered in fragrant lotuses suddenly appeared. A small group of people stood on a stone terrace shaped like a boat protruding out into the water. On what appeared to be a small stage, two people moved to the melody of the pipa that the breeze carried intermittently to Shao Jun's ears. It must be a play.

Under the Yuan dynasty, a golden era for *zaju* opera, plays were performed in every town, and it wasn't unusual for Jiangnan nobles to build private theatres on their properties, as the Hermit Who Touches the Clouds had clearly done. As she walked along the lake shore, Shao Jun wondered how to approach her host without putting herself in danger or causing a scandal.

When she was close enough to see them, she saw that the two actors wore ordinary clothes rather than theatre costumes. What's more, for the combat scene they were currently performing, they used sticks of ash instead of stage weapons. Shao Jun also noticed that they used real attack and defense techniques, meaning they had been trained in martial arts. Behind them sat a beautiful and elegantly dressed pipa player, a wizened old man, and … the young lord who had struck Shao Jun two nights before!

Completely perplexed, she remained rooted to the spot.

"Who goes there?" called a voice behind her.

The young woman looked behind her without turning.

She had been seen by two large young men who held their sticks horizontally behind their heads, as they often did in the army. Many military martial arts techniques began from this position, such as *Golden scissors,* a paired attack where the two attackers crossed their weapons to better corner their prey. Adopting this position, the two men were threatening and ready to fight.

But they didn't expect Shao Jun to leap towards them in a flash and hit the upper "scissor blade" as she flew through the air, sending both sticks flying to the ground. She could have knocked them both out if she had wanted to, but she had no intention of fighting. However, before she had a chance to speak, she noticed a new attack coming from behind.

The two fighters exchanging theatrical blows on the stage on the Greenfinch veranda had jumped to the bottom of the terrace, using their momentum to execute their own *Golden scissors* attack. While they were much more skilled than the previous two, Shao Jun was able to free herself with a kick. The actors attacked again, allowing her no respite, while the first two aggressors, startled out of their stupor, pressed their own offence. When the young woman dodged all the blows at the same time, the four sticks hit one another with enough force that they broke. She was almost injured by the flying pieces of wood.

Alerted by the noise, the old man sitting on the terrace suddenly stood. This skill of this intruder who had appeared from nowhere worried him. As long as it wasn't an assassin... Just as he seemed ready to join the fight, the young lord shouted out.

"Stop! Let her approach!"

When he stood, the refined young noble looked as tall and imposing as a mountain. His authority had immediately cooled the tempers of the fighters, two of whom had descended from the stage and now felt embarrassed at having been beaten so easily – and by a woman no less – despite flaunting their talents only moments earlier. The lord ignored them completely as he addressed Shao Jun with a warm smile.

"You're finally here!" he exclaimed as if speaking to an old friend. "Has your wound healed?"

"But who are you?" she retorted.

The old man began to protest at this lack of respect, but the young noble gestured at him to stop.

"I was planning to introduce myself when you were better," he responded. "Your arrival surprised us, but please know that you are safe here. But you will have to fight me first if you want more information than that."

A rack at the edge of the platform held wooden training weapons. The young lord took an ash stick, then hefted a bamboo cane, and, after judging it sufficiently light for Shao Jun to wield despite her injury, held it out to her.

"Take it."

"What kind of person are you?"

"Fight me and I'll answer your question."

He untied his belt to remove his outer robe as the young woman silently railed at him, her amazement having given way to a sudden burst of anger. This arrogant man who had surely never seen anything of the world thought that she couldn't hurt him with a bamboo cane? When he had hit her on the boat, she had been exhausted from her run, the blocking of her pressure points, stress and blood loss, but tonight it would be very different. While she wasn't on top form because of her shoulder, her mind was clear. In addition, she could wield weapons equally well in either hand, and her agility allowed her to compensate for her slight handicap. No, she wouldn't have any trouble overcoming this pompous noble, soft from living in luxury.

That said, she still didn't understand his motivation, which disturbed her. The young lord had treated her and left her to the care of an apparently unsuspecting Yanfei. Free of his robe, he wore only a short vest whose shimmering fabric reminded Shao Jun of her time at the imperial palace. But now he was ready to fight, weapon in hand, his eyes became as piercing as a cat's. His body tense with a seemingly fierce desire to kill, he was completely different from before. The young woman had the feeling he didn't have any regrets about hitting her two nights before, and that he would happily do it again. Perhaps this duel would be more intense than she had expected.

But just as she climbed onto the stage, she heard someone running up behind her.

"Who goes there?" called the two men patrolling the shore.

"It's me!" replied a high voice. "Master, it's Yanfei!"

The slave had followed Shao Jun all the way to the lake. Even though her feet weren't bound, she had learned to walk in the feminine way that was fashionable at the time, with short, hesitant steps, so she was now out of breath and her face was red as beetroot.

"Master, the lady wanted to come and see you and I- I couldn't stop her!" she cried.

"Hahaha!" the beautiful pipa player laughed, soon followed by the young lord, whose fierce focus had clearly been cooled by this unexpected interruption.

"It's fine, Yanfei," he said to his servant. "I simply couldn't wait to go up against the person who beat the Snake!"

"He knows I killed Wei Bin!" Shao Jun almost exclaimed

aloud. Her mind buzzed. What did this mean? But she didn't have time to think, as the young lord turned and pointed his ash baton at her, inviting her to take up a fighting stance. Their exchange could now begin. He wielded his weapon in the *Armies of the Emperor Qin waving their flags in six directions* style, but kept his right arm pressed against his body instead of using both hand as he should have done to balance out the opposing forces – yin and yang, fire and water – on which this technique depended. Shao Jun wondered why her opponent deprived himself of half of the advantages at his disposal. When she launched her first attack, she moved her left foot slightly in front of her right to pivot, avoiding the attack as she responded with her own. Even though she held her weapon in her left hand and was only at three-fourths of her normal capabilities, her level was still exceptional, and far above that of the first fighters. But she still needed to win this duel quickly, because she would tire fast in her current state. She had to move in closer because his ash baton was longer than her bamboo cane, but that wasn't a problem: her agility was made for this style of combat. When the young noble launched a new assault, she dodged and took advantage as he brought his baton back toward him – a mistake that no expert would make – to move forward and hit his wrist with four lightning-fast strikes of her cane.

The young woman was unaware, but her opponent had had the opportunity to measure himself against Wei Bin in the last year, who had beaten him flat in just three or four moves. Experiences like this are part of the learning undergone by any kung-fu fighter whose skill has not yet reached its height, and he was absolutely determined to face the one who had beaten the Snake. After all, losing to a peerless opponent was far more satisfying than an easy victory. And he was now in a difficult position. He needed to move forward to gain the upper hand, but any attempt to make even the smallest half-step was immediately rebutted by an attack he had to hurry to counter. He thought he was done when a particularly energetic blow sent his baton flying off to the right of the platform, but he rushed to catch it by the other end – fortunately for him, this weapon could be wielded either way round. He began to spin it in his hands; it almost seemed to multiply as it spun faster and faster.

Shao Jun was impressed with this level of skill. She hadn't strictly been trained in the use of the baton, but during their training sessions Master Zhu had briefly mentioned the *Six directions*, which resulted from the progressive development of the *Pear blossom spear* technique originally invented by Yang Miaozhan when she commanded the Red Coat army. This remarkable woman, whose kung-fu was greater even than that of her husband, the exceptional Li Quan, liked to say that no warrior under the sky could counter the soldiers she trained. When executed perfectly, this technique inspired by the movement of pear blossoms in the wind could make it seem as if the user wielded seven batons at once. The young lord only achieved three or four illusory weapons, perhaps because he refused to use both arms, but it was enough to cause Shao Jun problems.

Clack! The cane collided with the end of the baton, whose three or four ends immediately dissipated. The young woman seized the opportunity to force her adversary into close combat where he soon found himself in difficulty, unable to execute a series of moves freely. He was soon forced to descend from the platform. But if he had used both arms, he would have had a good chance of winning the duel. Was he also injured on his right arm? He seemed like he would prefer to lose rather than use his free hand. In this situation, Shao Jun didn't have the heart to beat him down, so she took a step back and said, "Lord, you'll never win against me if you wield your baton with only one hand, use both!"

"It's true, master..." added the old man from the side, who had up until now refrained from intervening so as to avoid the noble losing face.

His pride injured; the young man reddened. He was much less arrogant than when he began his challenge. The situation had got away from him, his *Pear blossom spear* had been defeated, and he owed his health to his opponent's mercy, after she refused to finish him despite leaving him as vulnerable as a sacrificial lamb on the altar.

"Be quiet!" he shouted at the old man. "Or you'll taste my *Three revelations of the baton*!"

CHAPTER 10

A cool night breeze, perfumed with the spiced scent of lotus blossoms, rose from the lake and revived Shao Jun.

Against all odds, she felt for the young lord on seeing his frustration at being unable to correctly execute his baton technique, having herself had a similar experience with Master Yangming. Despite the murderous gleam that had been in his eyes since the beginning of the fight, she had greater and greater difficulty believing that he could be affiliated with the Eight Tigers. His only objective really did seem to be to become a better fighter.

To encourage him and avoid increasing his embarrassment, she gripped her cane in both hands, raised it in front of her face and bowed.

"Lord, I am honored to have witnessed such a demonstration of your art."

She had never heard of these *Three Revelations*. There were thousands of baton techniques, but they were all based on the same six movements – lowering, raising, pushing, thrusting, rotating and covering – and knowing these alone was enough to counter all their variants. The young lord admired Shao Jun's calm serenity. "She is extraordinary. Now I understand why she causes Zhang Yong so much trouble," he thought.

He'd had the audacity to not even consider defeat, but how could he possibly have overcome the person who had triumphed over Wei Bin? From their very first exchange he had quickly understood that stubbornly refusing to use his left arm condemned him to failure. However, he had persisted rather than lose face. Perhaps the *Three Revelations* passed down to him by his master would allow him to regain the upper hand. He gripped the bottom third of his baton so that most of its length was behind him, took a deep breath and called to the pipa player.

"Play us *Man Jian Hong* written by General Yue Fei."

She began to play, plucking the strings which resonated with a jade-like purity to produce a soft yet powerful melody, gradually increasing in intensity. It was as elegant as the previous melodies but had an undeniably warlike rhythm. Shao Jun had never seen anyone hold a baton the way her opponent did, but the wizened old man sat to the side recognized the pose. "Oh dear…" he lamented internally. While the air was still warm from the heat of the day, an icy blast of air seemed to envelope the two combatants.

The "three revelations" which gave the technique its name were law, steadfastness, and wisdom, according to Buddhist texts, linked in a virtuous circle: the second results from the first, the third from the second, and the first from the third. Applying these in the field of martial arts required unshakeable foundations and impeccable purity of spirit, a far cry from this young man who had begun his Buddhist training so late – at the age of sixteen – and whose skill had yet to mature. Nonetheless, faced with the failure of his usual techniques, he felt he no longer had any choice if he wanted to win the duel. He risked injuring himself or Shao Jun if he made any mistakes, but his obstinacy made him blind to the dangers. Nothing could stop him once he had begun.

He began to weave like a dragon of legend, swimming through the air within the confined space of the stage. The two fighters had already circled seven or eight times within five bars of the pipa's song, at such a speed that they were reduced to blurred silhouettes for the onlookers. As the tension reached its height, the young lord let out a shout then leapt four or five feet into the air to perform a somersault as he twirled his baton, striking Shao Jun with the full force of his momentum.

This strike, known as the *Ship of samadhi,* took its name from a Sanskrit allegory in which the manifestation of the Buddha is compared to the appearance of a sail on the horizon. It was part of the *Three revelations of the baton,* which are a meditation tool; even in their martial form, logically, these techniques required the complete inner peace and detachment from passion specific to spiritual fulfillment. Noticing that the lord was far from being in this state of mind, the old man grew furious and almost got up to prevent him from making a mistake which he would regret. The attack would certainly hurt Shao Jun if it succeeded, but it was just as likely to turn against its user if used incorrectly. However, the insufficiently prepared young man was unable to wield his baton at the same time as he jumped, seeming almost to flounder, driven by his frenzy and the rhythm of the pipa.

Bam! The ash baton crashed down onto the bamboo cane, sending it flying into the air. The pipa stopped, the two silhouettes remained frozen in place, then *plop*! as the cane fell into the lake. "Phew! The master was the more skilled of the two!" the old man thought, finally relieved of his anxiety.

"I admit defeat," the lord declared disappointedly.

When he had performed the *Ship of samadhi,* he had lost control of his ash baton. Shao Jun had quickly realized that the attack would not hit and had thus immediately sent her cane towards her opponent's face. But she had slowed her strike as much as possible to avoid putting out his eye, which had allowed the young man to protect himself at the last second. He was aware however that he owed his safety to the merciful restraint of the one who should truly be recognized as the winner of the duel.

She was nonetheless pleasantly surprised by the grace with which he conceded his defeat.

"Will the young lord answer my questions now?" she asked.

The current had carried the bamboo cane toward the Greenfinch, so he bent down and caught it with his baton.

"Of course," he replied as he wiped it. "I would never break my word!"

He returned the two weapons to the rack and turned towards the pipa player.

"I'm sorry, Jouyi, I've made a fool of myself before you this evening."

The latter delicately hid her mouth behind her hand before she spoke, as all well-bred girls did.

"Lord, it's my fault, my interpretation of the *Man Jian Hong* was not very good."

"So, play it for me again another time," he gently offered before turned to the old man. "Mr Mu, please accompany Jouyi to the house so she can rest. I will join you very soon."

"But… Master… isn't it risky?"

"Mr Mu, you need not worry, this young lady is worthy of General Yang."

According to legend, under the Jin dynasty General Yang Hu – opposing General Lu Kang in a war against the Wu kingdom – had personally brought medicine to his adversary after learning he had fallen ill. Many had feared that it was a ruse, but it was not: General Yang was a man of who wanted to vanquish his rival – the two strategists were on an equal level – with honor. Ever since, his name had become synonymous with uprightness and respectability. Old Mu did not know the details of the story, but he was familiar with the expression, so bowed respectfully to Shao Jun before leaving the platform and leaving, followed by the four large guards with their pathetic broken batons. When they had all left the stone boat, the young lord parted the curtain of beads that separated a small room from the rest of the terrace.

"The crew of the *Greenfinch* is pleased to welcome you aboard this evening!" he smiled.

His joviality amused the young woman. The defeated duelist had forgotten his discomfort and now shone at the opportunity to display his charm. When Shao Jun entered the small area covered by an arbor, her host was lighting candles. The room, which could accommodate several dozen people, was more spacious than it appeared from the outside. It was probably suffocating during the day, but its proximity to the lake made it a very pleasant place at night. It was tastefully decorated with wooden Jiangsu seats surrounding a carved table encrusted with polished ivory, with a lovely blue-green celadon teapot sitting on the surface alongside a copper tureen on which pearled drops of icy water. Shao Jun had seen this type of thing at the palace. They usually contained crushed ice that had been stored in a cave since winter – a luxury that only the wealthiest houses could afford – on which were placed fruits and drinks that benefited from being served cool.

"If the young imperial favorite would oblige..." said the young lord, pointing at a seat.

She suspected he knew her identity, but the mention of her former rank nonetheless caused her to jump.

He drew a bottle from the tureen and filled two porcelain cups.

"When you lived in the palace, you must have drunk this type of grape alcohol, isn't that right?" he asked, handing one to his guest before emptying his in a single gulp.

Yes, of course she had drunk wine, but this golden-yellow liquid was nothing like those she had ever tasted or even seen.

"Lord, please tell me at last... Who do I have the honor of speaking to?"

"Wang Yangming didn't mention me when he gave you the jade pendant?"

Those words struck her like an avalanche. Momentarily forgetting that she was disarmed, Shao Jun instinctively reached to her waist to unsheathe her sword. The lord let out a small laugh and pulled out a long cardboard box from a niche behind him.

"Please, open it," he said.

It contained the young woman's sword and rope dart, as well

as the jade pendant, which immediately relieved the worry that had weighed on her since Chen Xijian had taken it from her. The stone and its cord had even been cleaned of the blood that had soaked them. Now she could be sure that this unknown person was not ill-intentioned.

"Excuse my impoliteness," Shao Jun persisted, "but what is your name?"

He poured a new cup of wine and said in a firm voice, "The humble lord before you is named Xu Pengju."

The young woman noted that he must therefore be a relative of General Yue Fei[13], which explained why he had such devotion to the man. But this name contained no useful information on its own…

"Pleased to meet you, Lord Xu," she responded.

He appeared to be disappointed. He had clearly expected to be recognized.

"My name means nothing to you?" he asked, pouring a new cup of wine to cover his embarrassment.

What kind of person, especially at that age, could expect that everyone would know his name? An unlikely idea suddenly entered Shao Jun's mind.

"Are you… the prince of Wei?" she guessed.

"Miss," responded her host with a satisfied smile, "you have before you the commander in chief of the troops of the prefecture of Nanjing, imperial guardian of the principality of Wei."

"So, you're a descendent of the king of Zhongshan… Which explains your high level of kung-fu."

---

13 *Pengju was the courtesy name of Yue Fei.*

The history of this seven-generation noble title was rich and complex. It began with General Xu Da, king of Zhongshan and the first prince of Wei, whose two sons had been officers in the service of Jianwen, the second Ming emperor, and whose daughter had married the prince of Yan. When the latter, who would later be known to the world as Ming Yongle, had entered the war of succession which would see him become emperor in 1402, the fates of the two brothers were rather different… The younger, Xu Zengshou, had caused the defeat at the battle of Nanjing by failing to prevent the leak of key information – and had been beheaded for this mistake – while his elder brother, Xu Huizu, had always remained loyal to Jianwen even after his fall.

He thus refused to submit to the victorious Yongle, but rather than kill his brother-in-law – whose father was a close friend of Hongwu, the founder of the Ming dynasty – Yongle chose to strip him of his titles and pass them on to the son of Xu Zengshou. He could not however remove his status as the prince of Wei, which resulted in the division of the Xu family into two noble branches, that of Beijing and that of Nanjing, from which Pengju descended. He had himself become prince of Wei ten years earlier, during the thirteenth year of Zhengde's reign. This title, in which he took great pride, and which drove him to study martial arts, made him the official supreme guardian of the peace in Nanjing. Nonetheless, there were many in the nobility and administration who secretly saw him as nothing more than a meritless upstart who liked to see himself as a hero. Shao Jun's compliment on the quality of his kung-fu delighted him. He felt the beginnings of a certain bond between them.

"Miss, you flatter me." He emptied his cup. "You must be eager to know what happened to the old eunuch… Do not fear, he now enjoys the supreme happiness of the other world, where he will be forever silent!"

How could such a young and well-raised young nobleman speak with the coolness of a professional assassin?

"Lord Pengju, why are you helping me?"

"If I am not mistaken, Wang Yangming entrusted you with his pendant with the recommendation that in the event of great difficulty, you find the master of the Temple of the Jade of the Five Virtues."

So, he did know everything! And he couldn't have got these details from Chen Xijian, because Shao Jun hadn't told him the name of the place where she had planned to take him, nor had she mentioned her master.

"It is a little-known fact," explained the young man, "but the Temple of the Jade of the Five Virtues was founded by my family. Moreover, please forgive me for striking you… I had no idea who I was attacking until the old eunuch said too much!"

Everything was suddenly clearer. This was exactly where Master Yangming had sent her! Historically, the prince of Wei was the guardian of Nanjing, the commander of the city troops, and thus the most influential man in the region. Zhang Yong would never dream of finding the former imperial favorite in his home.

"I thank you again for taking me into your protection," she said respectfully. "But may I ask what connects you to Master Yangming?"

"Wang Yangming is a close friend of my instructor. Both of these mutton fat jade pendants were made from a single piece of flawless jade which was accidentally shattered when it was brought back from a campaign against the invading Mongols. The great sculptor Gu Sunian carved three identical pendants from its remnants at the request of my master, who kept one and gave the other two to his closest friends. Each bears a different inscription, which is why I immediately knew that yours, on which is written the word *Education,* belonged to Wang Yangming. My master's is engraved with the word *Nature,* and the third with the word *Dao*. The old eunuch was clearly ignorant of the details of this story, or had no idea that I was connected to it, because he bragged with such audacity as he showed off the item he stole from you, even promising to denounce the protector you came to find… The first time he told me of these pendants, my master told me to treat anyone who presented me with one as I would treat him. Ha ha!"

The three ideas represented by these jade pendants originated directly from the opening of the Zhongyong: "What Heaven confers is called 'nature'. Accordance with this nature is called the Dao. Cultivating the Dao is called 'education'."[14] Xu Pengju said that while these three pendants symbolized the friendship that united the three men, the fact that they were engraved with different characters also represented their divergence as well as the nebulous nature of philosophy. They had conceived the idea after spending an entire night debating their respective interpretations of these basic notions without agreeing on the subject. "Now I better understand why Master Yangming was so sure that I would be safe here," Shao Jun thought to herself. She thanked her host once again, who burst out laughing.

---

14 The *Zhongyong* or Doctrine of the Mean is one of the four classics of Chinese philosophy.

"If Heaven falls on our heads, my home will still be left standing. Please, rest here until your wounds are completely healed. And when you're better, I will seek your teaching in martial arts again."

"Lord Pengju, what is your instructor's name?"

"Yang Yiqing. Did Master Yangming tell you about him?"

"Oh... It's Master Yang!"

The first time Shao Jun heard of this person, Emperor Zhengde had just received a note from him exhorting him to be less idle and dedicate himself more seriously to governing the empire, which had made him furious. "Silence this insolent!" he had shouted, throwing the missive across the room. But after he had calmed down, he had picked it up before murmuring, "The barbarians would have invaded us long ago without this man." Yang Yiqing's outspoken and inflexible nature had put him at odds with his superiors on several occasions, and his animosity towards Liu Jin, founder of the Eight Tigers, was notable, but none could contest his value and skills as a military strategist, as recognized as those of Master Yangming in the area of negotiation. His attributes were numerous and had continued to grow over his career, but he was especially known for directing the armies at the borders, a key task for maintaining the empire's stability. Shao Jun had always heard Wang Yangming, eighteen years his junior, mention his name with the respect and deference due to elders, but she didn't know they were so close.

"I also had some lessons from Master Yangming," Pengju added, "which makes us sort of co-disciples! You have absolutely nothing to fear from me."

The young woman drank a mouthful of wine. Every day since

her rushed departure from the palace, she had felt like she was constantly running for her life, staying one step ahead of one threat or another. How long had it been since she had been able to relax like this evening? Years, perhaps.

"Yes, and I'm so grateful to you…" she whispered.

She was unused to drinking alcohol, and the wine, sweet and fragrant, sent a pleasant wave of heat through her body. After sheathing her sword and attaching her rope dart to her belt, she leaned back.

"Thank you for your hospitality, Lord Pengju. I will rest, for now."

"I will return as well, it grows late. Please stay at the house, as I fear they will be looking for you in the city, and it would be imprudent for you to go there… I will accompany you myself when you are completely healed."

"They're looking for me?"

"Of course! Uncle Yu arrived in the city yesterday, convinced that you were responsible for the old eunuch's disappearance, and told me to order the garrison to search Nanjing for you. To show my cooperation and goodwill, I increase the patrols and guards. Prudence is required, he has informers everywhere…"

"Are you speaking about Yu Dayong?"

"Indeed."

"Does he often come south?"

"Yes, I heard that he was in business with the Portuguese."

Despite being governor of Nanjing, Yu Dayong was seen very little, and Xu Pengju avoided him as much as possible. But for Shao Jun, whose goal was to eliminate the Eight Tigers, his presence in the city was an unexpected opportunity.

"Lord, I wanted to ask…"

"Let me be clear," he cut her off. "I am happy to welcome you under my roof and ensure your safety, but I will not be mixed up in your dispute with the Eight Tigers."

Now that was unexpected. Because he had the trust of Wang Yangming, because he had killed Chen Xijian to protect her, because he had treated her and was prepared to offer her his hospitality despite her status as a fugitive, Shao Jun had quite naturally supposed that the young lord would be completely allied to her cause…

He stood and invited her to leave the terrace with him.

"Miss, if you will…"

Without saying any more, she left the stone boat under a starry sky. No breeze disturbed the water of the lake, and the silence of the night was broken only by the frogs croaking from their water lilies.

For once, no nightmares troubled her sleep. Chen Xijian was dead and couldn't reveal her secrets, and she was under the protection of a man whose influence in Nanjing exceeded that of Zhang Yong… Deep down, she could even understand why he refused to commit to her cause, which for him would require a significant number of sacrifices. He had probably killed the old mausoleum steward to protect himself as much as the young woman, but she was no less grateful to him for doing so.

Yes, she would stay here for a time to allow her wounds to heal, while waiting to be able to review next steps with Master Yangming.

When she arrived back at the house, she found Yanfei waiting in front of the door to the library. The young slave ran to meet her as soon as she saw her arrive.

"Miss! I hope you didn't fight with the master!"

“You should go to sleep, Yanfei.”

“The master promised to wait until you were healed before dueling you. He fights with such passion… I hope he didn’t injure you at least?”

Touched by her concern, Shao Jun smiled reassuringly at the young girl.

“No, and don’t worry, he didn’t hurt me. Now go to bed. I should rest too.”

CHAPTER 11

Xu Pengju visited Shao Jun every day during her convalescence. Each day, he spent fortunes having the best dishes in the region brought to the house by runners, but never bragged about it to his guest, even going as far as to pretend that the succulent exotic fruits came from his own gardens. Instead of speaking about the serious issues that preoccupied her, he spoke of lighter subjects, and seemed particularly interested in hearing of the young woman's journey to Europe, questioning her about Western landscapes and customs. He dreamed of visiting Italy, but it was difficult for him to even visit the empire's capital due to his considerable military and administrative responsibilities. Each discussion revealed a new facet of his personality.

Shao Jun also enjoyed the presence of Yanfei, who was unaware of the terrible business she was involved in and had shown no interest in knowing. The young slave nursed her with care, and after several days the ointments and infusions seemed to gain the upper hand over her wounds. When she removed the dressings to clean off the dried blood, the young girl was surprised by what she saw.

"Miss," she marveled, "the wound is completely closed!"

"You're right," Shao Jun responded as she stretched her arm, "I seem to be healed. Thank you for looking after me so well."

"It's incredible! Last month the cook sliced off the end of his finger cutting vegetables, and it's still not better. But it only took you several days to heal up!"

"But cutting off a finger is much more serious!"

"No… When you arrived, your wound was as wide as the mouth of a newborn crying for milk! It was awful… But now it's healed, and in just a few days too!"

Yanfei emphatically waved two spread fingers under Shao Jun's nose. This servant must be well treated indeed and unfearful of her master to be so open and talkative. The young woman wanted to know more.

"What does your master do, normally?" she asked.

"Umm… He seems bewitched by this Jouyi! Have you met her? She's not really very pretty, she just knows how to use makeup. He spent three thousand two hundred taels to buy her, but I really don't see what's so special about her."

The young slave's jealousy reminded the former imperial favorite of her years in the harem. After she was noticed by the Emperor, many of the concubines who had previously been friendly to her had changed completely. And while during that period Shao Jun had experienced love and happiness for the first time, she also knew that in Zhengde's eyes, she had never been more than simply one of the many in his entourage. She was his spy, and her usefulness was her value, and that was all. She had very rarely seen tenderness in her master's eyes.

She let out a small, bitter laugh. Why was she suddenly thinking of her old life? She wasn't the type to dwell on the past.

Xu Pengju called from the doorway.

"Yanfei, you impertinent little thing, what are you saying behind my back, hmm?"

In reality he hadn't heard anything, but the young slave turned bright red and began to panic.

"Master, I wouldn't dare!"

The lord entered the library and handed her a wicker basket.

"Peel these nuts," he ordered, "then crush them and have them boiled with milk. Tonight, we will drink delicious fresh nut milk."

Didn't he know that preparing the drink was not as simple as he made it sound? It was completely impossible to make nut milk in half a day, but Yanfei, still worried about being interrupted as she spoke badly of Jouyi, didn't dare protest and rushed to take the basket to satisfy her master's desires as best she could.

When she left, he sat down next to Shao Jun's bed.

"How is your injury?"

The young woman noted that he seemed more preoccupied than usual.

"Is something wrong?" she asked.

"I received a letter from my master, who has been recalled to a post at the border despite his age and declining strength."

"What does he say?"

"Nothing in particular. The barbarians don't dare invade the empire, the city of Tourfan submitted, and the days pass without incident."

So, why was he so worried? Shao Jun waited silently for him to open up to her.

"I'd like your opinion on something."

"I'm listening."

"Zhang Yong said the empire was sick, eroded by pressures on the borders and internal rebellion. According to him, only radical measures, a 'shock to the system', could overcome these dangers, like how a storm must break before good weather can return. Do you think it's true?"

Thrown by his frankness, the young woman considered carefully. While she was older than her host, she was far below his level of study. On the other hand, she had gained real experience of the world through her travels, something that was inaccessible to a noble of good family who had never left Nanjing. But they were both disciples of eminent Confucian scholars, which at least enabled them to speak from a common foundation. She looked out of the window and answered quietly, "In the West, I journeyed several tens of thousands of lis through over thirty countries. Some were prosperous after experiencing ruin, while others were in ruins after experiencing prosperity. It takes longer than a single night for a lake to ice over completely, and it takes longer than a single day for a young tree to grow to a hundred feet; there is no medicine to heal these maladies, and no man can cure all the evils of a country. Governance requires inventiveness, listening, and much patience. A leader must listen to the people and effect change over decades before seeing results."

"Is that the teaching of Wang Yangming?"

"Of course. I am not in a position to develop my own informed opinion on the subject."

"Master Yang once told me that the fate decreed by Heaven cannot be evaded. We can neither predict nor oppose it."

While the young lord was perfectly calm, to Shao Jun these words were like a bolt to the heart. If Yang Yiqing saw the world this way, then he was not opposed to Zhang Yong.

"And what do you suggest?" she asked.

"I think in my situation the best course of action is to *seek advice and consider the options*."

The young woman recognized the quote from the *Discourse on Teaching*, although the meaning of the words had always escaped her. Xu Pengju had however omitted the beginning of the passage in question, which stipulated that "the disciple should not aspire to equal the master, nor the master to be as competent as the disciple". Like many men his age, the young lord often overestimated himself, but he had boundless respect for his master, who would never have been able to accept such a suggestion.

One day Zhang Yong had come to visit Yang Yiqing while the prince was training, and the prince had the honor of being present for the discussion between the two men. According to the first, national affairs were in a deplorable state, and the country must be treated like a patient suffering from buboes: bursting the abscesses to disinfect them with strong alcohol. Xu Pengju disagreed, thinking it was better to trust fate and not fight against the inevitable or risk making things worse. Treatment such as that mentioned by Zhang Yang might certainly heal the patient, but it could also hasten their death. Instead, why not consolidate their natural defenses before subjecting them to a violent treatment?

But, too unsure of himself and so affected by the presence of his elders – the Tiger was in the process of becoming the most influential minister in the country's history – he hadn't dared open his mouth and his questions remained stuck in his throat like fish bones. And so, he had been unable to resist the desire to question Wang Yangming's pupil. Shao Jun's master was the greatest philosopher of their time, revered even more than Yang Yiqing in the field of literature. When Xu Pengju was finally able to express his thoughts to his guest, he was delighted to discover that she echoed his own conclusions.

He continued, despite the young woman's strange gaze.

"I still haven't explained why I refused to help you eliminate Yu Dayong."

Shao Jun never knew quite where she stood with him, so she found it very strange that he brought up such a delicate subject again. She felt like she was walking on eggshells.

"And do you have any intention of doing so now?"

"As I told you, the pendant Master Wang Yangming gave you was part of a trio..."

"Yes."

"And so, the one with the character *Dao* engraved on it belongs to... to the venerable captain general of the imperial guard, Zhang Yong."

Despite the seasonal warmth, the young woman couldn't hold back a shiver. Master Yangming, Yang Yiqing and... Zhang Yong! The idea that the three men could have been so close stunned her. A lot of things made sense in light of this new information. Master Yangming had always referred to the leader of the Eight Tigers as "Uncle Zhang", a mark of respect, while he referred to the others by their last names and was evasive every time Shao Jun had asked why. For the wise scholar, seeing a close friend become such a cruel monster was unacceptable. He must have insisted that the young woman seek refuge with

Xu Pengju only as a last resort because he feared that Yang Yiqing's disciple may side with Zhang Yong. Fortunately, the young man's views seemed much more aligned with those of his guest's master.

"I had no idea," Shao Jun murmured.

"Do you blame me?"

"No… Everyone must carry their own burden."

The lord was greatly relieved because his mind had been whirling ever since Yu Dayong's visit to Nanjing and the letter from his master. In the current situation, it had been impossible for him to maintain his neutrality: handing his guest over to Zhang Yong was to oppose Master Yangming's cause, but hiding her was to oppose the Eight Tigers. And yet, now he was free of the troubles that had weighed upon him, he saw more clearly, and was grateful to Shao Jun for not holding it against him.

"Miss, you must know that my master also informed me of something else in his letter."

"Oh?"

"Yes. Zhang Yong recently visited him to ensure he could still count on their friendship. He even mentioned their pendants."

"But why?"

"In my opinion, he only made the effort to travel as far as the frontier because he already has suspicions."

"Lord Pengju… does anyone know of my presence here?"

"Chen Xijian didn't have time to tell anyone. I heard that Yu Dayong found a body in the mausoleum, but my informer couldn't tell me whose it was. Was anyone else with you?"

"No. The body was Ma Yongcheng's."

Xu Pengju grimaced. The assassination of a person of such rank within the Xiaoling mausoleum would be an embarrassment. It wasn't surprising that Yu Dayong hadn't made the matter public.

"Did you kill him?" he asked.

"No, it was Chen Xijian."

"I see… The old eunuch wanted to claim your capture and all the glory for himself alone."

"Exactly!" Shao Jun responded, impressed by her host's perceptiveness.

"Yu Dayong certainly didn't know the details of the affair, but now I understand why Uncle Zhang pursues you so relentlessly…"

That explained Zhang Yong's visit to Master Yiqing. Instead of capturing Shao Jun as he hoped, he had two bodies, and his prey had disappeared into the ether once more.

"But how did Zhang Yong know about the jade pendant?" the young woman persisted.

"Perhaps he knows nothing. Bleeding on my boat, Chen Xijian proclaimed loud and clear that he had taken the pendant from you, but all those who were there that night have my trust, and none of them has left the house in the last few days. Also, if the leak had come from here, Zhang Yong would have come to me directly instead of visiting my master on the border. He can have nothing but suspicions, simply wants to reassure himself that he can rely on his old friendships…"

Yang Yiqing had written his letter innocently unaware of the torment he would inflict upon his disciple. By killing Chen Xijian, the latter, who had convinced himself that he was the modern equivalent of the great General Yue Fei and thought his decisions infallible, had become involved in a situation he would rather have avoided. And until the arrival of the fateful missive, he had believed that he had managed to act without risking the slightest reprisal. Now he was surrounded by chaos and had no idea which way to turn. Zhang Yong's visit to his old friend was something to be concerned about, but it was also entirely possible that it was just a coincidence. Yes, the young lord concluded, it was better not to jump to conclusions.

Shao Jun was more circumspect. Knowing the extent of Zhang Yong's power, she found it hard to believe in chance. It was hard to imagine such a calculating and meticulous person, who hadn't hesitated to have the Leopard Quarter burnt as a precaution, making a long journey just to speak to an old friend. It was simply impossible. One way or another, he had learned that the young woman had one of the pendants and had suspected Yang Yiqing. Now he knew that his old friend still had his, he could deduce that his adversary was none other than Wang Yangming – he might even already be on his way. Struck by the urgency of her situation, the young woman leapt up. She had to get the pendant to her master before the leader of the Eight Tigers reached him.

"Lord Pengju," she announced, "I must leave Nanjing immediately!"

"So suddenly? But your injury–"

"It's healed, I'll be fine. Can you help me leave, quietly?"

"I think it will be difficult while Uncle Yu is looking for you in the city… Are you sure you can't wait?"

"I doubt I will make it in time even I leave now. Lord Pengju, what was the date on Master Yang's letter?"

He had sent it from a post on the northwestern border, several thousand lis from Nanjing, a distance that even the fastest couriers would take two weeks to cover. Zhang Yong could already be almost halfway to Guangxi, where Wang Yangming was pacifying the Tianzhou rebellion.

Shao Jun's panicked expression amused Xu Pengju, who quickly reassured her.

"Even if Zhang Yong left immediately, you'll be in Tianzhou long before him. My master wrote his letter the day before yesterday."

"The day before yesterday?"

"Yes, we send our correspondence by air using the gyrfalcons I raised. Master Yang also uses them for the army on the three borders. The small birds are remarkable, they can cover a thousand lis in one night!"

"Does he mention how soon after Zhang Yong's visit he sent his message?"

"No, he only said 'recently'. A handful of days past, at most."

Shao Jun heaved a sigh of relief. Even if the letter was five or six days old and the horses were pushed to their last strength, it would be impossible to reach Guangxi in so little time. She still had a chance.

"Lord Pengju, this can't wait. Please, take me to the city gates."

If she stopped only to change mounts, it would take her a month to cover the three thousand lis between Nanjing and Tianzhou.

"Very well, but I will have to give you up if Yu Dayong questions me."

It took two hours to prepare Xu Pengju's departure: the prince of Wei's retinue had to have a certain prestige, regardless of the importance or distance of travel. A majestic parade of thirty people soon made its way towards the Treasure Gate, one of the thirteen points through which all travelers entered or left Nanjing. According to legend, the gate had been built in honor of Emperor Hongwu by Shen Wansan, then known as one of the richest men in the country. The Emperor, jealous of seeing his own fortune exceeded in such an outrageous fashion, secretly sent men every night to destroy everything that had been built during the day. He hoped that not only would the site appear cursed by evil spirits, but that Shen Wansan would ruin himself by constantly trying to reconstruct it. However, the Emperor was unaware that the wealthy man had a magical pot that refilled with coins every day, and apparently, he "took gold at midnight, and then found more in the morning". When he learned of this, Hongwu had the precious object entombed in the foundations of the wall as it was built, which is why the gate came to be known as the "Treasure Gate". It now sat to the south of the city, large enough to hold a thousand soldiers and featuring numerous arrow slits.

"Who goes there?" the sentry demanded.

Mu, the general steward, urged his horse forward, outraged by the question.

"Are you blind?" he cried. "The prince of Wei, commander-in-chief of the troops of Nanjing prefecture, comes to burn essence in the Porcelain Tower. Have you eaten a lion, to be so bold as to bar his way?"

"It's just… Governor Yu ordered us to allow no one out," the poor soldier stammered. "I'm only following orders. Just a moment, please, and I'll inform him of your presence."

"Governor Yu is here?" Xu Pengju interrupted before his steward grew angry.

Then Yu Dayong appeared.

"Prince Xu!" he called. "You wish to leave the city?"

The young lord greeted him, bowing with his hands clasped together. The Tiger's position was not the highest rank in the hierarchy, but he still had authority over all civil servants in Nanjing and the armed forces at the edges of the prefecture.

"Governor, glory to your zeal! Don't worry, I am simply visiting the Porcelain Tower to burn some incense. Will that be a problem?"

"How could I stand in the way of such a noble intention? Filial piety is the glue which holds our civilization together. Nonetheless, Uncle Zhang insisted that no exceptions could be made… Would you oblige me by opening the curtains on all your carriages so I can take a look?"

The Tiger had watched for a reaction from the young lord when he mentioned Zhang Yong, but he'd given nothing away. Yu Dayong had the feeling he was hiding something, but had no inkling that the prince was directly involved in the affair. As the governor was of a lower rank, his powers were limited in this specific situation, but he could at least inspect the prince's retinue… There were around thirty people, most of whom were mounted on horses while the rest rode in one of the four large carriages in the procession which could have held twenty people between them. Instead of opposing the request, which he could have rightly taken offence to, Xu Pengju smiled amiably.

"But of course," he responded. "I would hate to go against Uncle Zhang's orders. All I ask if that you are careful not to damage the paper horses carried in some of the carriages! They are for my ancestral mother."

According to tradition, paper offerings were burned as sacrifices to the deceased. When these houses, vehicles, utensils, and even sacrificial servants were engulfed by the flames, they flew to find the deceased relatives like horses of smoke galloping into the sky, hence the figurative name. As the prince of Wei's family was the greatest in Nanjing, his paper horses were also the finest. Yu Dayong was impressed to see an entire carriage full of these votive objects, which even included seven slaves made with such care that their faces seemed as if they might come to life at any moment. "The young lord spares no expense when it comes to the rites," he thought to himself.

Although he was not particularly intelligent, the Tiger was capable of brief moments of insight, and so he bent to examine the interior of the carriages from the ground. If someone were hiding among the paper horses, their feet would be immediately visible. He saw nothing but the delicate and finely sculpted legs of the paper objects, as well as the food which was undoubtedly for the banquet offering; the meals were vegetarian, and the monks at the temple were too greedy to be satisfied with such a frugal menu, particularly from the prince of Wei. Yu Dayong closed the curtains as he finished checking each of the carriages in turn.

"Lord Xu," he said, "please excuse my rude interruption. I wish you safe travel. May your ancestral mother lack for nothing!"

Their high rank made many of the Tigers haughty and disdainful, but Yu Dayong had always maintained a lively and direct way of speaking, so it was a particular effort to address the prince of Wei, a man who was young enough to be his grandson, with such deference. As he wished him safe travels, he suddenly felt as if he was being watched and spun to look behind him but saw nothing but the carriages and the procession. His arrogance, so deeply rooted in him after years spent as a high-ranking civil servant, prevented him from examining the lord's soldiers. If he had done so, he would have noticed that one of them wore their hat particularly low over their forehead, hiding their face. And if he had drawn closer, he would have discovered that it was Shao Jun, staring at him with hatred in her eyes.

This subterfuge was the prince's work. He knew that leaving the city would draw the attention of the authorities, and had filled his carriages with paper horses and offerings so that inspection of the procession would focus on those rather than the guards surrounding it... And that was exactly what had happened.

The young woman struggled to control herself as she stopped herself drawing the sword hidden under her saddle and stabbing it into the back of Yu Dayong, who had now shed his suspicious air.

"Will Lord Xu spend the night at the Porcelain Tower?" he asked.

As governor, he should be warned if the head of the garrison planned to spend the night outside the walls, as the amount of food in the carriages seemed to suggest.

"Yes," Xu Pengju answered. "And if you have the time, you are welcome to come with me, we can relax together for a while."

Yu Dayong chuckled. Given the importance of his current business, he had no time to waste burning incense sticks. He politely declined the invitation, opened the gate, and allowed the procession through.

The Porcelain Tower of Nanjing was built in the tenth year of the reign of Emperor Yongle on the foundations of a previous monument, which had itself been erected by the State of Wu during the Three Kingdoms era. Alongside the Luoyang Temple of the White Horse, it was one of the oldest Buddhist temples in China. Its central tower, over thirty *zhangs*[15] tall and fully painted, was the pride of the empire. By day, it shone like porcelain – hence the name – and glowed like a thousand flames at sunset.

The head priest ran out to greet the procession when he learned the prince of Wei had come to make offerings at his temple.

He also hastily ordered that the visitor apartments be cleaned, and requisitioned all the remaining monks to leave incense ready to burn everywhere in the building, which suddenly buzzed with activity. It was of the highest importance that this eminent visitor felt at home.

On arrival, Xu Pengju invited Shao Jun to enter a carriage with him.

"Miss," he said, "our paths will soon diverge, and I don't know how long it will be before we can meet again. Will you do me the honor of one last duel?"

The young woman burst out laughing. After receiving such generous support from him, she regretted that she was unable to agree to his request. The poor man, already prepared to draw his weapon, still clearly smarted from her defeating him using only one arm. But she would have been lying if she pretended she was fully recovered.

"Friends always find one another again," she responded. "Next time you'll teach me the *Three Revelations of the baton*."

"You're still not in a condition to fight? How is your shoulder?"

---

15 *Unit of measure equal to around 3 meters.*

"Better, thank you. But I don't think I'll be able to use my kung-fu properly for another five or six days."

The prince's disappointment was obvious, but his steward appeared at the carriage door holding a package before he could say more.

"Is everything ready, Mr Mu?" Xu Pengju asked.

"Yes. Tao Zhenting has arrived, here are the clothes and papers."

The package contained a blue coat and a letter bearing the seal of the messenger network.

"Miss," said the young man, "messenger Tao Zhenting has a physical appearance similar to your own. You can use his identity to remain safe on your journey."

Under the Mings, freight was mainly sent by river or sea, but urgent messages were carried by riders who galloped from one messenger outpost to another, changing mounts and riding at a grueling pace – only stopping briefly to eat and rest as needed. If she used the same horse for the entire journey, it would take one or two months to cover the three thousand lis between Nanjing and Tianzhou, but with her disguise and official seal, Shao Jun could use the messenger posts, which would allow her to reach her destination in two weeks. She removed her soldier's cloak to put on her new uniform, with which she would be able to pass completely unnoticed. She owed the prince of Wei a huge debt for his help. Hands folded together, she bowed before him.

"I don't know how to thank you, Lord Pengju."

"You won't draw any attention dressed like that. Tao Zhenting will take your soldier's cloak and join the escort so there will be the same number of guards as there were on my arrival. I saw Yu Dayong counting them as we left the city gate."

"I can't believe he suspects you!"

"I think it fits perfectly with his tendency to be excessively meticulous... He can find a needle in a haystack. I fear he will be the most difficult Tiger to take on, after Uncle Zhang."

Shao Jun shuddered. Like many, she had been taken in by Yu Dayong's simple-minded façade, so this remark reminded her that she should not underestimate him in future. She had to admit that the young man had consistently behaved as a true friend, even when they seemed destined to be sworn enemies. After all, the prince's master was a close friend of Zhang Yong.

"Lord Pengju, I'd like to ask you a question," she ventured.

"Go on."

"Given his long friendship with Zhang Yong, might your master be angry that you've helped me, if he learns of it?"

"You forget that he is just as close to Wang Yangming! And besides, I'm able to make and take responsibility for my own decisions!"

Shao Jun was moved. She saw in the fiery gaze of the prince of Wei that he spoke with complete sincerity, and took her leave, untroubled by her previous concerns. She could be sure he wouldn't betray her.

Xu Pengju felt strangely depressed as she left. He had never been refused anything in life, everyone around him always acceded to his every desire, but this time he would get no satisfaction. He had been fascinated by his guest both for her beauty and her martial arts skills, and it was for her sake alone that he had chosen to indirectly support Wang Yangming's cause rather than that of Zhang Yong. Yet she remained frustratingly inaccessible despite growing closer over the few days they had spent together.

When the prince was depressed he liked to recite a line from a poem by Jiang Yan of the Song dynasty – "*Alcohol relieves your sorrow and your heroism evaporates*" – but for the first time, the poet's words seemed vain and empty, powerless to soothe his melancholy.

Chapter 12

A hot, unsteady wind blew towards Tianzhou. For the southern borders, which only experienced a hot season and a cold season, the nuances of spring and autumn were unimaginable dreams. Yet the warm gust chilled Wang Shou to the depths of his being as he looked toward the forests.

Founded near the border with Annan[16] by Emperor Tang Xuanzong, Tianzhou had always been the fief of the mandarins of the Cen family. Their first rebellion, which began in the fifteenth year of Hongzhi's reign, ended with the death of their leader after three years of fighting against imperial troops. Then the remaining members of the clan rose up once more during the third and fourth years of Jiajing's reign; their troops numbering twenty-four thousand men. When Advisor Yao Mou sent imperial representatives to the area to reclaim control of the region, the Tianzhou insurgents, with the help of Annan,

16 *An old name for Vietnam.*

raised an army of two hundred thousand men, in response to which the imperial troops were forced to beat a retreat.

Wang Shou remained unsettled despite the victory. He knew he could count on the famous valor of the Wolves of Tianzhou, the local soldiers he led alongside Lu Su, but the Annan troops were a makeshift army of press-ganged peasants and vagrants who would die like flies against any battle-hardened opposition. The respite they had gained was only temporary, the central government would never leave the region to the rebels.

More educated than his comrade, Wang Shou had been deep in thought for what felt like hours. Was it possible to avoid the coming war? That question tormented him like no other.

His younger brother, Wang Zhen, interrupted to inform him that Lu Su was going to launch an attack against the imperial troops and needed his support. "What is wrong, big brother?" he said impatiently.

"Lady Wa leads some of the imperial troops."

"What? She came all the way here?"

"Yes. The empire clearly wants to be certain of the outcome."

After the leader of the Cens died during the first revolt, his son Meng had inherited his position as head of the clan. Then only nine years old, he placed himself under the protection of the Zhuang clan, which had the effect of reconciling Tianzhou and the empire, and thus pacifying the region for a time. To cement this alliance and reward the young man for his loyalty, the Zhuang chief gave his daughter, Wa Shi, meaning flower, in marriage.

Despite the femininity her name suggested, she tended to masculine pursuits. After the wedding she chose to be known as Wa, named for the varnished roof tiles whose strength and brilliance she claimed to possess. She bore Cen Meng an elder son, Bangzuo, but her husband chose Bangyan, another of his children with a concubine named Lin, as his successor.

A generation later, when Meng and Bangyan were both killed in a new revolt, running the city fell to the son of the latter. Cen Zhi was much too young to assume the position and Miss Lin was uneducated, so it was Lady Wa who used her intellect, charisma, and authority to take the situation in hand. Then, once the united armies of Lu Su and Wang Shou had taken possession of Tianzhou, she fled the city with the successor to protect him, when any number of less honorable women would have taken advantage of the situation to kill him in revenge – after all, Cen Zhi symbolized the injustice that had been dealt to her own child. Wang Shou himself respected the integrity and political skills of this woman to whom he once pledged allegiance. Her presence with the imperial army was worrying.

"Big brother," Wang Zhen said quietly, "I fear war is inevitable."

Wang Shou knew it. For him, Tianzhou's sovereignty was non-negotiable, but the idea of sacrificing its troops and citizens to the Emperor's armies repulsed him. It was why he refused to accept that the dice were already cast, and still hoped to find a bargaining chip with which to reopen negotiations. He nodded.

"If war is inevitable, we must ensure we keep our losses as few as possible."

But the Wolves knew their terrain well, and their commanders knew how to exploit it to carry out numerous ambushes. No, the hardest part would not be limiting losses on their side, but ensuring they didn't kill anyone too important in the opposite camp, to avoid falling into a war where a peaceful resolution was impossible.

While the insurgents prepared to trap the imperial forces in a pincer movement, Wang Yangming was studying topographical maps of the region from the campaign quarters. The maps, too imprecise to be truly useful, showed impassible and difficult terrain with forests, mountains, and rivers.

"Lady Wa!" he called.

Sitting nearby, she quickly stood. Although she was a noble, she wore military uniform and carried a helmet decorated with an insignia attesting to her position.

"Yes, Mr Wang?"

"Please, sit. Do you know this Lu Su and Wang Shou who currently control the city?"

"Yes, they are both natives of Tianzhou. Lu Su's daughter is married to my little brother, and I know Wang Shou personally."

"How are they likely to act, in your opinion?"

"As if they have nothing to lose," she answered hesitantly. "Lu Su is ambitious, Wang Shou cultivated, and they have never rebelled before… Their profile is different from the sovereigntists we have dealt with in the past."

"What you say is very true. To be precise, I think they are preparing to catch us with a surprise pincer attack. I saw flocks of birds flying up near our front lines – they must be moving significant numbers of troops there."

His prediction was soon proven true as a cry of alarm rose from the vanguard deeper in the woods. Lady Wa shuddered at the thought that the imperial army, whose relentless charges across open ground were its greatest strength, would be completely caught off guard by this type of attack. But Wang Yangming remained unperturbed as he sat, visibly indifferent to the urgency of the situation.

"You're right, Lady Wa," he declared calmly, "those two are no ordinary rebels."

Trained like a man in the practice and theory of martial arts, Lady Wa knew that the Wolves of Tianzhou were much more ferocious than the elite troops led by Wang Yangming. Did this scholar really understand what was happening right now? Once the defensive lines were broken, the entire army would rout, and they would have little chance of escape. She couldn't remain silent.

"Pardon me, Mr Wang," she said, "but would it not be prudent to recall the troops before it's too late?"

"Don't worry, Lady Wa, I have employed a technique known as *The guest acts as host*. When the rebels break through our lines, it is they who will be trapped."

The arrogance of the Wolves' commanders, who did not even consider the possibility of defeat, would be their downfall. Wang Yangming had guessed that Lu Su and Wang Shou would choose to embark on a show of force from the outset to discourage the imperial forces. Their knowledge of the terrain had a double advantage: it not only allowed them to carry out multiple surprise attacks to compensate for their lower numbers, but also to retreat without being pursued. However, they certainly didn't expect that their prey would actually be a trap. Wang Yangming's only mistake was to have slightly underestimated their strength, but his plan was unaffected. For her part, Lady Wa had had no idea that imperial troops had been posted to bait the trap.

"I bet that Lu and Wang would carry out a pincer move on our front lines," Wang Yangming explained, "then attack the middle line from the right."

He had therefore ordered the front line to open the way, then for the rear to attack: an unusual strategy that the Wolves couldn't have predicted. However, the front lines played a key role, so it seemed extremely risky to expose them needlessly.

"Mr Wang," Lady Wa insisted, "if I may, why not send reinforcements to the front lines?"

"Because that would complicate our victory."

How could it be easier to win with fewer men? A blast quickly answered this question: the imperial artillery had entered the fight. This was Wang Yangming's secret: he'd had firearms sent to this remote region, something which had surely never been seen before! Small detachments equipped with them had been placed outside the camp and the front line. When the Wolves had broken through the imperial troops, they had unknowingly thrown themselves into the line of fire, their legendary valor meaning nothing when at the mercy of these weapons. Their trap had been turned against them. The guest had acted as host.

Lady Wa nonetheless shuddered at each new detonation, as the soldiers, rebels though they were, were her countrymen and she could not rejoice in their deaths. While she was opposed to the rebellion, she had never wanted it to end in a bloodbath.

Noticing her paleness, Wang Yangming sought to reassure her. "Don't worry. Most of these weapons are loaded with blanks. My aim is to frighten the enemy, not kill them."

"Thank you, Mr Wang," she said gratefully with a deep bow.

"When His Majesty charged me with pacifying this region, I studied its history, and it felt natural to take your side."

Indeed, it had been unthinkable for him that the leadership of Tianzhou had not been given to a member of the Cen clan, governors of the city for generations. Because even once the leaders of the rebellion were defeated, their soldiers would never recognize the authority of a foreign magistrate. He had therefore had an official imperial recommendation drawn up for the people of Tianzhou so that Lady Wa could be recognized as the legitimate descendant of the Cen clan. If she was assigned to the position which should have been hers by right, relations with the central power could be reestablished. In summary, as the problem was local, it required a local solution. Following this logic, he had then placed his own troops under the command of Chen Xi, who had been operating in this region for a long time and knew the terrain well.

The shouts of the Wolves decreased in intensity as they grew closer and became embroiled in a situation they were completely unprepared for. Too sure of their formidable attack strength, they had no backup plan, and their strategy was as simple as it was radical: fight to the death. Their leaders had not yet been found or brought down, but it looked like it wouldn't be long now.

Lady Wa seized upon the option of surrender offered by Wang Yangming, convinced of the merit of his thinking.

"You are completely right. I'll go into the city myself to persuade the civilians."

"Madam, I've heard much of your great moral integrity, and I am honored to witness it for myself. Commander-in-Chief Zhang You will escort you. I hope he'll forgive Lu and Wang for being unable to discern good from evil."

Zhang You was a strong, smart and resourceful man from

Guangzhou. He had a good background and had studied military treatises, acquired perfect knowledge of Sun Tzu's *Art of War*, and led strategic operations as an adolescent. He had greased the palm of the rebel leader during the previous revolt in Tianzhou to quickly establish peace but had been betrayed at the last minute and imprisoned in the enemy jail before he finally managed to escape. Then, despite his ingenuity and feats of arms, he had been dismissed from his position for acting outside the regulations and resorting to bribery.

To carry out his mission, Wang Yangming had sought to surround himself with intelligent young people who were able to suggest new ideas, so Zhang You's profile had immediately stood out. He had sent him to the back lines, while assigning Chen Xi to the front; his two most trusted officers. Lady Wa would be well protected on her return to Tianzhou.

As she set off, Wang Shou was retreating to the same destination. An icy chill ran through him as he cast a final glance at the forest behind him.

His defeat was bitter, but when the Wolves had turned back, the empire's soldiers had not pursued them, as if out of some form of clemency. What game was the commander of the imperial army playing?

He was shaken out of his thoughts by the arrival of Lu Su, escorted by several rebels.

"Are you well, older brother?" he asked.

They didn't like one another but called each other by this nickname to show their closeness – their cause was shared after all, and it was important for them to support each other.

"I'm well," Wang Shou responded.

But that was only very relative. Certainly, they had few injured and dead, but the Wolves had been forced to flee the field of battle with their tails between their legs, which in itself was a terrible blow.

"Older brother," Lu Su breathed quietly, "they didn't act as expected..."

He didn't need to explain more. Even an idiot would have noticed that the imperial army had let them escape.

"How do we respond if they offer peace?" Wang Shou asked.

"We give them nothing! Yang said that the Fourth Cen was non-negotiable!"

Yang Siwei was Lu Su's mentor, and thus the hidden instigator of the current events. He refused to allow the central government to impose a magistrate on Tianzhou, whose governance, in his view, could only fall to Cen Zhen's successor, Bangxiang. The latter was still young, and his mother a concubine, so his legitimacy was easily contestable... But Lu Su had blind faith in his master, and thus refused even the idea of discussing these decrees, which worried Wang Shou.

"Let's wait and see the imperial army's next move," he said cautiously.

Night fell and the imperial camp set up such a formidable guard that the Wolves, despite their reputation for devastating nocturnal attacks, had no choice but to remain within the city walls. They were greatly surprised when they saw Commander Zhang You and Lady Wa approaching. Their stupefaction only grew on reading the demand for surrender sent by Wang Yangming.

It detailed the government's three demands: that Tianzhou be renamed Tianding; Cen Bangxiang would become the prefect; and the prefecture would be divided into sectors that Lu and Wang would be responsible for inspecting.

Wang Yangming had heard and understood the rebels' demands, but his real stroke of genius, the one which persuaded them, was the official recognition of Cen Bangxiang.

He was very relieved to see Zhang You and Lady Wa return to the camp safely, and to learn that the surrender would be ratified the next day. While he had been careful to give nothing away, he had in reality been plagued with terrible anguish. After all, as everyone knew, he had been sent here to crush the rebellion and set an example, if necessary, by massacring the rebels in a way that would be remembered for generations so that the city would finally be peaceful.

Wang Yangming suspected that this idea had been quietly suggested to the young Emperor by Zhang Yong, who was incapable of the humanity needed to negotiate a peaceful solution. This situation would certainly have ended in a blood bath if he had been in charge.

And yet, when Zhang Yong became leader of the Eight Tigers, Wang Yangming had nurtured the foolish hope that he could reason with him and finally bring an end to the age-old quarrel between his group and the Society of the Mind. But everyone has their own strengths and weaknesses, and the mentor knew those of his friend and rival only too well. He was not a man whom it was possible to make peace with.

"And yet, Uncle Zhang and I have a common destiny..."

But that way lay sadness. He had accomplished his main task but there was still much to do, and each change made in Tianzhou would test the strength of the newly established peace. While Wang Shou seemed very satisfied with the resolution to the conflict, perhaps Lu Su did not completely approve of the compromise in having Cen Bangxiang lead the city as an imperial civil servant rather than as an autonomous governor. What did Cen Bangxiang himself think of it? After all, not every eventuality can be planned for, and not even the immortal Taoists were immune to mistakes!

Not to mention the shadow of Zhang Yong, still looming over the ashes of the Society of the Mind and causing an icy wind to blow whenever his name was mentioned…

The following morning, the sun burned through the misty humidity of the south, promising a warm and pleasant day to come. The gates of Tianzhou opened to reveal two rows of Wolves ready for inspection, with Cen Bangxiang, Lu Su, and Wang Shou standing before them. Wang Yangming, who had little fondness for large military demonstrations, presented himself to them simply accompanied by two young aides, and followed by several other important figures from the imperial delegation. The evening before, the best local craftsmen had erected a beautiful multicolored pavilion in front of the city's reception hall, where the official peace talks would take place.

A banquet with all kinds of foods and drinks had been laid out in the great hall. Wang Yangming sat at the end of the table, Zhang You on his left, Lady Wa and Chen Xi on his right, while Lu Su, Wang Shou, and Cen Bangxiang sat opposite. It was Lady Wa who had suggested that meetings take place in this building, but it was originally the official residence of the prefectural magistrate, and Cen Bangxiang would live there if the administrative process proceeded smoothly. The latter was very nervous in her presence, as he knew that she might consider him a traitor to his line and expected to see her take her vengeance at any second.

Wang Yangming untied the white silk ribbon that fastened the surrender letter and quickly scanned it. He was willing to show sympathy towards Cen Bangxiang, as his ancestor Cen Zhongsu, a valiant general of the Song dynasty, had like himself been from Yuyao. But he was shocked at the rough calligraphy on the document. This thick and graceless writing did not do justice to the importance of the occasion.

"Who wrote this letter?" he suddenly asked.

Cen Bangxiang well knew that if Wang Yangming hadn't seen fit to place him at the head of the city, the rebels would now be nothing more than cripples and a pile of bodies. In addition, this impetuous young man of fifteen or sixteen years felt overawed by the authoritative aura of the greatest scholar of the imperial court. Embarrassed by the question, he couldn't help but lower his gaze before his elder and superior.

"Mr Wang..." he stammered piteously, "I must... tell you that it w-was Y- Yang..." He pulled himself together. "Mr Yang is my secretary, who noted down my dictation before writing this letter."

"I'd like to meet this Mr Yang."

Lu Su straightened, surprised. To his uneducated eyes, the commander of the imperial army was just another military man, and not the most eminent scholar of his time. But the day before, after choosing to accept the armistice and writing the letter of surrender – of which he was the author – Yang Siwei had asserted that Wang Yangming would ask to see him. Lu Su couldn't explain his master's confidence, but his prediction was about to come true!

"Secretary Yang is outside," answered Cen Bangxiang. "He awaits his orders."

"Then have him enter, please."

Now that was unusual. Wang Shou hid his surprise as the small old man with the long, sparse beard entered the hall, quickly prostrating himself before Wang Yangming as he trembled.

"The humble Yang Siwei presents himself before the honorable Master Wang," he said humbly.

Lu Su was even more perplexed. Why was his master, usually such an assured and confident man, giving the impression that he was presenting himself in society for the first time? Was it because the representative of the empire intimidated him that he suddenly found himself unable to articulate three words correctly? But he had little time to dwell further on the matter, as a bloody shout rang from outside the building, causing everyone in the gathering to freeze.

Lady Wa leapt to her feet. Chen Xi did the same and gestured at her to stay where she was.

"Don't move madam, I will see what is happening."

He strode out and returned a few seconds later accompanied by guards carrying two bodies which they laid on an empty table. Lu Su and Cen Bangxiang wordlessly fell to their knees, paling at the sight of the lifeless corpses.

"Mr Wang," Chen Xi cried, "these men have been killed!"

Wang Shou managed to remain composed, and immediately glimpsed the possibility that the imperial dignitaries suspected a trap set by the rebels and decided to defuse the situation as quickly as possible before it exploded.

"Mr Wang," he said calmly, "stay safe here while we catch the killer."

Wang Yangming regarded the corpses with the alarm.

"Chen Xi," he asked, "did you see the culprit?"

"No, they were already lying on the ground when I went out..."

Nothing here made sense. Logic dictated that an assassin would focus on the leading figures, but the death of these simple guards had no political or strategic value. It would take much more than the murder of anonymous soldiers to disrupt the peace process, as neither side could seriously be accused of the crime. Unless it was a diversion... Chen Xi suddenly saw the frail Yang Siwei, to whom no one was paying any attention, stop his trembling and launch himself at Wang Yangming like a speeding arrow.

The plan, which had not been conceived by the old man, was brilliant. It began with the deliberately grotesque writing of a document of the highest importance, an incongruity which would pique the curiosity of a great scholar, academic, and diplomat such as the founder of the School of Mind. Once the author of the letter was close to his target, he would feign physical weakness and a lack of confidence so as not to arouse suspicion, then launch a surprise attack after the pointless murder of the guards at the entrance distracted everyone in the room. Zhang You was untrained in hand-to-hand combat and so was unable to react, and Lady Wa, while formidable when wielding the knives she wore at her waist, wasn't able to draw them in time. Yang Siwei was already in the process of striking, armed with two thin, poisoned blades drawn from folds in his clothing. Even the slightest scratch would be certain death.

This fighting technique was named *Pricking the lamplight*

with a hairpin, referencing a poem written by Zhang Hu of the Tang dynasty:

The gates of the forbidden palace are closed to the moon. Charming eyes see nothing but the nests of herons; Prick the lamplight with a hairpin and extinguish the flame to save an insect.

The reclusive concubine extinguishing her candle with a precise motion of her hairpin had inspired the wielding of poisoned blades, as any martial artist who pushed this technique to its apex could pierce their adversary's heart with a single movement of their delicate weapon, killing with a single pin prick.

Wang Yangming instinctively reached for the sword that normally sat at his waist, but he had left it behind as a sign of peace. How could he have expected a fight at the signing of a peace treaty?

Nonetheless, his finely-honed reflexes allowed him to parry the attack with a powerful sweep of his left arm. The poisoned blades missed their target. The person who ordered the assassination had said it well: taking his life would be no mean feat.

A wise man would have fled when a surprise attack failed, but Yang Siwei did no such thing. On the contrary, he leapt into the air to launch a second attack, but Wang Yangming seized him by the leg, pressing firmly on his artery to reduce the blood pressure and render him harmless. As he did so, at the last second, he saw the gleam of another blade flashing towards him.

CHAPTER 13

When Yang Siwei unexpectedly attacked, Chen Xi was taking the pulse of one of the victims who had been stabbed in the chest and whose heart, unsurprisingly, no longer beat. He was about to pronounce them dead when suddenly, the second "body" stood and surged towards Wang Yangming – and unlike the soldiers posted in the room, this one was armed. He hurled his dagger as his target was occupied with disabling Yang Siwei, their two-pronged attack so well coordinated it have been fatal to any ordinary man.

But the mentor of the Society of the Mind was no ordinary man. Despite his surprise, he reacted quickly to catch the blade in its middle, where its blade was not sharp. The assassin felt as if his dagger was being pulled down by an incredible force as electric shocks ran up his wrist – Wang Yangming's inner energy attacking his meridians.

The person who commissioned the attack had warned of the threat the target posed, but his warning had fallen on the deaf ears of one too sure of his own skills. The strong young man, muscles tensed and face red with effort, was now at the mercy of the placid old man paralyzing his arms. Powerless in his agony, he felt as if his entire body were about to explode. Wang Yangming did not have a violent character; he was as implacable and imperturbable as a river with deep and powerful currents. But to catch the blade he had been forced to let go of his captive's leg, and Yang Siwei had taken advantage to jump six or seven feet into the air and launch his ultimate attack, the tips of his blades pointed straight towards the top of Wang Yangming's head.

Chen Xi froze. He had barely had time to unsheathe his sword and was too far from the attack to intervene... but someone else did it for him. Just as the situation seemed desperate and the fight unfairly balanced, a flash of steel stopped poisoned needles in their path, and Yang Siwei let out a piercing scream of pain. The fingers holding his weapons had just been sliced through by one of Wang Yangming's young aides.

Seeing the old man tumble to the ground like a wet rag, Zhang You quickly took the decision to cut his throat. He had been somewhat traumatized by his imprisonment during the previous rebellion, and generally never took risks with this type of high-level combatant. The intruder who had posed as a corpse had also managed to let go of his dagger and free himself from the grip of the energy technique. He spun round ready to run for the door, when Lady Wa's twin daggers sank into his back. While she had taken some time to react, she was now ready to unleash her hatred on the man who had tried to destroy the peace accord that she held so dear. The assassin desperately rushed towards Wang Yangming once more, striking him in the chest with all his strength, a blow which he couldn't avoid due to Lady Wa blocking his view. He absorbed the full impact, but then quickly replicated it by grasping his assailant's arms, forcing them to bend at an unnatural angle. They broke with a sickening crack, and the man collapsed to the floor writhing in pain. Chen Xi hurried to him, pinning him to the floor by pressing the tip of his sword to his throat.

One of the assassins was dead and the other injured. Lu Su, not wishing to be associated with his master's betrayal, was the first to break the stunned silence of the stunned.

"It's got nothing to do with me!" he cried.

"Nor me!" Cen Bangxiang echoed, for the same reasons.

Having just sliced Yang Siwei's throat before he could confess the reasons for the attack or the person who ordered it, Zhang You also feared suspicion of being involved in the plot. His loyalty to Wang Yanging had been unwavering ever since the man had allowed him to rejoin the army, so he feared he had made a terrible mistake. The esteemed scholar soon calmed the simmering tensions.

"Sirs," he announced, "let's not get carried away. I am sure that these assassins were not sent by any of you."

"Mr Wang," Wang Shou responded with admirable calm, "let me also assure you that we had no idea of Yang Siwei's vile treachery."

"I'm sure all three of you are sincerely pleased by this agreement, so I can't imagine any reason you would wish to see it terminated." He turned towards the guards. "Behead these two assassins, publicly."

Zhang You was surprised he didn't seize the opportunity to

interrogate the living assassin, but said nothing. Before the man with the two broken arms was taken outside, Chen Xi bent to his ear to whisper, "It's too late to be scared now!", and the room returned to relative peace.

Lady Wa did not feel calm. She was very aware that trying to help Wang Yangming with an insufficient level of kung-fu had been a mistake, and that without her clumsy intervention, he would not have had to suffer the violent blow to his chest.

"Mr Wang..." she began.

"Thank you very much for coming to my aid," the master kindly cut her off. "In view of what just happened, I hope that you will never forget to always be on guard, even within your own walls."

"I will."

From this day forward, she would have complete loyalty to the imperial government, even going so far as to send the Wolves as reinforcements against the invasion of Japanese pirates. And their respect for Wang Yangming would lead the descendants of the Cen clan to have unwavering loyalty to their country for many years to come.

When those involved in the peace negotiations had composed themselves, Cen Bangxiang, Lu Su, and Wang Shou led the imperial dignitaries to inspect the troops and ensure the execution of the assassins was clearly communicated to the local population as a strong message of support for the central government.

On returning to the main hall, Wang Yangming began to stagger. His two aides moved to support him then took him to a small adjoining room to rest.

"Master, what is happening to you?" one of them asked.

This voice had nothing masculine about it, and for good reason: it was Shao Jun.

"A-Liang, make me a bowl of invigorating soup," he told his real aide, who quickly left the room.

"Are you injured, master?" the young woman asked, helping the mentor sit.

He had practiced martial arts for his entire life but the years had not spared him; every autumn that came he grew a little weaker and more out of breath.

In the general confusion, Shao Jun hadn't seen the violent blow he'd taken to the chest.

"It's nothing," he chuckled. "I only met Luo Xiang on a few occasions, but his talent was impressive."

"He was the assassin?"

"Of course! The character *Luo* is composed of *Si* and *Wei*, and *Xiang* can also be pronounced as *Yang*... When the secretary was introduced as Yang Siwei, I immediately knew I was dealing with the Tiger Luo Xiang."

"But his beard looked so real..."

While it had certainly been very well made, it moved unnaturally just before he made to attack, something only a sharp eye would have noticed. The young woman wouldn't have recognized him with or without this artifice, as Luo Xiang was the only Tiger she had never seen. Wang Yangming let out a sigh and used the writing equipment on a nearby table to sketch a face which he showed to his pupil.

"Looking at this, do you recognize the face of the man who played dead?"

"It's him!" she exclaimed, impressed by the quality of the drawing.

The master picked up his pen to add a long, sparse beard to the face.

"And now?"

The portrait was now a picture of Yang Siwei, alias Luo Xiang! The young woman was even more astonished.

"Brothers?" she asked.

"That's the conclusion I came to. Even I was surprised."

Shao Jun had reached Wang Yangming two days earlier to warn him that Zhang Yong had visited Yang Yiqing to check he still had his jade pendant. The mentor had therefore been prepared for an imminent attack of some kind, but had expected something like a potential assassin hidden among the men under his command, and not among the entourage of the Tianzhou rebels! The day before, he had sent Shao Jun to spy on Wang Shou and Lu Su to gauge their opinions regarding peace before sending them Lady Wa and Zhang You. It was then that he had heard of this mysterious Master Yang who seemed so determined to precipitate a change in government. The disguised Tiger must also have had unusual self-control to dedicate himself to the minutiae of establishing a role and position which would quickly be reduced to nothing when the time came to act.

It was probably Zhang Yong who had given him the role a long time ago, just like he had persuaded the Emperor to send Wang Yangming to pacify the resulting revolt. It was a patient and long-term strategy, which used pawns cleverly placed in position several moves ahead. And without Shao Jun's unexpected intervention, the assassination would certainly have been successful. The mentor of the Society of the Mind couldn't help but admire his opponent's ingenuity.

"So that was why you didn't interrogate him before his execution!" exclaimed the young woman. "You already knew that he was acting on the orders of Zhang Yong, who had you sent here solely to have you assassinated ..."

"To begin with I think he just wanted me out of the way so you would be easier to capture, but then he ordered my death when his suspicions were confirmed after his visit to Yang Yiqing."

Everything was clear now: the leader of the Tigers had told Luo Xiang to light the fuse in Tianzhou as a pretext to send Wang Yangming, which would surprise no one due to his impeccable record of service and his old friendship with the captain of the imperial guard. And if he later turned out to be the mentor of the Central Plain Brotherhood, it would be easy to put an end to him there, while lamenting his death as a tragedy resulting from the rebellion and with no direct link to Zhang Yong. It was best to avoid spreading news of the affair to prevent the region from falling into chaos once more and avert any crisis at the court. But a confrontation between these two enemies was becoming inevitable now that Luo Xiang was dead.

"What can we do now, master?" Shao Jun asked after a moment of reflection.

"It's time to catch a sea turtle!"

"Pardon?"

"All Zhang Yong's scheming, his quest for the Precursor Box especially, are connected to the scroll engraved with the characters *Dai Yu*. We must act quickly if we are to thwart his plans and find the sea turtle before he does."

Wang Yangming was alluding to the legend in which the islands of Dai Yu and Yuan Jiao were broken off from the other sacred mountains and drifted to the North Pole, after giants from the dragon realm caught the turtles that carried them. Her master's perpetual mischievousness never failed to amuse Shao Jun. She was delighted to see his eyes sparkle with the impish gleam of a teenager impatient to embark on a new adventure.

"Very well, master, but how will we go about it?"

"Do you still have the jade pendant?"

"It never leaves my side."

"Even better." He drummed his fingers on the table. "The imperial troops will leave the region now that my official business here is complete. When we arrive in Guilin prefecture, you will wait in Hongqimen, a fishing village to the southeast of Guangzhou. On the day of the dragon boat festival, you will find a certain Tiexin, to whom you will show the pendant to prove that I sent you. We have men there ready to fight for us."

Shao Jun was stunned that the mentor had these secret troops at his disposal – such a level of preparation was worthy of Zhang Yong. If these men supported their cause, rebuilding the Brotherhood would be easier with their help.

"This Tiexin and these soldiers, are they your disciples?" she asked.

"Not at all. We can use them, but we can't trust them."

There was a famous saying that contradicted this: "Do not doubt your allies, and do not ally with those you doubt", but the master refused to explain further.

"For my part, I will only arrive in Hongqimen just before the festival," he added.

"You won't stay there with me?"

"No, I have three armies to return to their garrison."

Touched by Shao Jun's concern, he tried to reassure her.

"Young girl, there is no time to waste, you didn't even know where to go when you arrived in China…"

It wasn't a reproach, just the simple truth. She had left the country in midst of extreme chaos, and after Zhu Jiuyuan's death in Europe at the hands of the Tigers, she had wandered aimlessly for two years… but on her journey, she had matured and perfected her kung-fu. Certainly, neither Ezio Auditore nor Wang Yangming had been able to give her the clear answers she thought she needed, but her understanding of the world in which she lived had only grown since her return. Yet the more clearly she saw, the more her faith in her ability to rebuild the Brotherhood decreased.

"You're right, master," she responded. "I will trust your judgement and follow your instructions."

"You alone are responsible for the path you take. Just as Master Auditore did not instruct your return to China, neither will I impose my own decisions on you." He looked straight into her eyes and finished in a soft, fatherly tone, "Young girl, your life is your own."

While these words were meant to be comforting, they sent a chill through Shao Jun, suddenly reminding her that her path would continue to be as solitary as it always had been. "It's true," she thought to herself, "I thought I had to follow in my master's footsteps, but his path is not mine. I must make my own way."

The Society of the Mind had been her first real family, but it had been torn apart by the Eight Tigers. She would never forget the pain and sadness she had felt, which had driven her to swear to rebuild the Brotherhood despite having no idea how to proceed. Now, though the task seemed as difficult – if not more so – than ever, she could at least see it more clearly, which only increased her determination.

"Understood!" she responded simply.

"After everything you've done recently, take some time to rest. We will meet again in Hongqimen for the dragon boat festival."

The young woman remained silent for a moment before bowing, hands clasped before her chest.

"I will follow your instructions," she eventually said before withdrawing.

The decisive battle would soon commence.

Once alone, Wang Yangming was overcome by a coughing fit and brought a hand to his mouth. When he took it away, it was spattered with blood. It wasn't surprising: his protective technique had been broken by the strike of the twin disguised as a guard. While he was tougher than the average person, the fight had sapped his strength; he was now on the verge of fainting. He would require a good month for his *neigong* – his internal energy – to fully replenish, and he would need everything he had to face Zhang Yong's next attack. The leader of the Tigers would be furious to learn of his acolyte's death, but he was probably still unaware of Shao Jun's location, a key advantage which should be maintained. This was also why the mentor insisted that their paths should diverge as soon as possible.

When A-Liang, the young aide who had left to find some soup, returned with a steaming bowl, he was alarmed to find his master in such a piteous state. As Confucian values demanded, he had deep respect for his instructor.

"Master Wang, what happened?"

"It's nothing. Just temporary fatigue, that's all. Go and rest."

"But master… where is A-Jun?"

This was the name Wang Yangming had used to introduce Shao Jun to the young disciple who had followed him for so long.

"A-Jun has gone to rest, do not disturb him."

A-Liang had to hide his disappointment. A curious young man, he burned with impatience to go and ask his "comrade", who he took to be male, where he had learned his kung-fu and if he could teach him some.

When the aide withdrew carrying the empty bowl, Wang Yangming relaxed on his chair and, hands resting on his knees, began his *neigong* exercises. Implementing his plan would take time, and Zhang Yong would surely launch his next attack before he was fully recovered. Was this how it would all end, with the failure of the last hope of the Society of the Mind? No, he smiled to himself, their chances weren't zero. In a long-ago discussion with his two old friends, their respective world views had continued to surprise one another. And that was how he would continue to face his opponent: by developing strategies that his mind, brilliant though it was, would be unable to conceive of.

The country had over a thousand messenger posts. In addition to the two capitals and the thirteen prefectures, every large town had its own, which ensured urgent missives never took longer than ten to fifteen days to reach their destination. When a rider arrived, they exchanged their mount for another of equivalent quality before continuing their journey. The largest posts had up to twenty-four, but the smallest only five or six, which in busy periods could force messengers to accept a lower-quality mount than the one they arrived on. As the one Xu Pengju had given Shao Jun was one of his best, she had been able to reach Tianzhou using only the highest quality horses. However, her current journey would not be as fast, as the approach of the dragon boat festival meant reduced availability of high-quality mounts.

The young woman took the main road out of Guilin towards the southeast and had just left Pingle to travel a quieter path, frequented more by hares and rabbits than by humans. She should then pass Wuzhou and Zhaoqing before finally arriving in Guangzhou, but the tracks which crossed the uncivilized parts of Guangdong and Guangxi were treacherous and uncertain, overgrown with abundant vegetation encouraged by the region's gentle, moist climate, so she was unable to gallop constantly. Rocking with the rolling gait of her mount, she had plenty of time to lose herself in thought.

When she returned to China, the Tigers were seven in number. And while four had since lost their lives, their leader was as unfathomable as a bottomless well. The assassination attempt he had ordered in Tianzhou proved his talent for strategy and the extent of his political power, as well as his ability to make decisive choices without hesitation. Shao Jun couldn't help wondering if Wang Yangming would have survived without her intervention. But nothing could shake the respect she had for her master, and she was convinced he was right: their only chance of victory lay in finding the famous isle.

Her thoughts were interrupted by a plaintive moan around the next bend, just a little way on. She spurred her mount, rounding the corner to discover what looked like an unfortunate accident: at the foot of a large tree lay an overturned cart and the mule who had pulled it dead in a pool of blood, and a middle-aged woman in a flowered jacket and unbound feet. It was she who was moaning in pain.

"Is anyone there?" she called as she heard the approaching footsteps. "Help!"

Shao Jun forced herself to shake the idea that this could be a trap. Despite the demonstration of her kung-fu, no one knew her or could have recognized her in Tianzhou, then once in Guilin, she had left the imperial troops with the greatest secrecy. What's more, the road she had taken was so deserted that no one could have followed her without being seen from several lis away.

But the tension wouldn't leave her. She soon realized what was bothering her: despite her rural accent, the peasant had spoken in Mandarin, when it was Cantonese which was most prevalent in the southern regions of China. In addition, their inhabitants were generally looked down upon by the rest of the country; "Fear not the heavens, fear not the earth, but beware the Cantonese speaker" advised a popular saying. Shao Jun thus remained on her mount as she approached.

"Are you injured, madam?" she called out.

Her horse suddenly whinnied and fell with its rider into an enormous dark hole.

So it was a trap after all!

Despite her panic, her combat reflexes allowed her to react quickly: she removed her feet from the stirrups and grabbed a root protruding from the side of the earth as her mount continued its fall and crashed down below her. Hanging in mid-air, the young woman remembered with horror that her sword was beneath the saddle… but better to fight barehanded against whoever waited above than risk being trapped in this pit. Spying a low branch above her head on the tree she had seen earlier, she sent her rope dart to catch onto it and, slick with sweat but determined not to give in to panic, tried to climb towards the surface as fast as she could. She saw a figure emerge from the foliage, then felt herself suddenly falling back towards the bottom of the hole: they had sliced through her rope!

Her fall was cushioned by the body of her injured horse, which certainly prevented her from breaking any bones as she landed. Judging by the labored breathing of the poor beast, which weighed several hundred kilos, it must be gravely injured. Shao Jun had enjoyed the company of the strong and docile mount she had acquired at the last messenger post, but she knew it was as good as dead now. She drew her sword, felt the animal's chest to find its heart, and thrust her blade firmly between its ribs to end its suffering.

Crash! Everything suddenly turned black. Looking up, she saw they had moved the upturned cart over the opening like a cover, with the only light a tiny ray filtering between two planks.

The walls of the hole were earth, irregular with numerous hand- and footholds she used to jump from one to another to reach the top. Once there, she wedged herself as best she could, and tried to create an exit by pushing with all her strength against the rough wood covering the hole. She rejoiced as she felt the cart move a little, but her triumph was short-lived: the barrier was immediately moved back with force, and she fell back down to the bottom of the hole – though this time she was able to control her descent to land lightly next to her dead horse. Barely an instant later, she heard a *bam! bam! bam!* as the bandits threw stones on top of the improvised cover to ensure their prisoner wouldn't be able to move it back. That peasant, if it was she, was surprisingly strong.

"Miss Favorite," another voice called out, "are you still alive?"

Shao Jun recognized the timbre of the voice of Qiu Ju the Demon, Zhang Yong's bodyguard! It was he who had cut her rope dart, because he knew how much the former imperial favorite relied on this tool. It was also certainly he who had concocted the crude trap she was now cursing herself for falling into. How she regretted trusting the false Mandarin-speaking peasant in the middle of Guangdong!

"We must deal with her now!" she heard him shout. "This viper killed my two brothers!"

"The venerable captain general wants her alive," replied Qiu Ju. "And, you should know that it's dangerous to attack the imperial favorite in a rush… Uncle Luo, I understand your anger, but you can be assured that your twins will be avenged when Wang Yangming dies at our master's hand."

Uncle Luo? Shao Jun was stunned. So, Luo Xiang wasn't just one person, but three brothers! Now that was a secret so incredible that there had been no chance of the mentor discovering it. The last survivor must have been following her since Tianzhou, patiently reining in his anger to avoid ruining the Tigers' plans. The most worrying thing was that she now had irrefutable proof that Master Yangming had been unmasked, and that Zhang Yong was probably already on his trail. Did he know just how close the danger was?

The higher-ranking Qiu Ju addressed Luo Zang with a mix of pity and mockery.

"Come on, what are you so scared of? The girl is disarmed, harmless. And Uncle Zhang said he wanted her alive… he said nothing about whole!"

Luo Xiang came from a poor family which had sent two of the three triplets to the palace as eunuchs. There, their intelligence and the opportunities provided by their similarity drew the attention of Zhang Yong, who called the last of the brothers to his service – it was he who had been disguised as the female peasant. His level of kung-fu was the weakest of the three and now he feared losing his place among the Tigers: what use was he without high-level fighting skills or his siblings to carry out missions with? His hatred for Shao Jun knew no bounds.

"Perfect," he growled. "I'll tear her apart..."

Interrupted by hoofbeats on the road, he had no time to say more as a rider sped towards them. Travelers were rare in Guangdong – ten to fifteen days could pass between one person and the next – so Qiu Ju and Luo Xiang immediately agreed that the newcomer couldn't be in the area by chance. They set up an ambush. From the bottom of her hole, Shao Jun thought that it must be a man working for the Tigers come to help them in their grisly work. From the way the horse was galloping, she guessed it was a high-quality destrier and not the mount of a simple commoner. At first, she feared it was Zhang Yong, but the Tigers said that he had left to attack Wang Yangming. So, who could it be?

"Who are you?" Luo Xiang called out harshly.

A few seconds later the young woman heard him let out a terrified shout, then a heavy weight fell onto the cart with a bang. Had the Tiger just been killed? *Cling! Cling!* The sound of a rapid exchange of weapons rang out. Fighters of Qiu Ju's caliber didn't just appear on rural roads, but surprisingly the two adversaries seemed to be of equal skill. Could it be Master Wang himself, come to help his protegee? The idea was crazy, but she knew of no one else who would be able to take on this kind of fight.

She climbed the walls of the pit once more to push against the upturned cart. Unfortunately, it was still weighed down with stones and didn't budge an inch.

"Master!" cried the young woman. "Is that you?"

A shrill screech seemed to answer her question. Distracted by this unexpected interruption, Qiu Ju was injured. Gritting his teeth, he hissed in his irritatingly shrill voice, "You have no shame… to conspire in this way… Ahh…"

Now that was interesting, a member of the Eight Tigers who dared injure a fellow conspirator. A sword fell onto the cart with a crash and the Devil let out a final groan. The rider had killed him too! Shao Jun began pushing at the cart again to catch sight of her savior, but her feet slipped on the sides of the hole and she fell back to the bottom of the pit. Outside, she heard the stones being moved from the top of the wooden barrier. She could finally escape! Head tipped back, she waited to see the sky reappear… in vain. After a moment, she heard the horse stretch into a gallop. Incredulous, the young woman climbed to the top of the hole for a third time, breathed deeply, pressed her feet against the earth and pushed with all her strength to gain the space to finally escape the trap. Fearing a new ploy, she quickly slipped out, her sword held above her head to parry any incoming attack, but she was well and truly alone.

Feet planted firmly on the ground; she inspected the scene. Luo Xiang, cast from the same mold as his brothers, lay on his back with a gaping wound in his chest, still dressed in the peasant costume. Qiu Ju lay face down on the ground, his back torn open to reveal his ribs. He still breathed slightly. He was in no condition to talk, so Shao Jun ended his suffering with a quick sword slash. Tiger or not, she couldn't bear seeing his agony.

She threw the two bodies into the hole and rolled the large stones that had been piled on the cart over them. It was a cruel irony shared between only her and the heavens that the pit they had dug to trap the former imperial favorite had become their grave. There were only two Tigers left to vanquish, but she was still uneasy. She had no idea of her savior's identity and worried about the danger closing in on Master Yangming.

As she tortured herself with worry, the sound of hooves hammering on the road rang out again. It was a magnificent destrier, saddled and riderless, galloping towards her at high speed. Taking no time to question this new mystery, she rushed towards it and leapt into the air to precisely land directly on its back. Clearly well trained, the fiery mount slowed its pace. It had to be Shao Jun's anonymous savior who had sent her this horse. But why did they refuse to reveal themselves? "Never mind" she told herself, "Whoever it is, I'm sure there are good reasons to keep their identity secret."

All her thoughts were focused on Master Yangming as she set off.

CHAPTER 14

After Guilin, Wang Yangming travelled towards Nanchang to return the imperial troops to their garrison. His orders were then to return to the capital, though he first planned to visit his disciple in the village of Hongqimen to ready her for the surprise attack they were preparing to launch on Zhang Yong's island lair. Following his route, in Yongzhou Shao Jun learned that the army had continued towards Binzhou; in Binzhou, she heard that they had struck camp the day before she arrived, and she would need to cross Guangzhou to reach her destination. The young woman was filled with anxiety throughout her journey. If Zhang Yong got to her master before she did, she couldn't allow herself to think of the consequences.

She moved quickly, riding day and night without a rest, soon crossing the Dayu mountains as she travelled from Guangdong to Jiangxi and reached the small province of Nan'an, which marked the frontier with the semi-wild countries of the south. These remote regions were separated from the imperial power of the Central Plain by five mountain ranges, which inspired countless artists. One of them wrote the melancholy poem *Passing Through the Dayu Mountains* at the beginning of the Tang dynasty:

Travelling the mountainous peaks to the rebel countries,
I pause and yearn for my family.
My soul soars with the birds escaping to the south,
My tears remain hanging from the branches of northern trees.
Threatening rain rises up the mountain,
The clouds on the river flow into a thick fog.
I will return one day,
But the mountains of the south will remain in my heart.

While the regions evoked in the text were not as wild as they had been at the start of the Tang dynasty, they were still very sparsely populated, and the post where Shao Jun stopped to the north of Mount Dayu was small and dilapidated. There she was relieved to learn that Master Yangming had passed through the day before, which meant he was still alive. Reinvigorated by the good news, she left as soon as she could and the next day reached the town of Huanglong, which sat between mountains to the west and a river to the east – charming but far too modest to justify the opening of a messenger post. She soon spied the military encampment nearby and hastened towards it. As she approached, she recognized Master Yangming's escort, arms filled with kindling.

"A-Liang!" she called out.

The young man initially recoiled fearfully, failing to recognize her immediately.

"Oh, it's you! A-Jun, why are you dressed as a messenger?"

"Don't worry about that. Is the master here?"

"He just left to take a walk with an old friend."

"Who was it? Was anyone with him?"

"It was a thin old man I've never seen before, and he was alone. He ordered me to warm up the tents just before leaving with the master."

Shao Jun sighed. Perhaps it was a false alarm. She didn't think Zhang Yong would attack alone, and as Wang Yangming had many friends in the region, it was entirely possible that he had used his time there to reconnect with one of them. For example, it was likely to be someone like Wang Qiong who he had promoted to inspector general of Nan'an prefecture several years earlier. At the time, the surrounding provinces had been invaded by seemingly indomitable armies, and the empire, as often happened when faced with this type of situation, had sent Shao Jun's master to take care of the situation. His strategy had been two-fold: he had studied the local manners and customs to better understand and overcome his adversaries, and had then ordered schools to be built there so that the older insurgents and the younger generations who followed them could harmoniously integrate into the empire. Because, as he said, "it is easier to break a mountain than a twisted heart."

But just in case, it was better for the young woman to warn Wang Yangming of the threat he faced as soon as possible.

"Do you know when he'll be back?"

"I'm not sure. They'll return by the end of the day at the latest, for dinner."

What should she do? Leave and search for Wang Yangming, or wait here until nightfall? Although he was officially a count, the master liked to remain a simple man at heart, which could endanger him in this type of situation; no other person of his rank would venture so far from the military camp without an armed escort...

"A-Jun," A-Liang ventured, "I'd like to ask something which I'm worried will offend you."

His youthful concern amused Shao Jun.

"Don't worry, I'm listening!"

"A-Jun... Are you also an uncle?"

The young woman laughed aloud. It was true that recently she had been covering her tracks well of late. When she left Nanjing, she even wore a false beard to avoid being recognized by Yu Dayong's men. Then, playing the role of one of Master Yangming's aides, she had blended into the almost exclusively male crowd of the imperial delegation. But even disguised as a messenger and on horseback, she couldn't hide her fine features or her figure, which gave her a decidedly androgynous appearance and so led some to think that she might be an "uncle", in other words, a eunuch. The issue could be delicate, because few eunuchs had chosen their situation for themselves: most came from poor families who had, so to speak, sold them to the palace when they were children.

The young woman abruptly stopped laughing as she was hit by a sudden realization.

"A-Liang," she said, "you asked me if I was *also* an uncle... Does that mean the master's old friend was a eunuch?"

"Yes, he was an uncle."

Shao Jun ran towards her horse and leapt into the saddle.

"Quickly!" she called to the youth. "Come with me! Where did they go?"

"I... I don't know... The master said that they would talk as they admired the landscape." He pointed to the horizon with a finger. "They left in that direction."

The horse set off at a gallop in that direction, followed with great difficulty by A-Liang, who was completely confused and didn't know what to think. This mysterious "friend" who was at that very moment alone with Wang Yangming could be none other than Zhang Yong! How he had followed the trail of the jade pendants was still a mystery, but it was very clear that he had discovered the real identity of the mentor of the Central Plain Brotherhood, and that he had decided to use all means at his disposal to eliminate him. And after the attempt on his life in Tianzhou, the mentor was certainly in no fit state to face the formidable kung-fu of the leader of the Eight Tigers, who was among the best in the world. Particularly as his old adversary would not settle for a simple duel.

No, he would set a carefully planned trap, the way he always removed any obstacles to his will…

Shao Jun's heart froze. She feared she would fail to save her master when they were so close to their goal, and this single thought seemed to fog her vision, like a cloud of despair hampered her ability to fight. She pushed her mount to its limit, but the poor beast had already carried her across the land without rest, food, or water. She was at the end of her strength, and the panicked exhortations of her rider made no difference. What's more, the young woman had nothing but a vague direction in which to travel and had no time to formulate a plan of attack. But nothing else mattered to her just then. The risk didn't matter. Her life didn't matter. She had to save her master!

Meanwhile, Wang Yangming was relaxing on a small sailboat

a short distance from the town. The breeze sent ripples across the surface of the water and rustled the reddened leaves of the luxurious trees that bordered this section of the river. The scent of Mount Dayu oolong tea wafted from the canvas cabin erected on the boat where they were playing a game of Go by the light of a red lantern. Black and white counters spread over the board.

"Zhang, my friend, what brings you to this remote region?" Wang Yangming asked as he brought a steaming cup to his lips.

He placed a black counter with a malicious smile, taking the upper hand. After a long journey in his famous palanquin borne by twenty-four porters, Zhang Yong was alone and dressed in a simple gray chemise. Neither arrogant nor cruel, he was no longer the noble captain general of the twelve battalions of the imperial guard, but an ordinary old man. His white counters, spread in the grand dragon formation, waged a bitter struggle in stark contrast to his calm indifference, but victory was less important to him than the pleasure of playing the game.

"Now the Emperor is the clear monarch," he answered, "the world is at peace. Particularly since your political and military genius calmed the troubles in Tianzhou. I know you once administered the region of Ganzhou, and I was delighted to see a copy of *Passing Through the Dayu Mountains* in your tent."

Wang Yangming was no fool: his old friend-turned-rival would not travel thousands of lis to speak of poetry and play Go. "*The world is my heart, my heart is the universe,*" Liu Xiangshan had professed in the Song dynasty, a doctrine which had inspired his own as the founder of the School of Mind. Applying it to the world of martial arts required the user to avoid being dependent on their eyes to examine their surroundings, and instead use their inner energy, which was capable of much greater acuity. For example, when he was tracking her, Gao Feng had made himself almost invisible to Shao Jun, but he had been unable to hide from her master, who had not relied on his eyes to discover him. This was what he was doing now, searching for attackers hidden here or there in the vegetation, but his "heart" confirmed what his sight and hearing had already suggested: he was well and truly alone with Zhang Yong. Even Qiu Ju, normally ever-present at his side, was absent from the scene. Was it possible that news of Luo Xiang's death had not yet reached the leader of the Eight Tigers? Caution was still warranted, because after the strait, their boat would enter the maritime area that the captain of the guard knew like the back of his hand from his years fighting bands of pirates.

"When this town was built," Zhang Yong said, "the lake of Precious Jade protected it from invasions. Today its people are oppressed. Peasants and farmers work the mountainsides. Young and old alike burn incense. Brother Yangming, no matter how much I do against these pirates, they still hold me at bay. I await troops returning from a long voyage, and they will be warmly welcomed."

He had quoted a passage from *Passing Through the Dayu Mountains* after reading it in Wang Yangming's tent. What a shame that such a brilliant man bore such dark intentions.

In the time when they were connected by bonds of friendship, they respected one another's differences, although one achieved his aims with benevolence and conciliation, and the other often resorted to torture to achieve his own. Their fraternity, while unofficial, had been cemented during a night of discussion between the three – Yang Yiqing had also been present – on the future of the empire and their common desire to see China become a haven for all, as it always should have been. As great thinkers, they were not so naïve as to believe that realizing such a dream would be easy, but each thought himself capable of guiding it to this destination if he were given the means, or if he seized them.

Even when Zhang Yong became the leader of the Eight Tigers, the age-old enemies of the Central Plain Brotherhood, Wang Yangming had still believed it possible to reconcile their visions, and why not, put an end to the conflict between their organizations at the same time. Sadly, he had lost all hope for this after the Great Rites controversy. Was today to be their last game?

"Why so quiet, Brother Yangming? Did I make a mistake in citing the poet?"

"No, on the contrary, I'm impressed by your memory. It commands respect. I was remembering the beginnings of our friendship, that was all."

"So, you imagine then that my visit is not a sudden whim, but a well-considered decision." The atmosphere suddenly became tense, and the Tiger's play style reflected the menace in his words. The counter he placed after speaking put his opponent on the back foot. But the latter was not so easily beaten: before responding, he placed a counter in defense.

"Ah! What troubles you, my dear Zhang?"

"What troubles me?" he chuckled before drinking a mouthful of tea. "The criminal Shao Jun!"

"Oh, you have news of the imperial favorite?"

Here Zhang Yong had used one of his favorite tricks to expose his enemies under the guise of discussion. He had suddenly cut straight to the heart of the matter to study the reaction of the person he spoke to. The Tiger's eyes were sharp and piercing, his gaze peeling the mask off his victims like a knife peels fruit. The slightest nervous tremor, the tiniest wrinkle of worry, and Wang Yangming would betray himself. But he too was a master, and controlling his emotions was one of his specialties. He gave nothing away, the victor in this silent and motionless duel. Even when he spoke, his voice had been as light as possible, as if the exposure of his protegee meant nothing to him. As if, and that was the message he wanted to communicate, there were no connection at all between them.

But Zhang Yong hadn't finished yet.

"Yes," he answered. "The whore is surprising. She was spotted a few days ago near the Xiaoling mausoleum, where she injured several people before being arrested. We executed her the same day."

"How unfortunate! It's a shame that Emperor Zhengde's former favorite has fallen so low."

"I agree. But she reaped what she sowed. If she had come quietly, she could have ended her days in an imperial prison camp. But her master will receive no such mercy."

The Tiger's voice had grown colder as he spoke.

"Her master?"

"But of course! Shao Jun grew up shut in the Forbidden City, she had never spent any meaningful time outside the palace before her disappearance. She had neither the resources nor the education needed to plan and implement the plot to assassinate the former Emperor on her own."

"But supposing this master exists, and also that they are so powerful, why would they choose to manipulate the imperial favorite?"

"Perhaps precisely because no one would be able to trace it back to him, or because she would achieve his aims, whatever they were. When Shao Jun disappeared, I ordered that all members of her clan be eliminated, but I always suspected that their mentor had escaped us. And now I'm certain."

"Have you tracked him down?"

"Gao Feng was killed by a sword thrust to the heart. I inspected his wound myself, and I'm sure that his killer stood between five foot five and five feet eight inches, just like you. Shao Jun is only five foot one, which suggests she didn't kill my disciple. It was her master who was responsible!"

"Oh? Wasn't Gao Feng's body found at Mount Wolong, behind Jishan University? The man you're looking for must have been through my establishment!"

"I think so too. Which was why I asked my best man to investigate all the men of this height at the university... Which was like looking for a needle in a haystack. However, when Wei Bin was killed, the number of suspects was significantly reduced."

"How so?"

"Because the bitch led him into a trap after finding out about the Record of Blood Spilt for a Righteous Cause at the Imperial Academy, then disarmed him using the magnetized palm of the Buddha of Healing in the Temple of the Understanding of Law. A plan whose only flaw was to be too brilliant: it could only have been concocted by someone of great scholarship, which ruled out the imperial favorite."

"My dear Zhang Yong, one might think you were leading up to accusing me."

A cold wind swept across the small boat. The leader of the

Eight Tigers caressed the pendant at his neck.

"Brother Yangming," he said, "you were one of the seven people I trusted the most, until I found this object on Shao Jun."

He placed the jade pendant on the table between them, the motif of waves and plants facing upwards.

"This pendant?" asked Wang Yangming.

Zhang Yong laughed coldly.

"No, this is mine," he responded.

He turned the small stone over to reveal that the other side was engraved with the character *Dao*. Their famous night of passionate discussion had begun with a debate over the opening passage of the *Zhongyong*: "*What Heaven confers is called 'nature'. Accordance with this nature is called the Dao. Cultivating the Dao is called 'education'.*"

Yang Yiqing had argued that people should conform to the nature conferred on them by Heaven at their birth, while Zhang Yong had been convinced that not only could nature be fought, but that it could not be accomplished painlessly. For Wang Yangming, only by increasing knowledge and its accessibility could humans overcome the limits of their nature. In his wisdom as the elder of the group, Yang Yiqing hoped that the three of them would be able to put aside their differences to work together for their shared objective and had thus had made three identical stones engraved with different characters to symbolize the bond which united them. That evening they had come to an agreement and agreed to eliminate Lin Jiu by having him accused of treason. The atmosphere at court changed immediately and dramatically, and the Ming empire prospered once more while Zhang Yong, up to then the discreet and unassuming Tiger, rose to lead the group and revealed the ferocity which had been bubbling under the surface. After Zhengde's death, the Great Rites controversy corrupted the spirit of their accomplishments as well as their relationships.

Gently caressing his pendant, Zhang Yong began to explain.

"Before being demoted to being a warden at the Xiaoling mausoleum, Chen Xijian was the steward of the Leopard Quarter. It was thus inevitable that Shao Jun would go to find him, and so I devised a trap for her. And it would have been a success if that wretched underling hadn't sought to take advantage of the situation when his kung-fu abilities didn't live up to his ambitions."

He looked Wang Yangming straight in the eyes.

"When the imperial favorite gutted him, she must have dropped the bloody pendant on him, and the engravings on the stone were printed on him like a stamp on the clothing of the dead. Looking at it closely, you could make out a motif of plants and waves. It was then I knew that my adversary was one of my closest friends."

"So that is what made you suspect me…"

"My doubts first turned towards Brother Yiqing, as it was in the fief of his young protege, the prince of Wei, that Shao Jun disappeared without a trace. However, when I visited him, he immediately showed me that he had his pendant. It was then I ordered Luo Xiang to leave for Tianzhou, but when I arrived myself, you had killed him too.

"Did you know that in some circles he was known as 'the man with three shadows?"

Behind his impassive façade Wang Yangming was on high alert. For Zhang Yong to so openly speak of his underhanded affairs, he must have almost no doubts left, and was ready to play his final cards. With the approach of the now near-inevitable confrontation, the tension was growing palpable.

"No, I didn't know this nickname. How did it come about?"

"He was one of a set of triplets who constantly exchanged roles. Surprising, isn't it?"

The question required no real answer, so the two men remained silent. Then, the leader of the Eight Tigers spoke with a mix of bitterness and weariness, "Brother Yangming, your greatness is equal to any king. Not even Brother Yiqing himself could live up to you. I know you consider both of us to be monsters completely lacking in human sentiment and emotion, but the affection I hold for you blinded me for so long. I never saw nor pursued the truth when I should have done because I denied it. Now my delusion is at an end. Your ability to remain impassive no matter the situation is worthy of both respect and admiration, but nothing is perfect: when I put my pendant on the table, your leg trembled very slightly, which rocked the boat almost imperceptibly and confirmed my suspicions."

There was nothing to add, so neither said any more. After a long sign, Zhang Yong continued.

"Brother Yangming, I'd like your opinion and advice on a poem I'm writing."

Before Emperor Xuande charged the Imperial Academy with teaching them, the eunuchs had not had the right to learn to read or write. Even now, while most could recognize a hundred basic characters and a handful were properly instructed, those that could be considered to be scholars were as rare as phoenix feathers. Wang Yangming had of course known that Zhang Yong was lettered, but not that he knew how to write.

"With pleasure," responded the mentor. "Should we abandon our game?"

"Not before we see who the victor is."

He placed another counter on the board, then said quietly, "Determination does not equal success after all."

Wang Yangming had long thought the opposite, convinced that his determination would be enough to save his friend from the darkness of his own soul, and it had taken the massacre during the Great Rites controversy to prove his error. The Tiger seemed to read him like an open book. He had left no escape route, either on the Go board and or this conversation. It was no longer a question of knowing if he would close the trap, but when. Unexpectedly, he chose that moment to sing his poem in a rough voice.

"Youth is driven by the winds of ambition; with age all that remains is a violent breeze."

As he declaimed it, he traced the character for violent on the table, made from the hardest jujube wood. Then, as if the varnished surface were being struck by the carpenter's chisel, chips of wood suddenly began to fly in all directions and the teapot vibrated to the rhythm of the lines and dots. The speed of Zhang Yong's precise gestures sent his wide sleeves flying as if in a silent breeze, which had no effect on Wang Yangming, who remained as unperturbed as ever. In trust, the lines weren't particularly profound. Their rhythm and structure were correct, and they could have been presented by a candidate for the imperial exams, but that was the extent of their merit.

"My dear Zhang," he said simply, "you have an admirable talent for poetry."

While Zhang Yong's martial arts were intrinsically Buddhist, his own spirituality was yelikewen, a Christian faith painfully imported to China in the twenty-sixth year of the Yuan dynasty by the Jesuit Jean de Montecorvino and which had not been welcomed by the Nestorians, who had been present in the East since the Tang dynasty. The latter, who counted the descendants of Genghis Khan among their ranks, considered the yelikewens to be even more dangerous heretics than the Buddhists, and had quickly persecuted and exterminated them, before disappearing in their turn during the fall of the Yuans. Between his arrival in China and his death, Jean de Montecorvino been proclaimed bishop of Cambaluc – the old name for Beijing – and had been emulated in the highest spheres of power. His faith persisted over the generations, particularly among idealistic eunuchs like Zhang Yong, who claimed to be Templars with aspirations such as reviving the legendary order of holy knights.

By studying the many Taoists works contained in the Imperial Academy, he had discovered that the way of the heart practiced by Wang Yangming had common origins with a tantric kundalini technique taught by Singgibandan, the *Fire of the lotus*. He had then spent over a decade perfecting his mastery of the technique at each of its various stages: *hidden, inflamed, bright, obscure,* and *invisible*. And so, while the two men's philosophies were entirely opposed in some areas, their respective preferred internal energy techniques were actually from the same source, which made their confrontation especially fierce. It was invisible, and an uninformed spectator would have seen only two elderly scholars absorbed by their game of Go. In reality, while they played, Zhang Yong repeated a meditative mantra to himself – "Fluid as water, burning like fire, the mountain sheep walks without leaving a trace" – and on each repetition unleashed waves of *neigong* towards his adversary, who would have exploded on the inside if he hadn't used the way of the heart to protect himself. The counter was just as ferocious, and sorely taxed Wang Yangming's reserves of strength. Nonetheless, he in turn placed a counter as if nothing was wrong.

"Brother Yangming," Zhang Yong said, "compared to you, I'm not worth a Buddha's fart. I shoot my bow time after time, but each arrow I shoot only serves to further expose my deficiency."

Expression dark, face streaming with sweat, he began to engrave the eight lines of *Passing Through the Dayu Mountains* on the table with the tip of his finger. For once, events were proceeding as he had planned. His opponent's power was far beyond what he had expected, and if he continued to push so hard, he might cause his own downfall by exhausting his own resources. Yet he had to persevere, he had come too far to stop now. His face creased, and he seemed on the verge of coughing up blood. When he arrived at the end of the poem, he was visibly confused. His mind needed a tether in order to stay grounded. He began to write the character *resolve* on the table, and, without ceasing etching the wood with his right index finger, with his left hand he picked up a counter and slowly moved to place it on the board. When his hand was above the square he planned to occupy, he found he was unable to release the stone. Paralyzed by the effort, his body refused to let go.

Wang Yangming weathered the storm with exemplary stoicism. He maintained his calm even when the tumult of the energies on the boat seemed to affect the atmosphere around the two men, draining it of color as if under the light of the moon. To him it was clear that his adversary, by attempting to write and play Go at the same time as attacking, was dividing his attention and depriving himself of the stability required for a *neigong* battle of this magnitude. His breathing was ragged, and his waves of energy increasingly irregular; Wang Yangming could have defeated him in the blink of an eye if he had wanted to take advantage of these interruptions to launch counter attacks. Only his sentimentality prevented him from doing so. In any case, it could not be clearer that *Fire of the lotus* would not be enough to overcome the way of the heart.

Zhang Yong clenched his teeth and slammed his counter down. *Crack!* His imperfect control of the strength of his motion caused him to punch a gaping hole in the Chinese pine of the table beneath the board. The counters flew in all directions and clattered onto the deck of the boat. In losing control, he had no choice but to gather his remaining energy and release it in a final attack which would put an end to this battle between titans, one way or another. His internal wounds were growing more serious, and he knew he was losing, but refused to accept defeat without pushing himself to the ends of his abilities. Wang Yangming however, still displayed the same intolerable serenity as he had throughout their entire fight.

"Really, my dear Zhang," he said quietly, "does this game of Go merit such suffering?"

A drop of blood formed at the edge of Zhang Yong's mouth.

"Brother Yangming," he gasped, "your entire life you thought you were striving for good. It's a delusion, each light casts its own shadow. Even if I die, a part of me will live on forever. You lost this fight before it even began."

CHAPTER 15

What had happened to the master?

Shao Jun's heart felt like it would explode, like that of the horse beneath her that was breathing heavily and trembling with exhaustion. Despite being mad with worry, the young woman knew that she needed to stay calm, keep a clear head, and make the right decision. She stopped her mount and looked around.

Wang Yangming always had his troops camp a good distance from villages on their route to avoid troubling the inhabitants, so he was unlikely to be in Huanglong. On the other hand, he could be at the Buddhist temple in Lingyan, nestled in the valley to the west of the town. It would take Shao Jun some time to get there given the state of her horse, and she wouldn't be able to make it back to the camp before nightfall. The entire day would be wasted if she went the wrong way.

Wang Yangming had visited this temple around twelve years before, just after he was named inspector general of Nan'an, Ganzhou, Tingzhou, and Zhangzhou. He was immediately approached by a priest who told him an incredible story: at the end of his life, a high-ranking monk had predicted that his reincarnation would erect a pagoda there in his memory half a century later. When he heard this tale the monk had been dead for exactly fifty years, and he had looked exactly like Wang Yangming! Intrigued, the latter asked them to open the room in which the author of this singular prophecy had died, and found a corpse who could have been his twin sitting in a Buddha pose. Impressed, he acquiesced to the old monk's will and had a pagoda built on the site, then composed this poem:

A half-century later, I open a door that another self had closed.
The mind remembers what the body forgets; Buddha guides us in all things.

When Shao Jun heard this unusual story, she had asked her master if he really thought he was the reincarnation of the deceased monk, and he had answered that some mysteries would always be beyond conventional understanding. Of course, the priest had set the scene hoping to extract money from him for the construction of the pagoda, and if in doubt it was always better to avoid angering the dead. And to prevent any future problems, he had decided never to return to the temple… The young woman concluded that there would be little chance of finding him there. So where to look?

Exhausted and foaming at the mouth, her mount whinnied plaintively, as if complaining about being so mistreated by its rider. She realized she hadn't allowed her mount to drink for some time, so she dismounted and led the horse to the riverbank. There, a young man called to her, standing next to a well with a bucket of water on each arm.

"That water isn't clean enough for such a wonderful horse," he called out, "let it drink here!"

"Thank you, big brother!" Shao Jun responded, clasping her hands in front of her chest.

The man had a distinguished air despite the deplorable state of his tunic. He generously offered her horse one of his buckets of water, which quickly plunged its head in and drank deeply.

"It'll make you wet, big brother," the young woman said. "You don't have to…"

"It's no problem! But tell me, steward, did you arrive with Mr Wang Yangming's garrison?"

The mention of her mentor's name took her by surprise.

"Why?" she wondered.

"You look like part of Mr Wang Yangming's entourage! Once, I was bold enough to attend one of his lessons in the town, but I wasn't educated enough to understand everything… Do you know if he plans to give another lecture? I'd love to listen to him again, even if I don't understand all of it!"

Shao Jun was moved to see the young villager speak of education and culture with such fervor and burning passion in his eyes.

"Yes," she answered, "I'm looking for him. I'll ask when I find him."

"Oh, I just saw him! He was on a small boat; he must have been travelling to see the red-leaved trees downstream."

"You saw him?"

"Yes, around two lis further down the river, near Emerald Dragon pass. At this time of year, the maples look as if they're on fire, it's very beautiful…"

There was no time to lose: the young woman leapt onto her

horse and spurred it to a gallop in the direction indicated by the villager. He stood there, indignant at her rudeness as she sped off.

Emerald Dragon pass was only two lis away, a distance her horse covered in less time that it took to say the name. As she left Huanglong the earthen track was bordered by luxuriant trees whose leaves were reflected in the river as far as the eye could see, like a long, undulating dragon. While it was emerald in spring and summer, at the turn of the season it took on the fiery hues of fall. Shao Jun saw a small boat with a black sail, three meters long at most, floating gently near the left bank.

She didn't dare act immediately. If Master Yangming and Zhang Yong really were there, they weren't visibly fighting. The young woman led her horse to the edge of the water to better observe the scene. Four men immediately surged out of the water, violently breaking the smooth surface. They rushed towards the boat, then one of them was launched towards the bank as if struck a sudden blow. *Splash*! He hit the water like a sack of bricks and floated to the surface a few seconds later… before suddenly stirring and swimming back towards the boat at speed. The awning on the boat went flying, revealing its occupants: a small, stocky figure, and a larger one… Zhang Yong and Wang Yangming! The first was in the bow and the other in the stern, cornered by three disarmed attackers he kept comfortably at bay with his sword.

What was happening? Everything Shao Jun had just seen seemed inconceivable. Despairing, she decided to join the fight. She spurred her horse and pulled back on the reins. The beast neighed, reared, and bounded towards the river, where it quickly sank six feet into the water. Drawing level with the man with the superhuman abilities who had crashed near her a few seconds earlier, Shao Jun leapt from the saddle and threw herself on him, stretching her rope around his neck to strangle him. Despite this he was unperturbed and continued to swim towards the boat as if he hadn't even noticed. When he jumped aboard just behind Wang Yangming, the young woman was still on his back, hands clenched around her sinew and silk rope, feet pressed against her victim's back for leverage, but nothing happened – by this point any normal man would have a broken neck or his throat ripped open. The mentor was facing a similar problem: despite hitting the mark every time, none of his blows seemed to affect his opponents.

Shao Jun's left boot had a hidden blade which she had never used, given to her by the mentor some time before. It was difficult to wield and the idea itself seemed too underhanded for her liking, but given the situation, its use seemed completely appropriate. She rotated her ankle sharply and ejected the blade with a *cling!*, thrusting it into the man's neck with all her strength. She'd aimed for the dazhui, an acupuncture point located in the hollow of the seventh cervical, which usually caused loss of consciousness when struck. Unfortunately, the steel barely penetrated halfway into his rock-hard skin, and while blood ran from the wound, the superhuman brute continued to move towards the mentor.

Wang Yangming was already occupied by the three combatants facing him, and the strangeness of the situation disturbed him. The way of the heart allowed him to detect a mosquito at ten meters or a leaf swirling far behind him in the wind, so why hadn't he been able to detect the presence of four men just meters away under the water? How had they held their breath for so long? No kung-fu technique had such power. The phenomenon was beyond his comprehension despite his vast knowledge, as was the complete indifference the fighters showed as they allowed themselves to be stabbed and slashed all over, seemingly unaffected by their wounds. If they had used the *Golden mask* and *Iron shirt* techniques, he would have been able to respond appropriately, but their supernatural resistance seemed part of them, and not the result of any training or skill. His sword was useless against such adversaries.

Using one of his most destructive techniques, he plunged his sword into the shangzong point – or sea of breath, in the center of the chest – of one of the combatants and sent subtle vibrations through it. In doing so, he blocked the internal energies as the tip oscillated to maximize damage to the vital organs; if the victim survived, he should at least be incapable of moving or breathing until he received treatment. Perfected over long years of practice, Wang Yangming's swordsmanship had allowed him to achieve a style that was both strong and flexible, as fast as lightning and more terrible than thunder. Unfortunately, the devastating technique had no effect on his opponent, and worse, the blade remained trapped in his body!

Suddenly deprived of his weapon and dumbfounded by the terrifying phenomenon he had just witnessed, the mentor's attention briefly lapsed, and he took a powerful blow to the chest. The breath was knocked from his lungs. He had no time to recover from the shock as *thump!*, the man Shao Jun was vainly trying to control behind him gave him a powerful slap on the back. It sent him flying forward straight towards a dark shadow slipping between the three giants to brutally assault him with a punch to the chest. Wang Yangming had inherited the miraculous powers of Mount Kailash kung-fu thanks to his way of the heart, including the ability to withstand almost any hit struck by normal martial artists. But the attacker was Zhang Yong, and Zhang Yong was no average martial artist.

The Tiger had needed a few seconds after losing the inner energy battle to gather his strength, regain his breath, and reevaluate the situation, only possible thanks to the intervention of his four yuxiao – his tireless soldiers. He had known that the meeting would end in a fight if, as his growing suspicions suggested, his old friend was revealed to be the mentor of the Central Plain Brotherhood. He had left behind his palanquin carriers and even his loyal Qiu Ju to avoid raising suspicion, accompanied only by his four yuxiao which were undetectable even to the greatest masters. And for good reason: they didn't need to breathe. And though they were still imperfect and used only around a hundredth of their potential, they were still more powerful than any ordinary human.

He had been annoyed to recognize Shao Jun on the riverbank. After the failed assassination attempt in Tianzhou, he had sent Ju and Luo Xiang to lay a trap while he interrogated her master. The young woman's presence here suggested that the two other Tigers were dead. "Damned imperial whore!" he growled into his beard. He needed to act quickly and decisively if he were to avoid risking his plans any further. While Wang Yangming was occupied with the yuxiao, Zhang Yong noticed that he seemed to pay special attention to protecting his chest. From this he correctly deduced that Luo Xiang had successfully wounded him in Tianzhou, despite the failure of the mission. It was a weakness that could be exploited.

When the captain of the guard had realized the mentor of

the Brotherhood still lived, he'd initially had five main suspects, including his two old friends with the jade pendants. He had only focused on them after examining Chen Xijian's corpse, particularly the small splash of incriminating blood on his clothing. After that, all he had needed to do was isolate them by using his political power to assign them military missions, then visit them when they were at their most vulnerable. Despite being uncertain as to his enemy's true identity, his determination to rid himself of the mentor was such that he had sent Luo Xiang to assassinate Wang Yangming while he himself was on his way to meet Yang Yiqing. He had been prepared to mistakenly kill an old friend and live with that weight on his conscience. Besides, their methods were so different that it was inevitable they would face one another in unpleasant circumstances one day.

Until then, no one of importance had known that Luo Xiang was three separate men. Each of the brothers had a special quality: one was a skilled swordsman, the next had powerful inner energy, and the last was a master of disguise. They generally avoided showing themselves in public so as to maintain their secret, but the attacks they carried out together were always a success – which was why they had become the ace up their master's sleeve, the card he would play as a last resort. He had already cleared Yang Yiqing of guilt when he received the message telling him that two of the brothers were dead and had decided to solve the problem himself. He was certain now: he could never put an end to Wang Yangming on his own, but the latter was cornered, and his defensive movements suggested that the assassins in Tianzhou had at least managed to injure him. Zhang Yong broke into laughter. How ironic that such a formidable opponent would be betrayed by such a small detail!

The mentor of the School of Mind could use the way of the heart to instantly protect any part of his body that he focused on, but it demanded considerable concentration which was difficult to maintain during combat. After he was hit by the two successive blows, his internal energy barrier momentarily disappeared. It was at that precise moment that his adversary inflicted a powerful palm strike on the exact spot where he was injured by Luo Xiang several days earlier.

Crack! Three of his ribs broke. Spurred by his success, the leader of the Tigers repeated the strike with his right hand mercilessly and at tremendous speed, while his left reached for the small package that hung at his victim's waist. He almost couldn't contain his excitement as his fingers closed around it; after all the years of searching and fighting, the Precursor Box would finally be his! But his excitement was short-lived. Steel flashed in front of his face, forcing him to jump back to avoid being sliced in two.

Shao Jun had leapt to her master's defense, striking a blow with the blade attached to her boot.

After being hit in the back, Wang Yangming had thrown the half-strangled yuxiao with the neck wound into the water, apparently managing to incapacitate it for good – its inert body now floated on the surface of the river. The young woman took it upon herself to face, or at least occupy Zhang Yong to gain Wang Yangming a respite, which he sorely needed now his ribs were broken. Her attack was so fast and precise that she managed a shallow cut on the leader of the Tigers' forehead, from which a narrow stream of blood began to run. He was amazed to realize that he had greatly underestimated the former imperial favorite.

Until then, he had considered her to be a simple decoy, a means to reach his adversary, but it was clear that she was a skilled fighter in her own right. She had got the better of Wei Bin, the last of the Luo Xiangs, and Qiu Ju. Despite her youth and slim stature, her victories spoke for themselves. Zhang Yong very rarely encountered adversaries of her caliber, but here she was. A murderous gleam entered his gaze. It was an unlooked-for opportunity to kill two birds with one stone by ridding himself of both people most likely to revive the Brotherhood.

While the young woman didn't lack in courage, she lacked confidence, which was not helpful in this extraordinary fight. The boat was unstable, the superhuman strength of the men that had emerged from the water a huge source of worry, and her weapon was under her horse's saddle again… but when the yuxiao stabbed by Wang Yangming sent a punch towards her, she surprised it by parrying with little difficulty. She absorbed the impact and seized the guard of the sword in her adversary's chest. Pressing her foot against its body for leverage, she pulled on the sword to release the weapon from the vice of flesh, muscles, and bone. Behind her, her master succumbed to exhaustion and passed out. The situation was becoming increasing desperate. She kicked out with such power that the heel of her boot sank into the yuxiao's ribcage with a sickening crunch. It was thrown backwards into the water as the blade was finally freed.

Sword in hand, Shao Jun felt her courage swell. She was surprised to be so easily rid of the monster when the one she tried to strangle had given her so much trouble, but now wasn't the time to stop and think. A metallic whistle rang out, and one of the two superhuman warriors still on the boat quickly jumped into the river as if responding to a signal. Even more surprisingly, Zhang Yong jumped onto its back, then they rushed away from the boat at high speed thanks to the yuxiao's swimming skills. It made no sense. Wang Yangming was hovering between life and death, and the Tiger had undoubtedly held the upper hand. Why flee instead of finishing off his opponent? She had no chance to pursue them, because the single warrior remaining on the boat launched itself at her, face inexpressive and body gleaming like a demon.

The young woman didn't know what these inhuman monsters were, but she was determined to use every tool at her disposal. She nimbly dodged its charge, using the railing to pivot, then brought her sword down to slash at its shoulder with all the strength she could muster. The blade sliced through the fighter's flesh and severed its spine at the base of the neck. Not even the strongest man could survive such an injury. Its arms flailed for a moment, then it stiffened and fell backward into the water.

Upstream, Zhang Yong had nearly reached the bank, too far away for any pursuit. At the beginning of the ferocious battle the young woman had believed the four colossi were identical, but she realized that she had been mistaken. The one she had just killed hadn't caused her any great difficulty, while the first she had attacked had seemed invincible. Despite their varying levels of resilience, their numbers and considerable toughness combined with the leader of the Tigers, had been enough to seriously injure Master Yangming.

She approached him and rested her hand on his back to transfer some of her own inner energy to him. The technique was even more effective because they both practiced the way of the heart, and little by little, the mentor's near-empty chenmai meridian regained some semblance of vitality. However, when he opened his eyes, his pallid skin and feverish tremors sent his pupil spiraling into the depths of sorrow.

"Young girl ..." he murmured.

"Master..."

He sat up and tidied his clothing.

"I am not worthy of your trust, young girl. I am deeply sorry."

Shao Jun then understood that Zhang Yong had stolen the Precursor Box, the box she entrusted to her master for safekeeping. The young woman grabbed the boat's oars.

"Don't speak such nonsense. I need to get you to a doctor."

"No, young girl. It's no use ..."

The response was soft but firm. Final.

Further up the river, the yuxiao carrying Zhang Yong stopped swimming five or six feet from the bank and sank down into the water. The leader of the Tigers jumped for the bank, but the warrior, who was at the end of its strength and would soon be stiff as a corpse, made for an unstable platform. He landed several feet from the bank and had to walk to reach it, the bottom of his robe wet and both boots soaked. Standing in the grass, he could still see the small boat one li away. It seemed even more dilapidated from this distance.

Brother Yangming had been caught in his own trap.

Zhang Yong had finally acquired the Precursor Box and vanquished his enemy. Instead of rejoicing at what seemed to be a crushing victory, he felt as empty as if he had failed. All his yuxiao were dead, he had failed to kill the imperial favorite, and he had fled as soon as he grabbed the box to avoiding losing a fight against her. He was also painfully away that he would never have been able to beat his old friend without resorting to trickery. He had lost the game of Go, but the shadow of the Brotherhood continued to loom large over the leader of the Tiger's plans. Full of bitterness, he turned. He heard Shao Jun calling her horse as he moved further away.

Horse and rider had bonded over their long journey together. When she leapt into the water from its saddle, the destrier had returned to the riverbank and patiently waited. She called it, and her mount leapt into the river to meet her as she swam, returning to the bank together. There, the young woman set her heels to its sides to set off at a gallop. She had to force herself not to turn around, because she knew that the agonizing sight of her master alone on the boat would snap the narrow thread of determination she was clinging onto.

As for Wang Yangming, he bid her one last farewell.

He began to cough up blood, staining the front of his clothing red. That final blow had damaged his heart, and he knew his time had come. He had tried to remain as calm and dignified as possible in front of his beloved pupil, but now she was gone, he could finally let go. As the life drained out of him, he remembered the Lingyan temple nestled in the mountains. In the poem he composed at the time, he had written "I open a door that another self closed". Now it was his turn to retire. With a final effort, he picked up a white counter lying near him. It was the last one remaining on the boat, all the others having been knocked into the water along with the board. It was strange to think that only a short while before this small vessel held nothing but two friends playing an innocent game of Go, like the good old days. He finally took the time to read the poem Zhang Yong had carved into the table:

Youth is driven by the winds of ambition;
with age all that remains is a violent breeze.
Metal horses scattered across the border passes,
flags waving under the oceans. My path is obstructed
by a parade of profiteers;
supremacy by the sword,
all nations at my feet.

A poem just as aggressive and proud as its author. Wang Yangming's mind returned once more to their night of discussion in the company of Yang Yiqing. Zhang Yong argued that world conquest went hand in hand with pacifying the country, while the master of the School of Mind saw the intelligence of the people as the solution to all ills. How could the path to nirvana be through a sea of blood? It was chilling to think that a man who held such beliefs was now close to realizing his vision.

"My dear Zhang," he said aloud, "the darkness gives way to light. You may have won this time, but the game is not over yet. Someone else has already taken my place, and I know she will get the better of you."

The thought made him smile. The white counter dropped from his hand into the river, breaking the surface for a moment before the water stilled once more.

CHAPTER 16

Yu Dayong didn't like women, but he did like to eat. His position as governor of Nanjing was a walk in the park, allowing him all the comforts he could expect from one of the empire's two capitals. He had been worried about travelling to Macau which he imagined as a vast mosquito and snake-infested swamp, but had been pleasantly surprised by the culinary specialties of this fishing village.

He lifted a small piece of still-sizzling roast goose to his lips and savored its flavor. His entire body relaxed as he sighed with pleasure. It was impossible to find this kind of food in southern China. The geese of Macau spent their days pecking at crustaceans and small fish on the beach, which gave their flesh a unique taste that was all its own. Once killed and plucked, the animal was covered in honey and roasted over a fire fed with kiwi wood, then left to marinate in plum puree. It was his faithful Mai Bing who always took charge of preparing this meal for him. Unfortunately, the supplier who normally provided it had encountered a problem, and he had been forced to hastily resort to less qualified, but less busy providers. There was a clear difference in the quality of the meal.

He was interrupted by a sudden gust of wind as the door swung open. Yu Dayong allowed no one to disturb him as he ate; his subordinates were required to knock three times and wait for permission to enter even if they brought urgent news. He leapt to his feet in a fury, ready to launch a stream of invectives, but stopped himself when he saw his visitor.

"Venerable captain general!" he greeted him, bowing.

While he hadn't expected Zhang Yong until the next day, he was particularly surprised by his disheveled appearance, sweating face, and pale complexion. He had never seen the leader of the Tigers, a man normally so collected and impeccably attired, look so defeated.

"Venerable Uncle Zhang, what brings you here so soon?"

"Yu the Cruel, prepare to set sail."

Zhang Yong spoke in a rasping voice that betrayed the magnitude of the internal wounds he had suffered. Nervous and agitated, he looked all around him, checking each corner of the room as if he expected to find a threat hiding there.

"Venerable captain general, the meal has barely begun ..."

"It doesn't matter. We must reach the Dai Yu island without delay."

"Very well, venerable captain. Follow me."

Macao was a small peninsula, but the Portuguese man Pyros had fallen in love with its estuary the moment he laid eyes on it. Yu Dayong had driven out the dozen fishing families who lived there, and the port was now reserved for exclusive use by the Tigers and their allies. Since they didn't expect to leave until the next morning, the sailors were relaxing alongside their large junk, bragging about their exploits at sea. Their leader, Feng Renxiao, sharply interrupted their chatter as soon as he saw their employers arrive.

"Uncle Zhang, Uncle Yu," he said, hastening to greet them, "please accept my humble greetings."

"Prepare your men, Renxiao," Yu Dayong ordered. "We leave as soon as you are ready."

The sailor didn't like the authoritarian tone and the airs and graces of these soft-faced dignitaries, but he knew his place and simply bowed deeply.

"Understood." He turned to his men, "Hurry up, prepare to weigh anchor!"

The crew quickly got to work on the boat, a Fujian merchant junk around twenty meters in length, which could also be used a warship thanks to its pointed prow and wide poop. In the time of Emperor Yongle, the ships used by Admiral Zhenghe and his fleet to navigate the western seas measured over a hundred meters and held just as many men. Far from being a noble commanding a fleet, Feng Renxiao had as good as grown up on a junk in Fujian and had under his command a group of lively and agile sailors who had served him for years. They unfurled the sails and raised the anchor with confident and precise movements, difficult maneuvers which had become second nature to them. As soon as the Tigers were seated in the cabin, the junk set out to sea.

Zhang Yong looked around, massaged his chest, and let out a long sigh. Yu Dayong had never seen him in such a state. He knew his superior wielded a sword better than he and even better than Wei Bin. His inner strength was also known to be almost inexhaustible. Who could have injured him so?

"Yu," the captain said quietly, "please inspect the junk. Ensure no stowaways have slipped aboard. And be meticulous, I want everywhere searched with a fine-toothed comb."

While he found the order completely stupid and senseless – it was impossible for anyone to have sneaked on board –, the governor acquiesced and bowed deeply before leaving the cabin.

At the ship's wheel he asked Reng Renxiao to give him two men to accompany him belowdecks, which he found to be completely empty; in the absence of trade goods, it contained only a few provisions for the journey. The top deck housed the luxurious main cabin, those of the sailors, and a small storage area for miscellaneous equipment. None of these rooms contained anything suspect. And the entire top deck could be easily examined with a single glance. His inspection completed, he returned to knock on Zhang Yong's cabin door.

"Venerable captain," he called, "I've inspected the ship from top to bottom, and there is nothing to report."

"Enter!"

Yu Dayong entered and found his master sat at the table, staring ecstatically at a small parcel he had placed there.

"Venerable captain?"

"Open the package, Yu."

The Tiger quivered, then untied the string and parted the fabric to reveal an ancient box that looked nothing like a traditional Chinese box.

"Venerable captain, what is it?" he asked uncertainly.

"It's the object Pyros spoke of."

The Precursor Box! He had heard much about it, but he had never expected it to look like this. The Templars, of whom

Pyros was one, and the Brotherhood had been fighting over this box for almost a thousand years.

"V- Venerable captain, you found the imperial favorite?"

They knew from a reliable source that the box had passed through Ezio Auditore's hands, and had guessed that he passed it on to the last person he saw before his death: Shao Jun. Their suspicions were confirmed when she requested a copy of the *Record of Blood Spilt,* which mentioned the box, at the Imperial Academy. So, had Zhang Yong faced her?

"The whore escaped me," growled the latter. "But if I can deal with her mentor, I can easily deal with her as well."

Yu Dayong was stunned. So, his superior had finally discovered the identity of their mysterious adversary, the distinguished figure of the Brotherhood who had moved in the shadows since the Great Rites controversy.

"Venerable captain, who was the mentor?" he asked.

"It was Wang Yangming. But don't worry, he's history now."

Wang Yangming! Who would have believed it? And Zhang Yong had killed him? What terrible news. The man had been the greatest scholar of their time, so his death would have repercussions on many levels. To start with, the reputation of the leader of the Tigers would be greatly affected, with civilians and the military alike, as well as with imperial dignitaries, many of whom liked the character, scholarship, and fine mind of Jishan university's director. They would never forgive his murderer, whether or not they had the power to act against him. As for himself, Yu Dayong knew that his position depended on his master's influence; if it waned, he would suffer too.

"I probably killed Wang Yangming, but Shao Jun was the only witness. The whore only survived because of my injuries and the inadequacy of my four yuxiao." He laughed cruelly. "Don't worry, I'll get rid of her in the end."

"I didn't doubt it for a moment, venerable captain general."

Even if Shao Jun had followed the trail of the leader of the Tigers, she would hit a dead end at the port, Yu Dayong reassured himself. Thinking of Macau reminded him of his loyal Mai Bing and all the food that would have to be thrown away, filling him with bitterness.

"Venerable captain," he said, repackaging the box, "you should get some rest. I'll return to inspecting the ship."

After taking his leave and exiting the cabin with Zhang Yong's permission, he let out a long, silent sigh. He was too worried to rejoice in the death of their greatest enemy. In his eyes, it would have been easy for them to capture Shao Jun on her return to China if they had thrown all their forces at her. Instead, their leader launched a secret personal campaign to discover the Brotherhood's surviving mentor. He had used Gao Feng and Wei Bin as bait to achieve his goal, not even warning that it could mean their death. It appeared to be a logical continuation of the implacable coldness with which he had previously betrayed Liu Jin and taken his place. Yu Dayong feared for his future. Would it soon be his turn to be sacrificed in the name of some unknown machination? After all, they did say that the greyhound loses its value when the hare is dead. He would have to find some way to continue being useful in order to stay alive.

Feng Renxiao hurried towards him, visibly upset.

"Uncle Yu," he said, "I must tell you something."

"What?"

"We're facing a bad headwind... and looking at the sky, it will only get worse..."

"Do we risk the ship sinking?"

"If we continue towards Dai Yu island, it will end badly. I highly recommend that we anchor off Guimen reef and wait until the winds are more favorable."

The sailor hadn't been able to plan for this situation in advance because, out of caution, Zhang Yong had led him to believe that they were travelling towards the Philippines, only informing him of their real destination once they were at sea. Nonetheless, Yu Dayong gave great credit to his skill, thanking him for the warning with the intention of sincerely considering his recommendation. Guimen reef, a miniscule islet of around three hundred meters around on which not even a single blade of grass grew, was halfway between Macau and Dai Yu. During his twelve previous journeys along this sea route, the Tiger been forced to shelter there against the wind and rain on two occasions. Last time he'd been forced to wait there for three days. On the quarterdeck he looked up at the sky, seeing for himself that the weather was indeed particularly bad.

"How much will we be delayed if we stop?" he asked.

"The wind will probably blow until tomorrow; it will take some time to calm. Under those conditions, we could set off again on the day after tomorrow and make landfall two days later."

Yu Dayong thought for a moment.

"The plans of man are nothing before that of the Heavens. I will inform Uncle Zhang of the situation. Set course for Guimen while we await his decision!"

Feng Renxiao's seafaring skills were such that when Zhang Yong was informed of the need to stop, the junk had already arrived at the reef. *Guimen* meant "demon gate", but really it was a very ordinary small and rocky isle which would have made a good port if its dimensions had been less modest and it had a fresh water source. Feng Renxiao had barely lowered the anchor and moored the ship when the wind roared its fury and unleashed itself upon the sea. The ship's beam allowed it to ride the surf better than narrower ships, but it was still tossed about by the increasingly large waves. Even though it was not his first sea voyage, Yu Dayong had rarely experienced pitching on this scale.

Concerned for Zhang Yong's ability to endure this discomfort in his condition, he rushed towards his cabin only to find him sitting quietly on his bench looking completely relaxed. Had he recovered? He didn't dare ask, and quietly retreated to allow him to rest. The sailors had also stopped work and retired to their quarters. Only Feng Renxiao remained in the wheelhouse to maintain a presence at the wheel throughout the night. Neither the wind nor the swell bothered the man, who had spent his life at sea and dozed peacefully on his seat in the darkness of the starless night.

Two hours after the junk left, three men escorting a dozen young girls arrived at the port. It was Mai Bing, Yu Dayong's subordinate, and two other eunuchs bringing new slaves aged from fifteen to thirty years old back to their camp. With their wrists tied together and roped into a single column, their faces were all covered in tears.

Yu Dayong had become involved in human trafficking to meet the demands of the Flemish on Lusong island who needed qualified craftspeople and women. Always keen to make new allies, the Tiger had acceded to their request and had regularly brought slaves for them from Nanyang ever since. While he initially communicated with them directly, he soon began to communicate exclusively through Pyros, who served as their intermediary. Two years earlier, when the famine ended and nearby villages no longer had any need to sell their children, he had been forced to resort to the Iron Sharks gang to kidnap girls and ensure a regular flow of merchandise. The ones who just arrived in Macau had been kidnapped during a celebration at the temple of Mazu. Yu Dayong wouldn't call himself a slaver as such because he had only one customer, but his trafficking had eventually become public, earning him the nickname "the Cruel".

Mai Bing walked along cheerfully. This type of trade became more difficult to sustain as time went on, as the local population didn't replenish quickly enough, so he congratulated himself for being lucky enough to score twelve beauties at once. Uncle Yu would certainly be pleased, as would the Flemish who would soon arrive by sea.

"Uncle Mai," cried A-Cai, one of the eunuchs in his escort, "the junk is no longer in the port!"

Mai Bing's jovial mood evaporated. He knew his master well enough that only an extremely serious situation could have distracted him from his lucrative trade with the Flemish, and the girls he had been about to deliver to them would have been worth their weight in coin. The small building used by the sailors also seemed exceptionally quiet. There was no doubt: the ship and its crew had weighed anchor.

"A-Cai, go check if Uncle Yu is home," he ordered.

A-Cai cursed his ancestors to the eighteenth generation. Their master hated to be disturbed and could exact severe penalties against anyone who bothered him, particularly if he was eating. The eunuch was obliged to obey nonetheless, so he knocked on the door as gently as possible.

"Uncle Yu, are you there?" he called hesitantly.

There was no response, but he heard someone moving inside to open the door. When it opened, he was surprised to see that it was not Yu Dayong. He had no time to consider this incongruity though, as a blade pierced his chest as the door swung on its hinges.

Shao Jun stood before him in the doorway.

Following Zhang Yong's trail, she'd arrived only a short while before and just missed him. Seeing Yu Dayong's men in the distance heading in the direction of the port, she'd decided to hide in the pavilion and lie in wait. She had no desire to become a cold-blooded killer, but the Tigers had assassinated her masters and hunted her as far as Europe, leaving her little choice in the matter. These ones were also involved in despicable slavery, which counted against them. And anyway, there were too many of them for her to allow herself any misgivings. As soon as the first fell, the second advanced on her, pulling a weapon from his sleeve. His throat was sliced through with a great gout of blood before he was even able to draw his sword. The young woman was merciful, stabbing him through the heart to finish him as he began to drown in his own blood, hands vainly clawing at his throat.

Retreating slightly, Mai Bing was caught off guard. At first he had waited with wicked anticipation to see A-Cai severely reprimanded by their master, but he was filled with terror when he saw his subordinate collapse to reveal Shao Jun. Over his time with Yu Dayong, he had learned the basics of kung-fu, but had no illusion as to his ability to fight the former imperial favorite. Had she killed his master? Behind him, the kidnapped girls began to scream, sending him into complete panic. Legs trembling, he fell to his knees and repeatedly pressed his forehead to the ground.

"Miss Favorite, please..."

His pathetic appearance quelled Shao Jun's anger slightly. If the eunuch had drawn his sword instead, she would have attached him without thinking. On the other hand, the idea of taking the life of a man who didn't fight back, repulsive though he was, disgusted her. She wiped her sword clean on one of the bodies and spoke with an icy calm.

"Uncle Mai, you look as well as when we last met."

Shao Jun's calm disturbed Mai Bing even more: used to Yu Dayong's fierce character, he was well aware that when someone spoke gently to an inferior who had erred, it could only mean that a terrible punishment was coming. Thinking Shao Jun would behave likewise, he felt ready to faint and banged his head harder against the ground as he redoubled his pleas.

"Miss Favorite, I was only acting on Uncle Yu's orders... Please, I beg you, show mercy..."

"Where have these girls come from and where were you planning to take them?"

"They were kidnapped in the area by the Iron Sharks gang on Uncle Yu's orders, and are to be sold on Lusong island. I didn't dare disobey, please, show mercy."

"Uncle Mai, you have a mother and a father, do you not? What would they think if they knew you were participating in such atrocities?"

"Yes, yes, yes, the favorite speaks true. I am but a poor, stupid beast beholden to the desires of Uncle Yu. I would never have done these things if he didn't have such a hold over me."

Shao Jun's pity turned to disdain. The miserable being wouldn't even take responsibility for his actions, turning all the blame onto his master instead. For a moment she toyed with the idea of ordering him to take the slaves back to their home villages but doubted she could trust such a fickle being to follow her instructions. She cut the bonds of the girl at the head of the column, who appeared to be twenty-five or twenty-six. Once freed, she fell to her knees in prayer.

"Great goddess, praise be upon you! You saved us."

The slave saw Shao Jun as the reincarnation of Mazu, the most revered deity in the entire Fujian region.

And for good reason: a famous statue depicting her wearing a cloak was named "Miss Favorite", the exact title used by Mai Bing to address her seconds before. All the girls and young women had been making offerings to the goddess when they were captured by the Iron Sharks, who normally prowled Guangdong and Guangxi. The south of the region was largely uninhabited at the time, though a temple dedicated to the goddess stood on a large hill overlooking the sea. When the Portuguese saw it for the first time, they heard the natives speak Mazu's name and took it to be the name of the region. Their thick accents deformed the word, and that was how the place came to be known as Macau.

Shao Jun caught the arm of the kneeling woman to help her stand. Being mistaken for the reincarnation of a goddess discomfited her.

"Big sister," she asked, "do you know how to get home?"

By chance, the slave understood Mandarin despite being

uneducated, allowing her to act as an interpreter for the rest of her unfortunate companions.

"Yes. We were kidnapped at the temple of Mazu, but the boat they put us on to cross the estuary is still moored back there. We can use it to return to our families on the opposite shore."

"Perfect. You should go back now."

Shao Jun was relieved that they could get home on their own, because she had her own business to attend to. Armed with her sword, she began to slice the rest of the prisoners' bonds. Most came apart easily, but after six or seven prisoners the ropes began to cause her trouble. As she bent to try a different angle, the girl at the front of the line shouted something in Cantonese.

Seeing the former imperial favorite was distracted and having told himself that the time of his execution grew near, Mai Bing found the courage to stand and launch an attack despite his fear. His kung-fu was not exceptional, but he had studied several techniques for surprise attacks and still had a dagger hidden in his right boot. This type of treacherous strike had allowed him to kill enemies more skilled than he in the past, and he hoped to repeat his success by sinking his blade into Shao Jun's back.

He hadn't counted on the reflexes the young woman had developed over her time as a fugitive. She didn't speak Cantonese, so she hadn't understood the prisoner's shout; but she heard clothes rustling behind her and saw her attacker's shadow falling over her soon enough to react. Without even turning round, she smoothly released her rope dart behind her. Mai Bing screamed in pain and fell to the floor as the dart sank into his shoulder. It didn't take much to dispel the scant courage he had managed to muster. When he tried to get up to flee, he received a violent blow to the head and fell unconscious. The captive who had been at the head of the line had just thrown a large stone at his head that his injury and surprise had prevented him from avoiding. All the other girls quickly followed suit; their terror transformed into hatred towards the vile being who had deprived them of their freedom for the sake of a few coins. They who, in their village, spent their time quarrelling had finally found common ground. They also felt protected by the living embodiment of their goddess. A hail of stones flew towards the eunuch, whose brains soon flowed onto the ground like white sauce.

When her rage subsided, the captive who instigated the stoning suddenly seemed to realize that she and the other women had just killed Mai Bing. She began to shake like a leaf. It wasn't easy for anyone to carry the weight of a murder, regardless of the reason it had been committed.

"That shovel-faced bastard… We killed him?"

Shao Jun had never heard this typical rural Guangdong insult before, but she understood the young woman's horror. She moved towards the body to stab it through with her sword.

"No, it was I who killed him. Go in peace."

The villager knelt once more; forehead pressed against the ground.

"Thank you for your kindness, my lady. When we reach our village, I will ask my husband to burn two long sticks of incense in your honor."

All the other girls thanked her in turn before fleeing northwards at a run. The former imperial favorite felt guilty at being unable to accompany them. She sincerely hoped that they reached home without any problems.

After leaving Master Yangming on the river, she had travelled on to Hongqimen to find the Tiexin he had spoken of and ask for the help of him and his men. She had then followed Mai Bing to Macau, where she hoped to keep Zhang Yong busy until her allies of the moment could launch their surprise attack, but she hadn't expected the leader of the Tigers to weigh anchor so soon.

She needed to change her plans.

She felt tired and slightly confused as she looked down at the three bodies on the ground. The eunuchs' deaths were not to be mourned, it prevented them from causing more misery, but she still hated taking lives. She dug a grave for the bodies using a shovel in the fishermen's cabin. A little exercise helped her to assess her situation and calm her inner thoughts.

When she showed Tiexin the jade pendant and told him that Master Yangming was no longer with them, she had the impression he was pained but not upset. Later, when they were discussing the details of their plan, he had insisted that Shao Jun attack the small port of Macau alone before he and his men, something she found suspicious. Did he plan to abandon or betray her? The mentor had warned her not to trust them, so she couldn't rule out the possibility. Now Zhang Yong was at sea, she wasn't sure that this doubtful ally would still support her if she pursued her enemy across the water.

Just as she was finishing covering the bodies with earth, a small boat approached the shore, moving so quickly it almost seemed to fly. The young woman was disappointed to see it didn't hold the small army she had expected. Instead, the boat contained only a seventeen year-old fisherwoman with unbound feet, pretty despite her suntanned skin. It was Tiexin's sister A-Qian. Ready for action, she jumped to the ground with unusual agility, looking around with a confused expression before walking towards Shao Jun.

"Huh? Why is no one here?" she asked.

"They had already gone before I got here. Is your brother not coming, A-Qian?"

"He warned me that the nasty old Zhang Yong would flee without waiting for the last of his men."

More mature and competent that her age would suggest, she was respected by her brother's men and was aware of all his business. She was also the first person Shao Jun had discussed the situation with in Hongqimen. The former imperial concubine was still surprised. At first she'd believed that Tiexin had sent her to attack Zhang Yong alone in the hope that he would kill her and take all the risks instead, but what A-Qian had just said suggested that in reality he had doubted there would be a fight at the port.

He must still have some plan in mind though, which was unsettling.

"Did your brother say anything else?"

"He thinks Zhang Yong is going to the Isle of Demons, but with the wind that will blow tonight, they'll have to stop at Guimen reef. It will be our only chance to intercept him, big sister!" Seeing Shao Jun's hesitation, the fisherwoman took her by the sleeve. "We must hurry! This small boat will be smashed to pieces by the waves if we're caught in the storm!"

The former imperial favorite felt she was hiding something, but the sky was growing dark with clouds, forcing her to make a quick decision.

"Let's go!" she declared.

"We can use them, but we can't trust them", Wang Yangming had said of Tiexin and his men. She kept these words in mind as she stepped onto the boat. Although surrounded by mountains and saltwater, the young woman felt as if her master's spirit was with her. She was also painfully aware that he could no longer watch over her as he had done before, and she could now only count on her own abilities for survival.

CHAPTER 17

Maritime laws had fluctuated significantly over the course of the Ming dynasty. As a result, during the second year of Jiajing's reign a dispute broke out at the port of Ningbo over whether to allow two Japanese ships, come to present their tribute, to dock at the same time. Maritime policy had become harsher since then, and, except for several small fishing vessels, ships no longer approached the shore, even on stormy nights. However, the small boat braved the poor weather and sailed through the moonless night towards its destination: the junk moored at Guimen reef.

In the stern, A-Qian proved to be an impressive navigator, slipping between the waves on a boat that was usually used to cross a peaceful strait. Without her, the imperial favorite would have quickly been sunk. Who would have guessed that the young girl would be as skilled as an old sea dog?

"Big sister, we've caught up with them!" she called quietly, pointing at the silhouette looming near the island.

Apart from the whistling of the wind, the Tigers' ship was shrouded in an eerie silence. On board shone a single lantern which must belong to the sailor on watch. Their skiff sped across the water, its small size making it difficult to spot in the moonless night.

"We must be careful, there's sure to be a lookout," Shao Jun warned.

A-Qian nodded then pulled on the rudder at the last second: the boat turned, brushing lightly against the junk before stopping soundlessly at its side. The alarm would have been raised immediately if the sailors had heard anything other than the sound of waves against the hull.

As the young girl skillfully executed the delicate maneuver, Shao Jun squinted to examine the swell around them.

"A-Qian, where is your brother?" she asked.

The fisherwoman looked all around.

"Oh!" she exclaimed. "They're still not here?"

"I find it hard to believe they got lost along the way."

"My brother knows the location of the reef very well. He also gave me two flares to signal our position, but I'd prefer not to for the moment..."

Tiexin and his men were supposed to be there before them, and with their lead should have arrived earlier despite the bad weather. The flares, impossible to let off without immediately betraying the boat's presence, were completely useless. The young woman raged silently. The coward had left her to do the dirty work and bear all the risks alone both here and in the port. It was too late to turn back now though and waiting could be dangerous. Zhang Yong was in reach and she had to take her chance now, with or without help. Even if she wasn't up to the task ahead, she owed it to her master to push on and do everything she could to stop her enemy reaching his goal. Jaw clenched, she turned to A-Qian.

"Stay here," she said, "I'll go up first. Light the flare if anything happens."

"But big sister, it's too risky…"

"Don't worry, but stay alert."

Shao Jun was perturbed by the fisherwoman's reaction. She seemed genuinely concerned for her safety. Could she really be sincere? If she was pretending, she was as good an actress as she was a navigator. Perhaps her brother hadn't told her his entire plan after all. Without her master to guide her, the young woman didn't know who to trust. Anyway, her decision was made: she began to climb the smooth, glistening side of the junk using every tiny imperfection for grip. *Click!* A movement of her ankle, and she stabbed the blade on her boot into the wood to help her climb. When she was halfway up, she heard A-Qian call out softly.

"Big sister, be very careful!"

The young girl was impressed by her passenger's smooth movements as she swiftly climbed the side of the hull. Her lack of knowledge of martial arts meant she was unable to truly comprehend just how exceptional Shao Jun was: her agility exceeded that of Wang Yangming or Zhang Yong; fighters like her appeared only twice in a millennium.

She checked the deck was empty before climbing over the parapet. The junk swayed violently with the wind, but it was moored firmly enough that the sailors could avoid tedious inspections of the ship. Consequently, there was not a single soul on deck. She slid on board like a curl of smoke drifting on the breeze, pressing herself against the wall of the cabin before silently climbing its roof to reach the wheelhouse, which held the only light on the ship.

When she entered, the sailor dozing over the wheel opened his large round eyes, but the point of her sword was at his throat before he had time to cry out. He felt as if a shadow had materialized before him like some supernatural apparition. Master Yangming had more than once counselled Shao Jun against her hesitation and tendency toward excessive mercy, but she couldn't bring herself to be a cold-blooded murderer.

"Silence," she motioned. "And I'll let you live."

With a cloak that was clearly of non-Chinese design, he had initially believed her to be Portuguese or some other Westerner, so he was surprised to hear the intruder speak his tongue. He nodded slowly and felt the pressure of the steel against his skin ease slightly.

"Is Zhang Yong on board?" the young woman asked quietly.

"He's in the cabin under our feet," the man answered thinly.

"Thank you."

The sword slid downwards, then pressed an acupuncture point on his heart with surgical precision to incapacitate him. Shao Jun leapt onto the deck, silent as a cat, and slid the end of her blade between the door and the frame to delicately lift the lock that held it closed. Everything had gone without a hitch up to this point, but she couldn't afford to let her guard down. There was no way for Zhang Yong to know she was about to attack him on the open sea, but he was still extremely dangerous despite being weakened from his fight with Master Yangming. Killing him would not be easy.

She took a deep breath and suddenly opened the door.

On ships hinges are always corroded by the moist, salty atmosphere, which makes them creak. Though it meant being spotted as soon as she opened the door, the young woman had bet on the element of surprise. Just as she was about to hurl herself into the inky-black cabin, something flashed in the darkness.

A sword!

So, she was expected after all. And vulnerable, trapped as she was in the doorframe. Instead of retreating, which her opponent surely expected, she dodged the blow and dashed into the room, slashing downwards with her sword. She refused to allow herself to be caught by a surprise attack. The blade cut flesh with a wet sound, and a hoarse cry rang out. The person who attacked Shao Jun could no longer hold a sword, but the voice wasn't Zhang Yong's. The young woman realized she had underestimated her prey. The leader of the Tigers clearly expected her to come, so he had placed one – or more? – of his men in the room while he remained elsewhere. Now, she was alone in the darkness surrounded by an unknown number of assailants. How could she escape?

She had no time to think because she was suddenly dazed by a glare of light, as if lightning had struck at her feet. Accustomed to the complete darkness of the room, brightness which could not have come from any normal lamp overwhelmed her vision. It created an opening for her attackers: one looped a cord around her right hand, another around her left, and her pitiful attempts to wave her sword at them blindly were to no avail. From their texture she could feel that her bonds were made from silk and sinew. The men holding them pulled with superhuman strength, forcing her arms to snap apart. *Clang!*

Her sword fell to the floor. Victory had been so close. She was suddenly overcome with guilt. She should have listened to her master's wise words and not underestimated Zhang Yong. The man never lowered his guard, even in the most unexpected situations. As unbelievable as it might be, he had spotted the boat before it had drawn up to the ship.

The strange light was extinguished, and a lantern lit the room in its place.

"Miss Imperial Favorite," an androgynous voice said sarcastically, "thank you for honoring us with your presence!"

It was Yu Dayong!

When Shao Jun's sight returned he was opposite her, hairless, stocky, and pot-bellied, his mouth twisted in an ugly rictus, holding a small copper cylinder in his hand – it must be the tool he had used to create the strange light. At his side stood a rough man who looked like a sailor, cradling his bleeding right wrist in his left hand. Seated on an armchair next to the wall behind them was a eunuch with white hair and a furious expression: Zhang Yong.

"Venerable captain general," Yu Dayong asked as he caressed the knife at his waist, "may I send the imperial whore after her beloved Emperor?"

He had dreamed night and day of ending the final survivor of the Central Plain Brotherhood. Bound by his leader's orders and driven by terror at the thought of being next to die after Wei Bin and Gao Feng, he fretted as his chest continued to swell with fear and hatred. He had been delighted when the leader of the Tigers had recently said to kill her on sight, and now here she was, bound and in reach of his blade. Internally he rejoiced even as his face remained as expressionless as ever.

He was considerably disappointed when Zhang Yong finally spoke.

"Don't be in such a hurry, my dear governor, I have a few questions to ask her first."

He moved closer but stayed at a distance, because the young woman's feet were still free.

"Shao Jun," he said after clearing his throat, "how fares brother Yangming?"

She didn't answer, but Yu Dayong was very surprised by his superior's respectful attitude.

The leader of the Tigers hadn't stopped thinking about his old friend, a refined and powerful man, loved by all, who had never used his immense political power against him despite their numerous disagreements. Their night of discussion also haunted him; it was a long-cherished memory that now filled him with bitterness. Still consumed by his thirst for domination, he was unable to feel the slightest compassion. Nonetheless, a spark of emotion, nostalgia perhaps, drove his desire to hear about Wang Yangming from Shao Jun's own lips before he finally took her life.

"You really have no scruples," she spat. "I will avenge my master."

He laughed loudly. She was undoubtedly a worthy successor for the mentor of the Central Plain Brotherhood!

"Don't mock me, Shao Jun. Your master couldn't resist the power of my yuxiao."

So that was what they were called. Although they were undetectable to the way of the heart, they were certainly not invincible, and only their numbers and the surprise combined with Zhang Yong's attacks had allowed them to overcome

Wang Yangming. The leader of the Tigers' *Fire of the lotus* would have never been enough on its own. Though he hadn't lingered on the riverbank, he had been convinced that there was no way his rival could survive his wounds. The martial aspect of the School of Mind would end today, he decided. He pressed his right hand against his left wrist, releasing a thin blade from his sleeve. The weariness left his gaze to be replaced by his habitual cruelty.

Yu Dayong grimaced. He had hoped to kill the imperial whore with his own hands and had even unsheathed his dagger in readiness.

He noticed a strange light in the sky, faintly illuminating the interior of the cabin through the closed shutters. But there was no sound from the storm and no clouds blocked the view of the stars. The eunuch shivered as he remembered that Guimen was sometimes known as "the demon gate" before realizing what he had just seen. A flare!

The entire room began to shake violently from an explosion or an impact from an enormous solid mass. The ship was moored on the reef and wasn't transporting any explosives. Shao Jun had arrived on a boat, and she would also be affected by any collision with the junk. Even Zhang Yong, who had anticipated Shao Jun's attack by asking his subordinate and three personal guards to remain with him, had no idea what was happening. The sailors slept in the adjoining cabin, so it would surely not be long before they joined them after being woken by the commotion.

Bang! A gaping hole suddenly appeared in the wall of the room, just where the leader of the Tigers had been sitting seconds earlier. The wall was made from wood too hard for any saw to cut. Yu Dayong's initial response was to think there had been an accident with some gunpowder, but the ship had none on board. While the group was still frozen in shock, an abrupt cry rang out and a man flew through the opening, feet-first and stiff as a board, in Zhang Yong's direction. He dodged at lightning speed and stabbed the human projectile with his long, thin dagger, causing it to collapse to the floor like a sack of potatoes. It was a corpse! One of the sailors from the junk. Though the victim hadn't been skilled in kung-fu, his silent death and conversion to a projectile was incredible.

A second man burst through the hole like a cannon ball. Zhang Yong's position prevented him from using his sword in time, and he was forced to quickly raise his arm to protect himself. At the last second, he realized this projectile wasn't dead, and he was going to be hit in the chest. Who was this assailant? What force had propelled him? And how had he got on board without being spotted? He had many questions, but they would have to wait. *Pah!* Zhang Yong intercepted the intruder's punch with his open hand. The impact reverberated through his entire body and sent him stumbling back a step, but he immediately counter-attacked using *Fire of the lotus* to send a flow of yin energy into his opponent's body and render him harmless. His adversary instantly reacted by opening his fist to exert pressure on the leader of the Tigers' artery and block his neigong. The witnesses to this exchange with martial arts knowledge were impressed by the unexpected intruder's speed. Under normal circumstances the captain of the guard's high-level kung-fu would have had no trouble overcoming him, but his internal wounds still limited his abilities and the element of surprise had worked against him. The stranger inverted the position of his feet for stability, then launched a new series of strikes that were crude yet so fast that they seemed to blur into one long, drawn-out strike too impenetrable to allow through any counterstrike. On this occasion, sheer speed made up for any flaws in the clumsy technique.

Recovered from her initial surprise, Shao Jun recognized him: it was Tiexin! As unbelievable as it seemed, he managed to force the leader of the Tigers to move back without giving him a moment's respite, dangerously weakening his internal organs each time a new shockwave travelled through his body. Aware that he needed to change his strategy quickly, Zhang Yong suddenly pivoted to disengage from the relentless assault. The next punches slammed straight into the stomach of the sailor who was standing just behind him and holding the roped arm of the former imperial favorite – he instantly spat out a stream of blood and collapsed to the floor. As soon as the young woman felt slack in the rope, she freed herself with a wide sweep of her leg, sending her foot blade stabbing into the chest of the man holding her left arm.

The tables seemed to have completely turned in the space of a moment. The leader of the Tigers thought his captive had planned this providential rescue from the beginning, and that the newcomer belonged to some new version of the Central Plain Brotherhood, but he was nothing of the sort. Tiexin hated taking reckless risks, he was there only for his own purposes. His motivations mattered little to Shao Jun. She simply planned to take advantage of the opportunity he provided to kill Zhang Yong, which was her sole objective. She slid the toe of her boat under a sword on the floor and flipped it up to her hand with a flick of her ankle. As soon as her hand closed around it, she felt stronger and more sure of herself, ready to jump back into the fight. Suddenly, the same light that had blinded her earlier dazzled her once more. No! She couldn't let herself be caught by the same trap twice! She lifted her blade and hastily closed her eyes, protecting herself from the effects of the powerful tool. Tiexin didn't have the same presence of mind and found himself blinded, striking out madly in front of him without being able to see to protect himself. He was also carried away by his zeal, convinced of his skill and certain he would be able to vanquish the head of the Eight Tigers himself.

Yu Dayong had developed the mirror-torch on Dai Yu island, with the help of Pyros, to compensate for the weaknesses in his kung-fu. Its intensity was exceptional, but it could only be used twice before it needed reloading. In the space of minutes he had seen two of his men die, both more skilled than he, and watched the powerful intruder gain the upper hand over his master. Crying out in terror, he grabbed the last remaining living sailor by the shoulder, the one with the bleeding wrist, shoving him at Tiexin as he and Zhang Yong fled. The poor man tried to protect himself with his good hand, which was instantly broken by the power of the attacks. Panicking, he lifted his other arm, and *crack!*, it broke in multiple places, sending small splinters of bone flying everywhere. The fractured radius tore his flesh, and a punch sank into his chest. He screamed and fell to the ground, a shredded, shapeless mass of impossible angles.

When Shao Jun opened her eyes again, she could see well enough to spot Yu Dayong disappearing through an open trap door in the middle of the cabin. Zhang Yong must also have rushed into it, as he was nowhere to be seen. She had to move, because Tiexin began to aim devastating punches in her direction after hearing her move. The boxing style he used was called *Toppling Mount Kailash* – a sacred place in Buddhism, on whose peak the celestial emperor supposedly resided at three thousand six hundred meters in altitude – and this particular sequence of attacks where one elbow followed the other relentlessly was known as *Celestial drums beat the thunder*. The most skilled users could usually maintain a sustained rhythm of four strikes per second with each elbow, but after years of exhaustive training he had achieved double this rate, earning the nickname of "Eight celestial drums". It was almost impossible for an opponent to escape once caught in this flurry of attacks.

Shao Jun's kung-fu relied on her vital breath, so she couldn't speak or cry out while simultaneously dodging the attacks coming towards her with all the speed she could muster. The slightest error could be fatal. Without relaxing her concentration, she cautiously began to retreat towards the cabin's exit, then mounted the deck, both eyes still fixed on her blinded assailant who was furious at being trapped just when he thought victory was in his grasp. Shao Jun's heel abruptly hit the railing: she had reached the edge of the deck and had nowhere else to go to escape the boxing machine approaching her. In desperation, she jumped to the other side of the rail; one more step would send her into the water. A high-pitched voice suddenly broke the night:

"Big brother! Stop fighting!"

CHAPTER 18

It was A-Qian, dagger in hand and clothes covered in blood. She was followed by Tiexin's Eight Celestial Kings, strong and courageous sailors who had just killed Yu Dayong's men in their sleep. Recognizing his sister's voice, Tiexin began to stop his attack, but the perpetual movement of the technique was so powerful that it was dangerous for the user to suddenly stop, so he simply redirected his blows downwards as he gradually slowed rather than stopping abruptly. As he did so, he broke the railing Shao Jun was holding on to. If she lost her footing, the pitch of the ship and the sea currents would be her end. Seeing her fall backwards, A-Qian rushed towards her and grabbed her sleeve at the last second. The former imperial favorite deployed her cloak, allowing her to float on the wind for a moment like a kite before landing back on the deck. Barely had she reached this relative safety when the junk shook, this time throwing the young fisherwoman overboard. Tiexin himself wavered, but quickly used his formidable energy to stabilize himself, sinking his fingers into the wood of the parapet and stretching his hand out to his sister, narrowly missing her. Her slim silhouette disappeared into the night but was caught at the last second by Shao Jun's rope dart. She was able to reel the girl, pale with fright, back onto the relative safety of the ship with the sailor's help.

All three gripped the railing tightly as they looked down: two lines of fire propelled a small boat that seemed to have burst out through the hull. On board they could clearly see the two figures of Zhang Yong and Yu Dayong. The two Tigers would have been at the Eight Celestial Kings' mercy without the completely unexpected and unpredictable maneuver, but they accelerated away at incredible speed and would soon only be a dot on the horizon, like a star fallen into the sea. The boat was a fiery dragon on the surface of the sea, a military invention developed under the Ming dynasty: huge, thick pieces of bamboo filled with gunpowder were attached to its deck to propel it across the water when lit. If loaded with explosives, this type of boat could be used as a mobile bomb against an enemy ship, in this case it was a very effective means of transport for making a quick escape. Shao Jun had heard about this naval weapon during her first sea voyage with Zhu Jiuyuan. He told her that the governor of Guangdong had used one to successfully push back the Portuguese who tried to invade his territory in the sixteenth year of Zhengde's reign.

As she retrieved her rope and wrapped it with a flick of her wrist, the young woman noticed the deck under her feet didn't pitch as it should. Instead of rising and falling with the waves, the prow seemed to slowly rise. It wasn't hard to guess what was happening: Yu Dayong and Zhang Yong must have punctured the hull before they fled. In the storm, simple fishing boats like those alongside the ship wouldn't be enough to reach the coast…

"We need to hurry to the reef," Shao Jun declared. "The ship is going to sink."

A-Qian came out of her stupor and shouted at her brother.

"It's your fault! What were you thinking, attacking big sister Jun?"

Out of an excess of confidence, Tiexin had left his men to await his signal before attacking and had boarded ahead of them to demonstrate his invincible kung-fu. He was aware his mistake had cost them, but he was too proud to take responsibility and unloaded his anger onto the Eight Celestial Kings.

"What about you, hmm?" he yelled at them. "What took you so long?"

Ye Zongman, the head of the small band, was his right-hand man and his sworn brother. Realizing his friend felt responsible, he chose to be diplomatic.

"I'm sorry, big brother Tiexin, we didn't train hard enough!"

This childish apportioning of blame was wasting time as the deck continued to slant, and the sinking ship was creating powerful eddies which would be certain death for anyone carried in the water. They needed to get to Guimen reef as soon as possible.

"Big brother," said A-Qian, "there is no one alive on this ship, let's get off, quickly…"

As she prepared to return to her fishing boat, she saw Shao Jun turn and reach the wheelhouse in three agile bounds.

"There's still someone in there!" she shouted to the young girl.

And she was right: Tiexin and his men had killed all the sleeping sailors, but the one she had immobilized when she arrived on the ship was still alive. He was a bloody brute who executed the Tigers' most abominable orders, but she couldn't simply leave him to die. The extreme terror he showed when she got to him dispelled any lingering doubts. She removed the energy block that prevented him from moving.

"Follow me now if you want to live!" she whispered.

The entire front of the junk seemed to be on the verge of rising vertically before it finally sank. The night was filled with terrible creaks and groans signaling the deck's imminent collapse. Shao Jun ran across the deck, followed by the sailor; two meters below floated the boat containing Tiexin and his sister, and a larger boat held Ye Zongman and the other Celestial Kings.

"Big sister, this way!" A-Qian cried.

Light and nimble, the young woman jumped into the boat without hesitation. She turned to look at the man still on board the doomed ship.

"Come, quickly!" she shouted.

The sailor knew he had no choice, so he opted to try his luck with his enemies rather than certain drowning. He followed her down and had barely reached safety when Tiexin leapt to his feet, fists up and ready to fight.

"Tiexin!" Shao Jun intervened. "Please, leave him alone!"

Although visibly upset, he calmed without a fuss because of the very real risk of being engulfed by one of the powerful eddies caused by the sinking ship. Each took an oar and set themselves to the task, their combined efforts allowing them to quickly cover the fifty or so meters to the reef, reaching it even before the others. A loud rush of water could be heard as they set foot on land, and by the time they turned not a single trace of the junk remained on the water's surface. A shiver which had nothing to do with the wind went through all of them. This was how ships died: first with tragic slowness, then with a frantic impatience in their final moments.

Despite its three-hundred-meter circumference, Guimen reef was really nothing more than an enormous, lifeless rock protruding from the sea. Without saying a word, Tiexin climbed to its narrow summit, where two or three people at most could stand, while Ye Zongman and the other Celestial Kings waited slightly below on a wide platform that could have held ten times their number. A-Qian and Shao Jun also sat there a little apart from the others. The young woman was filled with despair: she had been so close to her target, but Zhang Yong had escaped her once again, this time with the Precursor box. If Master Yangming were here, he would surely find a way to follow him as quickly as possible, then kill him on his island to finally rebuild the Brotherhood in peace. But he was no longer here, and his pupil was on a reef without fresh water nor a ship able to travel through the storm, with her only ally a sailor she wasn't supposed to trust.

"A-Qian, what can we do now?" she asked.

Just then, Tiexin called the fisherwoman up to his rocky promontory. She rose to join him, then turned towards the former imperial favorite.

"Don't worry, big sister, I'm sure my brother has a solution."

Shao Jun responded with a bitter smile. She was no fool and wondered if the members of this small band were more outlaws than fisherfolk. While she herself was hunted by the authorities, the idea of working with brigands didn't make her happy. They hadn't even said they were prepared to risk following the leader of the Tigers as far as his lair. For some reason, the memory of her anonymous savior near Pingle came to mind. Looking up at Tiexin, she wondered what he could be saying, amazed by the respect and even veneration accorded to him by his men. More than just a leader and a fighter, he must also have some kind of vision to so inspire those around him. Suddenly, his men all let out a fearsome battle cry and bowed with a military discipline that was surprising for a band of pirates. A-Qian then addressed one of them harshly, and he responded by bowing his head as a sign of humility. The wind changed and now Shao Jun could hear their words, but she didn't understand anything because they were speaking in a dialect unknown to her. A strange noise drew her attention to a corner of the rocky platform: the sailor she had saved from the junk was terrified, prostrate, immobile, and trembling against a wall. His eyes were wide, and his jaw clenched so hard his teeth ground together.

Tiexin seemed to conclude his discourse in a harsh voice. While his men applauded, his sister rejoined the former imperial favorite. When she spoke, it was hesitantly, which couldn't bode well from someone who was usually so self-assured.

"Big sister Jun, um…"

"What were you talking about, A-Qian?"

"The two eunuchs fled towards Dai Yu island. But now we've attacked them, they will surely have their revenge, so we must act quickly."

"The Isle of Demons?"

"Yes, it's their lair, shared with the Portuguese man. It's difficult to access, no one else has ever succeeded in landing there. My brother is prepared to try and risk our lives despite everything, but… big sister, if you don't want to…"

"Don't worry, I'll come with you."

After initially being so reluctant, Shao Jun wasn't going to complain if Tiexin now felt personally involved in the fight against the Tigers – and never mind if he was a pirate, as A-Qian had just subtly confirmed.

"Alright, I'll tell my brother you'll come with us," the fisherwoman said, reassured. "But there's one last thing…"

"What?"

"We can't let him live."

She pointed at Yu Dayong's man who threw himself at the former imperial favorite's feet.

"M- Miss," he stammered hoarsely, "you saved my life. I beg you, don't let them kill me, I'll do whatever you want. I've already been to the Isle of Demons several times, and I know where to land to avoid wrecking the ship on the reefs surrounding it."

"Do you really know the Isle of Demons?" A-Qian asked skeptically.

"Yes! It's shaped like a large stone cut in two, and smoke seems to rise from its rocky peak. Miss, without my help, your ship will simply join all the other wrecks scattered around its coast."

This description was enough to prove he wasn't lying, though he still hadn't mentioned anything about the place's evil aura and the strange noises that emerged and echoed for lis around, like cries of pain from tormented wild beasts. It was said that demons lived on the cursed isle, but none of the curious people who had gone to investigate had ever returned to speak of their experiences. Determined to kill the eunuchs, Tiexin had decided that he could afford no more mistakes, and therefore to leave no survivors in his wake. It was why he planned not only to kill the sailor from the junk, but also Shao Jun if she had refused to join his expedition. The young woman didn't suspect anything, while A-Qian was very aware of everything that was at stake when she had offered "big sister Jun" the chance to accompany them. She asked her to wait a moment while she went to plead the sailor's cause with her brother.

"How can you prove you really know the Isle of Demons?" the former imperial favorite asked him quietly.

"I can tell you that Uncle Zhang and Uncle Yu called it Dai Yu."

He didn't need say more to definitively and irrefutably prove that he hadn't lied. She felt her hope begin to rekindle. She might have a chance of beating Zhang Yong if she found him before he had time to completely replenish his internal energy reserves. Besides, she would have no reason to live if she failed. The thought comforted her, though she didn't let it show.

"What is your name?" she asked the sailor.

"I am the humble Feng Renxiao."

"Is that what your parents named you?"

Embarrassed, he nodded silently. His first name meant "kindness" and "filial piety", qualities which he certainly hadn't lived up to by transporting Yu Dayong's slaves to Lusong Island. But the young woman could see the remorse in his eyes and felt he wasn't fundamentally bad.

"I saved you because I couldn't just leave you to drown. Discerning good and evil is an essential knowledge. If you are ashamed of your actions and you have the courage to repent, I'll give you the chance. But if you betray me, I swear my sword will end stabbed through your heart."

Feng Renxiao was old enough to be her father, but her

aura and natural authority inspired deep respect. He already preferred following her orders to following those of Yu Dayong.

"Yes, miss," he said simply. "I will follow your instructions."

A-Qian and Tiexin arrived to announce that they had agreed to allow the sailor to show them where to go. So, he would live, at least for now.

"Let's not delay any further!" Shao Jun declared.

She wasn't completely sure she could trust this man, whose terror had surely altered his judgement. Who was to say he wouldn't turn against her once more once back in the company of the leader of the Tigers and his former master? Until then, they needed his help to land on the island safely.

"When this business is finished, you'll return to your village and life an honest life," she ordered.

"Yes, I promise…"

"Don't go back on your word."

Taken aback by the menace in the young woman's voice, he was only able to utter an almost-inaudible "yes" in response.

CHAPTER 19

"Over there, miss!"

Fearing that he would be killed by Tiexin and his men at any minute, Feng Renxiao hadn't left Shao Jun's side since their departure from Guimen reef two days earlier. But a dark shape finally began to appear on the horizon: their destination was in sight.

Dai Yu Island.

The long, ugly mass didn't resemble the verdant paradise full of fruit-laden trees that the young woman had expected. Master Yangming had told her the legends that made it one of the sacred islands, but she now understood why pirates saw it more as the Isle of Demons. At its center stood a dark mountain on which no plant grew, its peak shrouded in cloud.

A volcano!

During her travels in Italy she had seen one known as Vesuvius. Zhu Jiuyuan had told her that it had erupted more than a thousand years earlier, reducing the famous Pompeii and surrounding towns to ash and continuing to belch flaming rocks for centuries after. Apparently, there was also one in China. "In the southern seas lies a volcano where no plant grows, burning day and night", recounted the *Book of Marvels*. One day, in Shanxi, a volcano on which a temple had been built erupted, terrifying the monks who had naively believed that the roots of a tree had caught fire underground. Zhu Jiuyuan had warned his pupil of the strange stories invented by the ancients to explain phenomena they didn't understand and told her of the magma that bubbled under the earth, sometimes escaping through the thinnest sections of the Earth's crust. The monks, he had added, also believed that the sulfurous emissions from hot parts of the mountain were the breath of a dragon living in its depths. Volcanoes were fascinating but dangerous places: you never knew when they were going to awaken and cause a disaster.

As they approached the coast of the island under cover of darkness to avoid being spotted too easily, Tiexin addressed Yu Dayong's former man directly for the first time.

"Feng Renxiao, are other ships belonging to the Tigers on their way to the island?"

"No, only the junk should be there. The place is secret, so they limit the number of journeys to it."

"Why do you ask?" Shao Jun demanded.

"Because a ship has been following us for two days but made no attempt to catch us. They sometimes appear on the horizon."

Since the Ming empire imposed strict control over its waters, maritime traffic had decreased between seventy and eighty percent, and only pirates like Tiexin, the Japanese, the Koreans, and the Filipinos still dared sail. While possible, it was unlikely that the appearance of an unknown vessel was a coincidence. It would be difficult to do anything about it and as the ship didn't seem to be aggressive, the mystery could wait for now.

"Captain Tiexin," Feng Renxiao continued, "now we are no more than two lis from the island, we can only reach the shore by beating the surface of the water fast and maintaining a good speed to avoid the yuxiao patrolling there."

"The yuxiao?"

"That's what I heard Zhang Yong say: if intruders venture near the island's coast, the yuxiao will sink any that survive the reefs."

"Those hateful eunuchs domesticated demons?" A-Qian interrupted.

"I was nothing more than a humble sailor at Uncle Yu's command… I repeat these words without knowing their meaning."

While the surface currents invariably sent boats crashing against the reefs, those which were deeper avoided them. Beating the surface of the water sent the hull of the boat as deep as possible into the water, allowing it to be carried by the subsurface currents. The sailors lowered the sails, equipped themselves with oars, and began to row hard, propelling the boat along invisible paths which meandered between the perils on the island's shore. They would certainly have been wrecked without Feng Renxiao's wise counsel.

"Big brother Tiexin," Ye Zongman asked, "are there really demons under the water?"

Tiexin, whose name meant "heart of fire", preferred to be addressed as "esteemed leader", but none of his men ever used this title. They had spent their first voyages at sea together and seen many extraordinary sea creatures which might be considered mythological beasts by less experienced sailors, so they were not easily inclined to believe in the existence of demons. Tiexin was not convinced by the story, but he did know the dangers of the reefs and was grateful to Feng Renxiao for advising them to beat the surface of the water.

One of the Celestial Kings, a well-built young man who was never easily frightened, pulled on his sleeve with a trembling hand.

"Captain Tiexin," he stammered, "l- look, over there!"

A dozen meters away, the last rays of the setting sun showed a human head silently rising above the waves. Despite the growing darkness, there was no doubt: it was no manatee or other sea mammal, but a man who examined his surroundings with wide, staring eyes, seemingly without struggling, swimming, or sinking beneath the surface. Powerful waves sometimes broke over his head, but he ignored them as if they were nothing more than a gentle breeze. He soon reemerged, dripping and impassive, to continue studying the surface. What was this marvel? No ordinary man could remain so still in rough seas.

"Captain Tiexin," murmured the frightened Celestial King, "it's an umi-bozu!"

The man was convinced he was seeing a drowned sailor, a fantastical creature from Japanese folklore which trapped the oars of unwary boats to overturn them. But umi-bozu were supposed to be bald, and this head had hair.

"No, big brother," A-Qian said, "it's a yuxiao. Whatever you do, don't stop rowing."

It was the second time Shao Jun had heard this word. "Your master was unable to resist the power of my yuxiao", Zhang

Yong had told her after capturing her on the junk. It must refer to the terrible creatures he had managed to create using some ungodly process. Having already seen them at work, she knew these monsters were formidable, and that they would be even more so off solid ground. She had also learnt that they were not as invincible as might be believed from the primal terror they inspired. Their main weakness was undoubtedly that they appeared to be unable to think for themselves. What was the point of such phenomenal strength if it could only be set into motion by external orders? That said, while she had succeeded in killing them before, the young woman couldn't shake a sense of unease. Their very existence was unnatural.

Even the reckless and proud Tiexin felt his blood run cold. He had thought that the Eight Tigers were only dangerous due to their high level of kung-fu, but he never imagined that their powers or talents would also allow them to bind supernatural creatures with abilities beyond human comprehension to their service. Now he understood how they had got the better of Taki Choji and his pirates. And out of pure bad luck, the deep current the boat was currently following ran near the demon, which had not let its gaze waver ever since it had set eyes upon them. As they passed it, all the men on board gripped their oars a little tighter and held their breath, but nothing happened. The head remained immobile as a rock protruding from the water.

Feng Renxiao wiped the sweat that had beaded on his forehead.

"Miss," he said quietly, "we have just escaped the first trap."

"You doubted we would?"

"Well… the first time I came here was with Yu Dayong, on board a pedal boat. He ordered us to pedal quickly without stopping, because the yuxiao attacked anyone who stopped among the reefs, without distinguishing between friend or foe. That is why I advised that we move at speed, but really I couldn't be sure of anything."

"Are there other creatures like this on the island?"

"I don't know, miss. I normally remain at the dock. Yu Dayong only asked me to enter with him once."

Shao Jun found it strange that he spoke of "entering" the island, but before she had a chance to ask for details, the boat was approaching the shore through waters that were suddenly very calm. One hundred times bigger than Guimen reef, Dai Yu Island had a dock but seemed to have no other human constructions, and no sign of human activity. In the unexpected silence, Tiexin cautiously set foot on land and looked around, searching for any sign of an ambush. But there was nowhere any fighters could have concealed themselves. Could Yu Dayong's seemingly repentant henchman have lied to them after all? Furious, the pirate was ready to pounce on him when Shao Jun stood in his way.

"Captain Tiexin," she demanded, "what are you doing?"

"There's no one on this island, this snake lied!"

"No," replied the sailor, "I told you the truth, Captain Tiexin. It's because the entrance to the island is underwater, you must dive to enter."

"Underwater?"

"Yes, you must pull the chain in the middle of the dock to raise the transport, then use it to move under the water."

The idea seemed completely fantastical. The sailor who had mistaken the yuxiao for an umi-bozu addressed his captain in a language which the former imperial favorite didn't understand, the same he had used on Guimen reef. After a brief exchange, they ran towards the dock and there set a winch in action with a terrible grinding. No sailor had paid any attention to it up until then as it was an essential element of any dock, but Feng Renxiao's claims needed to be verified. And if he had lied, the Celestial Kings would kill him on the spot.

"For your sake, I hope you told the truth…" Shao Jun said to him.

"I wouldn't dare lie, miss. The only time I entered the island was this way, with Yu Dayong. But the mechanism is heavy, very difficult to move. Fortunately, Mr Tiexin and his Japanese friend are strong."

"He's Japanese?"

"But of course! I've spent enough years at sea to learn a few words, to recognize the language and its accent."

Ah, so that was it! The young woman had known that Tiexin and his men were involved in some illicit business, but she had never imagined that he would have any Japanese under his command…

As the two men worked the crank, their efforts finally began to pay off: a large black shape emerged from the waves at the end of the chain, like a gigantic fish caught on a hook. Impatient to see what they were bringing up, the sailors worked even harder, and *clackclackclack!*, something resembling a gigantic barrel rose out of the waves, black and glistening like a beast from the deep. Their captain climbed on top of it and, seeing a carefully wrought door, pulled on the handle with all his strength to reveal an opening.

"Captain Tiexin," said Feng Renxiao, "this is what I was telling you about. You need to get inside it to enter the island."

At a glance, at most six or seven people could fit inside the narrow compartment.

"Are there others?" asked the pirate.

"No, this is the only one."

"And how does it work?"

"The vessel is located near a current which runs along the reefs to an underwater entrance."

What an ingenious system! It made the island impenetrable to anyone who didn't know the system and prevented any mass invasion of the Tigers' base. They were all impressed, even A-Qian.

"Go, big brother!" she cried. "Get in!"

Tiexin grabbed her by the arm as she was about to rush into the opening. Even if Yu Dayong's former man was telling the truth, none of them knew what they would discover when they arrived at the underwater entrance. The risk was too great to expose his sister to it. He looked at Ye Zongman, whose intelligence had always made him the person he always turned to for counsel.

"I'll take several men and go first," he announced quietly.

"No," the captain objected. "We'll go together, and A-Qian will remain here."

"That's probably wise. How many men will we leave behind on the dock?"

"Three will be enough. A-Qian, you guard the boat, and be ready to weigh anchor at any moment."

"Alright," she answered discontentedly, but without raising any further protest.

Tiexin, Ye Zongman, Shao Jun, Feng Renxiao, and four of the Celestial Kings entered the vessel, pressed against one another.

Once the hatch was closed, the young woman asked, "How do we start this machine, Feng Renxiao?"

"I've only been this way once, miss, my memories are hazy..."

They lit the oil lamps on each side of a crystal porthole on the front wall, illuminating both the interior and the exterior several meters ahead. When the men on the dock detached the chain from the capstan, the vessel fell back into the water and began to move, carried by the current. Despite the hatred she bore towards the Eight Tigers, the former imperial favorite couldn't help but marvel at the ingenuity of the invention. Now she better understood the great respect her master had for Zhang Yong despite their differences: the Tiger's scholarship and passion made him one of the rare few Wang Yangming would count as his peers. Who knew what they could have accomplished if they had followed the same path? Contemplating this wasted potential only strengthened Shao Jun's resolve. This time she would kill him, even if it cost her life!

"There we go, miss, we're moving," Feng Renxiao announced.

As soon as they had boarded, Tiexin had stood behind him and not taken his eye off him since, just in case he suddenly got the urge to betray them. Controlled by two pairs of levers – for speed and direction – the vessel quickly progressed along the submarine current. It entered a tunnel where the darkness seemed absolute, before emerging into a slightly less dark basin and bursting through the surface of the waves. As the atmosphere in the vessel grew stifling, Tiexin rushed to unscrew the door and allow in fresh air. No noise came from outside, but it would have been foolish to imagine an attack was impossible.

"Balang," he said, "you go out first."

The man he addressed was the Japanese man. He had begun

his career blurring the line between trade and banditry, like the other Celestial Kings, but the restrictive measures implemented by the Ming dynasty had prevented him taking to the high seas to carry out his business; since then, he and his companions had limited their activities to the Chinese coast. The pirate captain asked Balang to be the first to exit the vessel because, like his sworn brother Taki Choji, he had grown up in the Buddhist Temple of the Benevolent Fields and learned the way of steadiness, a martial teaching rumored to be the best of all the defensive arts. This technique, with results similar to the *Golden mask* and the *Iron shirt* of the central plain, had allowed him to resist two full rounds of Tiexin's extraordinary boxing when they dueled for his entry into Tiexin's group.

The Shinshu Temple of the Benevolent Fields had been founded the century before by Master Shinran. When he died, his daughter chose not to continue teaching in the same location, instead choosing to do so in her own monastery which she established in a gorge in the eastern mountains, named "Temple of the Source" by Emperor Kamakura. As her father had done before her and as her descendants would do after, she taught the way of the ancestors. The last spiritual leader of this place of meditation was Rennyo, Shinran's distant grandson, driven from his sanctuary by followers of the Tendai way from China who invaded the building and made it their own monastery. The Temple of the Benevolent Fields thus seemed the last refuge of Japanese Shinshu Buddhism, and its monks had resisted decades of religious war by extending their practice to martial arts.

But they were unable to resist forever, and thirty years earlier their home had been devastated by followers of the Tendai way.

Only a few monks escaped the fire that ravaged the buildings; including two young trainees: Taki Choji and Balang. The former succeeded in obtaining employment with a lord, but the latter, whose social class was too low, turned towards banditry and crime before meeting Tiexin and his band. The captain had over a hundred men at his command, but it was the aimless young foreigner's mastery of the way of steadiness that earned his place among the Eight Celestial Kings.

He nodded, adjusted his belt, and exited the vessel with slow, careful movements. Outside, the air was hot and harsh but clearly breathable. He looked around to ensure there were no threats in sight, then spoke.

"It's fine, you can come out… Oh!"

It was an expression of astonishment, not fear. The pirate leader climbed out of the opening in turn and let out the same cry of surprise when he saw their surroundings. He was in a large cave measuring around ten meters, the top of which glowed with a faint fluorescent light. On the left was a huge iron door embedded into the rocky wall, and on the right, a small pool of bubbling lava let off considerable heat. Some sort of large metal basin gurgled loudly within it. It was this strange installation that caused the smoke that constantly wafted from the Isle of Demons! But he knew of no metal that could retain its solidity and consistency when exposed to liquid magma.

Balang curiously extended an arm towards the valve on the wall but had barely brushed against it when a shadow detached itself from the ceiling to drop towards him at high speed. Although the Japanese pirate's senses were not naturally acute, they were sharp enough to allow him to react without thinking. His right foot slid back a half-step, and he adopted the pose typical of monks in kesa[17] but lowering his hands to his waist rather than to his hips. This position was the foundation of the way of steadiness, supposedly allowing him to withstand even the most powerful attacks without flinching, how he had resisted Tiexin's blows during their only fight. His attacker, who must have been clinging to the crevices in the rock overhead like a bat, hit him on the chest with his fists. A force powerful enough to topple mountains reverberated through him, breaking a dozen of his ribs. He immediately coughed out his crushed viscera in a bloody torrent. His lower body froze in place, not moving an inch as the upper half sagged like a piece of boneless meat.

Tiexin, who had barely had time to exit the vessel and jump to the ground, was sickened by the scene. He quickly returned to his senses and threw himself at the man, who had his back to him. *Bang!* His fist hit a body hard as stone, and the absence of any rebound prevented him from beginning his favorite series of attacks. Balang's killer swayed, likely because of his small size, but barely. The pirate leader hit him again, this time feeling if his fingers were about to break. What monster was this?

The mysterious individual turned quickly, indifferently; eyes blank of all expression.

Tiexin was unable to hold back his shout of surprise when he saw his face.

"Katana!"

17 The robe of Buddhist monks, traditionally an ochre color.

CHAPTER 20

Tiexin sometimes encountered Taki Choji at sea, though they kept to themselves and avoided conflict due to a mutually beneficial unwritten agreement. Shortly before his death at Zhang Yong's hands, Taki Choji had gained possession of a certain item coveted by Tiexin. After the massacre of the pirates, the leader of the Eight Celestial Kings had ransacked their camp to find the item he desired but had turned up nothing. As he examined the bodies, he noticed there was one missing: Katana, Taki Choji's adopted son. Thinking he must have fled with the item, he agreed to join Wang Yangming's cause in the hope of finding him, then Shao Jun had come to ask for his help at the dragon boat festival. Tiexin told himself that it was an opportunity to take the item he had been looking for. Despite everything, it was extraordinary that the first person he encountered on the island was the teenager dropping from the ceiling in the depths of the Isle of Demons. It seemed the kid had joined forces with his father's killers.

He hadn't grown much since the time the pirate captain had first seen him but had traded his boyish physique for unusual musculature and a rough face, made even more terrifying by a complete lack of expression. When he attacked, his blows were phenomenally powerful, and their intensity increased with every second, as if driven by a simmering internal rage. Tiexin launched into his famous *Celestial drums beat the thunder*, the potent southern Shaolin technique that had caused even Shao Jun difficulty, and which almost no opponent had ever been able to resist. But Katana held fast, delivering blow after blow without seeming to tire. He stood firm against his adversary, who was unaccustomed to not immediately gaining the advantage in a hand-to-hand fight.

"What are you waiting for? Come help me!" he shouted at his men, who had by now all exited the vessel.

Knowing their leader's pride and strength, they immediately realized the situation must be dire for him to ask for their help. Ye Zongman told Chen Yuanping, the next best fighter after Balang, to help. He didn't need to be asked: he was already rushing at Taki Choji's adopted son at the exact moment Tiexin forced him to stumble back and brought his short sword down with all his strength on the adolescent's right shoulder. Any normal human's arm would have been completely sliced through, but to the pirate it felt as if he were stabbing his blade into a tree trunk.

It penetrated three or four centimeters into flesh and then remained there, trapped. What was most frightening was that the teenager seemed indifferent to the attack, just as he didn't react when he opened his hand and gripped the sharp edge of the blade in a clumsy attempt to pull it out. He finally managed to grab its handle with his injured hand and broke it in two like a twig. Then he stabbed the broken half of the sword into the chest of Chen Yuanping, who was too stunned by this display to understand what was happening and breathed his last believing he had been killed by a demon. When Katana, as unconcerned by the blood running down his body as if it were sweat, turned towards him again, Tiexin finally gave in to panic. The fruitless attacks had left his arms painful, and a wave of profound despair washed over him. He was convinced that he couldn't win against such a supernatural opponent. He took several steps back until his heels hit the edge of the pool of lava. He was cornered.

Just as he was about to give himself up to the molten rock, he saw a figure attacking his assailant with incredible speed. Shao Jun had finally joined the battle. She had exited the vessel last as a precaution and to avoid giving Feng Renxiao any opportunity to remain inside alone and flee. Once on the shore she had seen Katana kill Chen Yuanping and instantly realized he was a yuxiao. Having faced them before, she knew that while their bodies were practically impenetrable, their weakness of mind could be used against them. The inhuman monsters felt no pain, but they were by no means invincible. As she landed between the two combatants, she jumped again to execute a technique known as *Kicking the arm*. The kick used all the energy accumulated during the jump to strike down at an opponent's arm. The affected limb would instantly fall to hang limply at their side. She knew that normal techniques wouldn't work on this inhuman being, instead using sudden and unexpected techniques to plunge Katana's dull mind into complete confusion The adolescent's speed and strength had been increased tenfold by the process he had been subjected to, but his ability to respond with anything beyond the simplest of reactions was severely impaired.

The strategy paid off: her disconcerted opponent was forced to interrupt his barrage of attacks and began to vainly wave his left hand in the air. Shao Jun took advantage of his disorientation to perform a variant of *Swallow draws the veil*: she leapt upwards and spun in the air, but instead of unsheathing her sword in mid-air to slice her enemy in two as she should have done, she turned her feet towards his face, the boot with the dagger in front, and sliced both his eyes in a single move before landing behind him. Rivers of blood streamed from his blind sockets like bloody tears, but the boy didn't make a sound. His ability to fight was greatly diminished.

When Tiexin, shocked by the nightmarish spectacle, whispered the boy's name, Katana turned towards him to recommence his assault. Still unable to see, he must be relying on his hearing to find his prey. His random attacks were now too easy to avoid to be any real danger, and the pirate captain was easily able to escape. By slipping next to the yuxiao, he was able to grasp him firmly by the wrist using *Jade closes and metal locks*, a powerful incapacitation move in the *Toppling Mount Kailash* boxing style. He needed to question him to find out where the item Tiexin had been searching for was hidden.

Crack! Katana broke his bones as he attempted to attack as if nothing was wrong. Tiexin was in trouble, because he would have to let go to move away, which would immediately expose him to a fresh assault. He moved around Katana to stay out of reach of his other arm, leading him as if in some grotesque, lightning-fast dance. How could he get himself out of this impossible situation? In the end he didn't have to: Shao Jun buried her sword into the creature's back, stopping him completely. The heart was still the source of life, even in a beast such as he. He collapsed to the ground as the young woman withdrew her blade.

Seeing his last chance to his lay hands on the precious object he was seeking disappear – because extracting information from Zhang Yong was unlikely – the pirate chief felt a flash of hatred for the one who had just saved him. Nonetheless, he hid his resentment.

"Miss Shao Jun," he asked, "can you explain what just happened?"

"It must be Zhang Yong and Yu Dayong's work on this island."

"What are you talking about?"

According to Chen Xijian, the purpose of the experiments carried out in the Leopard Quarter had been to discover the secrets of immortality, though it was now clear that that Zhang Yong's true purpose had been to create yuxiao. Before he died, Wei Bin had mentioned a link between Dai Yu island and the Precursor Box. The most obvious answer was that it somehow allowed him to correct the final flaws in these soulless monsters. If they succeeded in creating enough to form an army, there was no doubt that the leader of the Tigers would be able to conquer the world. That was why Wang Yangming had strived to the last to prevent him carrying out his plans.

Shao Jun was filled with sadness. If her guess was correct, then the former Emperor must have been involved in this horror. After growing up in the harem, he was the first man she had ever met, and his tenderness, his kindness, had for her been like rain falling on parched earth. She still remembered his smile and their time spent together with nostalgia. How could she reconcile these images with the monstrous mutilated corpse that lay before her? She let out a long sigh.

"Help me move him," she asked Feng Renxiao as he stood next to her. "We'll find somewhere to bury him later."

As they moved the body to the bottom of one of the cave walls, Tiexin inspected the metal door on the left. Clearly made from the same metal as the large basin over the lava, it was completely smooth and had no handle. The only device nearby was the valve in the wall. As the pirate chief prepared to unscrew it, Feng Renxiao shouted out.

"Captain Tiexin, don't touch it!"

"What's wrong?" asked Shao Jun.

"Uncle Yu said everything would explode if it's used. To open the door, you need to do this..."

He trotted over to the door and crouched to lift a small stone at the foot of a nearby rock, revealing a metal handle polished smooth with use. He pulled it as hard as he could, but to no avail. Conscious that everyone was waiting for him to prove his word, he panicked, sweating profusely as nothing happened: the device failed to move.

"B- But... this is how Uncle Yu entered..." he lamented.

"Let me try," the former imperial favorite interjected.

Resting a hand on the handle, she felt a small slot underneath; she had hardly put her finger into it than the mechanism began to move on its own. *Screeeech!* The door began to open with a metallic squeal. Given that it had to weigh several tons, seeing it pivot on its rails was a wonder, but it was insignificant compared to the sight that awaited the small group on the other side: an immense open space at the center of which stood twin towers sixty meters high, made from intertwined metal rods. The left tower was equipped with ropes continuously moving up and down. So, the center of the volcano was hollow! The area was lit by strange objects attached to the wall. They looked like fat candles as thick as an arm, with no flame and no smoke, but blindingly bright if stared at.

Did the power and ingenuity of the Eight Tigers know no limit? How could they build such marvels? Where had all the strange materials come from? Shao Jun remembered a story told to her by Ezio Auditore. He had said that in ancient times there were giants of incomparable wisdom and intelligence who erected great monuments and mysterious installations all over the world, before an unprecedented catastrophe destroyed their accomplishments and erased almost every trace of their existence.

Members of the Brotherhood, including the one who wrote the *Record of Blood Spilt for a Righteous Cause*, called them... the Precursors. The Italian mentor had seen three vestiges that bore witness to their passage in the world, but the humans who had succeeded them were completely ignorant as to their techniques or even their purpose. And so, Shao Jun had become the keeper of a box from their time, without knowing what it was for or how to use it. Faced with this tangible manifestation of their heritage, she felt the presence of the members of the Society of the Mind. She wasn't alone.

At the top of one of the towers Zhang Yong, Yu Dayong, and Pyros stood around an inert man stretched out on a platform, fat and full of needles, his stomach oscillating slightly. The Precursor Box rested on a shelf made from the strange, incomparably strong metal – something between iron and gold – behind the leader of the Tigers. A decade earlier Yu Dayong had discovered the island and its installations, and their ingenuity never ceased to amaze him: boiling the sea water in the metal basin over the lava produced vapor which drove the mechanism in the left tower. It cooled as it reached the ceiling, then fell back down, free of its salt, in the form of potable water, while the system of ropes it set in motion provided the energy to power the cave's lights and ventilation. When Zhang Yong and Pyros first discovered this place, they realized that it had been made to accommodate the Precursors' research and spent two whole years transferring all the equipment from the Xifan pavilion after which A-Qiang agreed to hand over the Dai Yu scroll in exchange for her elevation in rank. The Precursor Box had been the final piece they needed to complete their project, and now they had it.

It was Pyros who told the leader of the Tigers of the object when they first met at court. According to his story, these small boxes with rounded corners could be used to decipher written codes. The Portuguese man had already seen several in various ruins of the Precursors' civilization, but he had no idea how to procure one which would allow them to fully decipher the scroll in Emperor Zhengde's possession. Zhang Yong had been forced to deploy considerable means and sacrifice a number of his followers to finally acquire Ezio Auditore's box, but now he had it, and his and Pyros' dark designs could finally be realized.

"My dear governor," Yu Dayong said, "pass me the scroll."

Chen Xijian had provided Shao Jun with some information on the document, but it was very incomplete. An idea grew in the young woman's mind: what if, instead of offering immortality for oneself, the scroll made it possible to create beings that were immortal? Centuries earlier, Persia had been famous for its army of invincible soldiers, so powerful that they had even overcome the alliance of Greek cities at the battle of Thermopylae. It was the debauched character of its king, Xerxes, that finally brought the kingdom to its knees after defeat by the Romans. Lost during the sack of Ctsiphon, the scroll had then been passed from hand to hand over the generations before eventually reaching Zhengde. Still young, curious, and hungry for power, he threw himself into a quest to discover the unholy science which could turn corpses into immortal fighters. In one sense, the project had clearly been a success, because it was certainly the first of these monsters which destroyed the Xifan pavilion and massacred the scholars and scientists working there. Realizing the horror of the enterprise he had undertaken, the Emperor then closed the pavilion, at least until he found a way to translate the entire scroll. Then after his death, it was Zhang Yong who took up the cursed torch.

In his youth he had studied medicine and developed a keen interest in acupuncture, supported by access to the imperial libraries granted by his rank. Meanwhile, Pyros was a renowned pharmacist in Portugal, and it was the combination of their respective talents and knowledge which allowed them to create warriors as invincible as the one which devastated the Xifan pavilion, but more docile. The first was born on an island in the Eastern sea, so the leader of the Tigers had named the soldiers after a local maritime deity: Yu Xiao. The human-headed bird, described in the *Book of the Seas and Mountains*, was often depicted with a bird in each talon reigning supreme over the East China Sea. But for all their destructive power, the yuxiao had a considerable flaw: their very limited lifespan. These monsters owed their semblance of life to a mix of opiates and acupuncture, but they became unusable and rigid as a cadaver after around twelve hours. The precious artifact taken from Wang Yangming, combined with the secrets of Emperor Zhengde's scroll, should finally resolve this issue and provide Zhang Yong with his immortal army.

When he manipulated the cover, three sides of the box opened up: it was empty. He dubiously brought it closer to the scroll, but nothing seemed to happen.

"Pyros," he demanded "how did the Precursors use these boxes?"

"Venerable captain," Pyros answered uncomfortably, "I've never seen these boxes in use. I was simply told they made it possible to read the language of the Precursors, in which your document is most probably written."

How annoying. Did the box only respond to a specific way of being handled? Was the scroll a fake? Since Pyros clearly was no help, the leader of the Tigers turned to Yu Dayong.

"Dear governor," he said, "let's see if your knowledge of mechanics can be put to good use!"

Flattered by the attention, the latter advanced slowly. While his knowledge of the mechanical sciences was in reality quite limited, he examined the object carefully. Running his fingers over it, he felt a small indentation on its underside, like some sort of groove, and slipped his nail into it.

The box startled the eunuch by suddenly emitting a bright light. The glow quickly ceased, but it was still a clear step forward.

"That's it!" Zhang Yong cried, taking back the box.

He unscrewed the cap of the small bamboo tube he kept against his chest and withdrew a small silver knife which he used to remove the thin layer of dried dust covering the shelf on which it had sat moments before. This feature, made from the same metal as the door and basin, had several curious protuberances on its otherwise smooth surface which had always intrigued him. Over time, the dust in the environment had stuck to these reliefs which, it seemed to him, might be essential for their purposes. When they were bright as mirrors, the leader of the Tigers carefully wiped the box and gently returned it to the shelf.

Click! A bright beam of pale blue light once again emanated from the artefact, and projected Zhengde's scroll into the air complete with identical text and diagrams. The image blurred for a moment, then became an entire book, this time written in Chinese!

"Good God!" Pyros exclaimed. "It's in Latin!"

"Latin?" the disconcerted Zhang Yong asked.

"Yes, I studied Latin as child, I know what I'm talking about… It's said that these boxes record all the information they are exposed to. This object really is the work of the Precursors!"

So, the incredible box did more than just translate the language of its creators, it could also display the result in the language of anyone looking at it. That was why they were referred to as magic artifacts! Nonetheless, the text remained relatively impenetrable even in Chinese. The style was confused, nebulous formulae one after the other with no apparent connection, vague terms and expressions all over the place. Zhang Yong had a revelation: instead of looking for meaning in the whole, he studied the sentences independent of one another, approaching the paragraphs as he would acupuncture techniques rather than as a written language. From this angle, he began to discover the scroll's secrets.

A quiet mechanical rumbling could be heard from below. The Tigers immediately recognized the characteristic noise of the main door opening.

Yu Dayong was confused. Between the deadly reefs and the yuxiao, this secret base was as good as impenetrable. But looking out of the tower window, he could see a figure entering through the doorway.

"Venerable captain," he called, "someone is here!"

"It must be Shao Jun! Kill her!"

Zhang Yong had spoken without turning, unable to take his eyes off the book of light. In his time, Wang Mang exhorted scholars and educated men to leave the dead in peace and concern themselves only with the living. This tradition had become a foundation of Chinese medicine for centuries to come and had caused the country to fall behind significantly in terms of anatomical expertise. Indifferent to superstition and thirsty for knowledge, Zhang Yong had not only studied all the works he could procure on the subject from the imperial library but had also dissected cadavers himself. As a result, his understanding of the human body was undoubtedly one of the most advanced in the Ming empire. Despite this, the unfathomable secrets of the book before him gave him the exhilarating feeling that he was on the precipice of a new journey of discovery. How could he see it otherwise?

CHAPTER 21

The door came to a juddering halt before it had fully opened.

"What happened?" Tiexin asked nervously.

Feng Renxiao would have liked to answer, but the only time he had followed Yu Dayong in the vessel, he had stayed behind and therefore had no idea how the device worked. Before he had a chance to speak, the heavy door began to close again with a metallic creak. Shao Jun quickly leapt through the gap, but the stockier pirate leader was unable to follow. He rushed to the side of the door to try to pull the handle which controlled the opening mechanism. Nothing happened: despite his colossal strength, it refused to budge an inch. Breathing labored and face contorted with effort, he couldn't even call his men to help. From her side, the young woman picked up a large stone and wedged in in the door's path to keep it open. Seeing her do this, Tiexin rushed to push against the door with all his strength, quickly followed by his men. But it was in vain. They seemed to succeed in interrupting the closing of the door, but not in reversing it, and they couldn't hold out for long. There was also no room for them to get through. Looking directly through the opening, Feng Renxiao suddenly saw something which terrified him.

"Miss, watch out!" he cried.

Shao Jun immediately realized she was about to be attacked from behind. Her sword was attached to her back, making it impossible to draw quickly enough to parry, so she threw herself forwards and kicked off the cave wall to give herself height. The cold whisper of steel passed several millimeters from her ankles. Her tendons would have been sliced through if she had been facing an opponent of Zhang Yong's level. Trying to quickly gain the upper hand, she caught the blade between her feet to press it against the floor as she landed, bringing with it the weapon's wielder: Yu Dayong. The Tiger cursed inwardly when he saw that his former employee had betrayed him. The group of men pushing against the door was also a source of worry, because while he didn't doubt the durability of the door itself, he was less certain of the strength of its pivot mechanism. He was a good swordsman, but he was far below the talent of one such as Qiu Ju. And now he was discovering at the worst possible time that he was also far less skilled than the former imperial favorite. Until then, he had taken her victory over Wei Bin as being purely down to her ambush. The fact that he had captured her with little difficulty on the junk had misled him, and now they were on an equal footing, the difference between them was brought into stark contrast. To think that his greatest fear as he descended the tower was that he would be attacked by a yuxiao. How had she reached such a level of kung-fu?

"Does this whore think her feet are stronger than my sword?"

he grumbled to himself before yanking on his weapon in an attempt to free it. It didn't budge an inch: Shao Jun was using *The arms open the door and the feet kick the man into the room* to concentrate all her weight into her feet, weighing the blade down like a sack of bricks. Realizing he had no chance of winning in this situation, the Tiger let go of his weapon and jumped back a short way, avoiding the young woman's right boot as she kicked towards him in a wide arc. The blow didn't hit, but she now had time to unsheathe her own sword and rush at Yu Dayong.

He had taken care to refill the powder in his mirror-torch when they arrived at the cave, so now he drew the precious tool from his pocket to brandish it like a magic wand that would assure his salvation. But this time his adversary was prepared for his trick. She closed her eyes and grabbed her rope dart. Master Yangming had explained to her that his School of Mind was directly based on Liu Xiangshan's way of the heart. More than just a style of martial art, it was a philosophy in its own right, its purpose to achieve a heightened state of consciousness. Its basic principle was to harmonize the heart and the universe, by matching their rhythms – inspiring the mantra "The universe is my mind, and my mind is the universe". Eyelids closed, Shao Jun concentrated on her breathing and suddenly perceived her surroundings more clearly than ever.

Yu Dayong believed his dazzling ray of light had won him the battle, but his lamp had barely extinguished when he felt a terrible pain tear through his left ankle. Looking down, he saw the head of a dart planted in it, and a rope circling his calf so tightly that his leg would have been severed if it hadn't been so fat. Blind with panic, he set off his blinding lamp again, using the last of the powder. This time it was his other ankle that was captured. He shouted in impotent surprise. How had the imperial whore been able to aim so precisely when she should have been blinded? With a small movement of her wrist, the young woman loosened the rope and sent the end whipping at the Tiger's hand, causing him to drop his precious tool. Before he could respond, he found himself pressed against the wall of the cave, the sharp edge of a blade at his throat.

"M- Miss..." he stammered pitifully.

"Open that door, and fast!" Shao Jun ordered.

"I can't! The mechanism is controlled from the tower."

She pressed her sword more firmly against the eunuch's neck. It would only take the tiniest movement to open up his throat.

"Really?" she persisted.

"Miss...T- The mechanism is at the bottom of the right... tower..."

Ma Yongcheng was known for his bloody reputation, Wei Bin for his deception, Qiu Ju for his swordsmanship, Gao Feng for his loyalty, and Luo Xiang for his mystery. As for Yu Dayong? He was a coward. His character repulsed the former imperial favorite, but he could be useful: she might be able to get some information out of him if he preferred to betray his master rather than lose his life.

"Hurry up and open it," she growled.

He hobbled to the tower on his injured legs and pulled a hidden lever.

"There, miss, the door will open."

A grinding could be heard as the door moved. Surprised by the sudden movement, Tiexin and his men, who had been pushing against the heavy metal, stumbled forward and nearly fell. "We did it!" he cheered internally, convinced that he had achieved the result with his own efforts. However, his triumph was short-lived as a loud splash suddenly echoed behind him.

"Brother Tiexin!" Ye Zongman shouted next to him.

In the pool where the vessel waited, an enormous human form had emerged dripping from the water and rushed at them. The pirate leader took a deep breath and began his *Toppling Mount Kailash* technique as he turned to face the assailant. *Thud!* He hit the creature with both fists. Unfortunately, it was he who recoiled from the impact, thrown several steps back towards the doorway. He would undoubtedly have been crushed against it if it hadn't already been partly open. It was a terrible disillusionment for a powerful man so used to being feared on both land and sea. His boxing had always been unbeatable before, but now two opponents in a row were completely unaffected! His confidence transformed into uncertainty.

The superhuman fighter attacked the other men near the door. The member of the Eight Celestial Kings he assaulted had neither the experience nor the resistance of their leader, and the difference was clear: all the bones in his hand exploded, first from fingers to wrist, then from wrist to elbow. The instantly limp and swollen limb hung loosely from his shoulder as he screamed in pain. The yuxiao ended his suffering by breaking his ribcage with a punch before turning to its next victim. Ye Zongman begged Tiexin to intervene, but he remained petrified in the face of the supernatural power before them. What could he do? How could he fight? He was powerless.

"Come in, quickly!" Shao Jun cried, breaking the stupor that paralyzed the pirates.

They all slipped through the door, then the young woman immediately ordered Yu Dayong to activate the closing mechanism. Barely a foot-wide gap remained, but the mechanism suddenly stopped: the stone she had wedged in it a few moments earlier was still there. Tiexin kicked it hard and managed to loosen it when two hands suddenly grabbed hold from the outside.

The yuxiao had found a grip and was pushing with all its strength against the door – something which a human would never have considered doing as the risk of losing fingers was significant. The door made a grinding noise as it opened several centimeters, and Tiexin shuddered in horror. It was crazy – just a moment before the strength of six men hadn't been enough to make it move. Frightened, he carefully moved to the doorway and punched the creature's stomach, but it didn't even flinch. The door began to open. The pirate leader punched again and again, but it made no difference.

He saw the gleam of a blade in the corner of his eye. Seeing the urgency of the situation, Shao Jun leapt to intervene, and pierced the monster's heart with a single stroke. The pirate leader took the opportunity to add several punches and, this time, deprived of its strength as its semblance of life evaporated, the yuxiao let go and was sent flying backwards. But instead of continuing to close, the door began to open! While the former imperial favorite was distracted, Yu Dayong had seized his chance and reversed the mechanism before running towards the tower as fast as his injured legs allowed. The young woman shouted at her companions to get the door closed as she set off in pursuit, but he had already reached the mechanical ladder that stretched up the side of the building. No sooner had he grabbed onto it than it rose towards the top on its own, probably driven by a system of ropes and pulleys.

Rather than try to climb the building hand over hand, which would have taken too long, Shao Jun threw her rope dart up five or six meters to catch onto the building, using it to follow in the eunuch's wake. She climbed several stories, then relaunched her improvised grapple to continue her ascent, threatening to catch the Tiger much sooner than he had expected. For the first time in a long time there was no one he could order to sacrifice themselves in his place. He paled with fright.

As Tiexin watched the vertical race and regretted being unable to join in, one of his men screamed in panic: the yuxiao which had been stabbed in the heart had returned to try to force the metal door open. He succeeded in catching hold of the Celestial King who had cried out, snapping him like a twig as he crushed him in a deadly embrace. The pirate leader despaired. That was the third member of his group to die on this cursed island. He hadn't expected so many problems, nor such danger. He no longer had a choice; he must fight or die now that escape seemed impossible. And he had learned from how Shao Jun had dispatched Katana: while these monsters had superhuman strength and resistance, they still relied on their senses to find their targets and know when and where to attack.

The Vimalakirti Sutra said that "the inexhaustible oil lamp is like a lamp that lights a thousand candles: it banishes the shadows with its infinite light". This parable of Mahayana Buddhism encourages the spreading of the faith, but in China it had also given rise to a kung-fu technique. Its most illustrious practitioner was Jiechi, a Southern Shaolin monk. According to the legend, one day he struck a wall to reach a meteor hammer master hidden behind it who planned to ambush him. Driven through the bricks, which held the imprint of his punch, the power of the blow struck the hidden assailant with such power that he began to cough blood and fled as fast as his legs could carry him. This wall of the Imprint of Infinite Light, as it was later named by the monastery, was irrefutable proof of the teachings of the Vimalakariti Sutra. Tiexin had trained hard to master the Inexhaustible oil lamp, and used it now to hit the yuxiao through the body of the sailor it still held.

With its extremely limited intellect, the monster was thrown off balance by the unconventional attack and rained blows down on the body of the dead Celestial King in its arms, unable to see the pirate leader. The poor, inert body quickly began to disintegrate into a quivering mass of bloody flesh and broken bones. Its accelerated destruction would certainly put an end to the ruse and Tiexin would be deprived of his makeshift shield. What should he do now?

"Hurry and push the monster outside!" Ye Zongman yelled, as if in answer to his unspoken question.

The latter had rushed to the base of the tower where he thought he saw Yu Dayong a few moments earlier and found the door's closing mechanism. But he didn't dare activate it, fearing he would trap the yuxiao in the same room as himself and his companions. Too focused on his boxing to think or talk, the pirate leader chose to blindly follow his second's instructions. Aching and covered in sweat, he'd already executed the equivalent of seven out of the eight rounds of *Celestial drums beat the thunder* he normally performed. The superhuman fighter would kill him and the remaining Celestial Kings if he didn't force the superhuman fighter back. He summoned his last reserves of strength and struck like a man possessed. *Thud!* With the corpse of his man reduced to shreds of flesh, he could now attack the yuxiao's body directly, and struck it directly in the chest. He summoned something divine and profound from within himself, a will to survive that was almost transcendent, to deliver that final blow which forced his adversary back several paces. It stumbled then fell on its back, legs straddling the rails the door was mounted on. They were crushed by the heavy metal door as Ye Zongman activated the mechanism, but the monster, unable to feel pain, paid no attention and continued struggling like a demon with the sailor's broken remains.

Covered in blood and sweat, Tiexin contemplated the hellish scene. With Katana dead, Zhang Yong was his last hope of finding the item he sought, but it was unlikely. In his exhaustion, he wondered if it was really worth continuing. Only two of the Celestial Kings that had accompanied him were still alive, and he knew they would have no chance of escaping if another yuxiao appeared.

Bang! A man crashed to the ground at the bottom of the tower, falling to his death from a higher floor. It was Yu Dayong. It was terrifying to see a man of his stature meet such an end. Though the pirate leader prided himself on never giving up a fight, he would do it this time. He shuddered, then turned to Ye Zongman, who always gave good advice.

"Come, big brother Tiexin, let's go!" he said to him, pale and trembling.

"Good. Open the door."

He didn't need to be asked twice: the door began to open again to reveal the upper half of the yuxiao which had been sliced in two. The pirate leader kicked it out of the way, then as they passed through the opening, turned back to his second and ordered him to close it behind them.

Feng Renxiao shivered as he heard these words.

"But Captain Tiexin... Shao Jun is still inside!" he protested.

While he had neither the talent nor the courage to help Shao Jun directly, he also felt unable to abandon her to her fate as if there was no way out. Unable to leave things to chance, the pirate leader moved towards the valve embedded in the wall and prepared to turn it. According to Yu Dayong, this mechanism controlled the self-destruct mechanism for the cave. He had always thought it was an oddly accessible place for such a dangerous mechanism, but of course the Tiger had not been responsible for choosing the location of the devices in the cave. He had not understood even a quarter of them. But this one's purpose seemed obvious, which was why he had assigned a yuxiao – Katana – to protect it.

"No, Captain Tiexin! Don't!" Feng Renxiao cried, standing in front of the valve.

"Do you want to die?" the pirate asked coldly.

Stunned by his tone, Yu Dayong's former man moved away while Ye Zongman closed the door. Tiexin began to operate the mechanism.

"If I use this, then everything explodes?" he asked.

"Yes, but I don't know if it's immediate."

The bandit repaid him with a devastating punch which reduced his ribs to pieces and tore apart all his organs.

"Big brother Tiexin, why did you kill him?" exclaimed his second.

"He was no longer useful. And I did my duty to Wang Yangming by ensuring his disciple had a companion to accompany her to the other world."

When the mentor of the School of Mind had sought out the

small group to ask for their help, the Celestial Kings had been astonished by his eloquence and profoundness of his spiritual lessons and had unanimously agreed to assist him. Their leader had his own reasons for agreeing: to gain possession of Taki Choji's cargo. Now he had given up on it and Yu Dayong's former employee, who might have testified to his acts of piracy, was dead, he saw no reason to remain on this cursed island or risk his life further. He felt able to activate the vessel alone, and he knew how to safely leave the island using the current which passed near to the tortoise-shaped reef.

He glanced around one last time. The miraculous light which lit the cavern had begun to dim slightly, the first sign of the complete destruction which would undoubtedly ensue. Closing the hatch of the vessel on himself and what remained of his men, he felt a certain satisfaction. After all, he had told Wang Yangming he would help dispose of Zhang Yong, and there was no way the man was leaving this island alive. He had kept his word.

CHAPTER 22

As she climbed, Shao Jun wondered why Zhang Yong hadn't come down to help Yu Dayong. Faced with the two Tigers and the yuxiao, the pirates hadn't stood a chance. It was pure luck which had allowed the former imperial favorite to emerge unscathed from her encounters with the captain of the imperial guard at both Emerald Dragon Pass and Guimen reef. Something must have kept him above, but what could be so important? Soon she would reach him, and only one of them would come out of it alive.

The openings in the tower wall revealed a new floor every three or four meters, each mostly destroyed but scattered with strange and unfamiliar objects which seemed as likely to date from the previous millennium as they might the next. Having already passed the governor of Nanjing, the young woman rushed into the eighth level of the tower and waited for her enemy to appear in front of her as he ascended. As soon as he passed on the mechanical ladder, she hit him on the shoulders with two precise sword strikes. It was a technique known as *One hundred purples and a thousand reds,* a martial acupuncture technique which caused the victim terrible pain and paralyzed their limbs. He would almost certainly have fallen immediately if he hadn't been firmly wedged into his bucket.

An official despised by all and devoid of any respect for the people he administered, he had spent his entire life torturing and killing, taking sadistic pleasure in interrogating the unfortunates who displeased him in some way or another. One of his favorite techniques was "yellow cards", where he glued a small square of card onto the prisoner's face for each question he asked, continuing until even their nose and mouth were completely covered and they eventually suffocated. The result was unbearable psychological torment combined with slow and painful agony. And yet, like many torturers, he was unable to cope with pain himself, letting out a shrill scream as the joints in his shoulders were severed.

Shao Jun grabbed the ladder a few bars below and began to climb towards the top of the tower. When Yu Dayong reached the sixteenth floor, a blade pierced his throat. It was Pyros' sword, waiting there to kill anyone who would threaten him – of course the one he really expected was Wang Yangming's disciple, and not Zhang Yong's acolyte. With a muffled hiccup, the Tiger tilted backwards, trying to drag the young woman down with him as he fell. She pressed herself against the bars of the ladder at the last second and flew like a swallow towards the opening as the eunuch crashed to the ground. She unsheathed her sword as she entered and executed a lightning-fast thrust which opened the Portuguese man's throat. His unpredictable Western fighting techniques could have made him a dangerous opponent, but he didn't even have the chance to react. He stepped back, collapsing into a chair where he silently breathed his last.

Standing in the empty room next to the corpse, Shao Jun let out a long sigh. Seven of the Eight Tigers now lay in the past, and her brothers in the Society of the Mind would soon be fully avenged, but she felt no joy, only a great feeling of emptiness. Killing him brought her no satisfaction. It wasn't surprising that the wisest men, Wang Yangming included, only resorted to violence after exhausting all other means. Perhaps that was why he tried to keep her away from the capital after Wei Bin's death, when the young woman wanted to launch an immediate attack on Ma Yongcheng. He had wanted to protect her, not from the Tiger, but from the savagery itself.

It didn't matter now, soon it would all be over.

She returned to the ladder to resume her climb past the final two floors which separated her from the top. *Clang!* The ladder suddenly stopped, and the young woman leapt onto the top floor brandishing her sword, but the attack she was expecting never came. Zhang Yong, who must have been aware of her imminent arrival, had his back turned to her and was staring at a strange blue light in front of him, standing next to a table on which lay a naked man. She momentarily froze with confusion. What was the leader of the Tigers doing?

The man was one of the greatest martial arts masters of their time, so it seemed strange for him to be so negligent. The idea of hitting him from behind unsettled the former imperial concubine, but the stakes were too high for her to allow her morality to deprive her of such an opportunity. Ending her hesitation, she leapt forwards like an arrow, sword pointed in front of her.

Just before she reached her target the weapon was intercepted by a figure flying in from her right. The yuxiao lying on the table had unexpectedly come to life! It grabbed her blade in its left hand while simultaneously chopping down like an axe with its right, snapping her sword clean in half. *Clang!* The technique belonged to no known school, and for good reason: no normal human would have dared use it. Palms bloody, the monster stood between the young woman and the last of the Tigers.

"Shao Jun!" he exclaimed. "You're here at last!"

Zhang Yong spoke softly, not even deigning to turn his head. The box translated not only the scroll he had given it, but the entire document it had come from. He had no idea how long he had to take in this knowledge, so he refused to waste a single second, to the point of sending Yu Dayong and Pyros to their deaths. Even if he couldn't memorize it all at once, his reading had already provided him with a number of keys to solve the problems he had encountered, as well as a better understanding of the Precursors' technology. Using this newfound knowledge, a moment before he had taken the opportunity to practice the new acupuncture techniques to improve the resurrection of the corpse laid out on the nearby table. Thanks to the information he had just acquired, he exploited an unusual meridian to breathe life into a new monster that would outperform any he had created before, though Shao Jun had arrived before his preparations were complete. He named this new fighter "yujing" after the sea god Yu Jing, the legendary western brother to Yu Xiao.

"Kill her!" he ordered.

The monster suddenly widened its eyes, revealing the icy gleam that burned within. It was a being whose sole reason for existence was to kill. It rushed at Shao Jun, who quickly leapt through the window and sent her rope dart flying to catch on the tower's roof, which was decorated with a strange, enormous leather ball. Her rope secured, she began climbing towards the top, closely followed by her assailant which climbed the building with disconcerting ease. Zhang Yong listened to the action with an attentive ear as he continued to devour the tome of light.

"So, Shao Jun," he called in a satisfied tone, "would you have risked coming here if you knew what awaited you?"

Above his head, the young woman was engaged in a deadly game of cat and mouse, flying at the end of her silk and sinew rope to escape her terrible pursuer. She knew she would tire first despite her agility, and the Tiger's provocations did nothing to help.

"You betray Zhengde with these unnatural experiments!" she retorted. "The Emperor trusted you!"

It was true. He had begun to suspect the captain of the guard on his deathbed, despite allowing and encouraging his meteoric rise over the previous years. Such ingratitude disgusted the former imperial favorite. She would have reentered by the window to confront her sworn enemy, but the supernatural warrior on her tail left no room for maneuver. She jumped to catch onto the wall a little further down the tower, at the seventeenth floor.

"I had to kill him to achieve my aims!" Zhang Yong shouted to her. "But do you know what the Emperor noted on his scroll?"

The young woman felt a cold shiver run down her back, but she was forced to redirect her attention to the yujing hurtling down the wall towards her.

"He recommended a subject whose body would make a perfect yuxiao..." the Tiger continued. "You, his favorite concubine!"

These words struck Shao Jun like a blade to the heart. The Emperor had occupied a special place there ever since he took her as his consort. He had been the first to show her true kindness, and while he never invited her to his bed, she had truly loved him. After his death, she was the only one to let her tears fall in silence while the rest of the harem echoed with loud and ostentatious wailing. She had never cried for anyone close to her before. Could Zhang Yong's claims be true? She refused to believe it, but still felt as if the earth crumbling under her feet. Whether he lied or not, Zhang Yong was trying to throw her off balance and he had succeeded. In her turmoil, she let down her guard just long enough for the yujing to close its hands around her throat with such force that not even Tiexin himself could have removed them. As her vision blurred, the Emperor remained in her thoughts. Had he really intended to use her so? If it was true, then she might as well give in to the darkness.

Just then, a deafening roar reverberated through the right tower and a gear the size of a man flew into the air to violently hit the left tower. Identical to the first building externally, it held nothing other than the mechanisms that drove the island's installations, and Tiexin had just triggered the self-destruct. With this vital part now gone, the lights went out. Surprised by the unexpected darkness, the superhuman monster momentarily relaxed its grip, giving Shao Jun a chance to pull herself together. She sent both her feet flying into her attacker's face, forcing it to release her and lose its grip, tumbling to crash into the ground at the bottom of the tower. Meanwhile, the young woman used her rope to propel herself to the upper floor.

Yu Dayong had told Zhang Yong about the fateful valve designed to set in motion the island's inexorable destruction, so he immediately understood what was happening, though it took the disappearance of the Precursor Box's miraculous light to plunge him into confusion. "The bitch is still alive!" he thought. He grabbed the precious box and headed to a trap door leading to the roof, but the former imperial favorite threw her rope dart at him from behind. He reacted with cat-like reflexes, smoothly avoiding it as he unsheathed a small dagger and rushed at her. He knew the way of the heart's weakness was the chest and that he had the advantage in close combat. He could already feel the scent of blood tantalizing his nostrils and reveled at the idea of Wang Yangming's disciple dying at his hand.

Instead of the jubilation he expected, a searing pain ripped through his wrist. Surprisingly, Shao Jun had attacked him using what remained of her sword, which she had kept hold of even after it was broken by the yujing.

Impossible! Zhang Yong wanted to cry out. Not even the mentor of the Society of the Mind had been able to avoid his attack, yet somehow the young woman had developed her own style. She had combined her mastery of Eastern martial arts with the Western techniques learned from Ezio Auditore, to create a hybrid that was as cutting as ice and fluid as a river. If her sword hadn't been so shortened, she would have sliced through the Tiger's forearm. He was dumbfounded: no one had ever managed to injure him. He had no choice but to flee now he could no longer use his dagger properly. Grabbing the Precursor Box with his uninjured hand, he rushed through the trap door that led to the roof.

When the former imperial favorite followed him, she discovered him already out of reach, travelling upwards in a large willow basket attached to the strange leather ball she had seen earlier. She was briefly stunned with awe at the sight. The balloon quickly rose towards the mouth of the volcano, carrying its passenger to safety out of range of the cave's scheduled auto-destruct. Who would have expected such a thing?

There was no way she could just let this happen. Broken or not, the weapon on her back had been given to her by Wang Yangming, and the memory of her master gave her the strength to carry on, to fight to the end without giving in. She ran to the tower's edge and jumped into the air, straight towards the cave wall six meters away. Just before she jumped, she threw her rope dart to anchor firmly around a rocky protrusion, allowing her to safely reach the rocky wall. She began to climb as fast as she could to reach Zhang Yong's balloon, now the only way to leave the island.

The latter knew victory was in his grasp. The loss of the Precursor installations and equipment was regrettable, but he still had the box, and he now knew how to make yujing. While he admired her spirit and talent, he knew the former imperial favorite would never reach the balloon in time. Still, he couldn't help gripping the handle of his dagger even as he saw his pursuer's figure growing smaller and more indistinct.

"Shao Jun!" he shouted. "You are incredible, but Dai Yu will be your grave!"

Defeat was a bitter pill to swallow for the last member of the Society of the Mind, and Zhang Yong's laugh rang cruelly in her ears. Realizing that she wasn't climbing fast enough, she decided to give up and try climbing down the wall when an enormous cracking noise echoed through the cavern. She couldn't see it, but the metal basin had finally exploded. The two towers began to sway dangerously, and the entire cave seemed to shake. The young woman was forced to wedge her boot into a gap in the rock to avoid falling. Faced with no alternative, she resumed her ascent towards the mouth of the volcano as a hot, thick black smoke rose towards her. If she must join the Emperor, her master, and her fellow disciples, she would go with a light heart, but she would never simply abandon herself to the abyss. She would fight to the very last breath!

Unfortunately, it was her breath which failed her when she was still a good twenty meters from the top of the volcano, climbing the narrow chimney which led to it. Air became scarce, her vision blurred, the heat began to burn her back, and her hands constantly threatened to lose their grip. Was this how it would all end? The opening above her appeared round as a black moon, seeming more distant than ever. She suddenly noticed some of the smoke around her escaping through the wall only a few meters away! It was a small, rocky tunnel that led to the outside! Finding reserves of strength she didn't know she still had, she sent her rope dart towards the tunnel and hoisted herself up with a quick, powerful movement. The hole couldn't be more than a meter in diameter, but it was all she needed. She climbed in, and a few seconds later she was able to breathe freely. She moved to the side of the rocky opening just in time to avoid an eruption of searing ash.

The sun was beginning to peek over the horizon in the east, and the sea stretched around fifty meters below her feet. It was still too dark to see Zhang Yong's balloon, but she could make out a speck of bright sail on the black expanse of water. It must be Tiexin's ship moving away from the island. She was sure it hadn't taken the coward long to abandon her to her fate. She mentally apologized to her master. Not only had she failed to revive the Society of the Mind, but she was also going to die on this cursed isle. She closed her eyes, ready to abandon all hope… and her eyelids were suddenly lit by a bright flash. She immediately recognized the color of the long incandescent tongue: A-Qin's distress flare! It was still too dark to see the source, but it certainly hadn't come from the Celestial Kings' ship.

The memory of a conversation with Ezio Auditore quickly dissipated her concern and hesitation. The Italian master had been reassured to learn that there was a Brotherhood in China and was impressed by the young fighter to whom he revealed everything he knew about their shared goal. In his villa surrounded by vineyards, he had asked her if she knew how to choose the path she should follow.

"It's not easy," he had said, "because in this world, all is an illusion. Everything is as superficial it is important."

"So, what should I do?" Shao Jun had asked.

"Act as your heart directs you," he had answered simply.

The sun rose on the horizon, slowly flooding the east with blue while the west still slumbered in the darkness of night. The young woman stood on her small stone on the mountainside and opened her arms wide, jumping into the air as she faced the dawn. Hands gripping the edges of her cloak, she floated on the powerful sea breeze as boiling water full of ash was projected out of the volcano's openings, falling around her in a warm, gray rain.

Light and graceful, Wang Yangming's pupil turned in the air like the mythical Peng bird, momentarily freed of all her pain, both physical and spiritual.

As her glide brought her closer to the sea, she brought her arms together and dove into the water. The spray glittered like diamonds in the slanting rays of the rising sun.

EPILOGUE

"Big sister Jun!" A-Qian cried.

She watched with anguish from the prow of her small boat as Shao Jun dove into the waves at high speed. *Splash!* In the middle of an area peppered with reefs, she could crack her head open like a coconut falling from a tree on the numerous rocks hiding under the water. To her great relief, the young woman soon rose to the surface and swam to the boat, accompanied by A-Qian's cries of joy and encouragement.

"You didn't leave?" she asked as she climbed on board.

"My big brother didn't want me to wait… but I knew you'd make it out!"

Barely escaping the cave with their lives, Tiexin, Ye Zongman, and the last of the Celestial Kings had boarded the ship and immediately prepared to leave. While the pirate leader's sister had pleaded with them to wait for Shao Jun, he refused to listen. He would have abandoned A-Qian there and then if they hadn't been siblings. Faced with her unyielding determination, he had agreed to give her one of his ship's lifeboats and to wait a while just beyond the reefs, but his patience wouldn't last. The former imperial concubine knew how much the young girl respected her brother and appreciated the determination she had shown to save her all the more. She had felt like she could never trust anyone again after Wang Yangming's death, but A-Qian had proven herself worthy.

"How can I thank you…" she panted. "Let's go, quickly!"

They easily spotted the tortoise-shaped reef pointed out by Feng Renxiao and allowed themselves to be carried by the current as Dai Yu island finally exploded. Fearing they would be caught by the rocky debris raining down, they rowed as fast as they could. The sea suddenly became chaotic: a thick, acrid fog rolled over the surface of the water, angry waves began to form, and showers of lava fell and brutally cooled on contact with the saltwater. They didn't dare stop to rest until the sun had fully risen. Even at this distance, they could still feel the burning heat of the disaster at their backs, like the menacing breath of a dragon hot in pursuit.

"Big sister, have we made it?" A-Qian asked.

"I think we have!" Shao Jun answered with a small smile.

They had reached the halfway point between the reefs. Ahead, the hazy shape of a large ship appeared through sea mist filled with volcanic ash: it was Tiexin awaiting their return. Comforted by the sight, they both let out a deep sigh of relief.

"Big sister…" A-Qian asked, "is Master Yangming really no longer with us?"

"Unfortunately not."

"So, we'll never hear his teachings ever again..."

When Wang Yangming had come to ask for the pirates' help, he had gained Tiexin's respect thanks to his kung-fu, while his pearls of philosophical wisdom had drawn A-Qian's. Despite her young age, she understood that humanity had just lost one of its wisest men. Shao Jun herself was overcome with emotion at the mention of her master's name.

"His wisdom lives on through his disciples," she said reassuringly.

"Yes, you..."

She was cut short by a sudden impact, almost falling overboard: the boat had just hit a reef. The former imperial favorite caught the young girl just before she fell into the sea, but water was already bubbling through the gaping hole in the hull. Rowing at speed to escape the island's explosion, they had departed from the safe currents recommended by Feng Renxiao and must now face this new danger.

"Quickly, climb onto the reef!" Shao Jun shouted as the front of the boat sank beneath the waves.

The rock was large enough for them to both stand without wetting their feet, though their troubles were far from over.

"Big sister," A-Qian said anxiously, "what do we do?"

"Do you still have any flares?"

"I only had two..."

She had used the first at Guimen reef, and the second shortly before the island's explosion. She saw the outline of her brother's ship in the distance.

"Oh no! He's leaving!" Overwhelmed with panic, she began to shout in the direction of the ship. "Big brother! We're here!"

It was a wasted effort. The distance between them was too great for her voice to be heard, and Tiexin believed his sister dead after seeing the scale of the disaster. The young girl burst into tears as she saw the gray sail unfurl. How could they fail so close to their goal? Shao Jun took her in her arms.

"Don't cry, A-Qian."

"It's all my fault, I was distracted! We hit the reef because of me. We were so close to being saved!"

"Master Yangming once told me that there is still hope even in the most desperate situations, if you really want to believe."

"So… do you think my big brother will turn around?"

She knew her elder brother too well to think him capable of taking such a risk without any real reward. Despite the former imperial favorite's wise words, she found it difficult to avoid despair. Then something miraculous drew her attention.

"Big sister Jun!" she cried. "He's coming back! He's really coming back!"

Unbelievable though it was, a ship with ashen sails was coming towards them. But the closer it came, the more obvious it was that it was not the Celestial Kings. Would its passengers see the two survivors, or pass by without noticing them? A voice called in their direction from the ship before they even had a chance to start shouting for attention.

"Is anyone there?"

"Here! Here!" A-Qian cried, waving her arms.

The ship stopped several meters short of the first reefs, and five or six sailors began to row towards the two castaways in a small lifeboat.

"Miss Jun," said a reedy voice, "is it really you?"

"Who are you?" she retorted, keeping her guard up.

"Thank the heavens and earth! It's her! Miss, it's me, it's Yanfei!"

The face of the prince of Wei's young servant was soon visible through the fog. She was no navigator, but she gestured at the sailors and the small boat quickly approached Shao Jun and A-Qian.

"Miss Jun, there you are!" Yanfei exulted. "Quickly, get in! The master would have been furious if we hadn't found you! Ah, watch out, the boat isn't very stable!"

The servant was as talkative as the former imperial favorite remembered. It amused her to note that the girl hadn't got her sea legs yet, because despite her words, the boat was really quite stable.

"Yanfei! How did you get here?! Did Lord Pengju send you?"

"Miss, my master has been worried about you ever since you left Nanjing. He wanted to accompany you, but there was no one who could stand in for him... He eventually decided to follow you anyway, because he thought it was too dangerous for you to travel alone. He took a big risk! Someone might have reported him! You didn't see that he was following you?"

The young servant hid her mouth behind her hand and rolled her eyes, clearly embarrassed by doing nothing but talk about her master. Nonetheless, this short, confused account helped Shao Jun realize that it was Xu Pengju who saved her from Qiu Ju and Luo Xiang on the road. The prince of Wei had a great heart underneath his carefree airs. He truly was worthy of being Yang Yiqing's greatest disciple.

"Yanfei," she said, "take me to your master so I can thank him..."

"Yes, oh... if you want... The master is on board the ship, but he brought that airhead with him, and given the time, she must be singing him his favorite songs right now... I don't think it's really worth listening to..."

The mundane gossip brought the former imperial favorite a strangely calming sense of familiarity. She had spent the last few hours fighting for her life, nearly died a hundred times over, and had thought herself lost for sure when A-Qian's small boat sank, but now everything seemed back to normal. Perhaps it was not just the dawn of a new day, but of a new chapter in her life. She noticed the distressed look on the face of Tiexin's younger sister.

"What are you thinking?" she asked.

"It's nothing..."

Her chagrin was understandable. The child had had enormous respect for her pirate brother, but he had abandoned her to her fate without even a backward glance. She was pleased to be alive, but this betrayal weighed heavily on her.

"Don't worry about it, A-Qian," said her adoptive "big sister", "life is a path we must all follow alone."

Shao Jun sympathized with the young girl's confusion. She had once been lost like that, first when she left the safety of the Imperial Palace, then more recently when Wang Yangming bid her farewell. Now her fog of doubted had lifted; she knew the path to take.

"Master, you may longer be here to guide me," she thought as looked at the remains of Dai Yu island, "but I will continue on my way without doubting my every step."

Her mind was calm. She had found people she could trust in this cold and hostile world, and she knew she could rely on them to help rebuild the Society of the Mind. It would be a long and difficult road, but she would never again lose sight of her objective.

The rays of the rising sun glinting gold and silver from the waters united sea and sky.

About the Author

YAN LEISHENG has had a special interest in science fiction since an early age, but it wasn't until his thirties that he was first published. Since then, he has published twenty books, including novels, short story collections, essays, and poetry. His most famous trilogy "Heaven Prevails" has sold over 500,000 copies in Chinese.